CARLO GÉBLER was born in Dublin in 1954. He is the author of the memoir *Father & I* (2000), the narrative history *The Siege of Derry* (2005), novels including *The Cure* (1994), *How to Murder a Man* (1998) and *A Good Day for a Dog* (2009), as well as several plays for radio and stage, including *10 Rounds*, which was shortlisted for the Ewart-Biggs Prize (2002), and most recently *Charles & Mary* (2011), a play about Charles and Mary Lamb and the writing of their classic collection *Tales from Shakespeare*. In addition he also co-wrote *My Father's Watch* (2009) with Patrick Maguire, youngest of the Maguire Seven, has written several books for children, reviews widely and occasionally directs programmes for television. His film *Put to the Test* won the 1999 Royal Television Society award.

Carlo Gébler is currently writer-in-residence in HMP Maghaberry, Co. Antrim and teaches at Queen's University Belfast and Trinity College Dublin. He was elected to Aosdána in 1991. He is married, with five children. He lives near Enniskillen, Northern Ireland.

❧

The Dead Eight

THE DEAD EIGHT
First published 2011
by New Island
2 Brookside
Dundrum Road
Dublin 14

www.newisland.ie

ISBN 978-1- 84840-094-8

British Library Cataloguing Data. A CIP catalogue record for this book is
available from the British Library.

Book design by Ruby July.
Printed in the UK by CPI Antony Rowe, Chippenham and Eastbourne

New Island received financial assistance from
The Arts Council (An Comhairle Ealaíon), Dublin, Ireland

10 9 8 7 6 5 4 3 2 1

The Dead Eight

a novel

CARLO GÉBLER

**NEW
ISLAND**

For Georgia

Acknowledgements

I would like to thank: Peter Grimsdale and Jason Hartcup for information supplied on motorcars; Hannah Simpson for her advice on the historical background, for reading the first draft and correcting numerous errors; Patrick MacEntee for advice on legal practice; Jason Thompson (A8086) for his incisive and creative copy editing of the first draft; Dermot Bolger for his felicitous and generous interventions; and Emma Dunne for preparing the manuscript for publication. All mistakes are my own.

For a note on my literary source (and my debt to this source) please see the afterword.

Portions of this novel previously appeared in a different form in *Fortnight Magazine* and in a special edition of the *Princeton University Library Chronicle*, volume 72, No. 1 (Autumn 2010).

Carlo Gébler

Lies are the quickest way to hang a man.

Irish proverb

Prologue

My father had been named Daniel, yet he called me Hector. No boy in New Inn was called Hector. They had ordinary names like Liam or Peter.

One evening when I was nine my father returned from a day mending roads for the council and I told him: "I'd like to be called Eamonn, not Hector." Eamonn was the new president's name and an excellent choice I thought.

"Oh," said my father. "I don't think Miss Cooney will go for that."

This was a surprise. The Cooneys though Catholics had once been big local landowners. But there was only one left now. This was Anastasia or Anna Cooney, though no one used her Christian name and everyone called her Miss Cooney. She lived in the old Cooney place, Garranlea House, and father and mother and I lived in a lodge on the Garranlea demesne.

Miss Cooney was old woman and she always produced a Fig Roll (my favourite biscuit) from her pocket when she came to visit and she always asked me questions in her nice English voice. She liked me. I felt certain she would not mind if I switched to Eamonn.

"She really won't mind," I said.

"I wouldn't be so sure," said my father. "In fact I'd go so far as to say she'd be very disappointed."

Disappointed! Disappointed was what the master Mr Murdoch was if a boy did a really bold thing. It meant sad and let down. How could a change in my name do that to Miss Cooney?

"Why will she be disappointed?"

"Hector's a name she particularly likes," my father said.

"There must be other names she likes just as much. What about Eamonn?"

"Hector is her favourite: if she'd ever had a son her plan was to call him Hector."

Ah. I was called Hector to please Miss Cooney. That I could just about grasp but I knew there was more to this than that, and there was something else about the name that made it special. My father saw my puzzled expression and decided to give me the answer I sought.

"Do you know who Hector was?" he said.

I did not.

"Back in the days of the ancient Greeks he was a warrior who fought for Troy and was killed by Achilles."

This meant nothing to me.

"He was not the greatest warrior. Achilles killed him after all. But he did not lie and he stuck to his word and that is more important than anything else."

This meant even less.

"Miss Cooney says we need more men like Hector and less men like Achilles and we won't have a better world until we do."

So in some ancient war the loser had been better than the winner and I had his name. Now I was completely lost.

*

Miss Cooney came often to our house and had intense conversations with my father about our family history that lasted late into the night. He loved their talks and he always wrote down afterwards what was said and he attached these words to the newspaper clippings and letters and documents that Miss Cooney brought him and he kept all these papers in a box on top of his wardrobe and it was drilled into me and mother that if the place caught fire everything could burn except that box. In the event of a fire we had to save the box.

*

These precious papers all related to my father's mother. As I grew older my father slowly revealed them to me and in the 1950s and

1960s I met many of the people involved in her story, still living in the houses and farms of New Inn.

My father did not believe her story could be published while he was alive. But one day Ireland would be different and then it could be told and, as I was his only child, this would be my task. That was why he insisted I stay at school to do my Leaving Cert. That was why he insisted I become a teacher of history and English: to prepare me for the job.

*

Just before he died my father told me there was a letter for me in the box. After he was buried in the Roman Catholic graveyard in New Inn beside his wife, my mother, I got the box down and read his letter. It was very short. It said: "Remember, you are a Hector and your duty is to tell the truth, the whole truth and nothing but the truth."

To tell the whole truth I have to start with my great-grandmother Mary McCarthy. It was she who tipped the fate of everyone to come. Once her story is done I can tell her daughter Moll's story (she was my grandmother, my father's mother), and Badger's and the stories of all the others who got tangled up in this mess.

Will it be the truth? Well, all the dates and names will be correct. Still, even if this were a novel would you believe it?

1

Mary McCarthy was born on 12 January 1870 in the bedroom in Marlhill Cottage near New Inn in County Tipperary. She was the last of five. Her father was Edmund McCarthy and he was an under gardener at Garranlea House (home of Mr Cooney, his landlord) and her mother was Jane though Mary never knew Jane. Jane died within hours of giving birth to her daughter and her father reared Mary.

A few years after Mary was born the Cooneys sold off many of their properties to their tenants. Edmund bought the two-room cottage at Marlhill and the two acres that went with it and Abraham Slattery bought the seventy-five-acre Marlhill Farm that surrounded the cottage.

Edmund's bigger children grew up and went out into the world, but Mary stayed home and looked after him. When my great-grandmother Mary was fourteen her father remarried: his new wife, Alice, was the widow of a soldier who had died of fever in Egypt. She was a small woman with crooked teeth and two children: Albert, a boy of seven, and Victoria, a girl of eight. Alice expected Mary to take orders from her but Mary would not. After months of hot words Mary lifted the poker one evening and threatened to hit her stepmother a whack across the gob. Edmund took the poker off his daughter and sent her to stay with her oldest brother, Michael.

2

Michael McCarthy, my great-grandmother's brother, lived with his wife in a labourer's cottage outside the market town of Thurles. He was a quiet man of slight build who worked in a stable where several officers from the regiment garrisoned in the barracks in Thurles kept their horses.

One evening a Lieutenant Heaton from Liverpool called to Michael's house with a broken saddle he needed stitched. Michael was known as a man who did a neat tidy job.

Michael was out but Mary was in. Now aged fifteen, she was small and round and soft-spoken. Lieutenant Heaton liked what he saw.

After that Lieutenant Heaton called to see Mary on a regular basis. He brought gifts – hair clips and ribbons and shiny buttons – and he took her for walks in the woods where they gathered wild flowers together.

After three months Mary let him kiss her. After four she let him touch her through her clothes. After five she let him slip his hand under her blouse. After six she let Lieutenant Heaton put his hand up her skirts.

One summer's evening Lieutenant Heaton called to collect Mary. He carried a satchel. On the edge of the wood they found a flat piece of ground beneath an ash tree and sat down. The sun slanted from the west and lit the leaves from below and made them shine.

Lieutenant Heaton opened the satchel and produced two horn beakers and a brown bottle. On the label there was a picture of plump yellow grapes with writing below. Mary could not read the words but Lieutenant Heaton read them out to her: "Madeira Wine – imported and bottled by Clarke's of Cashel." Then they drank. Mary had never drunk alcohol before. When they had finished the bottle Mary felt strange. Wherever she looked she saw objects in duplicate or sometimes triplicate.

Lieutenant Heaton removed his jacket and folded it into a pillow and told her to lie back.

Mary obeyed. She lay back and closed her eyes. She smelled hair oil and saddle soap and gun oil on Lieutenant Heaton's jacket mixed with leaf mould and wet earth and old stone from the ground underneath. She felt Lieutenant Heaton's hot breath on her face. She smelled the drink on him. She felt her skirts as they were lifted high. She thought of the hair that grew between her legs: golden and thin and fine. She felt Lieutenant Heaton between her legs. She knew the months of walks and talks had all led up to this moment. She wondered why it had to be now and what would happen if it were not. Well, if it were not to be now, then she would need to push him off. She would need to stand up and walk away and then when she got back to Michael's house they would ask her questions. Where was Lieutenant Heaton because did he not always walk her home? Had she and the lieutenant fallen out? Then her brother and his wife would say it was to be hoped that they had not because only a foolish girl would fall out with nice, kind Lieutenant Heaton ... This was the future if she stood up and walked away. Was that what she wanted? She did not think it was. What was more, she did not have the energy to think any more. She wanted to be still. She wanted an end to this endless turmoil in her head. She wanted calm. She wanted quiet. And she wanted to be loved. Oh yes, she wanted to be loved. She wanted Lieutenant Heaton to love her, and was this not how to get him to love her? Oh yes, this was the way so no more thought, no more thought. The thoughts hurt her and her head was filled with jagged pains brought on by the thoughts and she swirled, she swirled around and around as she lay on the ground with her head on Lieutenant Heaton's coat and the ash tree with its leaves lit by the slanting evening sunlight shimmered above her.

She closed her eyes. She heard a wood pigeon coo: deep and throaty and restful. A second wood pigeon called in reply. She felt Lieutenant Heaton as he pressed down on her. She felt a sharp stab of pain. She hurt and she did not hurt. She knew what this was. She had gathered from the talk of older women that pain was always suffered when this happened. So that was what this was. It was the pain that came with love and it would have to be endured because otherwise Lieutenant Heaton would not have what he wanted. It was wrong of course to give in as she was; on the other hand, to be loved: was that not something and was this not the way to be sure she would be loved by Lieutenant Heaton?

She heard the wood pigeon again. There was the first one and then the second joined in. She wondered if they were mates. Did they say wood pigeons mated for life? Or was that blackbirds? She could not remember. She heard Lieutenant Heaton's hot urgent cries. They grew louder and fiercer. Then she heard two intense cries followed by a long drawn-out shriek of a sort that she had never heard before, which must be the special noise made by men at these times, she thought. She felt wet as well as strange and a little dreamy.

She opened her eyes and looked past Lieutenant Heaton's big hairy sideburn and his small white ear and the side of his head at the leaves above, bright silver in the sunlight. She felt Lieutenant Heaton shudder. It was not a big movement. It was a faint one. She felt Lieutenant Heaton go still. She saw the green flesh of the leaves above and she saw the thick dark veins inside the flesh. Lieutenant Heaton rolled away and sat up. She heard Lieutenant Heaton as he closed his trousers and fastened his belt. She felt Lieutenant Heaton lift her skirts back and drape them over her legs. She still felt moist as well as sore and strange and different and nervous and relieved and surprised. The wood pigeons cooed away in the distance and the leaves above were shiny new sixpences and shillings that rained down on her head, and she imagined a soft whisper in her ear as Lieutenant Heaton said, "I love you, I love you."

3

Without warning Lieutenant Heaton left with his regiment for Dublin. Mary borrowed money from Alice and followed. By the time she found their barracks the Second Munster Fusiliers had shipped out to India and Lieutenant Heaton was gone.

Another soldier, a Sergeant O'Neill, now took up Mary. He supported her for a few months and then he grew distant and told her that he did not love her any more. He did however know another sergeant who liked her very well, he said. This man was from the north of Ireland and he was called Armstrong and he was a nice kind man, a good sort, a Protestant.

Armstrong's arrangement with Mary lasted another few months and then there was another soldier and then another, and on and on it went except for those times when Mary burned down below and it hurt to pee and her undergarments were stained brown and yellow and she had to go to the special doctor and stop what she did and wait until the ache went away and there were no more brown and yellow stains.

4

It was two days after her thirtieth birthday. It was mid morning. The sky was low and grey. There was rain.

Mary trudged along Dublin's North Circular Road. The rain-wet paving stones were oily and lethal. She dreaded she might slip and then when she got up she would have a sodden behind for everyone to see, so she moved with care.

She reached The Swan. It was a red-brick public house on the corner of Eden Street. Above the main entrance a hand-painted sign announced that Philip Herring Esq. was licensed to sell beers and ales and wines and spirits and tobacco on the premises. Below the sign was a pair of doors with frosted glass panes and brass handles that opened into the front bar.

When she had first started to work out of The Swan years before, Mr Herring had told Mary he would prefer her to use only the back door and the back bar rather than the front door and the front bar. She knew Mr Herring would exclude her entirely from The Swan if she defied him so the back bar it was.

She slipped down Eden Street and opened the door of the back bar and went in. She took off her wet hat and put it on the table behind the door. She liked this table. From here she could see any man as he came in before he saw her and if she thought he was a possibility she would start a conversation with him.

She went to the counter.

"Mary," said the barman.

His name was Billy Donovan but the regulars called him Big Van. He was a huge heavy man with small watchful eyes and a red face and a curtain of flesh that wobbled under his chin. Sometimes customers called him The Turkey instead of Big Van but only behind his back.

"Usual, Mary?" said Big Van.

"Yes."

He moved away to get her drink and Mary inclined her head towards the partition: the front bar was on the other side. If she heard young male voices she would go in and pretend to look for someone and then return. If a man were interested he would follow her back. As long as she did not linger in the front bar or actively solicit there, Philip Herring tolerated these forays.

She tuned into the susurrus of speech beyond the partition. It was too low to understand the sense but she heard enough to know that all the talkers were old. She decided there was no need to go next door and to pretend to search for someone.

"There you go."

Big Van pushed a port-and-brandy towards her. She paid and carried the glass to the table where her hat was and sat down on the banquette seat. It was covered with dusty red velvet.

She sipped at her drink. Big Van spread a newspaper on the counter. As he read he ran a finger under the newsprint and muttered the words. She had once taken Big Van home. Given his weight, his ardour had surprised her.

A post-office boy came in and handed Big Van a telegram. Big Van set it on the shelf above the cash register. Telegrams often came to The Swan for customers. She moved on her seat. The boy left. If she sat the same way for too long she got a pain in her back. She felt one now. When she was younger she never had such problems. It was undeniable: she might not be old yet but she was definitely getting older.

She finished her port-and-brandy. No one had come in since she had started to drink. Well, that was the rain. God, she hated the stuff. Not only did it keep nearly everyone indoors but also she could not work outside in it. She had to bring clients to hers or go to theirs and that made everything always take longer.

"What are you having?"

Mary looked up. The speaker was a thin man in his early forties with a military haircut and an unremarkable face. Where had he come from? He must have been in the front bar all the time and she had not realised.

"I might be having champagne," she said.

"I doubt The Swan can rise to that," he said.

His accent sounded Kildare and his demeanour suggested ex-soldier.

"Port-and-brandy," she said.

"They'll manage that."

He went to the bar and ordered. She studied him from behind. His boots were clean and they had new heels. His trousers were made of material she did not recognise. They were dark and there was a stripe in them. When it was time to pay he drew a wallet out of his pocket and she saw that a chain attached it to something although she could not see what that was, perhaps his belt, perhaps a button. One thing was for sure, however: oh yes, he was a careful one.

The man returned and set the drinks on the table and sat down on the stool opposite. His was porter in a straight glass.

"Your health," he said. "Horace Conway."

"Mary McCarthy."

Each took a sip and then, as she always would in these

situations, she began with the questions. These were circumspect and she kept her voice low when she spoke. The function of the questions was not only to elicit information but also to give the impression that she was a good listener and had a pliant and agreeable temperament.

Horace did not seem surprised and his answers were expansive. He was born in 1852 in the town of Athy and he was the youngest of six, he said. His father was in the Leinster Fusiliers and died of frostbite in the Crimea. At fourteen he enlisted. At seventeen he shipped with the Fusiliers to Calcutta. A few years later he married Florence, a widow whose soldier husband had died of snakebite. Florence had children from her first marriage and with Horace she went on to have two more: a boy named Victor and a girl called Theodora. After twenty years of marriage an infection in Florence's right leg led to gangrene. The leg was amputated and she died. Horace's son Victor joined the Indian Army and Theodora married a corporal in the Connaught Rangers.

At the age of forty-eight, after he had served thirty-two years, Horace left the army and came home to Ireland. His mother was dead and there was no one in Athy except a sister he had never really known. He bought a house in Grattan Parade in the north Dublin suburb of Drumcondra. It was a small red-brick house with two bedrooms. He rented one to a ledger clerk who worked in the accountancy firm Quigley's whose offices were on the Quays.

The glasses were empty. Horace went to the counter and returned with another port-and-brandy and a pint of stout and a plate of sausages with a puddle of bright yellow mustard on the side and two forks. He gave one fork to her. She looked at the sausages. They were coated with a shiny film of grease and were steaming slightly. As she knew very well, The Swan served two kinds of sausage: mutton or beef. She saw that Horace had bought beef ones, which were better quality and more expensive.

He did not skimp. He was not mean. She liked that. Now she knew for sure that she would go home with him.

After a third round of drinks he invited her back. A figure was agreed. They left The Swan and walked through the rain. The sky that blew across the River Liffey smelt of porter and yeast. They passed a railway station and turned into Grattan Parade. They reached Horace's house. The front door was Buckingham Green and very dark. He unlocked the door and they went in. The hall smelled of lamp oil. It was a fishy smell. She did not like it. As she followed him towards the stairs she glanced into the parlour. There was balled newspaper and kindling and black nuggets of coal laid in the grate for a fire. They started up the bare wooden stairs. Their feet made dull hollow booms on the treads and she got a whiff of marmalade and paint.

"Back room," he said when they got to the landing. The lodger had gotten the good room at the front, she realised.

She went in to his room and he followed. He closed the door and pulled the blind. It made a brittle noise as it dropped. It was made of stiff yellow material. The wheels of a train clattered in the distance. Closer to hand she heard girls in the street chant as they turned a skipping rope and another girl jumped. They undressed. They went to bed. When they kissed she noticed his teeth. They had sharp edges and with the bottom of her tongue she could feel that his lower teeth had grooves worn in them by the upper ones.

While she waited for him to finish she listened to the sound of the rope as it dunned the pavement outside. She heard the steam whistle of another train, high and hard and shrill. She had always liked the sound of trains and now here she was with the sound of one in her ears while she waited for Horace to spend himself. It was a good omen.

Three days later Mary wheeled her possessions around to Horace's in a handcart and moved in. Her arrangement with Horace was that she would not see other men and she would keep the house for him. In return he would feed her and clothe her and keep her and he did not have to pay any more. As far as his neighbours were concerned she was his sister. She was a childless widow and her name was Mrs McCarthy. That was the story they agreed. As for the lodger, he was in no position to carry tales. Horace had asked him to go and he did the day that Mary moved in.

5

It was spring. May. Four months had passed since she had moved in with Horace. Mary sat and darned in the scullery. She heard the front door open and close and Horace as he clumped along the hall.

"Mary?"

"In here."

"There's a telegram."

He came into the scullery. It was a small dark room at the back with a single window that overlooked a small yard. There was a washing line outside and on the line hung a single white shirt of Horace's that she had washed.

"I called into The Swan," he said, "when I was in town." His voice was gentle; she knew that something bad must have happened. "This came for you."

He showed her a buff telegram envelope. She saw her name on the front. She recognised the shape of the letters. That much she managed but the rest of the writing was a mystery to her.

Mary was not able to read or write.

"I read it," Horace said.

She already knew that. The top was ragged where he had opened it.

"It's from your brother in Thurles."

"And he sent it to me at The Swan?"

"He did."

So Michael knew that was the public house she had worked out of. It was incredible how precise pieces of information travelled from one place to another in Ireland. It all went to show that whatever you did to hide it, your parish and your family always found out your business in the end. Maybe she ought to have gone to England when she was younger. Several English soldiers had wanted to take her across. Yet something had stopped her going. What was that, love of her nation? She had never known exactly, yet whatever it was it had kept her home.

"Shall I read it out?" he said.

"Go on, get it over with."

He pulled a sheet out and unfolded it.

"'Father and Alice died yesterday. Funeral Friday. Please reply. Michael.'"

A few minutes later Horace walked to the post office and sent Michael a telegram on her behalf. It read: "Coming tomorrow. Your sis. Mary."

While Horace was away Mary made a black armband and sewed it on to the sleeve of her summer jacket.

The next day Horace gave her fifteen shillings and she bought a second-class return ticket and caught the train. In Thurles she got a lift with a carter out to Michael's house. When she got there he was sat by the fire with a cup of tea cradled in his hands. His wife had taken the children to stay with her mother. Michael told Mary how their father and stepmother had been killed. They had been out in the trap together. Something had stung the horse: it was maybe a hornet, he thought, but nobody knew for sure. The horse had bolted and the trap had overturned and their heads had been dashed on the road and they had died. She had missed their wake. It had been nothing to write home about, he said.

Mary spent the night in the tiny bed on the landing that had been hers back when she had lodged with Michael as a young girl.

6

The next day Michael rented a trap and they went over to New Inn for the funeral in the Catholic church. Within minutes of the start of Mass Mary felt bored. She began to gaze at the tablets on the walls that showed Christ's progress up Calvary. For a while she was happy and then she sensed that the eyes of Old Mrs Dunphy in the pew straight across the aisle were on her. Old Mrs Dunphy was a publican: she watered her beer. Old Mrs Dunphy had a reputation as a gossip. Mary realised that she needed to cry.

She closed her eyes and remembered Lieutenant Heaton, the soldier she had loved when she was fifteen and who was the only man she had ever loved, she thought. She remembered how she had felt when his regiment marched away suddenly and how she had felt when she went to the barracks gate in Dublin and found that they had shipped to India. Her stomach knotted and tears welled up. She opened her eyes and angled her head towards old Mrs Dunphy and with a sense of relief felt a fat tear roll down her cheek; it left a wet trail behind.

7

Two days later Mary was alone at Michael's house. There was a rap at the door. She swung the door back to reveal a young man in his twenties with fine brown hair. He held a bowler hat in one hand and an envelope in the other.

"Miss Mary McCarthy?"

"Yes."

He proffered the envelope. "Letter from Mr Burke."

Mr Burke was a solicitor in Cashel. She remembered she had once gone with her father to his office in Chapel Street. Her father had left her to wait in the street and gone in. In her memory she had waited a long time while he did whatever he did.

She took the envelope.

"If you wouldn't mind giving your reply now, we'd be most grateful," the man said.

She opened the envelope and pulled the letter out. Then she patted the pockets of the smock that she wore over her dress as if looking for something. Whatever it was she did not find it. She glanced around the room.

"I'm as blind as a bat without my glasses," she said. "I don't know where they've got to."

She smiled at the young man.

"Shall I read it to you?" he said.

He had put his hands in his pockets. Young men were so predictable, she thought.

"Would you?"

He took his hands out of his pockets. There was change in one and it clinked as he did. She would have some of that, she thought. He took the letter and unfolded it. He cleared his throat.

"'Re: Mr and Mrs Edmund McCarthy (deceased). Dear Miss McCarthy, I am writing in connection with the estate of Mr and Mrs Edmund McCarthy. I would be extremely grateful if you could present yourself at our premises, address above, at the earliest possible opportunity. Yours sincerely, Patrick R.J. Burke.'"

She looked over his shoulder. His trap stood in the lane beyond the tiny front garden. "Can I come now?" she said. "Would you convey me in your trap?"

"Yes."

"Well, come in for a moment while I get ready."

She stepped back and opened the door wider and as she did she glanced at the place below his waist. The fabric was stretched because of pressure from behind.

She closed the door behind him and turned the key. A look of surprise crossed his face. She ignored it. She wanted to be sure that if her brother came back he would not burst in and find them. She took his hat and the letter. She put them on the table by the breadboard. She turned back and touched him through the fabric of his trousers. He made a small noise. She undid the buttons and pulled him free and pushed back the loose skin from around the tip.

A smell rose up to her: an odour that men often gave out from under there. It was yeasty. He was already a bit damp. That was the excitement. Before a man came something else came out. She had often noticed this. She grasped him. He made another couple of noises like the one he had already made only louder.

"Oh God."

Her wrist and the sleeve of her dress were wet. She waited. He wilted. When he was small again she folded him away and buttoned him up. She took off her smock and dried her hand on it. She found her gloves and hat. It was a straw hat with a sprig of roses made of coloured glass attached to the band.

"Shall we go?" she said.

Half an hour later they arrived at Burke's Chapel Street offices. The clerk drove the trap into the yard at the back. He stopped and pulled on the skidpan.

"Oh no," she muttered. "I've forgotten my purse."

She gave her nice smile. "What's your name?"

"Vincent Figgis."

"I'm sorry to ask, Vincent, but ... could you rise to sixpence?"

He pulled coins from his pocket and separated a silver round and popped it into her gloved hand.

"Thank you," she said and slipped it inside her left glove.

He opened the trap's door and folded the steps down. She climbed out.

"Go through that door," he said. He pointed at the top of the yard. "You'll find Mr Burke at the front of the house."

As she crossed the yard she sensed his stare on her back. She went inside and found Mr Burke in his office. He was a small man with a red face. She introduced herself. He told her to sit. He went away and came back with a box of documents.

"Your late father and stepmother's will," he said.

The text was short and pithy.

Her father and her stepmother were troubled by her occupation. They wanted her to give it up and in order to make this possible they had decided to make provision for her.

Thus they bequeathed her the Marlhill cottage and its two

finger-shaped acres and everything else they possessed in the hope that she would leave Dublin and return home to live a good and pious life.

Mary began to cry. This was not grief. This was shock. She had always assumed her stepmother would have persuaded her father to leave it all to her son Frank. Yet she had not. Her father and her stepmother had agreed together that it would be hers. What was so extraordinary was the way their secret had remained a secret. All those years without her ever knowing, this will had sat in this office and at any point in that time somebody could have brought her father and stepmother some outrageous piece of gossip about her from Dublin that could have made them decide to change their will. It had not happened, although it could have done, and then without her knowledge she would have lost what she had never known she had. Oh, there was no doubt about it: Ireland was a land of tremendous secrets; secrets so extraordinary that those whom they concerned could not begin to imagine their existence.

After a few minutes Mary felt better and her tears dried up.

"I need to send a telegram, Mr Burke, but I came out without any change. Would you send a telegram? I can settle up with you another time."

"Certainly," said Mr Burke. He dipped his pen in the inkwell. "Who's it to?"

"Horace Conway Esquire, 2 Grattan Parade, Drumcondra, Dublin."

Mr Burke's pen scratched as he wrote.

"The message reads: 'Detained here. Must stay. E.'," she said.

8

She went out and found Vincent waiting.

"Will we go?" he said.

She wondered if her eyes looked red. "Yes," she said.

She got in and the trap rose and fell with her weight. They left Burke's yard and sallied through the town. She noticed Vincent wore heavy boots and each bore a shiny silver chain of nail heads.

The last house slipped by and they passed into the country. There was a strong smell of grass and a faint smell of milk. She looked at the sky. It was filled with big white clouds.

"There's Lambert's pub," said Vincent. "Will you take a drink?"

She saw the pub ahead. It was a country pub with grey slates and red windows and doors. She smiled and nodded. She knew where this was headed.

He pulled up and went in and came out with a jug of porter and two glasses. They sat in the trap and drank together and watched the swallows as they flitted through the air around them. They finished the porter and he returned the jug and the glasses to Lambert's and they went on. It was late afternoon now. The sun slanted across the fields and every leaf in the hedgerows touched by its light shone a brighter green than usual. Vincent sang "I Know Where I'm Going" and she sang with him.

Vincent turned down a lane and pulled up by a wood. They climbed down from the trap and began to follow a path strewn with dry leaf mould and bits of twig into the middle of the wood. Here and there bright shafts of sunlight shot through the murk. They lit up the midges and motes they caught and made them gold and silver and when they hit the forest floor the shafts made odd-shaped squares of light that trembled as the leaves above were stirred by a faint wind. These patches on the floor of the wood were like piece of broken mirror, she thought.

Vincent wanted her to lie on the ground but Mary said, no, it would wet her dress. She leaned against a tree and lifted her skirts. It was soon over. As they walked back towards the trap she asked for another sixpence.

A few days later Mary moved in to the cottage at Marlhill and over the weeks that followed Vincent came to see her several times. By the end of July she was pregnant. On the evening she broke the news, Vincent explained that quite by chance he had actually come to tell her he could not see her any more. His family had made it clear to him that he must stop. Then he said goodbye and left.

When she reflected later, Mary decided it was probably true. He had come to break it off on the very same evening she had chosen to break the news that she was pregnant.

Mary never saw Vincent again, ever, though she did hear later that he went to Boston.

9

On 4 April 1901 Mary went into labour in the bedroom where she had been born. After an easy labour she delivered a girl with red hair. Mary named her child Mary McCarthy, although to avoid confusion she put out that her daughter would answer to Moll. She suckled Moll for a while but by the spring of 1902 she was tired of her life at Marlhill and she missed Horace and she believed that her feelings were reciprocated.

She let the cottage at Marlhill to some of Michael's wife's people and arranged for Mr Burke to pay their rent into a bank in Thurles. It was a private arrangement that only Mr Burke knew about. She arranged for Moll to go into the girls' half of St Bridget's Orphanage in Thurles. Mr Burke was on St Bridget's board so this was easy to expedite. Then she took the train to Dublin and walked to 2 Grattan Parade and gave the knocker two sharp raps.

Horace opened the door. For a moment when he saw Mary he was surprised. She saw it on his face. Then she saw his mouth move and his eyes glow. Oh yes, she had been right to imagine that he still wanted her.

"I knew you'd be back," he said.

"I knew you knew I'd be back," she said.

He had a girl living with him. Ethel was twenty-two. Her hair was blonde and she had a big brown mole on her upper lip. She was gone within an hour.

10

When she arrived Moll was given a cot in the St Bridget's girls' dormitory and an older girl was assigned to look after her. When Moll was six the older girl left and Moll got a standard bed with an iron frame and a mattress that smelled of carbolic and pee.

The girls in the dormitory went up to the age of sixteen and the woman in charge was Mrs Johnston. She was ancient and leathery and she slept in an annex separated from the dormitory by a thin partition.

If a girl cried in the night and Mrs Johnston liked the child then she would take that girl into her own bed and pet her.

However, if she did not like the girl then Mrs Johnston would call out: "Quiet, now, or the Devil will have your eyes out with his pin." Sometimes for the sake of variety she would call: "Quiet, now, or the Devil will slice your tongue off with his cut-throat razor." If she were very cross it would be: "Shut up, or the devil will cut off your girl's parts and you'll never have a baby."

Moll was round, small, freckled, red-haired and gap-toothed.

As these were qualities Mrs Johnston disliked (she favoured willowy girls with yellow hair) she was never one of Mrs Johnston's favourites and the old woman never took her into her bed. As a result Moll learned to cry in silence and in time she became adept at that.

The orphanage had a classroom and a master. However, as most girls were expected to go into service either in a Big House or the home of a strong farmer at sixteen, they were given chores to prepare them. The work of the girls also made the orphanage money.

Shortly after Moll had gotten her own bed she was assigned to the poultry. Every morning thereafter, once she had put on her regulation dress and smock and drawn on her itchy woollen stockings and slotted her feet into her heavy clogs, she would go to the scullery and lift the egg basket from the nail on the back of the door and run to the small kitchen garden with its nice high walls that kept out the foxes.

Her first job was to let the birds out; her second was to lift the trapdoors around the sides and the back of the hen house and rummage in the nesting boxes for warm fresh eggs. Her third job was to carry these inside to the cook, Mrs McSorley. Now she would eat her breakfast of bread and dripping and strong unsweetened tea (for sugar was forbidden the girls in St Bridget's) and then before she joined the other girls in the classroom she would return to help Old Arnold the poultryman to feed the birds. He was a garrulous, bandy-legged pipe smoker who was prone to fits and sometimes he would have one when she was out with him in the little kitchen garden as they doled out the mixture of meal and water that the birds were fed on.

When he fitted, Old Arnold would fall to the grass and writhe and thrash and froth would come out of his mouth, white and heavy like egg white, and she would have to run into the orphanage and find the master, Mr O'Shea, or the cook, Mrs McSorley, and together they would run back out, and then the grown-up would turn Old Arnold on his side and slip a finger into his mouth and pull his tongue forward, and then the grown-up would go and leave her to wait with Old Arnold until he came around.

When Moll turned ten Mrs McSorley said that she was now old enough to cope with Old Arnold's fits on her own and not to come any more for Mr O'Shea or for her but turn him on his side and pull his tongue forward herself and the next time and every time he fitted thereafter she did as she had been told.

1 1

By the time she was eleven Moll's red hair was very long and her body had begun to change. Curves had begun to show. She had noticed this. Others had noticed this as well and there was an alteration in the way that everyone spoke to her. She had always blushed but now her blushes were more frequent and more virulent. This was something to do with getting older. Why this should be was a mystery, but there it was. This was how things were and there was nothing else for it but to endure.

One day she was in the kitchen. She was on a chair reaching up for a pan on a high shelf.

"Look at those legs," said Clare Corrigan. She was sat at the table peeling potatoes. "Some man will love those, I'm sure."

Moll felt her face redden. She got down from the chair and handed Mrs McSorley the pan.

"My, Moll, you have gone red," said Mrs McSorley. "You're as red as a fox."

"Foxy Moll," said Clare Corrigan.

"Foxy Moll," said Mrs McSorley, "that is good. Oh yes, I like that. Foxy Moll McCarthy has a nice ring, doesn't it? Do you know what? I think that's what we'll have to call you from here on. We'll call you Foxy Moll, won't we, Clare?" Foxy Moll was what Mrs McSorley called her from then on and before long so did almost everyone else at St Bridget's.

12

A new gardener came to work in the orphanage. He was called Willie Garret. He was a small man with very black hair that he wore parted on the left and a symmetrical face and a strange manner that was somewhat charming and somewhat wheedling and somewhat boastful and somewhat apologetic. None of the orphans liked him. He had no wife or children.

One bright March morning after breakfast and before school Foxy Moll was in the little kitchen garden. Old Arnold was pouring meal from a pail into a feeding trough when he began to shake and stagger. He dropped the pail. The meal spilled everywhere and the hens darted forward to feed. Then he collapsed and the hens scattered away. Old Arnold began to writhe on the grass. The twine around his waist worked loose. His trousers slipped down below his hips and Foxy Moll saw his belly button and the line of hair that ran downwards and the wedge of hair at the bottom. The hair was grey and wiry and thin and the skin behind the hair was white like a mushroom. The sight frightened her and she closed her eyes when she turned Arnold onto his side and she kept them closed when she slipped her fingers in and pulled his slimy tongue forward. When she finished she panted hard from the effort and she did not hear the door of the little kitchen garden open and close or the sound of the footsteps that approached.

"What's wrong with Old Arnold?"

Foxy Moll started at the unexpected voice and opened her eyes. She saw Willie Garret's pale face and black hair; the slick at the front dangled in front of his right eye. He stood opposite on the other side of Old Arnold.

"He has turns," she said.

"Ah ha."

"And when he does, I put him on his side like this and he comes right as rain after a bit."

"Is that so?"

Willie stared down at the figure at their feet and then looked back at her.

"By the looks of things, you were doing more than turning the poor fellow. If you weren't such a nice girl, I think I'd say you were taking advantage."

She felt her neck redden as the flush began and then, a moment after, the hot red sensation crept around her chin and up across her face all the way to the roots of her hair at the top of her brow. Her eyes watered. She trembled. She wanted to shout "No, no," but she knew that if she opened her mouth nothing would come out. No words, nothing at all. Yet still she opened her mouth and no words came out.

"Will you look at that?" said Willie. "You've gone red, girl, and, oh my goodness, that's a red I'd say you'd not see anywhere but on a fox. Oh yes, they don't call you Foxy Moll for nothing, do they? You are a red one, oh yes, red as a fox, so you are, red as a fox."

She closed her mouth. Why did this happen? Why did she

blush like she did? She felt embarrassed but at the same time this attention and the way he talked to her and the way he teased her was nice. She liked it.

With her face still aflame she glanced at him. She did not plan to do this. It just happened. Then she gave him the tiniest smile. Again she had not decided to do this but then had done it. It was not intended. It just happened.

Willie Garret smiled and winked back.

"Foxy Moll, my foxy girl."

The nice feeling that she had became stronger but so did her embarrassment and the heat of her face. She looked away. On the ground Old Arnold moaned and rolled onto his back and sat up and blinked and spluttered.

"You'd a turn, old timer," said Willie, "but our friend here, Foxy Moll, she took good care of you."

Old Arnold shuddered and wriggled and hoisted his trousers and that was a complicated process as he was still sat on the ground and then he retied the string looped around his waist.

"Ah, these turns, they're a damnation."

"Let's get you on your feet," said Willie.

Foxy Moll noticed that he spoke in an altogether different way than he had with her a few moments before. Gone was the wheedling soft tone and in its place was a hard, even curt, mat-ter-of-fact tone. Obviously he had two voices and one was for girls and the other was for anyone else, like Old Arnold.

Willie got his hands under Old Arnold's elbows and lifted him up. Willie may have been small but he was strong.

"Have you always taken turns?" said Willie.

"Only since the Crimea." Old Arnold dusted his clothes but he did not do a good job.

"Let me." Willie began to wipe Old Arnold's shoulders with one of his small hands.

"One of the Tsar's cannonballs clipped my head. I was out for days. They thought I was gone but I came back as good as new, but then the fits started and they haven't stopped since." He pointed at the wooden pail that he had dropped when the fit started. "Be a good girl and pass me that."

She picked up the pail by its rope handle.

"You're a good girl, Mary," said Old Arnold.

"Is she?" said Willie. "I don't know about that."

"She's always good to me."

To her ears Old Arnold sounded cross. She wondered why. He was not cross with her, was he? She had done nothing wrong. Then she understood. It was Willie Garret. Old Arnold did not care for him. That was why he sounded cross. But why did he not care for him? It was a mystery but then she had often noticed how adults were like that. They had notions and likes and dislikes that were way above her head.

"I've noticed you don't call her Foxy Moll, do you, like the rest of them here?" said Willie.

"No, I do not."

"Why's that?" Willie sounded disgruntled and resentful.

"I'll tell you why." Old Arnold took the pail and turned his old worn face towards the younger man and looked straight at him with his watery blue eyes. "She got her name when she was born, she got Mary McCarthy, and Mary McCarthy as far as I am concerned is what she is. Always was, always will be."

"But she doesn't mind. She likes it." Willie stared at her. "Sure you don't mind, do you? You don't mind, Foxy Moll?"

Whatever she said she was bound to annoy one or other man and she did not want to annoy either of them. The only way out of this was to pretend not to hear. She looked at the ground. The hens were back; they pecked at the spilled meal. She hoped it looked as if her attention was on them.

There was a long silence. Finally Old Arnold said, "Let's get the eggs."

Foxy Moll had already collected the eggs earlier that morning but she said nothing now and simply followed the old man into the hen house. Inside it reeked of hen: a sharp avian stink.

"That Willie one," said Old Arnold, "he's not a good lad. You want to take my advice, don't let him near you and don't you go near him, do you hear me? He's a serpent, slippery and dangerous. Very good with the talk but not to be trusted further than you can throw him, which wouldn't be far, even if he is a light little squit of a thing. And what is it with everyone and your name? You're Mary McCarthy, yes? But no, everyone has to meddle with your name and they call you Foxy Moll instead. Why can't they leave your name alone?"

These were strange questions and she could not answer them. What did it matter if everyone called her Foxy Moll? Besides, why would they not? Her hair was red. Her skin was red. She was red. It made sense. In truth she did not mind. As for when Willie Garret said her name, the truth was she really liked it. It made her feel something she had never felt before. It was a funny feeling: as if she fizzed inside. Of course she could not possibly confess this to Old Arnold so Foxy Moll said nothing.

"I'd steer clear of him, if I was you," said Old Arnold eventually.

They began to search the nesting boxes for eggs but of course there were none there. They left empty-handed and went back out. Foxy Moll saw Willie Garret was gone. She felt disappointed but she did not let this show.

13

The next day, she saw Willie at a distance as he wheeled his wheelbarrow down the drive of St Bridget's. She guessed he was on his way to clean the weeds from around the gates.

The day after, she did not see him at all and she heard from Mrs McSorley he had been sent with the horse and cart to the coal yard for coke for the boiler.

The next day, he was on her mind as she took her basket and headed off first thing on her egg run. She did not see him on the way to the kitchen garden and she told herself he had not come to work yet and perhaps she would see him later. She hoped she would.

When she got to the hen house she undid the bolts and folded down the long trapdoor at the back. She reached inside the nesting boxes and began to feel around in the dry, scratchy straw for eggs. She found one warm and smooth and lifted it from the straw with care and put it in the basket.

"Ah, there's my favourite girl," she heard. She recognised

Willie Garret's voice behind her straight away. "Hello, Foxy Moll. How are you this morning?"

She decided to ignore him because she thought that would make him pay more attention and so she continued to rummage for eggs with her back towards him.

"Is Foxy Moll going to ignore her Willie?"

"I've got to get Mrs McSorley's eggs or she'll eat me." This was untrue but it was a serviceable excuse.

"But Willie Garret's got a present for his Foxy Moll, a tiny little present – surely Foxy Moll would like a little present, wouldn't she?"

She had no idea what this might be but she wanted it whatever it was.

"What is it?" she said. She turned towards him.

"Oh, so suddenly Foxy Moll is interested now, is she?"

She said nothing. She would just look at him and wait and if after a bit nothing happened then she would turn back and resume her search for eggs. She stared at him.

"It's this," he said.

He put his hand into his jacket pocket and took out a paper bag. Then from out of the paper bag he pulled an orange barley sugar in the shape of a shepherd's crook.

"You'd have a sweet tooth, I'd say. That's why I got it."

She stared at the barley sugar. It was a deep and lovely orange colour with a small but desirable pink ribbon tied in a bow at the point where the shaft started to curve. She wanted it very much. She had never had a barley sugar before but she had spoken to other girls who had and from them she knew that it was one of the loveliest things on earth.

"You want it?" he said.

In her stomach she felt a strange but pleasurable agitated feeling while inside her mouth her cheeks were wet with spit while all over her tongue there were little prickles of sensation that she recognised as need.

"Yes," she said.

"Will you be nice to me, then?"

She wondered what that meant. Nice? She would be courteous, she was sure of that. She knew what words she had to say to express gratitude. She would be polite. Was that what he meant by being nice?

As she pondered she felt herself pulled in different directions. The anxious part of her nature, the part that looked after her wellbeing, said, no, don't take it, don't accept it. What he means by nice isn't nice. He'll want things off you, things that are dirty and horrible, and the simplest thing, the easiest thing, the cleanest thing is to just say "No" now and turn around and go back to looking for eggs.

The other side of her nature, her greedy side, said the reverse: here was a present, a present of a piece of lovely barley sugar. Had she not always wanted to taste it? Yes, she had. Well, here was her chance. All she needed to do was reach out and take it from him. That was all. Nothing more. Then all she would have to say was "Thank you". She could do that, could she not? Yes, she could. Once she had done that she would have discharged her duties and in return the barley sugar would be hers.

Without thought, without any decision to make the movement, she reached towards him and opened her hand.

"Just as I thought," he said. "Little Foxy Moll has a sweet tooth. Isn't that right, my dear one, you've a sweet tooth? Confess it."

"Yes."

"Yes, what?"

Yes, what? What had he asked of her? What did he want her to say? She could not think. In her head she had only one thought: to get that twist of barley sugar and make it hers.

"Yes, what?" he said.

"Yes, Foxy Moll has a red tooth."

"A red tooth?" he said and snorted. "You mean a sweet tooth."

She began to flush. "Yes, a sweet tooth," she said. "Foxy Moll has a sweet tooth."

He put the barley sugar in her palm. She closed her fingers around it and then in one swift movement she slipped her hand into the pocket of her smock and put the precious barley sugar in the crease at the very bottom where grit and fluff collected.

"What do you say now?" said Willie.

"Thank you."

"No. It's 'Thank you, Willie.'"

"Thank you, Willie."

"Oh, Foxy Moll is learning some manners. And what a lovely thing it is to see her so mannerly."

He put the paper bag in his pocket and walked off with a smirk on his face. She went back to her egg hunt. Her face began to cool. She filled her basket and brought the eggs into Mrs Mc-Sorley. Then she slipped up to her dormitory, although she was not meant to go there in the day, and hid the barley sugar inside the pillowslip around her pillow.

That night in bed she listened to the breathing of the girls around her. Their breathing was normal but as time passed it became slower and more regular. After a while the point came when she felt sure that everyone was asleep. She pulled her barley sugar out from inside the pillowslip and undid the ribbon with care. She put the ribbon back inside the pillowslip so that she could use it in the morning and now at last came the moment she had anticipated all day. She slipped the end of the barley sugar, not the crook but the straight end, into her mouth and began to suck. At first the barley sugar did not taste of anything. The sensation she had was of something cold and glassy and hard in her mouth. But within seconds she was graced with a new sensation, a moist and extraordinarily sweet taste that spread through her mouth and down her throat. It was the nicest taste that she had ever tasted in her whole life.

In the morning after she had brushed her hair she remembered the ribbon in her pillowslip. She fetched it and tied her hair at the back.

Clare Corrigan saw the new coloured ribbon.

"Where did that come from?"

"It was a present."

"Who gave you a present? You don't know anybody."

"Willie Garret, the new man in the gardens."

"Oh," said Clare Corrigan, her eyes wide with what Foxy Moll recognised was a mixture of surprise and envy.

Envy, she thought as she ran downstairs, envy. No one had ever envied anything of hers before. The very idea made her feel giddy and powerful.

After breakfast Willie came and found her in the little kitchen garden.

"I like the ribbon," he said. "Do you?"

He touched the ribbon; it was only a gentle touch but her whole scalp tingled. She had never known anything like these feelings before. They were strange and powerful but not unpleasant.

"There'll be more where that came from," he said.

He walked off and, filled with elation, she went on with the work of egg collection.

14

Over the seasons that followed Willie brought her several ribbons of different colours and widths as well as buttons and cakes and coloured thread and a woollen shawl.

All these things, none of which she had ever owned before, gave her the same giddy, powerful feeling that the barley-sugar ribbon had. She was also gratified that Willie liked her enough to give her these things, and before long she decided that the very fact that he gave them certified his ardour and guaranteed he felt the way he said he did.

The gifts also affected the other orphans and how they treated her. As news of Willie's generosity spread she was treated with a respect that she had never known before. She who had been nobody had become somebody: somebody known as Willie's girl, Willie's Foxy Moll.

The next thing that happened was that she no longer looked forward to the gifts alone, as she had done, and rather than wonder what he would give her she began instead to look forward to when she might see him. What was more, when he spoke to her and called her Foxy Moll or asked her if she was a foxy one or used the other endearments that were part of his repertoire her heart raced and she felt a great bubble of happiness fill her up inside.

Then the anxiety set in: it was almost like jealousy. She had to see him and it hurt when she did not, as much as it thrilled her when she did. Then she began to wheedle. She wanted his assurance that he liked her most out of all the girls in the orphanage and in the town and in Munster and in the whole of Ireland. She asked and he gave her that assurance time after time and at first it satisfied but then it was not enough. It had to be more. He had to say that he loved her and her alone and no one else and, what was more, that he had never and he would never love anyone but her. For a long time Willie Garret would not tell her this. All he would say was that he liked her. Then all he would say was that he adored her. Then at last the day came when he told her that he loved her and the moment he spoke the words strange surges of feeling darted through her stomach. Her legs trembled and she felt odd between her legs: it was in some measure an ache and also to some degree something else that she had never known before and in her small nascent breasts she felt needles of pain.

Each Sunday afternoon the orphans were allowed to leave St Bridget's and walk out into the country for an hour. The Sunday after that she met Willie by arrangement and they walked out to a little wood. Here she let him kiss her. They walked out to this wood on more Sunday afternoons after that and many times he kissed her. Then came the time that he gave her the ring and promised to marry her. She had never felt so happy in her life and she let Willie lift her skirt. Then he did what he had been on at her to do for quite some time and even though she knew she should not let him she felt that she could not deny him now. When he was finished they walked back to the orphanage arm in arm. She was fourteen.

15

The next day was Monday but Willie did not turn up for work. Nor was he there on Tuesday or Wednesday or Thursday. On Friday a parishioner told a priest who told Mrs McSorley who told several of the orphans who passed through her kitchen, one of whom was Clare Corrigan, what had happened.

In the classroom Clare Corrigan's desk was behind Foxy Moll's. The master wrote on the blackboard; the chalk scratched as he did.

"Foxy Moll, did you hear?" whispered Clare Corrigan.

Pale and white and heavy with ache, she knew at once that this must concern Willie. She was desperate to have news of him and at the same time she surmised that whatever Clare Corrigan had to tell her must be bad.

"Willie was seen on Monday going into an army recruiting office in Limerick and then he was seen at the station getting on a train. He's joined the army, so he has, and he's going off to France to fight."

Foxy Moll bolted from the classroom and into the garden. She doubled over and out it flooded: the bread and dripping and tea that had been her breakfast and the kipper she had eaten for dinner at midday. The mess of undigested food formed a puddle at her feet.

The master sent Clare Corrigan after her. Clare found her outside and went to Mrs McSorley in the kitchen. The cook had greasy hands and was making meatloaf with sausage meat.

"Foxy Moll's sick."

"Where?"

"On the grass, round the side."

"That girl," said Mrs McSorley. "I'm only busy making the supper and now I have to stop because of her." Though nothing had been said, everyone in St Bridget's blamed her for Willie's disappearance and the adults complained it was a terrible nuisance to lose him.

Mrs McSorley brought Foxy Moll back into the kitchen. She found a bit of cloth in the rag box.

"Wipe your face with that," she said, "then throw it in the fire."

It was a scrap of old green curtain; the material was very rough. Foxy Moll wiped her mouth and threw the rag into the open fire.

"Here." Mrs McSorley handed her a tin cup. Bubbles floated on top of the milk inside. "Drink that. That'll settle you."

Foxy Moll sniffed the milk. It smelled of cow and pasture. It was heavy and rich and buttery and, she knew, impossible for her to swallow.

"I can't. It'll make me sick again." She put the cup on the table. "I'll take a cup of water, though. If you have it."

Late that night Foxy Moll began to shiver and sweat. Her teeth first chattered and then ground against one another. Then she started to murmur and before long she shouted. Her yells woke Clare Corrigan who got out of bed and lifted her heavy nightdress so that she would not trip on the hem and went to the annex.

"Mrs Johnston."

"What's the matter now?"

"It's Foxy Moll."

Mrs Johnston climbed out of her high wooden bed and threw a shawl around her shoulders and padded out into the dark dormitory. She heard Foxy Moll shout and thrash under the blankets as she approached. Mrs Johnston put her hand out in the darkness and found Foxy Moll's head and clamped her hand onto her forehead. It was hot and wet.

"At the side of my bed there's a candle," she said to Clare Corrigan who stood behind her. "Light it and bring it here."

Clare Corrigan went away and returned. By the pale fluttery light of the candle Mrs Johnston and the orphan saw that Foxy Moll was red-faced and she streamed with sweat.

"She's boiling," said Mrs Johnston. "I need a basin of cold water and a flannel, and we'll have to get the doctor."

The next day the doctor came in the afternoon and diagnosed a fever and prescribed isolation in case whatever it was that Foxy Moll had was contagious. A bed was made up for her in the attic under the eaves and she lay up there for a week and sweated and wept and slept and was tormented by a terrible feverish dream that repeated over and over and over again.

She was out on a dirt road that snaked across flat boggy ground under a sullen filthy black sky. Willie was there in front of her: he hurried on and she called to him to wait and tried to catch up with him but he did not listen to her cries. He moved faster and faster. She tried to catch up with him but it was useless. No matter how hard she struggled and how much she shouted and wailed and cajoled, he got further and further and further ahead of her until, in the end, he vanished and she was left alone in the middle of endless empty bog.

In the odd hours that she was awake and conscious she would

lie in her bed and stare up at the slanted slope of grey slates just above her head. She sometimes heard the scratches made by the claws of birds as they walked about on the roof outside. At these times she felt a pain in her chest more or less in the region of her heart. It was a powerful feeling: it excruciated and exhausted in equal measure. In comparison to this, Foxy Moll found that on balance she preferred her awful dream.

At last her temperature returned to normal and she was allowed to return to the dormitory. The first thing she did when she got there was to go to her shelf in the press where she kept her clothes and pull out the buttons and the ribbons and the shawl hidden under her things. At the sight of Willie's gifts those awful sharp stabs of pain that had tormented her when she had been awake in the attic hit her again. They hit her so hard that she felt her legs shake and she knew she needed to sit. At the same time, at the sight of all she had left that connected her to Willie, she felt something like relief.

She grabbed it all – the ribbons and the buttons and the shawl – and carried them to her bed and sat and cradled them on her lap. For a long while great gusts of pain and joy flowed through her. The feelings were terrible. They also comforted her.

16

Early in 1917 Horace Conway got pneumonia. One morning a man came to the front door. He told Mary he was Richard Rooney and his mother was Agnes Rooney *née* Conway and she had asked him to trace her lost brother Horace and by chance he had mentioned his quest in The Swan and Big Van had directed him to Grattan Parade and so now here he was.

"He's not well," said Mary.

"I'd gathered."

"Come in then."

They went up the stairs and into the darkened room where Horace lay in bed very still under the blankets. There was a strong, bitter vegetable smell that was the bitter brown medicine Horace took for his chest.

"I think he's still asleep," Mary said.

"No I'm not," said Horace. "Who's this?"

"Richard Rooney," said the visitor. "I'm Agnes' son."

"My sister Agnes? She's alive?"

"That's right."

Over the next week Agnes and her stout butcher husband and Richard and the four other Rooney children all came to visit. Horace was so happy to see them Mary felt sure he was on the mend. Then came the night throughout which he coughed and vomited and just as dawn began to show he died.

His will was read three days later. It had always been Mary's understanding that 2 Grattan Parade was to be hers but in the last week of Horace's life Richard Rooney had helped him make a new will and Horace had not told Mary he had done this, and so when the will was read it was with great surprise that she discovered he had left his little house to his sister Agnes and not to her.

Mary was forty-seven. She considered staying in Dublin but she did not want to be alone and doubted anyone would take her at the age she was. Her thoughts turned to Moll, her child in St Bridget's Orphanage in Thurles. On 4 April her child would turn sixteen. She had an idea that was the age all the orphans left and went out to work. She formed a plan. Her brother's wife's people were tenants still in the cottage at Marlhill. She would put them out. Mr Burke would see to that. She would send for her daughter. Mr Burke would see to that too. Moll would come home. They would live together. They would become allies and then friends and when she became old Moll would look after her.

Mary went to The Swan and Big Van wrote a letter for her to Mr Burke and set her plan in motion.

1 7

It was a May morning. Foxy Moll awoke but kept her eyes shut. Why could she not hear the familiar sounds as girls threw off their blankets and hurried off to wash in cold water? Why so quiet? Then she remembered.

She opened her eyes. The wall in front of her was rough and bumpy and a line of whitewash flakes lay in the crease where the wall met the floor. They reminded her of snow piled at the side of the road.

She lifted her eyes to the small window. There was green slime around the edges and the sky outside was grey. She heard a whisper. She knew the sound: it was the sound rain made as it fell on the grasses and the bushes and the trees around Marlhill. She was back in the bedroom in the cottage where she had been born. Her mother was in the other room: the kitchen. She was home.

She threw off the covers and swung sideways and put her feet down on the square of sacking that lay on the smooth hard cold earthen floor. She put on her day dress and smock which were the same ones that she had worn in the orphanage and pulled on her stockings and shoes and combed her hair and pinned it up and went out to the kitchen.

Her mother sat by the hearth with a black shawl pulled tight around her. A few minutes before she had thrown some turf sods on the embers left from the previous night and these had just caught and the smoke they made streamed up the chimney. The smoke was a dark grey like a storm cloud but so thick and substantial that it seemed liquid. Foxy Moll saw that her mother's settle bed had been folded up and put away.

"You slept?" her mother said.

"I did."

"I'd say you find a queer difference between here and the place you were."

"I do."

She recalled the quiet that had just struck her as it had every morning since she had come back home. "I do," she said again.

"Not quite so palatial," said her mother.

That was a strange word to choose. Obviously her mother had no idea what St Bridget's was really like. Not that she would say anything. As she had already discovered within a few weeks, the best course with her mother was to neither disagree nor contradict. It just led to trouble.

"It's raining," Foxy Moll said.

The sooty kettle hung from the crane and she wondered when her mother would swing it over the fire to boil the water for tea. She craved a cup of strong tea and hoped for a slice of bread and butter to go with it.

"Shall I go to the spring well?"

She thought that the mention of water might prompt her mother to put the kettle on. The spring well was two fields along the lane to Marlhill Farm. They got their water there by arrangement with Marlhill's owner, Mr Caesar.

"I was out already," her mother said. "I got water."

Foxy Moll pulled up a stool and sat.

"How's the form?"

Her mother gave a funny shrug. "You go sailing out into the world, but the sea always washes you back to where you started."

Foxy Moll nodded. Yes, this was true. Had she herself not been washed back to where she had started? She did not mind but her mother seemed to.

"What have I done?" Her mother gave another little shrug as if to add weight to her question. "What have I ever done?"

Foxy Moll looked at the wall at the back of the fire with its thick furry coat of soot and then at her mother.

"You've had me," she said.

"That's true, but would anyone know we're related?"

Foxy Moll was short and a little plump while her mother was taller than her daughter was and thinner and dark haired although now she was going grey.

"I'm McCarthy, same as you."

"I haven't your red hair or your figure. No one would ever call me Foxy Moll, but you, you're a red foxy one all right."

Foxy Moll wondered if she dared say it. She decided she would.

"Maybe I take after my father?"

"No, you don't."

As far as Mary could recall there had not been anything red about Mr Burke's clerk Vincent Figgis although she supposed there must have been red in his people somewhere and that was where her daughter got her colour.

The turf sods were ablaze now so Mary swung the crane and got the kettle into position.

"We'll have some tea," she said. "And I'll thank you never to talk about your father again."

1 8

Several hours had passed. Foxy Moll looked out the small kitchen window and saw the rain had stopped.

"The rain's stopped," Foxy Moll said.

"We need sugar," said her mother. "Will you go to Cassidy's shop?"

"I will."

"A pound will be fine. Tell them to put it down. I'll be in to settle up on Saturday, tell them. Oh, and a shop loaf, as you're at it, too."

A shopping bag made from a flour sack hung by its rope handles from the back of the door. Foxy Moll took it down and went outside.

The first thing she noticed was the smell that was a mix of wet earth and wet stone and wet thatch. Then she noticed the air. It was warm yet damp. When the sun shone after rain it always smelled and felt like that and in her mind this wet warmth was what made everything grow. Then she heard the drone of hundreds of bees in the bushes that separated the cottage from the road. It was the sound of life to her.

She went out their gate that was a wide farm gate, broad enough for a cart to pass through, and turned to the right onto the public road. The road ran north and about half a mile up on the right was the turn for New Inn but she was not about to go that way. There was a much quicker route to New Inn on foot.

A few yards further along the road there was a hand-painted sign nailed to a tree that read "Marlhill Farm". There was a lane here on the right and she turned into it. The lane was earthen but so compacted by the weight of the many people and vehicles and animals that had passed along it over the years that it was rock hard.

The lane passed behind her mother's cottage and ran in a straight line past the field with the spring well where they got their water, all the way to a farmhouse and some farm buildings in the distance. This was Marlhill Farm, the home of the man whose land surrounded her mother's finger-shaped two acres.

The owner of the farm was called Mr John Caesar and her mother had told her about him and the other people on his farm as they sat by the fire on the first night Foxy Moll had arrived home from the orphanage.

Mr Caesar had been born in Holycross, twenty miles north of New Inn. His people were strong farmers. He had several siblings but his favourite was his sister Catherine.

As a young man Mr Caesar had gone to New York to work as a labourer and his sister Catherine had married Thomas Gleeson, another strong farmer, and had twelve children.

In 1915 aged fifty-five Mr Caesar had come home and with the American dollars he had saved he had bought Marlhill Farm. Then he married a woman called Hogan from West Tipperary.

Mr Caesar was too old to manage the farm alone so his nephew Harry Gleeson, one of his sister Catherine's sons who had been reared by another Caesar uncle, came to Marlhill Farm to work as a labourer.

As Mr and Mrs Caesar were both over fifty now and it was too late for them to have children, it was understood that when they died Marlhill Farm would pass to Harry.

After her mother had finished her account she had said to her daughter: "This Harry is only a couple of years older than you. Marry him and one day you'll be a strong farmer's wife. There are many worse fates in life than that, I assure you."

Foxy Moll just nodded although she thought this was an awful idea. When she married it would be for love.

Foxy Moll started up the lane towards the Caesars' house and she soon passed the gate on her right to the field where they drew their water. The hard compacted earth of the lane was already dry after the earlier rain though there were puddles in hollows here and there and the sky was reflected in these. As she went along Foxy Moll stared down at the puddles and then up at the sky to compare the reflection with the original. That morning the sky had been hidden by a low lid of cloud but now all the cloud was gone and it was all blue over her head.

She felt cheerful. It was a lovely warm afternoon. All that she had to do was walk to New Inn and pick up the bread and the sugar and walk back. She started to hum and swung the bag first backwards and forwards and then around and around.

After a couple of hundred yards the Caesars' farmhouse appeared on Foxy Moll's right. It was a two-storey concrete-faced dwelling with a porch and casement windows and a single chimney that jutted up from the middle of the slate roof. There was a bench against the wall opposite the front door that faced south and Mr and Mrs Caesar were sat there.

"Lovely afternoon," Mr Caesar called.

"Lovely," said Foxy Moll. She stopped and turned to face the old couple.

"If you could bottle this sun and sell it to the Americans, you'd be rich," he said.

He had removed his jacket. His blue shirt had no collar. He was a heavy man and his belly pressed out from behind his shirt and hung over the thick brown belt he had buckled around his middle. He had a crinkled face and small yellowy eyes and terrible teeth on account of the sweet tea that he drank in vast quantities. The first time they met he had told Foxy Moll never to take sugar in her tea because of what it did to the teeth. She told him the girls in St Bridget's were forbidden sugar in their tea on grounds of cost and so she never had. "The world would be a better place if we all followed the example of St Bridget's," he had said.

"Now, why would the Americans want our sun?" said Mrs Caesar.

She was a small dark-skinned woman with a big pointed nose and a mass of grey hair that she wore piled up on the back of her head and secured with many pins. Whenever they met, Foxy Moll always imagined that Mrs Caesar's piled hair must be about to tumble but it never did.

"Haven't they enough sun of their own without adding ours?" said Mrs Caesar.

"They have sun all right, but not like ours," said Mr Caesar. "Look at it, will you, there's nothing to beat it in all the world, certainly nothing that comes out of America."

He looked at Foxy Moll with his small yellowy eyes that she thought were kind despite their strange colour.

"Isn't that right, Foxy Moll?"

"I don't know. But you've been to America, haven't you, Mr Caesar? So, you'd know."

"I have been. And I'm glad you brought that fact up. Yes, I am an expert on American sunshine," and here he turned towards Mrs Caesar, "which I don't believe you are. I believe if anyone knows what they'll buy over there, it's me."

"If I'd a penny, Mr Caesar, for every bit of nonsense you come out with, I'd say I'd be richer than the Queen of England."

Mr Caesar snorted. "You wouldn't make more than tuppence a day."

"Why wouldn't I?"

"Because I never come out with more than tuppence worth of nonsense in a day, do I?"

"How are you today, Foxy Moll?" said Mrs Caesar. "Settling in? Getting used to Marlhill?"

Foxy Moll nodded.

"Some change, I'd say, after where you've been."

Foxy Moll smiled.

"You running a message to New Inn?"

"Yes. Can I get you anything?" said Foxy Moll.

"That's kind of you to offer. No, I think we have all we need."

"I'd better head on, so."

"We've some more spuds for your mother. Have a word with the nephew, would you? He's in the yard."

Foxy Moll nodded and walked on until she came to an entranceway on her right. She turned here in to a yard surrounded by buildings and outhouses. She saw Harry sat on a box with a horse's collar on his lap. He was bareheaded and his cloth cap lay at his feet. He was lanky and long limbed.

"Hello," she called but he did not look up because he did not hear her. As she knew from her mother some terrible illness in his brain when he had been a baby had left him a bit deaf although strangely it had not affected his musical talent. She had been told he played the fiddle beautifully and could even read music.

She ambled towards him. His face was down as he concentrated on sewing the torn seam of the collar so that as she approached Foxy Moll saw the crown of his head. The hair about his ears was black but in the middle there was a band of white that ran from forehead to nape. That wide white streak was another consequence of his illness as a baby.

"Badger."

Because of the thick white streak that was what everyone called him rather than Harry. He still did not look up. She moved right up to him and she touched him on the shoulder gently and he looked up.

"Oh." He smiled briefly. "Hello, Foxy Moll."

"Hello, Badger."

He smiled. "Day's turned out grand, hasn't it?"

"Hasn't it just?"

She looked at his face. It was long and flat and his features were regular but small. It was not an unpleasant face but it did not stir her in the way that Willie Garret's face had, for example. She did not know much but she did know that this was not the face of a man whom she could marry, let alone love. She knew that much. He was a nice fellow, however, and she never minded stopping to say hello to him. She knew that too.

"Mrs Caesar said something about some spuds for my mother?"

"Yes, yes." His voice was a bit flat because of his deafness. "We've a couple of stone for you. I'll throw them over the gate by the spring well when I'm out counting the animals later. Will you be able to manage them from there?"

"Why wouldn't I?"

She said goodbye and retraced her steps. She wanted to thank the Caesars for the promised gift of the potatoes but the bench was empty. They had gone inside.

"Bye, Foxy Moll," she heard from behind.

She turned. "Bye, Badger."

She lifted the bag and waved it over her head.

Badger smiled. "Be sure you don't annoy any fairies."

There was a local superstition that people were not the only ones to use the Mass Path she was about to take.

"I'll take care where I step."

She went on and passed through a gate and skirted a little

pond full of very black still water on which a drake and a mallard floated and then she came to the old Mass Path. It wound away through the fields and high hedges of hawthorn and fuchsia grew along its edges. In the distance she saw the spire of the Catholic church and the tower of the Church of Ireland church and the roofs of the houses of New Inn grouped around the two places of worship.

The Mass Path was grassy but with stones embedded here and there. She would have to be careful not to catch her foot on one and trip. As she began to move along the path she hummed and felt happier still.

19

The Mass Path came into New Inn behind the Catholic grave-yard.

As she skirted the wall Foxy Moll saw the tops of some of the headstones on the other side. Her mother had given her an account of the McCarthys' family history and so she knew that her grandmother Jane and her grandfather Edmund and his second wife Alice were all buried together in there though she had not been to see their graves yet. Her mother had said they would do that one Sunday but she did not believe they ever would.

The Mass Path ended at Cross Street. Foxy Moll turned to the right here and walked down to the cross in the middle of the village and then she turned to the right again and went onto Main Street. She was now in the centre of New Inn where the shops and official buildings were.

She passed the Royal Irish Constabulary barracks on her right. It was a long building with a porch and a courtyard at the back. Then she passed the New Inn Cooperative Creamery. This was a square building with tall chimneys out of which wafted the smell of boiled milk. Then she passed several shops and pubs. Then she arrived at her destination.

Cassidy's shop and bar had a small window on either side of the front door with a range of dusty shoes and boots on display and dead flies in the corners. The way in was through a pair of pink swing doors. She pushed through them and entered a little vestibule with a tiled floor. There was another set of pink doors ahead. She passed through these and when they closed behind a bell rang above her head.

Cassidy's shop had two counters. The one on the left was for hardware and the shelves behind were stacked with different-sized twines and tools and overalls and boxes of nails. The counter to the right was for food. At one end there were boxes filled with loaves and a pile of *Tipperary Democrat* newspapers with the headline "Home Rule Plans Will Exclude Ulster" and on the shelves behind there were drums of tea and sugar and other goods sold by weight.

Halfway down the shop was a partition and Cassidy's bar was on the other side. She could tell there were people in there because she heard voices.

"My lovely wee dog," she heard a man say: he was local rural, doubtless a farmer and middle aged.

"Hold on, Mr O'Toole, there's a customer," said a woman. This voice belonged to Mrs Cassidy, the proprietor.

"Who is it?" This was the man again.

"Now, how would I know who it is, Mr O'Toole?" said Mrs Cassidy. "And I shan't, shall I, till I go and see?"

Mrs Cassidy came out from behind the partition that separated the bar from the shop and appeared in front of Foxy Moll on the other side of the counter. Mrs Cassidy was a widow. Her hair was dyed black. She had a long smooth face and very few wrinkles for a woman of her years. There were rumours that when she went on holiday to Galway she used a different name and shared her room with a man.

"Who is it?" the voice on the other side of the partition said again.

Foxy Moll felt embarrassed to be the subject of an enquiry but at the same time she felt a peculiar throb somewhere in her body, somewhere deep and intimate and mysterious, and the throb was not unpleasant and it felt strange to her to have both these feelings at the same time.

"Mr O'Toole, will you stop?" Mrs Cassidy smiled at Foxy Moll. "Yes? How can I help?"

"Well, if you won't answer my question," said Mr O'Toole, "I'll have to see for myself."

The door in the partition opened and Foxy Moll saw a man. He was in his forties. He did not have much hair and what little he had was grey, as was his moustache. He wore a black coat unbuttoned and underneath a suit and a tie. Earlier she had thought he was a farmer but now she was not so sure.

"Hello." He smiled.

She nodded.

"And who are you?" he said.

"I'm Mary McCarthy's girl."

Mr O'Toole tilted his head sideways and assumed a sceptical expression.

"Whose girl did you say?"

"You know the McCarthys," said Mrs Cassidy.

She spoke to him as if he ought to know. For Mrs Cassidy to speak to this man like that they must be very good friends, Foxy Moll thought. Only a very good friend would get away with talking like that.

"Do I?" said Mr O'Toole. "The McCarthys. Who are they when they're at home?"

"You know the cottage on the Knockgraffon Road just by the laneway for the place the Slatterys had for donkey's years that was bought by your man Caesar ... Marlhill Farm, there's a sign on a tree with its name and all. Anyhow, just there, small cottage, thatched roof, that's the McCarthys' home place."

Mr O'Toole frowned. "I think I know it."

"Course you do, there've been McCarthys there, oh, years and years … First, there was … Edmund – I think I have the right name – and Jane – was it Jane? I think so. They'd five children, the youngest was Mary, this girl's mother, and then didn't Jane die after Mary being born, and isn't Jane buried above in the graveyard here in New Inn? And then didn't Edmund marry again – I think the second wife was called Alice, wasn't she?"

Foxy Moll was quite amazed Mrs Cassidy knew as much as she did and that it was all correct and when she turned to Foxy Moll for confirmation Foxy Moll smiled to show that not only was Mrs Cassidy right but that she was impressed too.

"When Edmund and Alice died," Mrs Cassidy said, "the home place went to the daughter, Mary, who's living there now."

Mrs Cassidy turned away from Mr O'Toole and looked straight at her. Foxy Moll noticed that Mrs Cassidy had nice eyes, grey and shiny, and lovely clean eyebrows too, very neat and thin and black.

"You're Mary McCarthy's girl, aren't you, pet?"

Foxy Moll trembled with pleasure. Not only was her voice soft and nice but also Mrs Cassidy had called her pet. No one called her pet. Pet. The word made her feel lovely.

"Yes." she nodded.

"Don't they call you Foxy Moll?"

"Yes." She nodded.

"Foxy Moll? They call you Foxy Moll?" Mr O'Toole laughed long and loud and full.

"Will you stop that, Mr O'Toole? It's not nice to laugh at anyone's name, is it, Miss McCarthy?"

Foxy Moll wondered what to say. She did not mind. On the contrary she liked this strange man's mirth. It made her feel special.

"People often laugh the first time they hear me called Foxy

Moll," she said. "I'm used to it and I don't mind at all."

"So, there you are, Mrs Cassidy," said Mr O'Toole, "you can stop ticking me off. She doesn't mind."

Foxy Moll felt another dart of pleasure shoot through her. No one had paid her this much attention in ages. Not since the time that Willie Garret had wooed her. Unbidden a picture of Willie appeared before her mind's eye: the curtain of black hair that hung over his right eye and his lovely well-formed face and his small but strong shoulders. At any other time the image would have pained her but now it did not. Today as she stood with Mrs Cassidy and this man called O'Toole a picture that had always upset her when it forced itself into her mind made no impression at all. And why was that? The answer came immediately. She was happy.

"Are you a typical redhead?" said Mr O'Toole. "Are you mischievous, are you sly, are you a foxy one?"

Foxy Moll shook her head. Now the heat was on her and her face began to redden.

"Mr O'Toole, look what you've done," said Mrs Cassidy. "You've embarrassed her."

"Have I?"

He looked Foxy Moll straight in the eye. His gaze was warm and direct and amiable and affectionate.

She shook her head. Her face now burned red.

"You'll have to make amends, Mr O'Toole," said Mrs Cassidy.

"Oh, I'll make amends."

He stepped closer to Foxy Moll. She smelled something. It was the stuff that men put on their faces after they shaved.

"What are you getting?" said O'Toole.

"Sugar and a shop loaf."

"Pound of sugar and one of your long whites, Mrs Cassidy," said Mr O'Toole, "and put them down to me."

"Certainly."

"Oh, no," said Foxy Moll.

"Oh, yes," said Mr O'Toole, "oh, yes."

"He can afford it, don't worry," said Mrs Cassidy.

"Really?"

"Really," said Mrs Cassidy. "Now give me your bag."

He really had offered to pay for the bread and sugar and now Mrs Cassidy had confirmed that. When she got home and relayed this news her mother might thaw a bit. She might be friendlier.

She handed her shopping bag to Mrs Cassidy. The shopkeeper weighted a pound of sugar into a brown paper bag and wrapped a loaf in tissue and put both into the shopping bag.

"Is there anything else you need?" said Mr O'Toole.

Foxy Moll shook her head.

"Really? Is that all you were sent for?"

"Yes. Bread and sugar."

"Do you like honey?"

"Honey?"

"I'd have thought you'd be mad for the honey. Aren't foxy ones mad for the stuff?"

"Do foxes eat honey?" she said. "I thought they only ate chickens and rabbits."

"Throw in one of your honeycombs, Mrs Cassidy, and a pound of butter and half a pound of loose tea."

Mrs Cassidy weighted out the tea and put it in a brown bag and tied this with coarse twine and then she wrapped the butter and the honeycomb in thick greaseproof paper that was the same shade of grey as lead. She put these items in the bag with the bread and the sugar.

He turned to Foxy Moll. "Have you milk at home?"

Moll could not remember whether or not her mother had told her to get milk so she glanced sideways at the counter and made the smallest shrug by which she meant that in all likelihood they did have milk but she was not positive. Mr O'Toole did not miss this gesture.

"Throw in a couple of tins of condensed milk as well."

Mrs Cassidy put two cans of milk in the bag with all the other things.

"So, now," he switched to an English accent, "you have bread and honey to go with your cup of char."

He took the bag from Mrs Cassidy and handed it to Foxy Moll. "I hope I've made sufficient amends for any embarrassment I caused?"

"Thank you."

"So, it's the little house on the Knockgraffon Road beside the turn for Marlhill Farm?"

"Yes."

"Actually, why don't you show it to me now? My trap is out the back." He looked at the shopkeeper. "I can run her home in a few minutes, can't I, Mrs Cassidy? It's only a few minutes."

"Yes, Mr O'Toole."

"I'll bring her round to the front. Mrs Cassidy, can I have a word?"

He went into the bar and closed the doors behind while Mrs Cassidy sidled away behind the counter and vanished behind the partition. Foxy Moll heard whispers but she could not make out what was said. Then the whispers stopped and Mrs Cassidy was in front of her again.

"How old are you, pet?"

"Sixteen."

"Sixteen. You sure?"

Foxy Moll nodded.

"When were you born?"

There was a curious question. Still they had both been so nice, Mr O'Toole in particular, so what harm was there if she told the truth?

"April fourth, 1901."

"You look older."

"Everyone in St Bridget's said I looked younger than I really was."

"Did they?" said Mrs Cassidy.

The older woman stared up at the corner of the ceiling above the door to the street. Foxy Moll wondered if she was looking at something up there and then decided that was not the case: Mrs Cassidy ruminated.

"So you were in St Bridget's?"

Foxy Moll nodded.

"How did you like it?"

"Well enough."

The less said the better in this case but Mrs Cassidy did not ask any more questions. She just stared up and pondered until she was roused from her thoughts by the clip-clop of hooves outside followed by a loud "Whoa!" from Mr O'Toole and the ping of the skidpan spring as it was pulled on.

"The trap's outside," said Mrs Cassidy.

"Thank you," said Foxy Moll.

Then as she turned she wondered what she had thanked the woman for. Should it not just be "Goodbye"?

"Goodbye," she said.

"Look after yourself, won't you?"

"Why wouldn't I?"

"Because you're too young."

Mystified by this, Foxy Moll shrugged and pushed open the pink swing door and went forward. She could hardly wait to get outside to Mr O'Toole.

20

Mr O'Toole was in no hurry to urge the piebald on but let her move at her own rate. The trap moved at a slow pace. He sat on the right side half-turned towards the front and Foxy Moll sat on the left side opposite Mr O'Toole with the groceries on her lap. She smelled his smell better than she had in Cassidy's. Mr O'Toole smelled of soap and hair cream and pee. That was his tweed suit. There was also another smell: his unique one. The sun in the sky beamed down. They passed a field with a grey donkey at the gate. The animal scratched its head on the post.

"Look at him," said Mr O'Toole. "Can you imagine having an itch and no hand to scratch with?"

She considered this. "No."

"It must be infuriating. Poor old donkey."

"Poor old donkey."

"Poor old donkey is right."

The pony's hooves went clip-clop and the trap's wheels rumbled.

"Show me your hands," he said.

"My hands?"

"Yes, what are your hands like?"

She held her groceries with her left hand and offered her right to him. It was a little white hand with small square nails at the finger ends and big freckles all over the bony veined place behind her knuckles.

"Very nice paw. That's a fox's paw all right."

He did something with the reins so that they were all in his right hand and then with his left hand he ran his fingertips down her fingers and over her knuckles and across to her wrist.

An accidental touch was one thing but this was something else altogether. She felt odd. It had a purpose behind it and she knew what that was. Yet how could that be? He was so much older than she was and married, as the wedding band on the ring finger that had just touched her told her.

"Have you children, Mr O'Toole? I suppose they're grown up?"

Mr O'Toole gave her a brisk run-through of his family background. First he mentioned Eileen his wife, now bed-ridden with some disease that wasted her muscles, and then he covered their children: a son who managed a quarry and another son who was in the police and two daughters both married to farmers. He then explained that his farm was over one hundred acres but on account of his wife's illness he had let it, although he and Eileen lived on in the farmhouse while the tenant lived elsewhere. Then he asked her what she thought the loneliest time of the day was.

She imagined him alone at night in his kitchen as a lamp hissed and the coals settled in the hearth.

"Evening?"

"No. By evening I've had a day of it and so I'm used to it. No, the worst is the morning, waking and knowing I've only a day of chores ahead and nothing else and not a bit of company and never a kind word."

They passed through a green tunnel where the branches of the trees on either side above their heads met and formed a canopy. She could not think of anything to say so she just said, "Yes."

"But I don't believe anything happens without a reason," he said, "neither my wife's sickness, nor driving you home. Everything has a purpose, don't you agree?"

She saw the entrance to Caesars' lane and then their gate ahead and the yellow thatch that was so old it was almost brown on the roof of their cottage behind. It was a relief to be back because she had no idea what to say to Mr O'Toole.

"Here we are," she said. "It's coming up."

As the trap nosed through the gate and then pulled up Mary came out to see who was there.

"My mother," Foxy Moll said.

"Mrs McCarthy," Mr O'Toole said. "Just lifted your daughter here with a few groceries. She's a credit to you, by the way."

With a deft movement he turned and opened the little door at the back and hopped out and dropped the step down. Foxy Moll stepped down. Mr O'Toole folded the step away and got back on his seat and closed the door.

"I'd like to come over one day," he said. "Would that be all right, Mrs McCarthy?"

"Why wouldn't it?"

To Foxy Moll's ears her mother sounded warmer and friendlier than she had ever heard her be before.

"Well, if that's all right then, I will," he said. "Goodbye, Foxy Moll."

"Thank you."

Mr O'Toole waved at her mother. "Goodbye, Mrs McCarthy."

He turned the trap and went out the gate and started back in the direction of New Inn. Foxy Moll and Mary watched him.

"Who is he?" said her mother.

"Mr O'Toole."

"What have you got in the bag?"

The clip-clop of the pony and the rumble of the trap's wheels became fainter and fainter.

"A few things. And we don't have to pay for them. They're on his slate."

"What sort of things?"

"Sugar, bread, loose tea, butter, condensed milk and a honeycomb."

"A honeycomb?"

"Yes."

"What did you do to make that happen?"

"Nothing."

"You didn't do nothing," said Mary. "You must have done something and whatever it was you'd better make sure you go on doing it."

21

Mr O'Toole called a week later. He brought a cake of bread and a jar of damson jam for which he apologised and said that it was a year old and had doubtless lost its succulence on that account. He added that they should be careful when they ate it in case there were stones in the jam. You could break a tooth with a stone from a damson, he said.

Mary put him in the Windsor that was normally her chair because it had armrests and a thin cushion on the seat and she sat on the stool. The kettle was swung over the fire. Foxy Moll cut the bread and spooned out the jam and spread it on the slices (there was no butter) and as she did she checked that no stones lurked in it. She did find one and she lifted it out with the spoon and flicked it into the fire. Then she sat on an old orange box to wait for the water to boil and listened to the adults. They talked of the weather and of prices and of the indisposition of Mr O'Toole's wife.

It was dry inconsequential tedious talk and after a bit Foxy Moll no longer listened and she began to imagine things. First she thought of the trap and herself sat opposite Mr O'Toole and the noise as Mr O'Toole cracked his whip, although he did not have a whip in real life, and then she imagined that he urged the horses to go faster and faster and the wheels turned below and sang as they spun faster and faster and her hair streamed behind and Mr O'Toole laughed.

From this dream of heady speed she moved to a stream-bed strewn with moss-covered rocks and water that was sluggish because it was a stream in summer and dragonflies nosed through the air and there was a stand of willow trees and the warm air was gentle as it moved around her and the sun beamed down from high in the sky and warmed her hair and her shoulders and Mr O'Toole whispered what he felt about her: nice things, kind things, warm loving things, just the sort of words that she had loved to hear from Willie Garret and which she had not heard since he had fled to the army and which she longed to hear again. "I like you …" Mr O'Toole whispered, "I love you … you're the loveliest girl, you know, the loveliest girl in all the world, you know, and I can't live without you, you know, no I can't live without you, you know, you lovely, lovely, lovely girl…."

As the words which she imagined he said spun on and on, somewhere deep inside of her that was near and yet under and behind where her ribs ended and her stomach began this lovely sensation started: a warm and serene sensation that was small to begin with but got bigger and the more she imagined his words the more powerful it grew until at last she was filled up with a quiet delicious feeling of happiness.

"The kettle," she heard.

Startled by this, Foxy Moll blinked and the lovely feeling deep within started to wilt and shrink straight away.

"The kettle," her mother said again.

Foxy Moll saw and heard the lid vibrate as a cone of steam poured out.

"Yes," she said.

She stood. She swung the crane. The feeling was now gone. She warmed the pot and then started to spoon in the dark dry tiny leaves of black tea and as she spooned in the tea she noticed that a faint dust rose from the leaves. She felt like she sometimes felt when she woke: groggy and sleepy and dismayed that she had been torn from bliss to wakefulness.

After an hour Mr O'Toole got up to go.

"I'm passing the day after tomorrow in the trap, some time in the late afternoon," he said, "and if it's fine, we could take a spin out to the lake. It's lovely at this time of the year."

"Yes." Mary nodded.

Later that evening after Mr O'Toole had gone Foxy Moll and her mother sipped tea by the fire and her mother said, "Do you know what to do to make a man happy?"

Foxy Moll shook her head. "No," she said.

"Well I do, that's how I got by … I got by from making men happy … so learn from me. In the end, they'll always want certain things – and why not, why shouldn't they – and giving those things is how you make men happy, you understand?"

Foxy Moll had an inkling but she was not positive so she sat very still and waited for her mother to tell her what was what.

"But if you make a man happy," she said, "you've always got to get something in return, remember that too. Sometimes before you start, sometimes just after and sometimes a bit later but, whatever the case, you always have to get something back and they'll always be happy to pay you something because you've made them happy. You understand?"

Foxy Moll did not at first, not quite, but this was just the start of talk that went on for hours and over the course of the talk she came to understand what her mother meant and what she must do when the opportunity presented itself. There were things a girl did and they made a man happy and the happy man in return would give the girl something. She grasped this but as she did she wondered was that the only way things were. Yes, this might be her mother's way but was it the only way? Was it possible that sometimes you might want to do something and not get something back? What about love? Love must exist and love was selfless, she thought, not selfish. She came to no conclusions after she had these thoughts except in one regard: there was something about the way her mother saw everything that troubled her and that she did not like and that she thought was selfish.

22

Two days later Mr O'Toole called.

"Ready for the lake?" he said.

They were. They left the cottage and closed the door. They got in the trap. Foxy Moll and her mother sat on one side. Mr O'Toole sat on the other. He unfastened the reins from the keeper and released the skidpan and called to the pony, "Walk on."

The pony pulled them out through their gate and onto the public road. Mr O'Toole shook the reins and called, "Go on." The pony began to trot.

When they came to the lake Mr O'Toole parked the trap on a flat piece of ground where one or two other vehicles were parked and then they set off along a path that brought them to the top of a headland from where they looked across the calm flat water to the opposite shore where trees grew along the edge.

"Isn't that a sight for sore eyes?" said Mr O'Toole.

A swan appeared on their right and moved past, slow and sedate, and three grey chicks followed in her wake.

"I used to fish here when I was a boy, and we used to go out there to Gulliver's Island," he said. Mr O'Toole pointed at a green finger of land covered in trees a few hundred yards from the shore to his left. "We caught pike mostly, occasionally trout. Have you ever fished?"

"No," said Foxy Moll. She had never even held a rod in her life but she saw no need to say that to him.

"Well, there's an experience to look forward to then," said Mr O'Toole. "It's a lovely, calming pastime."

"I'm sure she'd like to learn," said her mother. "You'd like to learn, wouldn't you, Foxy Moll? Haven't you always said you'd like to learn to fish?"

Foxy Moll had never given fishing much thought much less ever spoken about it as something she wanted to learn how to do but after her mother's hours of talk about men and how to please men she knew that she had to give the answer now that her mother expected her to give and that was the only thing that mattered.

"Yes," she said.

"That's yes, you'd love to learn to fish?"

"Yes."

"Well, if she'll take instruction from an old fool, I'd be happy to give it," said Mr O'Toole.

"An old fool, I hardly think so," her mother said. "But thank you, and I'm sure Foxy Moll would love to take you up on that kind offer, wouldn't you, Foxy Moll?"

"Yes."

An evening and a time were agreed for Foxy Moll to go with Mr O'Toole so that he could teach her how to fish.

23

On the day and at the time agreed, Foxy Moll sat on the stool by the fire with her coat on. Her mother sat in the Windsor chair. The trap rolled up outside and stopped.

"That must be him," her mother said.

Foxy Moll got up and went to the small window.

"Yes, it's him."

"Remember to be nice, now. Remember everything I've said."

Foxy Moll opened the cottage door and went out. The sky was white. It was mild. There was the trap with the door open and the step folded down and she saw that Mr O'Toole waited by the trap. He wore a tweed suit with brown leather piping on the cuffs and the lapels and a bowler hat.

"Great evening for it," he said. Mr O'Toole doffed his hat to her.

Foxy Moll got into the trap; on the floor there was a rod in a canvas sock and a net with a cork handle and a basket made of thick brown wicker that smelled vaguely of ooze and slime.

Mr O'Toole got in and they set off. As they bowled along the lanes towards the lake, Mr O'Toole said nothing. Foxy Moll stared at the hedgerows and trees that streamed past. The motion and the speed of the trap excited her. For several minutes she had no thoughts at all. She was absorbed by the physical experience. Then for no reason she remembered that they were on their way to the lake which in turn prompted her to wonder about the depth of the water. If they went out in a boat, as she presumed they might, and it sank what would happen? She could not swim.

"Do you swim?" she said.

"Swim," said Mr O'Toole, "yes, yes I do. I don't suppose you can swim?"

"No."

"Well, don't worry. If you fall in, I'll fish you out."

"I'm frightened of the water."

"You're frightened of drowning, you mean. Different thing, that, to being frightened of water."

She felt reassured although she was not certain why she should.

Mr O'Toole passed the spot where they had stopped when she and her mother had walked with him to the headland and he continued until he got to a gap in the trees. He turned in here. There was a wooden hut and a hand-painted sign nailed to a tree that read "Fishing Club". He stopped. The skidpan went on.

"Look at that." He pointed at the surface of the lake. It was smooth and silver and very still. "It gets better and better."

They walked out along a jetty. Its boards were green but the green was dry and powdery, not slimy. At the end they came to a ladder with a rowing boat at the bottom.

"You first," said Mr O'Toole.

She went down the ladder and put her right foot into the bottom of the rowing boat. The boat moved in a way that alarmed her and she did not want to let go of the ladder.

"Just sit down," said Mr O'Toole.

She held tight to the ladder and gathered her skirts and sat on the nearest seat.

Mr O'Toole passed the gear down to her. Then he climbed in and the boat rocked and as the boat rocked he moved with it. He seemed not just familiar but quite at home with its strange motions.

"You need to go to the back," he said.

He put his hand out and she took it. Then he half steered and half pushed her to the rear where she sank down onto a wooden seat.

Mr O'Toole fiddled with the rowlocks and got the oars in place and then he undid a rope and pushed them away with an oar. Then as soon as he had clearance for the oars he began to row. His strokes were slow but even and the boat moved forward slow and sedate as the swan they had seen the last time they had come to the lake. Foxy Moll noticed that Mr O'Toole nibbled at the bottom of his moustache as he rowed.

"What are you looking at?" he said.

"You're chewing your moustache."

He smiled. "I do that when I'm concentrating on something, like I am now on rowing."

He smiled at her. She gave a tentative smile back. She raised her eyes and looked past Mr O'Toole. The water beyond the boat was darker than it had looked from the jetty: it was blacker and less silvery and in the near distance Gulliver's Island rose between them and the far shore and in the middle of the island she noticed that a roofless stone tower and stone buildings peeped from among the trees that covered it.

"Are we going to the island?" she said.

"Yes, and round to the far side," he said. "Very good for pike, round the far side."

When they got around there he assembled a rod and got a piece of sausage from the basket and baited the hook and paid the line out and gave her the rod to hold. He began to row again. She held the rod very tight. The hook dragged behind through the water. She heard the oars as they creaked in the rowlocks. She felt the motion of the boat as it slid across the surface. Her feelings churned. She wanted to be kissed and she wanted to please her mother. Was it possible if she was kissed and happy that she could also please Mary? She felt a tug and almost let the rod go. She squealed and tightened her grip. Mr O'Toole held the oars with one hand and leaned forward and tugged at the line with the fingers of his free hand.

"Yes," he said. "Nice. You've caught your first fish, Foxy Moll, the first of many, I hope."

She began to reel in. She saw something silver thrash about under the surface of the lake. The pike came closer and closer and then it was right beside the boat. Mr O'Toole lifted the oars and pulled them in and laid them in the bottom of the boat. Then with one deft motion he extended the net and scooped the pike from below and lifted the creature into the boat. The pike writhed in the net's coils. The movements of the pike terrified her. She thought it was about to leap up and touch her or bite her. Now Mr O'Toole had a cosh. He put his foot on the body and hit the pike's head. The fish went still. The cosh was smeared with fish scales and blood. He jiggled the cosh in the water and dropped it back into the basket, dripping and wet. He had a pair of pliers and he used them to pull the hook out of the pike's mouth.

The boat drifted into some reeds that grew by the island's edge. Mr O'Toole pushed the oars through the rowlocks and dropped the flat ends into the water and began to row back towards the middle of the lake.

From her place Foxy Moll stared at the pike on the boards at her feet. It was between a foot and two-foot long. It was heavy and fat and powerful and muscular. The spine and top were a boggy brown but the flanks were lighter and the belly lighter still and its skin was daubed with white spots as if someone had splashed it with a brush that had been dipped in whitewash. The mouth was ugly and pointed but also flat like a spade and the teeth that she could see because the mouth was open were sharp and white and looked very nasty.

"Would one of them pikes bite you in the water?"

"No, it would not," said Mr O'Toole.

"No?"

"A pike has no interest in us. It's other fish he wants."

"Oh."

"You don't know a lot, do you?"

He dipped the flat oar ends and pulled strong and smooth and sure. She felt the boat move and wondered how to answer.

"I don't know about the pike. That's true. I can read and write though."

He straightened up and pulled the oars in, which reminded her of a bird as it folded its wings against its body, and then he set the ends down. He looked straight at her. She met his gaze for a moment and then she looked away. She looked at the far shore, not at the fringe of trees but at a field that ran down to the lake. The field was full of cows and their young calves and the animals had come right down to the water's edge and some of them had walked out into the water. The water was up to their chests in some cases. There was a bull as well. He was behind his cows, stood on ground that was higher than they were. He was in profile. She saw his heavy shoulders and his large power-ful head against the white sky. The boat drifted and drifted. She wondered why Mr O'Toole was not rowing. Was he still look-ing at her? She looked back. Yes, he was. What was he staring at? What was he looking at her for? She looked away again. A dragonfly appeared in her line of sight. Its purple wings whirred. She pretended to watch the dragonfly and followed its iridescent passage as it swooped up and down through the warm air. She wondered if she would go red like she always did when she was embarrassed and she imagined that now that this fatal thought had popped into her head she would. She lifted her hand and covered her mouth. The flush started on her throat and began to slide upwards.

"Your red hair," said Mr O'Toole, "is the loveliest I've ever seen."

The blush accelerated and she felt her whole face start to glow.

"I love your red hair, you know."

She stared down at where the pike lay in the bottom of the boat with its silvery grey underbelly and its spiny fins and its open wet black eye that stared up at her and the sky above.

"Oh, what I'd give for a little kiss from the girl with the lovely red hair. Will the girl with the lovely red hair give me a kiss, will she give me a kiss, will she?"

She kept her eye on the pike. Her face cooled: a miracle. It was her impression that lately her blushes were less intense and of less duration. She must be outgrowing them, she thought, and then she realised the process had started, only she had not realised before now. Would the blushes ever stop entirely? Probably not but their power was on the wane. She was sure of that.

He took the boat back to the jetty and tied it up and stowed the oars in the bottom. The rowlocks came out and went into his basket. The rod was taken apart and slid back into its canvas sock. The reel went into the basket. The net was disassembled.

"Better see to the business end before we do anything more," said Mr O'Toole. "It isn't nice but it has to be done."

He got a knife from his basket and slit the pike from head to tail. He put his finger in and slid it along. The action made a sucking noise. The pike's insides tumbled out still attached. They were a mix of tubes and organs and bits of things that she did not recognise and all were the strangest muted browns and pinks and reds, so unlike any colours that she knew in life.

Mr O'Toole pulled the pike further apart like a book. Then he cut where the insides were still attached and the tangle of tubes and organs tumbled out. When they hit the lake's surface they made only a tiny splash. The lumpy mess floated for a moment and then as she watched began to sink.

Mr O'Toole rinsed the pike and wrapped it in a sheet of old newspaper and stowed it in his basket. He rinsed his hands and dried them on his knees. As he did she noticed his hands. She had not taken them in before. They were long and graceful and the fingers were long as well. He closed the basket and did up the fasteners.

Was he going to kiss her? She thought he might and then she thought that he might not. He was no longer the man who had whispered the way he had about her hair, her lovely hair. He seemed so purposeful now, so preoccupied with his tasks. In which case why had he spoken as he had when they had been out on the lake? It was a mystery.

"Shall we go?" he said.

She nodded. He indicated the ladder. She climbed to the jetty. He passed the basket and the rod and the net up and then he followed.

They got into the trap and set off. Mr O'Toole was silent. The cloud above was grey but in the west it had a white lustre where the sun behind shone through as it sank towards the horizon. She felt calm yet puzzled. What had all that talk in the boat been for when Mr O'Toole now seemed to be almost unaware that she was with him? He cannot have meant it, she decided. It had just been talk. Did she mind? She decided that she did not. He could kiss her. Or not. It was up to him and either way she did not mind but she would have liked it if he had talked some more. She had liked his praise. It had made her feel good right in the marrow of her being.

They got back to the cottage at Marlhill. Mr O'Toole cut three pieces from the pike and her mother began to fry them on the fire in the heavy black pan. Before long the room was filled with the smell of pike.

"Open the doors," said Mary.

Foxy Moll opened the front door and looked south over the Caesars' fields and on to the lands beyond that belonged to Mr Byrne and then she opened the back door and she looked north over Caesars' lane and on to the lands beyond that belonged to Mr Fitzgerald and both ways she looked she saw hedgerows and fields and trees, all of them a different colour of green. Marlhill was a green world. Then she went back to her place and sat and waited while the fish pieces sizzled in the pan.

When she got her plate later she was nervous. She had a vague idea that the pike was a dirty fish: it was a fish that ate rats. She saw her mother and Mr O'Toole had begun to eat and she did not want them to notice that she had not. She put a small piece of the flesh in her mouth. The meat was oily and Foxy Moll was sure that she tasted ooze and wet mud and reeds and old stones as she chewed but at least now she knew she would finish and she did.

"I'd best be away," said Mr O'Toole when he had eaten.

He threw the skin and the wet piece of bone left over from his portion into the fire. There was a sharp hiss.

He took the rest of the pike and rewrapped it in newspaper and put it in the basket. He explained how his wife was partial to pike and that the doctor had recommended fish at least twice a week because it would be good for her and it would help her to get better. He tramped across the hard earthen floor. Goodbyes were given and taken at the door and a few moments later Mr O'Toole's trap rumbled away.

Foxy Moll and her mother went back in and sat by the fire. Foxy Moll took the stool and her mother the Windsor chair.

"Well?" said her mother.

Foxy Moll looked across at Mary. With both doors open there was a through breeze and little puffs of turf smoke were pulled into the room from the hearth where they swirled in the air before they vanished. Foxy Moll looked out the back door and saw that the sky was dark grey the same as the smoke.

"What?" she said.

"You're being nice to Mr O'Toole, aren't you?"

She shrugged.

"I asked you a question. Are you being nice to that man?"

"Yes."

Her mother blinked. "This draught is playing the devil with the fire," she said.

Her mother got up and closed both doors. With only a small window at the front and another at the back the room went dark.

Her mother sat back in her chair and poked at the turf embers. They stirred and shivered in a way that was almost liquid, Foxy Moll thought. Her mother threw on a few new sods and a few particles showered upwards and Foxy Moll saw that they were very red against the sooty black back of the hearth.

"I'll wait a bit before I light the candle," said her mother. "There's a bit of light in the sky yet."

24

Over the summer Mr O'Toole brought her on several excursions. They went fishing. They went to Gulliver's island for a picnic. He lit a fire although it was warm and the sun shone. They explored the old monastic ruins.

"May I kiss you?" he said.

She consented and he kissed her once on each cheek and then on the forehead and on her mouth. His lips were closed. Over the autumn he took her to hotels and they had tea. At Christmas he gave her a lovely pair of pale grey stockings that she thought were very beautiful and a box of candied fruit which tasted sweet and sour and that she was not partial to although she told Mr O'Toole that she liked them very much.

In the spring they fished again and in the summer on the island he touched her through her underclothes and she was excited by this and then he touched her tongue with his and she was still more excited and she registered the excitement first as a tingle all over her torso and then, as it intensified, as a pain.

At the end of August Mr O'Toole promised a surprise. The day when it came was wet. A light mizzle of rain fell. He collected her and when they got into the trap he gave her a blanket to cover her legs and a black umbrella to hold over her head and he covered his own legs with another blanket but he could not use an umbrella because he needed both hands to hold the reins. They bowled along the damp lanes and the wheels of the trap splashed in the puddles on the road. They arrived at a small hotel called Feeney's. He drove to the stables at the back. A stable boy promised to dry the blankets that had covered their legs and to fodder the pony. They huddled under the umbrella together. The rain was heavier now and it plinked on the taut fabric as they went along a gravel path and in through a door at the back of Feeney's.

Once they were inside Mr O'Toole shook the umbrella dry over the step and folded the umbrella and put it in a porcelain holder at the door that she noticed was decorated with pictures of Chinese ships full of Chinese sailors with long ponytails and then they went up a set of back stairs together to another door on the first floor. Mr O'Toole not only knew his way around but he had the key to this bedroom door. She guessed he had already been to the hotel and made arrangements. This back part of the hotel smelled of cabbage and potato water. She guessed they were somewhere near the hotel's kitchen.

Mr O'Toole opened a door and she went in first and he followed. As he locked the door behind she looked around. There was a bed and a chest of drawers with a pitcher and ewer and a clotheshorse with a couple of rough thin towels draped over it.

She went to the window. There was a white lace curtain. She lifted it and looked out. She saw the wet gravel path below and the little indentations in the gravel that they had made with their feet as they hurried to the back door and then she lifted her gaze and watched threads of rain as they fell from the sky. She heard Mr O'Toole hang up his coat on the back of the door. He moved across the room. She felt him behind her. He buried his face in her hair.

"Oh, what lovely hair, what lovely, lovely hair …"

When he was done Mr O'Toole said, "Thank you, oh, thank you, thank you," over and over.

At first she did not understand but then as he repeated himself again and again it occurred to her that he must be lonesome on account of the invalid Mrs O'Toole at home in his house and that they never did this and that was why he was so grateful and he really was, he really was grateful. Oh yes, she could tell from the sound of his voice as well as from the words he said.

Then a truly unexpected and remarkable thought rattled into her mind hard on the heels of this realisation. If the invalid wife at home died then Mr O'Toole would be free to marry her and she would be the second Mrs O'Toole and would that not be a wonderful thing to be? Oh yes, so very wonderful, and as he lay in the bed beside her she stared at the white cracked ceiling overhead and tried to imagine her new life as the second Mrs O'Toole but she could only envision what she had already done with him: rides in the trap and picnics on the island and fishing and this in the bed in Feeney's hotel on a rainy afternoon.

A week after the hotel when the weather was warm and mild and dry as it often was at the start of autumn Mr O'Toole took her to the island and they did it on a blanket behind a tumbled-down building and Mr O'Toole was quick and urgent. Later when they got back to the cottage at Marlhill he lifted the seat on which he always sat when he drove the trap and pulled from the compartment below two packets of tea and a bag of sugar and tins of herring.

"We didn't want them at home and I thought your mother could use them," he said.

After that he always had something: a box of Seville oranges to make marmalade with and a box of cigarettes for Mary although her mother did not smoke and a pair of kid gloves which Foxy Moll thought were lovely even if they were a little big for her small hands and at Christmas a Dundee cake and a tin of biscuits with a painting on the front and a box of Christmas crackers to pull with her mother.

25

In April 1919 Foxy Moll turned eighteen and for her birthday he took her to a department store in Limerick and bought her two dresses: one with flowers on a blue background and the other black with white spots. After the shopping he took her to a hotel for tea. They ate crumpets with spicy apple jelly and Foxy Moll drank strong tea and he drank coffee, which was a beverage that she had never drunk in her life and she could smell the strange bitter smell of the coffee from her side of the table.

Mr O'Toole talked about his circumstances in a hushed quiet voice and whenever the waitress or anyone else was near he was careful to stop speaking and it was clear to her that this was because he did not want anyone to hear what he said to her. He had been unhappy, he said, and lonesome for years and now he was not unhappy or lonesome any more and it was all due to her and he thanked her from the very bottom of his heart. Then he asked her did she understand and she said she did. But did she really understand? She said she did. She said he was like a fire that had been about to go out and had come back to life. She had a way with words, he said, because that was just how it was.

The time came to go. He asked the waitress for the bill. She brought it along with a slip of paper that was folded in two and which had his name on it.

"What's this?" Mr O'Toole looked down at the folded paper in the saucer in front of him.

"I don't know." The waitress was a girl with a flat chest and large eyes and heavy hands. "A woman gave it to me."

"What woman?"

"She said she was your sister-in-law. She was in an awful rush to get the train and said would I give it to you and it was important and that was all she said."

Mr O'Toole swallowed and Foxy Moll watched his Adam's apple move up and down in his throat. The waitress went off. He lifted the note and opened it with obvious reluctance and began to read. His face was smooth and showed no emotion.

After a moment or two he began to blink. His colour changed. He became pale. He refolded the note along the creases that were already there in the paper and then he tore the note into small pieces and swept them with one hand into the palm of the other and then he put the pieces into his pocket. He said nothing. He turned the bill over. He drew change from his pocket and separated the coins to pay and put them on the saucer. He checked the bill again. He added another tuppence.

"We can go," he said.

He spoke in a hushed tone but despite the lowness of his volume there was curtness there; it lurked under the softness in his voice. He had something on his mind that needed his urgent attention and her presence was in his way: that was what his voice said to her.

"I'll take you home." He pointed at her parcels piled on an empty chair. "Don't forget them."

"Why would I?" she said and deep down inside she had a bad

feeling and she knew where it came from, that bad feeling: it came from the note.

The next time they were together he took her to a wood and they did it stood upright: brisk and functional. She had her back to a tree and she thought that it did not seem to make Mr O'Toole as happy as before or did she imagine things? She recalled the bad feeling that had struck her in the hotel dining room in Limerick. It was still there; in patient silence it trembled and throbbed somewhere deep in her body. When they got back to the cottage at Marlhill he gave her a brown paper bag with two oranges inside. No, she did not imagine things. The note Mr O'Toole got in the hotel in Limerick was the start of it and now something had shifted. Something had changed. When she presented the bag with the two oranges to her mother, Mary thought the same.

"What have you done now? Have you done something stupid?"

Over the months that followed they did it less and there were no more big presents just small ones now: on one occasion a roll of coloured thread and on another a hair comb with a bent tine that looked used and scuffed and which she guessed was his wife's and on a third occasion just a pot of blackberry jam. When she had opened it at home she found that a bloom of purple mould covered the surface.

One day late in summer he drove her to the lake but rather than go to the place with the jetty and his boat he went to the place they had gone to on their first outing when her mother had been with them: the place from which tourists were able to walk by a path to the top of the headland that jutted into the lake.

He manoeuvred the trap to a spot from which they were able to see the headland to their right and the jetty to their left and the water ahead of them. He pulled on the skidpan and looked forward. The water was dark. The sky was covered with dark grey cloud. It was not smooth cloud. It was bumpy cloud.

With its lumps and dips it reminded her of the pike's insides. He coughed. She waited. She knew that this was bad. Mr O'Toole began to talk in a low voice. It was worse than bad. There was gossip, he said, about him and about her. His sick wife's relatives were angry, he said. An ultimatum had been delivered, he said. He could not see her any more, he said. He could not be seen with her any more, he said. It was over, he said. His bloody relatives, his bloody wife's bloody relatives, they had bloody ruined everything. Foxy Moll had never heard Mr O'Toole use the word bloody before. She was shocked and to some extent the shock she felt at the way he talked masked the pain she felt deep inside which she knew she would later feel on the surface and that would take her over.

He would see her right, though, Mr O'Toole continued. He would see Foxy Moll right. Oh yes, he would be responsible. He would see that she was looked after. He was not a man who just cut his losses and ran. He was a man who faced up to his responsibilities. Oh yes, she could be assured on that score. He would have the leaky thatch that roofed the cottage at Marlhill removed and replaced with corrugated iron. He would have turf delivered, a whole cartload, enough for months and months, enough to take Foxy Moll and her mother right through the winter of 1919 and on into the spring of 1920.

Foxy Moll began to cry and wiped her eyes with the sleeve ends of her dress. It was one of the dresses he had bought her in Limerick: the blue one. She cried in a quiet way for a while and her cuffs got so wet with her tears that she had to fold them back. She stopped crying. Mr O'Toole began to talk politics. People had been killed: RIC constables and Irish Volunteers. There had been a general strike in Limerick. Sinn Féin had been suppressed in the county. Dáil Éireann would soon be declared illegal, he was sure of it. It was bad now and it was all about to get worse, he said, much worse, and the troublemakers were going to make Ireland ungovernable and an impossible place to lead a normal life. That then, he continued, was the other reason why he could not see her. The climate, the times they were in, they were against them. Foxy Moll did not follow this part of what Mr O'Toole said. She no longer cried. She ached. She ached in the exact same place as she had after Willie Garret had bolted. This was heartbreak, she thought. That was what she felt inside of her. It hurt like her heart literally was snapped.

She heard Mr O'Toole release the skidpan. He turned the trap and off they went back the way they had come. She wondered if it would rain then decided that it was not about to rain. Her ache throbbed. She turned her cuffs up again then rubbed her damp wrists. The cottage at Marlhill came into view. He turned the trap through the gate and tugged the reins and pulled on the skidpan. He had nothing for her. She knew that. There was nothing at all for her in the compartment under the seat.

"I promised I'd never talk to you again, so you mustn't talk to me if you see me," he said. "Do you understand? If you see me in the street in New Inn, I won't speak to you, I won't look at you."

He got out and folded down the steps. He held out his hand and she took it, not because she wanted to but because she felt faint and she thought that her knees might buckle. She stepped down. He withdrew his hand and folded the steps away and got in and closed the door and took the reins.

"The roof will be done, I don't know when, as soon as I can arrange it, and the fellow will be around with the turf tomorrow. Is the turf shed dry?"

He pointed to the corrugated structure attached to the far gable.

She nodded. "I think so."

As far as she could remember from the times that she had gone in there to fetch wood or turf it was dry.

He released the skidpan.

"Walk on," he said.

The trap moved off. He nosed through the gate. He called

again. His horse broke into a slow trot. Foxy Moll went inside. Her mother was in her seat by the fire.

"Oh, nothing today?" she said.

"He's going to corrugate the roof and give us enough turf for the winter."

"So, I suppose that means you won't be seeing him again?"

Foxy Moll decided to stand still in the middle of the floor and to say nothing.

"I'll take that as a 'no'. A man's only that generous when he's finished with you."

Foxy Moll tried to judge her mother's tone. She was not angry. No, to her ears it sounded as if she was a little irritated because Foxy Moll had lost Mr O'Toole while at the same time she also seemed quite pleased that Foxy Moll had lost him. Her mother's irritation Foxy Moll could grasp: Mr O'Toole's gifts had improved their lives so she could see why her mother would be disappointed that there would be no more of them; but the delight – why would her mother be delighted? Foxy Moll could not understand that at all. At least at first: later, though, when she lay in bed she had a startling thought. Her mother was jealous. Her mother wished Mr O'Toole had courted her rather than her daughter. This was an incredible idea but then it struck her that her mother only thought of herself and judged every situation solely in respect of how it would benefit her. That explained it. She had wanted Mr O'Toole to pay her attention because then he would have given her those things he had given Foxy Moll. Once Foxy Moll had had this thought she felt better. She liked Mr O'Toole because of what he was and how he made her feel and his smell and his hair and the touch of his fingers and all sorts of other tiny things and not because of what he gave her. She was not like her mother. She would always be different.

The next day one of Mr O'Toole's labourers came. He drove a cart piled high with turf. He stacked it in neat piles in the shed at the far gable end and covered it with sacking and when Foxy

Moll went to thank him he told her that she was lovely and when she heard his words she felt light and happy again and she forgot Mr O'Toole and they did it against the turf stack and they had just finished and buttoned themselves up when mother came out with hot brown tea and a plate of buttered bread for him.

After he left her mother said, "You don't have to be nice to everyone, you know, only the ones who are going to give you something."

"I don't know what you mean," Foxy Moll said. She did know of course but when necessary she was able to give a very good impression that she did not.

Two days after, a tradesman came and he took off the thatch and fixed corrugated iron in its place and he was nice and he told Foxy Moll how pretty she was and again she felt happy and forgot Mr O'Toole and they went into the fields and lay down. When she went back inside the cottage later, her mother said not a word. She just shook her head and went, "Tut, tut."

A few days later Foxy Moll expected her period to start. It did not. She did not worry. Sometimes it was a day or two late just as sometimes it was a day or two early. But a week passed and then a second and a third and she knew. There was a baby starting inside her. She knew who the father was as well. It was not Mr O'Toole's labourer who brought the turf or the tradesman who fixed the roof. It was Mr O'Toole. She decided that she would tell the baby that Mr O'Toole was the father when the baby grew up and was old enough to understand because that was the one thing she could never forgive her mother for: not telling her who her father was.

She hoped her baby would come on her birthday but in the event her first child was born four days before, on the last day of March 1920. Her mother wanted to call him Horace after Horace Conway but Foxy Moll would not hear of it because Horace was a soldier's name and she did not want a soldier for a son and she held out for Daniel Paul and that was what he was called,

Daniel Paul McCarthy. On the birth certificate the space for the father's name was left blank.

Two weeks after the birth she went to Father Murphy and asked him to baptise her child.

He scowled and said, "I'll do it when no one's about."

It was done one Sunday afternoon. Daniel's only godparent was his grandmother Mary.

26

A few weeks later a woman came by a trap that she drove herself. She knocked on the cottage door and Foxy Moll went to open it. The visitor had a sharp angular face and she wore a grey skirt and a grey jacket and a small hat on her head. It was hard to gauge her age. Foxy Moll guessed that she must be in her thirties or perhaps even her early forties.

She introduced herself as Miss Cooney of Garranlea House. She was in the Legion of Mary, she explained, but that did not mean she always agreed with Father Murphy. On the contrary, she said, she kept her own counsel. This was a phrase Foxy Moll had never heard before but she assumed it must mean the visitor was on her side and it turned out this was true because a moment later Miss Cooney said she had something for her. She went back to the trap and returned with a wooden box made of light thin white wood. Foxy Moll saw it contained baby clothes plus bread, a bag of tea leaves, a jar of jam, potatoes with patches of dried earth on them, cans of tinned milk, matches and candles.

"I thought Daniel might use the clothes," she said in her polite English voice, "and the rest might be of use to yourself."

Foxy Moll guessed she had learnt about Daniel from Father Murphy. That made sense. But how or why exactly that had led to the clothes and food Miss Cooney had brought today was not clear. It did not matter though. Foxy Moll was happy to have them. She invited Miss Cooney in for tea. As they sat by the fire and waited for the kettle to boil Miss Cooney mentioned that she had been a nurse in France and England during the Great War and after the war ended she had come home to Ireland to keep house for her father, Mr Cooney, now a widower. She also said that she had lost her Irish accent when she had been over in France and England and had never gotten it back. Later she asked to hold Daniel. When he fell asleep she laid him in the blanket-lined drawer from the chest that Foxy Moll used as a crib.

"I might have something at home that you could use for the baby to sleep in," Miss Cooney said.

After they had their tea Miss Cooney said she had to go and she was certain there was a crib knocking about Garranlea House.

Miss Cooney returned the next day. The crib was made of wood and had rockers and a tin canopy and was painted blue. As she left, Miss Cooney asked if she could come back the next time she had something: food or clothes or anything that she thought the McCarthys might use.

"Of course," Foxy Moll said.

A week later Miss Cooney brought over a pram for Foxy Moll. She had cleaned it up and it was quite serviceable, she said. Foxy Moll had never been so excited about anything for a long while.

"My own pram, my own pram," she said, "I never thought I'd have one. Thank you, thank you."

Miss Cooney said goodbye and drove away in her trap. After the sound of the trap's wheels had vanished her mother cleared her throat. She had something to say.

"You know what that one is?" said her mother.

"A good Samaritan?" said Foxy Moll carefully.

"Don't talk nonsense," said her mother. "She's Father Murphy's spy of course."

"How do you know?"

"Why else would she come like she does unless she was? It's obvious."

"Well tell me this," said Foxy Moll. "You say she's a spy, you tell me then what's she found out that she didn't know already? That we're poor, we don't have much, we live in an old cabin, but he knew all that before."

Her mother was silent.

"Go on, tell me, if she's a spy, what has she found out?"

"You won't like it."

"You've started so you may as well finish."

"She's found out she only has to give you a few baubles and she has you fawning: you're her creature."

"So her business isn't to spy, you're saying now?"

Her mother shook her head. She did that when she was outclassed and was cross about it.

"She wants to get me into the Legion of Mary, is that it, so then I'd be her creature completely, is that what you're saying?"

Her mother closed her eyes. This was what she did when she did not have an answer.

"I think she's kind," said Foxy Moll.

Her mother snorted and opened her eyes and looked at her daughter. "You should know by now there is no such thing as someone who is simply kind. Nobody does anything without a reason, and if you don't know that yet, that's your own look out."

Foxy Moll considered. Sometimes, yes, some people did what they did because they would get something out of you but the idea that this was true of everybody all the time, well, she did not want to believe it. There had to be some people on earth who did things for no better reason than that they thought they were right. Why must her mother think that everybody was pure selfish?

Daniel mewled in the new pram where Foxy Moll had laid him earlier. She told hold of the handle and jigged the pram. He stopped mewling.

It occurred to Foxy Moll then that what her mother really hated was that they did not see people the same way. It was her mother who wanted to make her daughter her creature. Foxy Moll also knew that would never happen. She knew it was wrong to think like her mother and she knew if she did she would never find love.

27

Foxy Moll had a second child. The father was a local farmer called Bell. The baby was a girl. Foxy Moll wanted to call her Judy. She went to Father Murphy to ask him to baptise the infant and Father Murphy said he had let her away with murder the once but he would not do so again and so he would not. Then, the Sunday immediately following, he condemned female immorality in his sermon. Foxy Moll and her mother were there in the congregation with Judy and Daniel. Father Murphy did not name Foxy Moll but it was obvious it was her that he meant. They stood up and they walked out and on the walk back to Marlhill they agreed they would never go back to the New Inn church, even if Father Murphy went and a new priest arrived and he came to the cottage and begged them to attend. They would never cross the threshold of the church again.

2 8

From the Tipperary Democrat, *Saturday 13 December 1930:*

ARSON SUSPECTED AT MARLHILL

An attempt seems to have been made Thursday last (December 11) to burn properties in Marlhill and Knockgraffon.

The primary target of the arsonists (and it is suspected that several people were involved) was a small one-bedroom property, the residence of Miss Mary McCarthy (60), her daughter Miss Mary ("Moll") McCarthy (29) and her three children whose surname is also McCarthy, Daniel (10), Judy (6) and Maria (2).

The other property attacked was an empty one in Knockgraffon and it was attacked, our sources tell us, in order to prevent the McCarthys from moving into it in the event that the attack on the Marlhill property was a success.

The matter is now in the hands of the police.

*

My name is Moll McCarthy, though I am known as Foxy Moll. I am 29 years old. I live at Marlhill, on the Knockgraffon Road. I live with my mother, Miss Mary McCarthy (who owns the property), and my three children, Daniel (10), Judy (6) and Maria (2). Daniel and Judy attend Knockgraffon National School.

Last Thursday night, December 11, I was asleep in my bedroom. I had Daniel and Judy in the bed with me and I had the baby, Maria, in the crib beside me. My mother was sleeping in the other room. The old collie we have was in with my mother as well. He's old, but keen for all that, and some time in the night he woke me with his growling. He growls when foxes come sniffing after our poultry. There's a fox, I thought, but our birds are locked away safe and snug.

Next, I heard commotion and the voices of men and the sound then of several people running. It was no fox the collie had heard, I thought. I smelt burning. It was kerosene. I know the smell. There's a little window in my bedroom and I was certain that I now saw flickering on the other side of the glass. There was a fire in front of the house. I was sure of it.

I jumped out of bed and ran into the next room where my mother was sleeping. She sat up in her bed as I came in. She's a light sleeper. "What is it?" she said. "Are you sick?"

"Not I," I said and I looked at the bottom of our front door. There's a gap between the floor and the door's bottom edge and I ought to have seen nothing, but I saw light. That's where the fire was, I realised. It was raging on the other side of our front door.

I got everyone up and in our nightclothes and with our feet bare and with nothing, only a broom and a carpet beater and a wooden pail and not even a lamp to light our way, we all rushed out the back door and ran round to the front. It was fortunate, the night we had of it. Yes, it was cold, and bitterly so, but it was clear and there was a moon and we had light to see where we were going and what we were doing.

When we got to the front, we saw there were rags burning on the ground by the front door. We also saw there was a fire in the turf shed, a little lean-to attached to the far gable. When we went to look, we saw more burning rags.

"Off you go to the Caesars' farm," I said to my son, Daniel. Mr and Mrs Caesar live at the top of the lane beside us and near enough to our place, but still it was pitch black but Daniel didn't baulk.

"I'll go for you," he said and off he ran.

I set about beating the flames, first at the door and then in the turf shed, with the carpet beater, while my mother fetched one pail of water after the next. My daughter, Judy, held the baby, Maria, and jiggled her in her arms.

We had the flames pretty much out when we heard voices and saw a lamp coming out of the dark towards us. It was Daniel and Mr Caesar and Mr Caesar's farm manager, Harry Gleeson, who is known to everyone as Badger. Mrs Caesar had given Daniel a big pair of water boots and Mr Caesar and Badger had just pulled on coats and boots over their sleeping clothes.

Badger took the broom and swept the rags and that into a heap.

"The Guards might want this as evidence," Mr Caesar said.

I inspected the damage with Mr Caesar. The lean-to door and doorposts were badly scorched. The turf was wet

through from all the water we had thrown on. It was mid-
dling turf in the first place, only now it would be no good
for burning. Mr Caesar promised he'd have Badger bring
us down a load.

"There's no call for that," I said.

"You're not to argue," said Mr Caesar.

Our front door was scorched badly too, along the bottom, and the paint had bubbled. We'd need a new door;
there was no doubt of that.

"You're lucky the roof was tin," Mr Caesar said. "Thatch
and kerosene together, it would have been fatal. The place
would have gone up in a jiffy. You'd all have burnt to death
in your beds."

Mr Caesar insisted we came up with him to the farmhouse. We dressed and went up. Mrs Caesar had the fire
lit. She gave us all tea and scones and butter. We all slept
in her parlour. In the morning, Mr Caesar took me to the
Guards' station and I reported the fire and the Guard in
the Day Room told me to come back on Monday. My
mother took the children back to the house. Daniel and
Judy didn't go to school that day.

*

Questioned by Superintendent Mahony:

QUESTION: You believe the fire was malicious?
ANSWER: I do.
QUESTION: Do you know who might have started it?
ANSWER: I don't.
QUESTION: How do you get on with your neighbours?
ANSWER: Good.
QUESTION: Are you sure?
ANSWER: Didn't Mr Caesar and Badger come down?

QUESTION: Your other neighbours, how do you get on with them?

ANSWER: They have no cause for complaint.

QUESTION: Why do you put it like that?

ANSWER: Like what?

QUESTION: "They have no cause for complaint." That doesn't sound like a very neighbourly way of talking.

ANSWER: I don't know what you mean.

QUESTION: Don't you?

ANSWER: No.

QUESTION: "They have no cause for complaint." That means that they could have cause for complaint if they wished.

ANSWER: I've done nothing wrong.

QUESTION: Did I say you did anything wrong?

ANSWER: You're tangling me up with your questions.

QUESTION: You said, "I've done nothing wrong." That's an interesting phrase. That means that you've got things on your mind, things that are right and, more importantly, things that are wrong.

ANSWER: I didn't set my own house on fire.

QUESTION: There you go again. Did I say you did? No. So what are you talking about here?

ANSWER: I don't understand.

QUESTION: Oh, I think you do.

ANSWER: No, I don't.

QUESTION: You don't?

ANSWER: No, I don't. I don't understand. I come in here and report a fire. Some people came and they laid a fire at my house. If it had caught, if my roof had been thatch, Mr Caesar said, we'd all be dead.

QUESTION: I didn't know Mr Caesar was such an expert on fires.

ANSWER: He's my neighbour. I'm reporting what he said.

QUESTION: You like Mr Caesar?

ANSWER: Yes.

QUESTION: He's a good neighbour?

ANSWER: Yes.

QUESTION: Mr Gleeson? You call him Badger. You like him?

ANSWER: Yes.

QUESTION: Mrs Caesar?

ANSWER: Yes, she's lovely.

QUESTION: They your best neighbours?

ANSWER: Yes.

QUESTION: What about the Fitzgeralds?

ANSWER: What about the Fitzgeralds?

QUESTION: They've complained here. Two of your goats got across the Caesars' lane and onto their land.

ANSWER: I told them sorry.

QUESTION: They had to fix a hole in their hedge where your animal went through. Does "sorry" fix a hole in the hedge?

ANSWER: They never said about the hole.

QUESTION: Not to you they mightn't, but it has come to our attention, here in the barracks. And your neighbours across the road, the Condons, they are not mightily impressed with your animal husbandry either.

ANSWER: They've said nothing.

QUESTION: Again, not to you they haven't. But here we hear things. We hear everything. Everything that is annoying people and eating away at them, they come and tell us. And we hear a great deal about you. A great deal. You're not liked. And it's not just your animals. Do you understand me?

ANSWER: No, I don't. I didn't set the fire at my house.

QUESTION: Would you stop and would you listen for a change, instead of opening your mouth every other minute and firing off the first thought that comes into your head?

ANSWER: I have said what I have to say.

QUESTION: But I haven't said what I want. Now listen. The

way you carry on, those children – three you have, isn't it? It isn't right, it isn't Christian and people don't like it, the women especially, because of how you carry on. It's their men, their sons, their fathers, their husbands you are leading astray. You have enemies. You need to watch yourself. This was a warning. And another fire was set at an empty house near Knockgraffon National School so you could not move in if your own house was lost. If you lived a different sort of life, your troubles would stop. I'm saying all this in a friendly sort of way, you understand? You help yourself and I'll try and find who did this. Do you understand?
ANSWER: Thank you, sir.

I have heard this statement read over to me and it is correct,
    Mary Moll McCarthy.
    Witness: Thomas Reilly, Inspector, 15.12.30
    Patrick Mahony, Superintendent, 15.12.30 at 11.50 a.m.

29

Her mother was poorly. She coughed a lot. She complained of the cold all the time. She barely ate. Foxy Moll put her to bed in her bedroom and lit the fire in there to warm the room.

"Would you take a drink?" she asked when the fire was going.

"I might," her mother said. She was deep under the bed-clothes with only her head showing on the bolster. "What is it?" Her mother did not care for spirits. They gave her a headache. She favoured fortified wines.

"Madeira," said Foxy Moll, delighted that what she had to offer was what her mother liked. Foxy Moll had just got a bottle as a gift from Mr Monaghan. He was an elderly widower whom she saw in his little house in New Inn from time to time. His bedroom was small and dark and he always had the shutters closed when she visited. The bedclothes smelt of mothballs.

"Madeira," her mother said slowly. "Bottled by Clarke's of Cashel?" her mother asked.

Foxy Moll was surprised by the question. She tried to remember. "I think so," she said. "I'm not sure."

"Madeira," her mother said again. She said the word as if it meant something though Foxy Moll had no idea what that was. "Clarke's of Cashel."

"I'll get it," Foxy Moll said. She went and got the bottle and a glass and came back to the bedside.

"Yes," she said. She looked at the label. "Yes, it is Clarke's of Cashel."

She pulled the cork and poured some of the dark yellowy-brown wine into the glass. She set the bottle down and lifted her mother from behind and put the glass to her lips and tilted. A small surge of drink bumped over the lip of the glass and ran over her mother's lips and disappeared into her mouth. Her mother closed her eyes and pursed her lips and nodded faintly. Foxy Moll let her head fall back onto the bolster. Her mother swallowed and Foxy Moll saw her Adam's apple glide up and then down.

"Oh yes," said her mother. "I have never forgotten that taste. How would I?" She opened her eyes and looked up at her daughter. "That was what I had, you know, the first time."

Foxy Moll decided she would not speak or move but she would stand very still and wait to be told.

"I was living with my brother Michael. Heaton was a soldier. We went to a wood and he gave me Madeira and then I lay down on his jacket. I made a terrible mistake. I believed he loved me. That was a mistake and I made it twice. Heaton first and then Horace when I should have known better. What an idiot I was. The only thing that counts is what you get. Promise you will remember that? Go on, say after me, the only thing that matters is what you get."

"Why are you telling me this?" said Foxy Moll.

"Because I want you to survive," her mother said, "after I go."

"I'll have to manage my way," said Foxy Moll, "the way I always have."

"You never listen," said her mother.

"Oh, I listen, I just don't agree."

"Is that it? I'll take another sip."

She put the glass to her mother's thin lower lip and this time her mother took two big gulps and emptied the glass.

"More?" asked Foxy Moll.

"No," said her mother and she closed her eyes. "That was very nice."

Foxy Moll listened to her mother's breaths. They were smooth and shallow. She would soon be asleep, she thought.

She poured a little Madeira into the glass and swallowed a mouthful and shivered and then stared down at her mother's face. It was long and thin and very pale and there were deep lines at the sides of the eyes and across the forehead and under the nose. It was the face of a woman who was angry and disappointed.

Well, what else would she be?

Apart from the two she said she loved even if it was a mistake, her mother had devoted her whole life to getting what she could from everyone she knew and now what had she to show for it? What ever happened to her, Foxy Moll was certain of one thing: this was not what she wanted her face to show at her end. She would not live the way her mother had.

30

From the Tipperary Democrat, *Saturday 15 August 1931:*

Householder Successfully Sues Council over Arson Attack

(From our court correspondent)

In our edition of Saturday 13 December 1930, we described the unfortunate experience of Mary McCarthy (then living though now deceased: she died Monday 6 April 1931 and her funeral was covered in our edition of Saturday 11 April 1931), her daughter, Mary "Moll" McCarthy, and her three grandchildren, Daniel, Judy and Maria McCarthy.

The previous Thursday evening December 11, as we reported, persons unknown laid fires at the front door and in the adjacent turf shed of the McCarthy residence, a modest cottage in Marlhill, New Inn, Co. Tipperary.

On the same night, another empty property at Knock-graffon was also set on fire. In both instances, there is good reason to believe the same culprits were responsible.

Since the attack, the police in New Inn have made strenuous attempts to identify those responsible. Unfortunately, their efforts have been unavailing to date. However, we understand investigations are continuing.

In the meantime, Mary "Moll" McCarthy (with the support of her mother until the latter's untimely death) initiated legal proceedings against Tipperary County Council alleging malicious damage and, on Tuesday last, August 11, the case was heard in the District Court in Caher before District Justice Seán Troy. The court accepted that the fires were malicious and £25.00 was awarded to the plaintiff. Tipperary County Council has until the end of the month to pay and was denied leave to appeal.

Speaking outside the courthouse afterwards, Miss McCarthy declared her intention to use the money to buy "good sturdy brogues" for her three children plus clothes for "the baby". She is expecting her fourth child in September.

*

From the Tipperary Democrat, *Saturday 21 January 1933:*

MOTHER SUCCESSFULLY RESISTS ATTEMPT BY STATE TO COMMIT HER CHILDREN TO CARE OF STATE

(From our court correspondent)
On Tuesday last, January 17, a melancholy case appeared before District Justice Seán Troy in the District Court in Caher. On behalf of the Guards in New Inn the solicitor Mr Frank O'Donnelly presented the court with an account of Mary "Moll" McCarthy's history, supported by sworn

statements from local people. The burden of this material (and the police case) was that Miss McCarthy's four children – Daniel (13), Judy (9), Maria (5) and Brendan (2) – have different fathers and she was an "unfit mother". The unsavoury relationships that produced these children, said the Guards' representative, were both a threat to public health and a cause of great offence to New Inn's inhabitants, especially its married women. In addition, said Mr O'Donnelly, Miss McCarthy was an inattentive mother. For these reasons, he concluded, the Guards moved for the committal of Miss McCarthy's four children to State care.

District Justice Seán Troy, having listened to the State's presentation, then cross-questioned Miss McCarthy. She vigorously contested the inference that she was unfit and negligent. Her children were fed and clothed properly, she said, and furthermore her children of school age attended Knockgraffon National School regularly.

She presented a testimonial from Mr Jack Hare, the Master at Knockgraffon, that Daniel and Maria enjoyed a 98 per cent attendance record. The master's letter also noted that Miss McCarthy's daughter Maria would start at Knockgraffon National School in September this year and that he was looking forward to welcoming this new addition to his school.

Miss McCarthy also presented a testimonial from Miss Anastasia Cooney of Garranlea House, which was read into the proceedings. Miss Cooney, who has known Miss McCarthy since she returned from nursing in France and Britain following the Great War, said she knew Miss McCarthy to be an excellent mother who went to extraordinary pains to care for her children despite having only a tiny income and very poor support from the State. Should the McCarthy children be committed to the State's care, Miss Cooney concluded, it would not only be a violation of natural justice but all over Ireland good parents of modest circumstances would start to fret, with good reason, that the State might take their children away.

The testimonials having been read, Miss McCarthy noted that her children were in the lobby outside the court and she asked if she might have them brought in so District Justice Seán Troy could see for himself "that they were in perfect repair", a suggestion that provoked considerable laughter.

District Justice Seán Troy thanked Miss Cooney for her contribution and asked the clerk to fetch Daniel McCarthy into the court. "Nobody is in a better position to speak about family life in the McCarthy house in Marlhill than Daniel," said District Justice Seán Troy.

The witness was introduced to the court and the questions began and, though but thirteen years old, we can report that young Master Daniel McCarthy answered the questions in a clear and resolute voice. He confirmed that life in the family home in Marlhill was modest, even frugal, but said that he and his siblings were fed, clothed and loved by their mother. When asked if she ever struck her children, Daniel said loudly, "No." When he was asked if she was ever drunk, Daniel said loudly, "No, never, she is never drunk."

District Justice Seán Troy thanked Daniel for his contribution. The Guards' application to have the McCarthy children taken into care was rejected.

31

It was a June night and Foxy Moll was in bed asleep when a tap at the window woke her. She looked at her little window but even though there was some light from the moon she saw nothing. She heard the taps again. There were four short and two long ones. She knew now who her visitor was. They had agreed that if he ever came in the night this was how he would signal to her that he had come. She found her slippers and a dressing gown and went to her window and tapped back. She was aware of him beyond and she heard his boots on the ground. His name was Cunningham. He was a farmer. He had two children and a wife called Carmel who he maintained did not understand him. She also did not sleep with him because she said it hurt her.

Foxy Moll opened her door and slipped quietly into the other room and stopped. She heard her children breathing in their sleep. She wondered whether to bring Mr Cunningham in or whether to go out. She heard one of her children murmur in their sleep. Not tonight, she thought. They would go round to the turf shed.

She lifted the latch, pulled the door open, slipped out and closed it in one seamless silent motion.

Mr Cunningham was immediately outside and his arms went around her straightaway and he pulled her against his middle. He was desperate. It was obvious.

"Hold on," she said. "Hold on. Wait."

She slipped out of his embrace and took his hand. She saw he was in his Blueshirt uniform under his light coat. She knew there had been a parade in New Inn earlier with speeches and a lot of marching. He had been there of course and once it was over he had come to her.

"How was it?" she said.

"What?"

"Tonight's parade?"

"Speeches and more speeches."

He took her hand and brought it down to his groin. Behind the material she felt he was stiff.

"It's been that way all night," he said.

They went to the turf shed. It did not take long. Afterwards he reached into his coat pocket and pulled out some badges. They were light tin affairs and they had a picture on them of O'Duffy the Blueshirt leader, he said.

"They're for your children," he said. "Tell them to wear them to school."

She nodded and said, "Thank you," but kept her counsel. Her children had a hard enough time as it was and if they got mixed up in politics it would make a bad situation a whole lot worse and that she would never allow. She would never let them wear these to school.

He left on his bicycle and she went in to the fire. She scraped back the blanket of ash to reveal the hot ember heart below. She threw the badges onto the embers. Then with the poker point she pushed the badges down into the embers until they were out of sight. In the course of the night the tin would buckle and the picture of General O'Duffy the Blueshirt leader would go black and in the morning when she threw them away with the ashes it would be impossible to know what had been on the front. She spread the ash over the embers. She went back to bed.

3 2

From the Tipperary Democrat, *Saturday 16 May 1936:*

FOR SECOND TIME NEW INN MOTHER SUCCESSFULLY RESISTS ATTEMPT BY GUARDS TO COMMIT HER CHILDREN TO CARE OF STATE

(From our court correspondent)
Three years ago, Miss Mary "Moll" McCarthy appeared before District Justice Seán Troy on the foot of an application by the Guards in New Inn to have Miss McCarthy's children committed to the care of the State.

Last Tuesday May 12, the Guards attempted again to have the children, Daniel (16), Judy (12), Maria (8), Brendan (4 yrs 8 months) and Dermot (1 yr 8 months), committed to the care of the State.

District Justice Seán Troy listened to the Guards' representations, then heard from a visibly pregnant Miss

McCarthy. She denied nothing except that she was a poor mother. She was an exceptional mother, she said, and she presented the court with testimonials from the master of Knockgraffon National School, Jack Hare, and Miss Cooney of Garranlea House. She also had a letter from her nearest neighbour at Marlhill, Mrs Caesar. This declared she was an "exemplary person".

District Justice Seán Troy then cross-questioned Daniel. He reported he had left school in June 1935 and now worked full-time for a family called O'Shaughnessy. Their farm in Knockgraffon was two miles from his mother's place in Marlhill yet he went home after work every evening to see his mother, seven days a week. His mother provided a stable and loving home, he said, and despite little income other than "the princely sum of six shillings a week in the form of home assistance", her children never wanted for clothes or went hungry. When asked whether she or the State would care best for her children he said loudly, "My mother will care for them best."

District Justice Seán Troy rejected the Guards' application to have the McCarthy children committed to the care of the State.

33

Foxy Moll was in a hat, a nice black one with a lovely brim that turned down at the back and up at the front and was styled a Tyrol and had attached to it a pheasant's feather that had a lovely arch to it and that trembled whenever she moved her head. She also had on a lovely new coat of brown astrakhan with heavy wooden buttons and good shoes and she felt wonderful dressed in such lovely good clothes.

Then she took the coat off and discovered that she had nothing underneath, no dress, no stockings, nothing. She was not certain where she was in the dream. There were people around but no one noticed her or paid any attention to her so she was not embarrassed. Not a bit. Instead she just thought, I have this lovely coat and hat and shoes but nothing on underneath, nothing at all, and after the thought a sense of great sadness flooded through her.

She opened her eyes and looked out the window. The light was thin and pale. She guessed that it was very early and the old alarm clock with the missing leg that Mrs Caesar had given her when Mr Caesar had gotten his wife a new one for Christmas would not ring for a while.

Foxy Moll closed her eyes. She felt a little puzzled by the dream and listened to the sounds that came from outside: bird-song and the faraway clip-clop of the Caesars' donkey Alfred as he pulled the cart down the lane. The clip-clop of his hooves and the rumble of the cartwheels grew louder and then came the sound that she connected to Mondays and Wednesdays and Saturdays, the days when the Caesars' milk went to the New Inn Farmers' Cooperative Creamery, and that sound was the clang the churns made as they jostled against one another. It was a strange sad high-pitched sound, the sort of sound that she imagined one might hear in heaven – not that she was certain there was such a place any more.

Now that the cart was level with the cottage she wondered who had the reins in his hands this Monday morning. Was it Badger? Maybe not. Maybe today it was the new fellow who had come to work at Marlhill Farm. His name was Tommy Reid. He was the son of another of Mr Caesar's many siblings and, though his second name might be Reid, Tommy had the Caesar looks: the long face and the small even features; and he had the Caesar manner as well, open and pleasant and amiable – at least that was her impression.

Foxy Moll was not sure of Tommy's age but somewhere along the way she had picked up (how, she had no idea) that he had been born in 1920 in which case he was eighteen. He looked eighteen anyway.

Tommy was the farm's labourer now and Badger was the manager and one day Marlhill Farm would be his. He was still a single man and that was a surprise to many around New Inn but not to her. Foxy Moll had always guessed that Badger was not the kind to marry. His manner told her that. He was too quiet, too reticent and his deafness left him a bit awkward, a bit shy. He was one of those men who just did not have the same interests as most other men.

She heard a flat voice shout, "Whoa." That was Badger's voice and she presumed that the cart had reached the public road but then she heard another voice that she recognised as Tommy's. She had not thought of that. Badger and Tommy were both headed for the creamery this morning. They must be on their way to bring back cattle feed or skimmed milk and the two of them were needed to load it onto the cart.

The hooves and the rumble of the wheels started up again. The cart turned onto the public road and headed for her. That was the routine on creamery mornings. A few moments later she heard the cart as it nosed through her gate and then stopped by her front door.

"Turn the cart and I'll drop the can." It was Badger who said this.

"Right, so." That was Tommy.

She heard Badger's footfalls as he came towards the front of the cottage and then the chink as he set a milk can by her door. Good old Badger, she thought. On creamery days he always left her a sup of milk and when she got up later she would heat some on the fire for the children to dip their bread in at breakfast.

She had a second can that she had washed and scoured and set out by the front door the night before. She heard the handle of this second can squeak now and she guessed Badger must have picked it up.

"Will you stop acting the mule?"

That was Tommy and there was laughter as well provoked by whatever Badger was up to. Badger was nearly forty but he had not grown up like other men who had cares had grown up. With no wife and no children he was still frisky and apt to lark around if the occasion was suitable and she liked that. It was what she most liked about him.

She heard the clip-clop of Alfred's hooves start up again and she followed the sound as the cart nosed out her gate and headed up the road towards New Inn. The noise of the hooves and the wheels began to grow fainter and then after a while she heard nothing and she dozed off and slept until the cart woke her again on its return from the creamery as it passed behind the cottage and rumbled up the lane towards the farmhouse.

She opened her eyes. It was later. The room was brighter. She squinted at the clock face. There were a few more minutes to go before the alarm would sound. She would lie on for a bit, warm and snug. She closed her eyes. She thought of the dream again, the one she had had earlier. Maybe she could go back to it for her last few minutes in bed and this time she could have underwear and stockings and a dress ... red – no, blue crêpe-de-chine, the fabric slippery and smooth and cool to the touch.

34

It was calm and warm that morning and after Judy and Maria and Brendan had left for school she got a bundle of old sacks that she had cut open to convert them into covers and carried them to the flags outside her front door.

The flags were quite new. She had had them for three years. They had been the gift of Mr O'Driscoll who was the father of her youngest child Helena.

Mr O'Driscoll was another farmer stuck in an unhappy marriage. When they had been together Mr O'Driscoll had promised Foxy Moll that he would leave his wife.

When she had fallen pregnant with what turned out to be Helena, Mr O'Driscoll's attitude towards her had changed. First he had become distant and then Mr O'Driscoll had told her that he could not see her any more. He had said that the strain was too much. He had said that his family was making difficulties. He had said that he feared the scandal would kill his mother.

Of course Mr O'Driscoll had also wanted to make it up to her. Whenever her men left her they always wanted to make it up to her. The way he proposed to do this, Mr O'Driscoll had said, was with flagstones.

She needed flagstones, he had said. With flags outside visitors would have somewhere to stamp their feet and get off the mud or grass that was on their shoes or boots before they went into Foxy Moll's. With flags around her house she would find her house so much easier to keep. With flags around her house her children would have somewhere to play. And now he was going to give her those flagstones, he had said, oh yes, he was. He was going to have flagstones laid around her house.

Everything that had happened with Mr O'Driscoll at the end, both the reasons why he had left her and his wish to make amends, had also happened with the different fathers of her previous five children, and indeed with all the other men who had promised marriage but then left her even though she was not pregnant, so nothing that happened with Mr O'Driscoll had surprised her. Except for those whom she knew for just a short time, it was always the same whenever she parted from anyone: they made promises to do things for her in order to feel better about their desertion of her.

She had therefore not been surprised when three weeks after Mr O'Driscoll had said goodbye a lorry had come: a Crossley flatbed loaded with big flat flagstones that were yellow in colour and gritty to the touch as well as heaps of sand and gravel. The workmen had unloaded it all and over the course of the next week they had cut away the turf around her house and laid a foundation of sand and gravel and then bedded the flags on top which was why her little house was now surrounded by this lovely collar of flagstones and her children had somewhere they could play outside without getting muck on their shoes or their clothes.

She spread the sacks that she had and arranged them into a nice square and then she called through the open door, "Dermot, Helena." The children came out. Dermot carried the box of coloured wooden bricks and Helena had a long wooden spoon.

"You're going to play with the bricks, are you?" said Foxy Moll.

The bricks had been Miss Cooney's gift the previous Christmas. They were from Clery's the department store in Dublin. Foxy Moll knew its name and what it was but she had never visited either the shop or the city in which it stood and she doubted that she ever would.

"We build them up and knock them down," said Dermot. Then he and Helena laughed together. They both plopped themselves down onto the sacks which their mother had laid flat for that purpose.

"Good for you," said Foxy Moll. "Build them up and knock them down."

Foxy Moll went into the cottage and opened the back door and all the windows to let air through. She mixed water and Indian maize in a bucket then carried the bucket to her first field. This was where the coop for her birds stood. There was an old tyre split in two in front of the coop that was more of the Caesars' bounty. Badger had delivered them a few months earlier. She used the two tyre halves as feeding troughs for her birds.

Careful to spread the meal in an even way she filled the tyres and then opened the door of the coop. The birds poured out and rushed to the tyres and with many clucks and jostles they began to feed.

She went into the coop. It smelled of bird; the odour pricked the back of her throat. She went to the first nesting box and put her hand into the straw and wood shavings and rummaged about. After a moment she felt a warm egg and pulled it out. It was brown and there were a couple of white feathers stuck to it.

With care she put the egg into the pocket of the apron that she wore over her work dress and then she burrowed in the wood shavings and straw again.

When she left the coop a few minutes later she had eighteen

eggs. They were heavy and she supported the pocket of the apron where they were all stored from underneath with both hands. The eggman from Cassidy's shop would call later. She decided that she would keep six and she would give him the rest.

She looked at her birds as they milled around the split tyres. Several white and brown feathers floated in the air above them or lay here and there on the grass. Feathers always flew at feeding time.

A donkey brayed. The noise was long and drawn-out and harsh and nerve-racking. That was Alfred's bray. She recognised it. She would have known his bray and the sound that his hooves made anywhere.

She thought it was funny the way you got to know certain sounds so that you could identify them as quick and sure as you could identify a voice.

With her eye she followed the ash trees that grew along the Caesars' lane to their house at the end. The roof slates were grey and dry this morning and black smoke rose from the two chimneys. She guessed that they burned coal because only coal made smoke that black; turf and wood made a thinner paler greyer smoke, although where the Caesars had gotten coal in the middle of a war when nobody else could and why they burned it on a mild day like this one were both mysteries to her. Perhaps they needed to heat water for baths or to wash clothes. The bray came again: a honk that was almost painful.

She retrieved her bucket and with it held in one hand and the eggs supported by the other she walked back to the house. At the front door she found Dermot intent upon the construction of a tower. Helena watched. Foxy Moll put the bucket down. The final brick went on. Dermot nodded to his little sister. Helena raised the wooden spoon and struck the base of the tower. With a noisy clatter the bricks collapsed into a heap. She laughed. He laughed.

"Again," Helena shouted.

"Again?" said Dermot. "Again?"

"Yes. Yes."

Foxy Moll picked up the bucket and went in. A few moments later as she cleaned the eggs she heard more laughter and another clatter as the bricks tumbled down once more. Then she heard footsteps and her children's laughter stopped. Was it the eggman from Cassidy's shop? He seldom came in the morning and if it was him, well, he would either have to wait a bit because she had not got all the eggs cleaned up yet, or he would have to come back at the usual time.

"Is your mother here?"

The voice was male. It was not the man from Cassidy's. Who was it? She turned. A man stood in her doorway. He wore a fawn-coloured trench coat and jodhpurs and riding boots.

"Hello," she said.

She knew him: not properly of course but she knew his name and he knew hers and they had spoken over the years whenever they had passed one another out on the roads or over in New Inn.

Indeed had she not seen him a couple of days earlier and had he not said that he would call up to see her? She had thought nothing of it at the time because men often said such things to her. They meant it when they said it but then later on they found reasons not to come. These reasons always had do with their wives and families and the men themselves would realise that they did not want to be spotted as they consorted with her and they did not want to be the subject of gossip and they did not want to have to put up with trouble at home.

This one, however, had said that he would be up and now here he was stood on her front doorstep: the famous Jimmy Spink, known as Jimmy Jodhpurs, the name often shortened to J.J., on account of the fact that he only wore jodhpurs.

Then her next thought came easy – he was not like most of the other men that she had known because of what he had done and continued to do and because of the organisation of which he was a member and because of his associates and because he had weapons hidden in this hedgerow or that attic; for all these reasons he did not need to worry about gossip. No one would dare gossip about him or what he did or whom he was seen with. If someone saw him with Foxy Moll they would be too frightened to pass the information on lest what they had said got back to him and he was then provoked to pay them a visit: a visit that they would not enjoy. Of course if something went on long enough and enough people saw then it became common knowledge but being known was quite different to being discussed and what no one would dare to do was talk about J.J. Yes, she was pretty sure of that.

This in turn led to another much more radical thought. If the people of New Inn were so frightened that they would not talk about him did that mean he would be different from all the other men she had known? Did that mean he would not baulk? Did that mean he would withstand the pressure from his family and his wife (whom everyone in New Inn knew he kept in Cashel and visited on occasion) to give her up?

"Hello," she said.

He nodded and stepped forward. He was bareheaded. He held his hat in his hand. It was a conventional men's hat, not a flat cap. It was obvious to her that he had removed it outside before he came in and she approved of that. She saw that he had shaved. She saw that he had combed his hair. His hair was wet with pomade and she smelled his pomade from where she stood. She liked pomade. It made her tingle. She liked his clean looks. He had made an effort. She liked that. Of course she knew why he had bothered. He wanted to impress. It was obvious but even when a man made the effort because he wanted to impress, because he was only after one thing, she still approved.

"Care for a walk?" he said.

Did she? It was not a walk that he wanted, was it? These

events only went one way. Oh why not? What had she to lose?

"Yes, only not now."

"Oh."

He looked baffled. Then he glanced round at where her children sat with the bricks. He turned back and looked at her and his expression changed.

She looked straight back at him. His nose was straight and his lips thin. He had grey eyes. It was funny how she had seen him many times over the years in passing but she had never looked at him, she had never paid attention to his features, no, she had never scrutinised his features so she had never realised that J.J. was actually a handsome man.

"I've to mind the children," she said.

"Oh, yes."

Behind him Dermot said, "Again?"

"Yes," Helena said, "yes, yes …"

Clack clack clack the tower of wooden blocks began to rise.

"My daughter will be home from school later."

"Is that Judy?"

"Yes, and how did you know her name?"

"My business is to know."

He recited the names of her other children and their ages. There's a good chance that he knows who their fathers are as well, she thought. He told her where Daniel worked and for whom and something about Daniel's duties and the provenance of his employer Mr O'Shaughnessy. At the finish J.J. described Mr O'Shaughnessy as sound. She was glad to hear it. It was not a good thing not to be liked by J.J.

"Do you know the Caesars?" she asked. "I suppose you do."

He looked at her shrewdly. She was not surprised. It was not an innocent question though she had tried to make it seem like one. J.J. had a reputation. It was said by many people around New Inn that he had organised the abduction of an informer whose remains were later found in a mountain bog with his hands tied and bullet holes in his skull. Mr and Mrs Caesar did not endorse such activities or the politics that lay behind them. She presumed J.J. knew this but what she did not know was how he regarded them. Was he hostile or did he take the view, like so many of his stripe, that people like Mr and Mrs Caesar were an irrelevance?

"Yes, I know them," he said. His tone was neutral. "Why do you ask?"

"No reason at all really," she said. She hoped she sounded blithe. "They're my neighbours and I just wondered if you knew them, that's all. You know everyone else about these parts."

"I ignore the Caesars," he said.

She nodded.

"And like ghosts I don't even see them when we pass in the street. I don't think they see me either."

"Ah," she said. So neither party acknowledged the existence of the other. That was better than either actively disliking the other. Yes, that was quite a satisfactory answer, she thought, cunning, yes, but reassuring.

"Tell me about Mr O'Driscoll," he said.

It was a moment or two before she realised the subject of the question.

"I'm sorry," she said. "Why would I do that?"

"You knew him. He paid for all those flagstones outside, didn't he?"

She looked him straight in the eye. "I've no idea what you're on about."

"My, you are a very discreet individual," said J.J. "I like that. Will I warrant the same discretion?"

"What does warrant mean?" she said.

"Will you be discreet about me?"

"Yes," she said quickly. Did he not know that from the answer she had just given about Mr O'Driscoll? What she did she did but it was never discussed with anyone, ever. That was a principle that never changed. "I never talk," she said.

"Good," he said.

She looked down at his hands: they were delicate and elongated and in that respect they were like his face, she thought. She could not quite see his fingernails as there was not enough light but she hoped that the ends were round and smooth and there was no dirt under them.

"So, what time then do I come back?" His tone was direct but not curt. She knew that he would be back at whatever time she said.

"Four."

He turned and looked into the sky. There had been a veil of cloud earlier but it had started to thin and to break up and now patches of blue showed.

"It doesn't look like rain," he said. "And the sun might even be shining by four."

"I hope so."

"It might be a fine evening."

"I hope so."

Of course he did not want it to rain. No of course not. As she knew from all those times that she had walked out with men in the past, if it had just rained or if it rained while they were out together then everything was difficult and fumbled and had to be done stood up with her leaned against a wall or a tree. When it was dry and the ground was firm it was easier and better. Of course there was nothing to beat the bed. Over the years sometimes her men had come in the middle of the night or very early in the morning and woken her with a gentle tap on the window and she had taken them into her own bed, or if that was too risky she had gone out to them and taken them into the turf shed, and on other occasions the men had rented bedrooms in small pubs or out of the way hotels and they had gone to them. She had also visited men in their houses but these were only men who lived alone. On the whole it had been out in the fields or against trees or old walls or in abandoned houses or in little woods or against rocks or down in the Dugout that she did it.

"So I'll come back later, then."

"Yes," she said. "How did you come, by the way?"

He put his hat on.

"Why do you ask?"

"I didn't hear a car or a trap in the road," she said. She aimed to sound bored. She was not sure if she managed it. Secretly she hoped he had a car and would take her out in it.

"You pay attention to such things?" said J.J.

"Not really." She still aimed to sound bored.

"So why did you ask then?"

"I don't know."

"I came on the bicycle, but I have a car. Is your ground in front firm enough to take a car, do you think?"

"I'd say so."

"But if I come back in my car I'm not proposing a drive. I'd like a walk."

She nodded. They understood one another. He left. The older children came home from school. She made them toast at the fire. There was no jam or dripping so they ate the toast dry with milky tea. Then Foxy Moll issued her instructions to Judy. There were turnips to peel and boil and potatoes to wash and boil. Daniel would be over after six. They were to keep him something to eat. She thought that she would be home in a couple of hours, three at the most. They were to keep the fire in.

3 5

Foxy Moll heard a car and went out. A Rover 12 came through the gate. It was black and quite big. She recognised most makes: Foxy Moll liked cars although she knew that she would never own one and had seldom been in a car other than the Humber that belonged to Miss Cooney's father and a few others driven by men who gave her lifts to or from New Inn. She liked their speed. She liked the sense of separation from the world outside that she got when she was inside a car. Most of all she liked to look out at the world as it sped by and know that the world, for as long as she was in the car, was not able to interfere with her.

J.J. stopped the car. She heard the noise of a spring stretch as he pulled on the handbrake. The engine died. J.J. got out.

"Afternoon," he said.

"I'll just leave off my apron."

She went in and hung the apron on one of the nails on the back of the door. She took her hat from a second nail and pulled it on. It was brown felt cloche cap with a little feather and nothing like that lovely hat of her dream earlier. She took a short jacket from a third nail and draped it over her arm. She told the children she'd be back later. She went out and closed the door. He waited by the car. He had left his hat on the dashboard in front of the steering wheel.

"Shall we go?" It was the same voice as earlier when he had said what time he would return at: not curt but clear and emphatic.

"Yes."

He motioned towards her paddock where her goats were. They walked over. He untied the string and they went through the first gate.

"You need a new gate," he said as he did the string up.

When he repeated the palaver at the next gate he said, "In fact, it's not one new gate you need, but two."

"Are you going to buy me new gates?"

"I might."

They set off along a track that ran south to the corner and which she knew cut through four more fields and ended at the Dugout. It was a nice ten-minute walk.

"Will you hang them too?"

"Ah, now," he said, "I'm not a tradesman, you know."

"Really?"

"I use my head not my hands. I'm an intellectual, you know."

They walked on. She heard soft creaks from the leather of his riding boots. She wore brown brogues with a small heel.

"So, an in– how do you say it?"

"Intellectual."

"– is a brain box?"

"Yes."

"So, you're a brain box?"

"If you say so."

"Do you think all of the time then?"

"I do."

She considered this for a moment and decided that she approved. Perhaps this one really would not be like the others.

"What do you think about?"

"Whatever I want. Our history, the future of this State, the function of government."

"Do you ever think about people?"

"What do you mean? Their actions, their deeds?"

"Yes, what they're like, really. I do think about people a lot … about their character."

"Oh, I see."

They passed through the gate and into the next field going south.

"Well, I've been thinking about you," he said.

"Me. Why – why have you been thinking about me?"

"I need comfort."

"Oh."

Conversation had been rare on these walks when she had taken them in the past and when it had featured there had never been talk of this sort.

"Comfort," she said.

She gazed ahead. The grass was very green and quite long. The animals were out of their winter housing but Badger had not brought them down here yet. "I'm letting the grass get up," he had said when they had met here the day before: him out to walk one of his greyhounds and her with the goat that had escaped but which she had caught and was bringing home on a halter.

"I've heard you give good comfort," she heard J.J. say beside her.

"You have?"

"Is it true?"

"I wouldn't know."

"Oh, I see, so I'm going to have to find out for myself," he said and he laughed.

The laugh was short and the pitch was quite high. That surprised her. As far as laughter went she had imagined something different from him: something bigger and deeper and more masculine.

"Well, will you try?" he said.

"I always try."

"That's good. And you've never disappointed."

"I wouldn't know about that."

"I'd say you've never disappointed. I'm told you've never disappointed."

On the outskirts of her mind she had a small furtive thought: she imagined the New Inn wives and Father O'Malley, the priest from New Zealand who had replaced old Father Murphy – not that he was any different: after Daniel, Father Murphy refused to baptise her other children and Father O'Malley when he arrived continued that tradition – and now she imagined how they looked at her, Father O'Malley and the women, and how they talked about her and how they judged her. It was an idea that she did not care for. Then she reminded herself of her rule.

She could not alter what these ones thought and therefore the best thing was not to think about them or what they thought or said. Not ever. She could think about nice people and their characters all right but she mustn't think about the bad ones and their ways ever.

"Look at that cloud," she said. She pointed into the sky. "It looks like the head of a donkey."

"You're right. There are the ears and the mouth and eyes."

They entered the next field. He had increased his pace, she noticed. Her forehead was warm. She stopped to catch her breath.

"I'm out of condition," she said, "and you're going too fast."

"It's a habit. Too many years on the run, you see. I'll slow down."

He stopped. They started off together again and walked slower this time.

"Of course I'm bigger than you, I've a longer stride. For every step I take, you probably have to take two," he said.

"Probably."

"How tall are you?"

"I don't know."

She had known once but she had long since forgotten.

"Five foot, five foot two," he said.

"I'm not sure."

"I'll bring the tape measure next time."

"My son, Daniel, is taller than me – isn't that rare, the child taller than the mother?"

"He must be six inches above you, I'd say."

"Oh yes, you know him, don't you? I'd forgotten."

"Only by sight, only to say hello to. The O'Shaughnessys are friends of mine and when I visit them I sometimes see him there, working, or I might be in the kitchen and he comes in for a cup of tea, that sort of thing."

"I see," she said.

They crossed the third field in silence and entered the fourth. She saw the stubble lines ahead where Badger had left the stubble to grow and provide cover for game and wild birds after he had cut the hay and in the far corner beyond down on her right she saw the Dugout: a low concrete structure that reminded her of a toad, a squat fat toad that waited and sat.

"The O'Shaughnessy family speaks highly of Daniel, you know," he said.

She wondered if his thoughts had been about her son the whole time as they had crossed the field.

"I hope so. He's a good boy," she said.

"A good worker. Doesn't cut corners. And a man of his word, they say."

"Yes."

She wondered where this was headed. What on earth did he want to talk about Daniel for? Had he recruited Daniel? Was that what this was leading up to? Was he about to tell her that? With all her heart she hoped not. Life was hard enough as it was if you were Moll McCarthy's child and to become known as Republican would only make a bad situation much worse.

"He keeps himself to himself, does Daniel," she said. "He doesn't interfere in other people's business. That's how I've brought him up. Other people have their ways but you pay no attention and you just do your best."

"And whatever you do, don't get mixed up with politics … Isn't that what you mean?"

"Just being my son is quite enough of a cross to bear. He doesn't need another."

"Political engagement as a cross. Well, if we all thought like that we'd all still be living in the Dark Ages, wouldn't we? Life can't be improved without a struggle, without taking up that cross, if you like."

"Well, I know my mind on this point and it's made up. I won't get involved with this struggle and I've taught my children to think like me."

He gave a snort and laughed high-pitched like the last time.

"I'm sure you've taught them well," he said. "But let's not talk about politics any more. I'm fed up with it all, I can tell you. In fact, I say we don't talk about it for the rest of the day. What do you say?"

They had reached the Dugout: it was a pillbox with room for a platoon built by the Free State at the bottom of Caesars' land during the Civil War. J.J. stopped and held his right hand out.

"Agreed?"

She put her hand into his. He squeezed. Then he pulled her towards him. He released her hand and put his arms behind her back and pulled. She felt his chest press against her face. She smelled his smell: the pomade and then something else, his natural smell, the smell of his sweat. He ground his pelvis against her stomach. He made a little noise. The signals were unmistakable.

She lifted her head and darted her mouth at his neck and kissed him. He stopped moving and held his head sideways: an invitation for her to kiss his neck again. This time she opened her mouth and put her lips against him and touched his skin with the end of her tongue.

They stayed like this for a few moments. Then he broke away.

"Come on," he said. There was the voice again: clear and factual.

36

The Dugout was low and wide, with a door at either end and an observation slit at chest height ran the whole length between the doors. J.J. opened the steel door at the right-hand end and pulled her in. Inside the Dugout smelled of earth and concrete. It also smelled of nettle and dung but those smells came from fields and not from within. He swung the door behind. The metal bottom scraped on the concrete floor as he did. When he pushed the door home it made a clang. It fastened with a metal arm that dropped into a keeper.

With the door shut the only light was what came in through the slit but there was enough for her to see the benches along the back and a rusty brazier in the corner and a metal table and two metal chairs.

He took her jacket and threw it onto the table. Then with deftness and speed that surprised her he lifted her up under her arms and stood her on a chair. He reached under her skirt and pulled her drawers down. She held his left shoulder and stepped out of them. He threw them on her jacket. He lifted her to the table and laid her back. Her hat came off and dropped to the floor. He fumbled with his flies. She hoped that her hat would not get dirty. It might be a poor hat but it was the only one she had. He pushed. She was ready enough. She noticed the heat of it. She registered his weight. She heard him pant. She felt him pump. She got a little shock when he cried out because his cry was so loud. He went still. She was wet below. He fell out of her but made no move to get up and go. He just lay on and panted a little. She wondered about her jacket. Would it stain? It was her best jacket. It was a present from one of her callers: a man called Jameson. He must move now, she thought. He cannot lie like this much longer. She found it hard to breathe as the weight of him bore down on her. She gave a quiet cough to remind him that she was still there. He lifted his head like a man roused from sleep and uncertain of his whereabouts. She felt his hands fumble about below although his weight still crushed her. At last he finished what he was at. He levered himself upright. She felt a great sense of physical relief as his weight lifted off her.

He held his hand out. She took it. His slim long fingers wrapped around her hand. He pulled and up she came. Now that she was upright she was sure that she had leaked onto her jacket. She reached her feet forward and jumped down. Her brogues found the ground. The concrete floor was hard. It had no give.

"You mustn't forget your hat," he said.

"No."

She smoothed her skirts down front and back even though she knew that in a moment she would in all likelihood lift them again to get her drawers on.

"I'll get it for you," he said.

He moved away from her. She found her drawers. She picked them up. They were ivory-coloured with white piping around the edges. Should she put them on? She heard him as he moved around behind her in his search for her hat.

"Where the hell's it gone?" he said.

"What?"

"Your hat's disappeared."

She glanced at her brogues. There was not enough light to see what state they were in but she knew that it would be a palaver to pull her drawers on over them. She looked at her drawers again. They had gone on clean that morning, she thought, so why get them dirty now? No the better plan was to take them home and put them on later when she could see what she was about.

"Ah," he said. "There you are."

She folded her drawers into a tight roll then slid them into the pocket at the side of her dress. The wet in her middle slid down the inside of her thighs towards the tops of her stockings. No matter, she thought as she turned and picked up her jacket, a quick rinse in a bit of cold water and they would be fine.

He appeared before her with the hat held out. "It had rolled right down to the other end."

She took the hat and ran her hand along the little feather to check that it was undamaged. She was worried that the fall might have bent it or worse broken it but it had not. The curve was a smooth unbroken line. She pulled it on and as she always did when she put on a hat she felt taller which was why she liked to wear them whenever possible.

He stepped away and pulled the door open. It clanged as he did. Light flooded in. He went through the door and she followed. Outside it was the same day that it had been ten minutes earlier. It was bright and warm and the sky was filled with huge bundles of white fluff that appeared to be afloat on a sea of blue.

It was also warmer, she realised, in the open than it had been in the Dugout. She had noticed the same thing with her cottage. When it was warm on the lawn as she called the ground in front of her house it was cold inside her four walls and when she had stepped across her threshold either to go in or to come out she had often felt that. Old walls, she guessed, must hold the cold.

3 7

They started to walk and followed the exact same route they had taken on their way to the Dugout. She could tell because of the way the grass had been ruffled by their passage through it.

"What are you doing tomorrow?" he said.

"Tomorrow?"

He was keen. He must be desperate. What was his wife's name? She had been told it. Could she remember it? Oh, yes. It was Nancy, yes, Nancy Spink, Mrs Nancy Spink or to be precise and use the proper title it was Mrs Jimmy Spink.

"Tomorrow?" she said again.

She tried to think. Would she be doing anything? Did she have any plans? Was it not just another day like the one she had just had?

"At about this time?" he said. "What will you be doing? Will you be at the house?"

"I should say so."

"I suppose you'd always be there when the children come in from school?"

"I would."

"That's the time, then, to find you, this time."

"It would be. In the week, but of course, Saturday and Sunday …"

"Those days I'm not usually free," he said.

Of course she should have thought of that. That was doubtless when he went home to see his wife. Did he have children? She tried to remember if she had been told when she had been given the wife's name. Yes, she probably had been. Her mind was like a sieve. Why did it not hold these things? Or perhaps it did but she had put the knowledge somewhere in her head where she could not locate it, like putting something in the back of a drawer and forgetting you had put it there. Perhaps. How old was he? Mid-forties, she guessed, or maybe a shade older, say fifty? If he had any children then they must be grown up and if that was the case they would surely be out in the world at this stage. In which case why did he go home on Saturdays and Sundays? Perhaps he had another woman somewhere and that was when he saw her. No, that was wrong. The pants she had heard in the Dugout told her that he had not had a woman in a while. On top of which he wanted to see her again. No, he had no woman, not at the moment, not of late – she was sure of it.

"Look at that, will you?" he said.

They both stopped and he pointed at a vixen ahead of them. She scrabbled at the earth with her front paws. She was dark red and her long tail looked heavier and bigger than her long lean body.

"What's she after?" said Foxy Moll.

The vixen heard her voice and glanced back. She stared at them and she did not move as she stared at them. She stayed quite still. Foxy Moll was struck by the animal's stillness as it gazed at them and gauged how far away they were and whether they were a threat and how fast she would have to scurry off if they approached. The vixen stared for several seconds and then as they did not move towards her she judged they posed no threat and resumed digging in the turf with her front paws. They watched as she worked: first she dug and then she snapped at her quarry, whatever it was; her jaw worked in a furious fashion and her teeth showed for a moment. What was it she was after, Foxy Moll wondered? Perhaps it was a mouse. Did they burrow in the earth? She had no idea. The fox's jaws stopped. What she was after had escaped. She pushed her snout down into the turned-up earth and scrabbled with her paws.

"She's going for worms," J.J. said. "She must be starving."

"She'd better not come near my birds," said Foxy Moll.

The vixen lifted her head and started to move away. She dragged her left hind leg behind and moved with an odd twisted gait. She was lame.

"She wouldn't be hard to shoot in that condition," said J.J.

"I've no gun."

"Get Badger to do it. He shoots these fields with Old Caesar's gun, doesn't he?"

"Yes, he does," Foxy Moll said, although she thought that Badger would more often than not be after something for the pot and not on the hunt for vermin when he took the gun out.

"Right," he said, "Badger can give her the dead eight, then."

"The dead eight?"

She was unfamiliar with the phrase and shook her head mystified. "I don't follow," she said.

"When you look at the end of a shotgun," said J.J., "the two barrels, side by side, what do they look like?"

She pictured the end of a shotgun, the two circles touching. "An eight?"

"But it isn't standing, is it? The eight is lying down, isn't it? It's dead. The dead eight."

"Ah," she said.

The vixen was still in view and she watched it now as it dragged its bad hind leg and she wondered. Shoot a creature that could just about walk? That did not seem right. Besides would it not die of starvation anyway soon enough?

Foxy Moll shrugged and wished that she had not said "She'd better not come near my birds." That had been stupid and if she had kept her mouth shut there would not be any of this foolish talk about shooting and guns.

'So, will you ask Badger?"

"Maybe," she said.

"You won't ask Badger," he said in a shrewd way, "because you're a female, you're sentimental and you think it's wrong to shoot a wounded animal. Am I right?"

Her face went red.

"I have my answer, I see."

The vixen squeezed under a hedge.

"With three legs she's not going to harm my birds."

"There speaks a true woman, who only a moment before was worried this vixen might come for her poultry."

The vixen was gone. They started to walk on again.

"If you think something won't harm you, you leave it alone, don't you?" he said.

"What's wrong with that?"

"I'll tell you. One, never assume anything; two, never predict because you're going to be wrong; three, don't make excuses, just do the correct thing. Those have been my watchwords and they've served me well. I leave nothing to chance."

She nodded as if she was interested but she was not. Lists bored her and besides her thoughts had turned to money and what she needed and what she would do if J.J. gave her money. She had seen some stockings with clocks on them in the haberdasher's that she rather wanted. Then she rebuked herself. She was not to think like this. He would not give her any money. He would give her something for the children perhaps but not for her, not yet. He would give her things like potatoes and flour and butter and tea and maybe whiskey. He would buy what he knew she needed for the house. Then after the end to assuage his conscience he would gift her something very big like a winter's worth of turf and if there were any money it would come then.

They moved on. Their steps were slow and neither talked. She did not mind because without speech she was free to listen to the sounds around her: the swish of their feet as they tramped along and the wind as it moved through the bushes and the bray of Caesars' donkey and the bleat of a sheep somewhere and the rumble of a lorry as it ground down the public road in the direction of Knockgraffon National School.

Some minutes later they reached her cottage.

"Will you take a cup of tea?" she said.

He looked at his wristwatch. It was a good one. The face was black with the numbers in white and the strap was leather and brown and sturdy. It looked military. Perhaps it was army issue. After the British garrisons had gone the new powers in the land, the victors (and J.J. at that point was one), expropriated much of the stuff the British did not take.

"I won't," he said. "I have to be somewhere."

He pulled a purse from his trouser pocket and unzipped it. He counted out five silver sixpences and a florin.

"For the children. They can buy some sweets. Sixpence should get them something decent."

She nodded.

"The florin is for Daniel."

He put the money into her hand. Yes, if she wanted those stockings she would have to find the cash from somewhere else.

"Until tomorrow," he said.

He got into his car and drove away. She went inside.

38

At two o'clock the next day she heard what she assumed was J.J.'s car pull up much earlier than she had expected.

She went out. She was surprised to see that he had two associates with him: Ned Quigg who was known as Screw and Eddie Duggan who was known as Nutley because that was his mother's maiden name. J.J. wore a trilby and the other two wore flat caps with peaks.

"Hello," he said. "This here's Screw and this one is Nutley."

She nodded at J.J.'s two associates.

"I've decided to see to that vixen," he said. "It shouldn't take us long."

He opened the Rover's boot. A dog jumped out but Foxy Moll did not recognise the breed. J.J. lifted out a gun-case made of rigid brown leather. The dog circled them. It was excited and energetic and sniffed and wagged its tail. J.J. opened a flap and pulled out a shotgun from inside the case. He put the gun-case back into the boot and reached into a cartridge box and selected half a dozen stubby dark-red cartridges and put these in his jacket pocket. Screw and Nutley each took an ash-plant from the boot. These whooshed through the air as the men swung them to test their strength.

"These ones have always wanted to try their hands at beating, so I'm going to give them a chance today," J.J. said. "If they're halfway good, they can always go and work on some big estate and make a few pound."

He lowered the boot. The lock engaged with a clunk.

"Come on," he called.

The dog ran to his heel and they moved away in a line: Screw first, then J.J., with Nutley last. She was struck by the way they moved in unison. Their appreciation of one another's tempos was perfect. It was clear that they were accustomed to going around together. Of course, she reflected as she watched them sidle through the gate and into her first little field, this should not come as a surprise. They had marched around the countryside about their business together for years.

She went inside and got back to work making scones. Later she heard gunfire: one shot and then soon after a second shot. Later again she heard voices. She went out. The dog and J.J. and Screw and Nutley approached. They came through the gate from the paddock and started towards her. They were not in a line and they did not move with purpose as they had done when they had set out. They sauntered and there was laughter. They were happy. The dog seemed happy too. She knew they had done it. They drew level with her.

"She won't bother you where she is now," said J.J. "Oh, yes."

"She got the dead eight," said Screw.

Screw had a small mouth and narrow lips that were not in proportion to his other features. His skin was flushed and damp with sweat. She did not like his manner. He seemed to her pushy and impatient and volatile as if there was a danger that he might at any moment explode.

J.J. handed his gun to Nutley who was a slight slim man with dark hair that was thin and that he wore longer than was usual with most men. He struck her as watchful and wary and reserved.

"Put the gun in the case, would you?" said J.J.

Nutley nodded.

"And here." He pulled four cartridges from his pocket and put them in Nutley's hand and then he jerked his head in Foxy Moll's direction. "I'm going to take this one down and show her our work. I'll be a few minutes. You can sit in the car."

He turned to Foxy Moll.

"Come on," he said in the voice that, although it was not curt, brooked no opposition.

They walked through the fields. He tried to quicken their pace but she dawdled. She wanted to delay what she knew lay ahead of her for as long as possible but what lay ahead of her could not be put off indefinitely and when they got to the fourth field she saw in the distance that something lay on the ground under the hedge. It was brown and at first glance she thought it was a piece of clothing.

"There she is."

"I don't want to see."

"Why?" He sounded surprised. "It's not gruesome. Got her clean. Come on."

He took her arm and walked her over. When they arrived she saw the way the vixen had fallen on her side with her legs splayed forward and her tail stretched behind so that she looked like she was on the run except that she lay flat on the ground. She had taken the blast in her face on the left side and where the pelt was shot away Foxy Moll saw bone and sinew and lines of sharp little teeth that stuck out of her gums. There were ticks on the vixen's body: small black jumping things. There was a smell too: a smell of old meat and fox.

"Dog raised her, drove her forward, and I got her square on with the second," J.J. said. "I wouldn't have thought she felt a thing."

Foxy Moll wondered about the first shot but decided not to ask.

They went into the Dugout.

"I haven't much time," he said. "The lads are waiting."

She unbuttoned him and did him by hand. His hat stayed on.

They went back to the car. The boot lid was up and the dog sat in the boot well. Screw sat in the front passenger seat. Nutley sprawled on the back seat. The windows were down and both men smoked. The smoke was white and because it was so still it hung in little clouds around the car before it drifted away.

J.J. went to the Rover's boot and lifted out a ten-stone sack of potatoes that she had not noticed when he had gotten the gun earlier. He set these by her door. He told her what day and at what time he would be back. He said it quiet so that the others would not hear. She nodded to show that she had heard. He went back to the boot.

"Lie down, boy," he said to the dog.

The dog lay down. He must have travelled in the boot many times before, she thought. She wondered if the dog had a name.

J.J. closed the boot lid.

"What's its name?" she said.

"What?" A second passed. He smiled. He pointed at the boot. "Oh, you mean him? Dixie ... yes, I know, hardly original."

He drove away. She carried the potatoes inside. As a rule when one of her callers gave her a gift she was happy – above all if it was food because that meant a feed for the children and that was great. She always got a good feeling when she filled their bellies and there was only one feeling she knew to beat it and that was the feeling she had gotten when her visitors had told her that they liked or even loved her and they would leave their wives and families and marry her and even though none ever had and even though she knew deep down that they would not do what they said she had always believed them at the moment they had said these things and then she was happy and trusting and certain until they broke the terrible news that the relationship was over and they said that they were not going to marry her, let alone see her again.

All through the evening that followed she was tired and subdued. She knew what the matter was. It was the dead vixen. The sight of the corpse had depressed her. After she had put the younger children into her bed she got out the bottle of puce plum poitín and mixed some up with boiled water and sugar and cloves and then she sipped the drink while she sat by the fire. She felt better by the time that she had finished. The alcohol helped her to sleep as well.

39

In the morning when she woke she had forgotten the vixen and her mood was restored and she knew she was recovered because no sooner was she up but she found that she wondered about J.J.'s next visit and what he would bring when he came. She needed tea and sugar and some arrowroot biscuits would be nice and she decided that she would tell him what she required. Men liked to be told what they could do to please her in the same way that they liked to tell her what she had to do to please them.

She dressed and got the fire restarted and woke the children and then went out to the spring well. As she filled the second bucket she heard a gun fire twice. It was quite close. She turned and saw Badger out in the lane with the gun over his shoulder.

"Hello," she called.

He stopped and leaned on the gate and called back to her with mock solemnity, "Good morning to you, Foxy Moll."

"You're up early this day."

"Early morning is best for the shooting."

She left the spring well and her second bucket and went to the gate. "How are you?"

"Well, you're a long time dead, so you're best making the most of the little time you have living and not complaining."

"Yes, Badger."

He snapped the gun shut and squinted along the barrels.

"I think the sighting might be gone on this old thing."

With its scuffed stock and scratched barrels it did indeed look old, she thought. J.J.'s gun, she remembered from the day before, was in much better shape.

"Mind you," he said still squinting, "a bad workman always blames his tools. Maybe it's my fault I missed."

"What are you after?"

"A couple of rabbits for the pot."

"But nothing yet?"

"Well, I loosed a couple, but that availed me nothing."

He lifted the gun down from his shoulder and began to examine the sights.

"So, no dead eight," she said.

"What?" Badger lifted his head and regarded her with his long flat face and his small blue eyes. "What did you say?"

"It's not loaded, is it?"

"No, of course it isn't."

She touched the barrel ends. "It looks like the number eight but it's lying down ... the dead eight."

"Right," he said. He sounded wary.

"I only heard it myself yesterday and it means killing something, giving it the chop. That's what I was told."

"That's a new one on me," said Badger. "Well, you learn something every day, don't you?"

"I try, but my noodle isn't so hot at holding things. I was useless at my lessons when I was young."

"Same as myself. I couldn't wait to leave school and get tore into work."

"Do you like it?" said Foxy Moll. She asked this in her solemn voice.

"I love it. I'm never bored, never tired."

"That's because you've no wife nagging you or children hanging out of you."

He chortled. "You'd know far more about that than me."

"What'll you do when this is yours and you're up there on your ownsome in the farmhouse every night?" she said. "You'll be lonely."

"I'll have Tommy."

"What if he marries?"

"I hadn't thought of that."

"I tell you what," she said, "I'll be your wife."

"What's that you say?"

He had not heard. On account of his bad ears he sometimes did not catch things. "I'll be your wife," she said. "You'll marry me, won't you?"

He laughed and looked down at his feet.

"I don't think I'll ever marry." He sounded sincere. "Not the marrying sort, me."

"Why's that?" said Foxy Moll.

"Don't know. It's just something I've always known wasn't for me. Wasn't my cup of tea."

"Oh, you've always known it, have you?"

"I think so."

"That's the trouble with you men. None of you want it. But I'd love it: I'd love a husband, though I think I've left it a bit late, now."

He lifted his face and he looked into her eyes and she looked back into his eyes and she had the feeling that for that moment he knew just how she felt and she knew just how he felt. They understood each other.

"Do you need a hand with your buckets?" he said.

"No. That's kind of you, but I can manage."

"Really?"

"Yes, really."

"Well, better push on," he said, "if I'm to get anything for tonight's pot. I'm going to try across the road. There are lots of burrows in the banks there."

She nodded. It was true. She had often seen rabbits on the Condons' ground across the road from her cottage.

"Good luck," she said. "I hope you get something."

He turned to go and turned back. "What's the phrase again?"

He pointed at the barrels to refer her back to what they had talked about before.

"The dead eight," she said.

"The dead eight," he said and walked away.

She went back to the spring well and grasped the bucket handles and started for her cottage.

40

For the next few weeks J.J. came to see her almost every day and they went to the Dugout together each time that he visited. When it was her time of the month she did him by hand or with her mouth.

One morning early in July they drove to the other side of the Galty Mountains where they turned up a track and stopped outside a whitewashed cottage. There were houses like it all over the county that had been built for labourers by local government at the end of the nineteenth century.

"Where are we?" she said.

"Ask no questions, you're told no lies," said J.J.

They got out. The door of the cottage opened. An old man came out and nodded at J.J. He wore a dark shabby three-piece suit with a collarless shirt and a flat cap. He had a pipe in his mouth and as he walked towards them he blew out a cloud of smoke. When he came close she saw that the bowl had a silver lid attached by a hinge. The lid was in the upright position.

"I'll be back in an hour," said the old man.

He clicked the lid down and set off along a track that ran away into the mountains. She guessed that he had been told in advance to make himself scarce.

"Let's not dilly-dally," said J.J.

They went through the door and into a little porch. There were two doors: both stood open. She saw the parlour to her left and the kitchen to her right.

"Go right," J.J. said.

She stepped forward. The kitchen was square with small windows front and back. There was a fire and a table and on the table, leaned against a butter dish, there was an envelope with writing on the front. There was a strong smell of burned potato and pipe and old man and turf.

"That way," said J.J. He pointed at a narrow stairs set against the back wall.

She moved across the kitchen. She wore a hat fixed with a hatpin. As she moved she took out the hat-pin and when she was close to the table she dropped it.

"Oh, butter fingers," she said.

She crouched down. The floor was brown linoleum. The pin was made of brass and it was hefty with a decorative head copied, it was said, from the Book of Kells. She picked the pin up and rose and as she did she read what was on the envelope: Mr J. Bermingham, Boolakennedy, Co. Tipperary. Bermingham must be a supporter of the cause, she thought, and this was a safe house.

She took off her hat and stuck the pin through it and put it on the table. Then she climbed the stairs. When she got to the top she found herself in a small room tucked under the sloped eaves. There was a small low bed. She undressed and got in. The blankets also smelled of burned potato and pipe and old man and turf.

After they had finished J.J. dozed off and she lay still. Sheep bleated somewhere close at hand and she listened to them.

"Hear the sheep?" she said.

"Uh huh."

"I like sheep."

"Why?"

"They rarely charge, they don't trample and they're not stupid."

"Oh."

"And when I see a lamb at his mother," she said, "with his little back arched and his little tail going like mad, it always cheers me up."

This was true. It was one of her favourite sights.

4 1

A couple of weeks later J.J. appeared in his car one afternoon and told her they were going to a public house. They drove to The Fighting Cocks, a country pub beyond Golden. They stopped outside and he pulled up the lever between them and the spring made the familiar clicks.

"I have to see a few lads," he said. This was a new voice. She had not heard this voice before. It was quiet and somewhat mysterious. "Sit in the saloon, say nothing and don't act like you know me. When I've finished, I'll come and sit with you."

He pulled his wallet out and opened it. "Here."

He held out a one-pound note: an Irish one with the sad lady on it. She sat in profile so that she looked out at something although Foxy Moll did not know what it was unless it was at her and of course that was daft because how could the lady on the one-pound note look at her?

He locked the Rover and they went in through a little door and into a little hall with two doors: one led to the saloon and the other to the public bar.

"I'm in here." He indicated the door to the public bar.

He went through his door and she went through hers.

The saloon was empty. There was a bar at the top and a partition with a door space in the middle. She went to the counter.

"A hot port," she said, "please."

"I'll bring it over," said the barman.

She found a seat in the corner from where she was able to see through the gap in the partition and into the public bar. J.J. sat at a table. His back was towards her. He could not see her. Screw and Nutley were with him. There were three other men at the table as well. She did not recognise any of them.

The drink came and she paid. She sipped her drink and as she sipped she observed the scene next door. J.J. talked. Alcohol and bars, she had noticed, brought out a man's loudness but J.J. was an exception. His voice was not raised and he did not wave his arms around or do any of the other things that men in her experience usually did when they were in a bar. He just talked in his quiet and serious way and the men around the table listened and nodded a lot. It was clear to her that J.J. was a man to whom others deferred. J.J. was a leader. No doubt about that. She rather liked that, even if the cause that he led had never interested her or impressed her very much either.

Oh, she understood the principles all right. After all, she had heard enough about it over the years and she had gotten more from J.J. She understood her life had been awful before when she had been oppressed or something and then after a struggle there had come liberty and some improvement. The trouble was that although she knew full well this was what she was supposed to believe she did not because when all was said and done what in fact had improved since the Treaty? The answer was nothing. Had there been no Troubles and had the soldiers not left and had the old RIC stayed and had the Free State not come in then would she be worse off? No, her situation would be the same as it was now and she would still live in her little cottage and tend her goats and chickens and care for her children and struggle to make ends meet. In which case what had all those men been killed for and what was all the conflict about and what was all the anger and the trouble and disruption for? What did it do?

Well, it put some new men in who it did not seem to her were any better than the ones who had been in power before and that in turn made ones like J.J. angry and bitter because they said that the business was botched and the job was unfinished and there was still the north to settle. J.J. and his associates hated the State and the way it had sold them and their ideals short while the State for its part hated them for their intransigence and called them criminals and leeches and thugs.

As she saw it, if there had not been any conflict in the first place then this state of affairs would not exist with the Free Staters in their corner and J.J. and his associates in their corner and would that not be better: to be free of all this bitterness and hatred and that way J.J. would have had more time for her. Of course this was a line of thought that she knew better than to share with J.J.

The meeting finished. The men melted away and Screw and Nutley nodded to her through the gap in the partition as they passed by. She finished her drink. She and J.J. went outside and got into his car. They drove to a wood she had never visited and did not recognise. He drove down a track and stopped. It was dark beneath the trees. He turned off the engine. He took her hand and kissed it. She was surprised by his gentleness and his care.

They got out and went into the back. He pulled her underwear down and threw it over the seats and into the front. Her bloomers landed on the steering wheel where they trembled for a moment and then fell to the floor. She lay back on the seat and he kneeled in some manner on the floor and that way they contrived somehow to do it and when it was finished and she lay still she heard the screech of some bird and she saw that the car windows were all misted up with their breath.

42

In September, just when she noticed that there was shortness to the length of the days and the leaves had just begun to brown on the trees around her cottage and on the hedgerows that bounded the fields, she found lovely puffballs, big and white and solid, in the ground behind her house. She sliced them like loaves of bread and fried the slices in her old black pan and fed her children with them. Her monthly did not come and she felt sick when she woke up in the morning and she knew then that she was pregnant.

Early in November when she felt she was about to show she told him just after they had done it in the Dugout.

"Oh," he said quietly. He did not seem perturbed or interested or indeed anything very much. "I see."

He went to the door and opened it and looked out. She saw his outline against the grey sky. It rained outside and she saw the little threads of rain come down.

"How long have you known?" he said.

"Since September."

"You didn't say anything."

"I wasn't sure."

"Ah. I suppose worse things have happened."

He continued to come to see her as her middle swelled although he never had Nutley or Screw with him. She supposed he did not want them to know that she was pregnant. He did not want word to get around and get back to his wife Nancy, Mrs Nancy Spink. They went to the Dugout and they went to the safe house whose owner smoked the pipe with the silver lid and they went to several other safe houses all located a few miles from her house at Marlhill.

Three days before Christmas he came in his Rover with a hundredweight of coal. It was in a sack with coal dust in the fabric. She went out and watched as he put on special gloves and an apron and hauled the coal from his car and into her wheelbarrow and then wheeled the sack to her turf house where he set it down. He got a knife from his pocket and slit the top open and pulled the sacking sides apart and revealed the big dark dusty lumps. Where and how he had gotten this coal was a mystery but he must have connections, she assumed, because very little coal came across from England now.

He returned to his car and took a small tree from his boot and then from the back seat he fetched a large box wrapped in red paper.

He carried the tree and the box into her kitchen and used stones to wedge the tree in a pail and stood the tree up and then he placed the box underneath. The tree shed needles and a few of the needles gathered on top of the box.

"You'll have to wait until Christmas morning before you open that," he said.

It was too cold to go to the Dugout and they sat and drank tea and she thought he seemed content. When he left he promised that he would be back to see her on St Stephen's Day.

On Christmas morning she went to open his gift. She untied the string and unwrapped the lovely red paper with slow care so that she could reuse them both at some stage. Inside she found Terry's chocolates in a big gold box. She opened the box and each of her children had a chocolate and she had a chocolate and then she put the box on the shelf. She thought it would be nice to offer him a chocolate the next day, which was St Stephen's Day, but the next day he never came and the box stayed on the shelf.

When she went to bed on St Stephen's night she felt sore in her chest and tired and a little stunned. Her throat hurt as it always did when she wanted to weep and when she was sure that the children were asleep she let herself have a quiet cry. She cried for a long time and then she fell asleep. She woke up early before the children were awake and she still felt sad and she cried again.

The hurt she felt in her chest around her heart lasted a fortnight and then a morning came when she woke up and expected to feel sad and expected to cry and to her surprise the pain had gone and she knew that she was not about to cry. He had come and he had gone and she had grieved and now it was over; it was finished and in all likelihood she would never see him again and she was over J.J. and she would not cry any more.

The third Monday in January she heard his car pull up outside. She knew the sound of his engine. She felt a little flutter down behind her stomach somewhere near her spine but it lasted only a second or two and then it was gone and she knew that they would talk and that would be that and then he would go and she would feel a little pang perhaps but nothing more, nothing serious, because this was good and finished and she had grieved enough already.

A few moments later she heard his knock. She opened the door. He wore a coat that he had buttoned up to the neck and he had his hat pulled down over his eyes.

"Let's look at your animals," he said.

She put on her coat and hat and went out. The sky was clear and the day was cold. There was a wind and the wind went through her clothes. They went past her turf shed and through the gate and into the first little field. The goats were all in the corner where they were best protected from the wind. The goats looked at them and they looked back at the goats. She noticed the smell of goat as she always did when she was near them, the smell strong and rank with something like old cheese in it as well as meat and goat's milk.

"I'm sorry this has to stop," he said.

She waited. She expected him to say something about his wife or his children or his family and the pressure they brought to bear to make him stop seeing her. That had always been what the men had said at this point but he said nothing more. He just continued to stare at the animals and they stared back at him and her.

"I really am sorry," he said.

"It can't be helped, I suppose," she said.

She heard him cough. Ah, she thought, he was going to speak. Would it be the excuse: was he going to tell her why he had to finish it? No, she thought, that was not his style. He had something else he wanted to talk about. She was sure of it.

"When we began," he said, "I asked about Mr O'Driscoll. I knew he gave you the flags but you wouldn't say anything about him when I asked."

So that's what this was about, she thought. Given his politics, he needed to ensure she would not carry any tales or information about him and his comings and goings and his associates to anyone else. But how strange he had to ask. No one had ever complained to her on that score and nor would they. She did not talk ever.

"No," she said, and it was true. She never said anything about anybody to anyone else. That was her way. It had to be because, as she knew only too well, she would not survive otherwise.

"So when the next man asks about J.J. will you give him the brush off like you gave me the brush off about Mr O'Driscoll?"

"Yes," she said, "and the brush off isn't the half of it. I never blab."

She felt disgruntled and she knew it sounded in her voice. She did not like to be angry as a rule but in this case she did not care. How had J.J. failed to grasp the sort of woman she was? Did he not know anything?

"I'm sorry," he said, as if he had read her mind. "I shouldn't have asked. No, of course you won't, you don't."

They remained as they were for quite some time and looked at the goats and the goats looked back at them and the wind pressed against their bodies and the cold gradually soaked into their bones.

"I have to go," he said finally.

He undid the top button of his coat and slipped his hand inside and produced an envelope from his breast pocket. The envelope was white and there was nothing written on the front except for the words "By hand" in the top left-hand corner.

"There's something here," he said, "to help you. I'm not promising, but I'll try and get some more."

They walked back through the gate to her door. She offered tea. He declined. He had to be away, he said, and if he did not go now he would be late for his appointment.

He got into his car and started the engine and then he dropped down the lever that was between the front seats and she heard its springy noise. Then he drove out the gate and the little yellow indicator arm came out on the right-hand side that meant that was the way he was about to go. He turned right and for a moment she thought he would wave but he did not and then he was gone and there was only the whirr of the engine as he drove away along the road.

She stood and held the envelope with "By hand" on the front and listened to the sound of J.J.'s Rover 12 grow fainter and fainter and then all she could hear was the moan of the wind in the trees. Then she went inside and opened the envelope. It contained ten green one-pound notes with the lady on the front who looked out at something from under the shawl that covered her head. Foxy Moll put the money in the Fyson's tin where she hid her cash and she put the envelope in the box where she stored things for reuse and where she had put the red wrapping paper and the string from the Terry's chocolates that he had given her for Christmas.

4 3

The midwife Mrs O'Hanlon delivered Foxy Moll's baby at Marlhill on 2 June 1939. Foxy Moll named her Edwina. She was small and light and did not seem to Foxy Moll to be very healthy but Mrs O'Hanlon said that she was grand and she just needed to fatten up. On the birth certificate the space where the father's name was supposed to go was left blank. She did not bring Edwina to Father O'Malley. Apart from her other children her only visitor after the birth and the only one to welcome Edwina into the world was Miss Cooney. She came to the house with a box filled with towelling nappies and soap and oranges and candles and tea and shop bread and a little basin in which to wash the baby. Miss Cooney also arranged for unused vegetables and pies and bread and leftovers from the kitchens of Rockwell College to be delivered twice a week to Foxy Moll's cottage by one of the school's porters.

Foxy Moll had never eaten as well as she did when she nursed this time but Edwina did not thrive no matter how well Foxy

Moll ate. Her feeds were laborious affairs and then most of what she had gotten down came up again. Colic was suspected. Miss Cooney sent Foxy Moll and her baby Edwina to Doctor Ferriter in New Inn. He asked if Edwina was feeding properly and she said no and he said that it was temporary and it would pass and she would be grand. Then he asked where the bill was to go and she said that the bill was to go to Miss Cooney.

As the months wore on Edwina got thinner and crankier and sicklier. Miss Cooney arranged for Foxy Moll to go back to Doctor Ferriter and this time the infant was weighed and she was examined and prescribed a tonic to be given with a little warm milk. This did no good. Foxy Moll went back to Doctor Ferriter several more times after that at Miss Cooney's insistence and there were more examinations and more tonics but none of it did any good and Edwina got worse and worse.

On Friday 22 December 1939 in the cottage at Marlhill at about two o'clock in the afternoon, just as the light began to go, Foxy Moll noticed that her daughter lay very still in her crib and when she went to check she found that Edwina no longer breathed. Foxy Moll did not go to the priest. He had not baptised her so she knew he was not about to bury her either. Mr O'Shaughnessy always let Daniel leave work a bit early on a Friday and when he came home around an hour later Foxy Moll asked her son to walk over to Miss Cooney with the message that Edwina was dead and she needed Miss Cooney's help.

An hour later Foxy Moll heard a motorcar pull up outside the cottage. She recognised the noise the engine made. It was Mr Cooney's Humber. A moment later the door was opened with respectful care and Miss Cooney came in followed by Daniel.

"I sent a telegram to the coffin maker," she said in a hushed tone. "He'll be down presently."

An hour later he appeared: a small man with a papery voice. He measured the corpse and went out to his van. He had a workshop in the back. In the cottage they heard him start the engine to power the electric lights followed by the sharp bangs and the coarse rasp of a handsaw. An hour later he reappeared with the coffin: small and short and covered with white satin. Miss Cooney paid and he left.

Foxy Moll dressed Edwina in a little muslin gown and laid her in the coffin. Everyone kneeled around the coffin and prayed. Miss Cooney went home. Foxy Moll put her children to bed and sat up with her daughter all through the dark night.

44

On Saturday morning the Humber pulled up outside the cottage at Marlhill and Miss Cooney and her father entered, both dressed in black and both subdued. The coffin lid was screwed down. Everyone went out and Mr Cooney carried the coffin. Everyone stopped at the car. Miss Cooney gave instructions. She would sit in the front passenger seat with Dermot and Helena, the two youngest McCarthys, on her lap. Foxy Moll and Daniel and Judy and Maria and Brendan were to go in the back. She opened the back door on the driver's side and everyone got in who was meant to get in and then her father laid the coffin over their laps and closed the door. His daughter got in the front and Dermot and Helena got onto her lap and Mr Cooney got in on his side and sat behind the steering wheel.

"Doors closed?" said Mr Cooney.

No one dissented.

"Sit back, everybody." His voice was English but not as English as his daughter's was. He had lost his accent in the British Army while he fought against the Boers in South Africa.

He started the engine and drove back to Garranlea House. He turned through the gates but then instead of going up the main drive he turned off onto a track that had grass in the middle and was seldom used. He drove with care and the tyres of his Humber splashed in the puddles that had formed here and there along the lane and after two hundred yards or so he stopped under some beech trees that dripped rainwater onto the roof of the car. There was a small stone building with a round roof and a metal door that stood open. It was the Cooney family crypt.

Mr Cooney left the engine on and got out and opened the back door and took the coffin.

"Will you come in?" he said to Foxy Moll.

She shook her head. Mr Cooney carried the little coffin under the dripping trees and disappeared through the open door into the crypt. Foxy Moll's children said nothing. Foxy Moll said nothing. Miss Cooney said nothing. The sound of the engine came from under the bonnet. A wind gust struck the side of the Humber and made the car rock. Mr Cooney reappeared. He closed the crypt door after himself and locked it with a big key and then he put the key in a niche at the top of the pillar on the right of the door.

Mr Cooney got back in the car and drove everyone to Garranlea House. There was a small fire in the living room. There was tea and scones. The scones went almost untouched. Mr Cooney drove everyone back to the cottage in his Humber. The fire had gone out while they had been away and Foxy Moll had to soak an old rag in paraffin and set it alight before she was able to get the turf to catch light. She thought that Christmas 1939 was the most miserable of her life.

45

The man got off the train at Tipperary station. It was early afternoon on a warm Tuesday in June 1940. Only a few passengers got off with him. That was how the man liked it. Always arrive in a quiet way and do not draw attention to yourself. These were his watchwords. In his line it paid not to be noticed.

The man carried his two suitcases along the platform towards the exit. The cases were dark brown leather. The man had bought them in Clery's in Dublin in 1928 just before he had gotten married. They had gone with him and Sheila on their honeymoon to Salthill and they had been with the man on every journey he had made since – and there had been many of them: so many given his line of work that he had lost count by this stage. The larger suitcase had two broad belts wrapped around it and tucked under these so that it was tight to the suitcase lid was a long canvas bag designed to carry the sections of a fishing rod. Anyone who scrutinised the bag would have noticed that there was something more than the sections of a fishing rod inside, something substantial and heavy and thick: it was in fact a pick-axe handle. The fishing bag and its unusual contents went with the man wherever he travelled in the twenty-six counties but as luck would have it no one ever paid any heed to the bag or its contents. Everyone just assumed that it was a fishing rod the man carried and that was fine by him.

The man came to the exit. The woman in front of him went past the ticket collector and handed him her ticket without either a break in her stride or a glance in his direction. Over her dress she wore a light raincoat belted around the waist. She left a smell after herself. The man sniffed as he stopped and put down his cases. The thought came. What would she be like? He glanced after her. She had heavy ankles. That probably meant thick legs but it was hard to judge her pins through the coat she had on.

The image came unbidden: a woman, this woman, every woman, any woman naked stretched on a bed. She had small breasts and a thickset middle and her legs were open. He held her buttocks and pulled her onto him and she let out a small sharp cry of surprise. All that had long since stopped with Sheila but it had not stopped his appetite for it.

"How are you?" the ticket collector said.

The picture in his mind vanished and his attention returned to the world around him.

"I've the ticket in my pocket," said the man.

The ticket collector was young. He wore his peaked hat pushed well back. Did the fellow not know how to wear his hat in the proper manner? If he had been a Guard and not a railway employee then the man would have said something for sure.

"Go on," said the ticket collector. "I don't need to see it, you've an honest face."

The ticket collector motioned with his hand that the man was to step through.

What had he said – he had an honest face? Too bloody right he had. He was a Guard but he was not about to say that he was.

He had a few days when nobody would know who he was and why he was there and that temporary anonymity was one of his main advantages and had to be preserved.

"Well, I do have a ticket," he said. "I'd never travel without one."

"I knew that," said the ticket collector.

He picked his suitcases up again and went through to the front annex of the station. Here there was a ticket office with a booking clerk behind the glass and benches around the walls with waiting rail passengers sat on them and tucked around the corner, invisible from the platform but all too bloody visible now that he was in the annex, a uniformed Guard who held a piece of paper with "Sgt Anthony Daly" written on it.

He sighed. He wore a blue suit and a light coat and carried two leather suitcases. He looked like a travelling salesman or a teacher or a government civil servant, perhaps from the Department of Agriculture, down from Dublin to look at milk yields in County Tipperary, who had brought his rod along to do a spot of Sunday fishing. Without doubt he did not look like a sergeant in the Guards whose speciality was to ferret out Republicans and beat them if the circumstances allowed and then deliver them to the State for prosecution and imprisonment.

However, once he stepped up to the driver and acknowledged who he was with a nod or a greeting and the driver shook his hand or worse addressed him as Sergeant Daly, well then the ticket collector behind him and the clerk in the booking office that faced him and the passengers on the benches and anyone else who happened to be about would have his name and there was a good chance, rather too good a chance if the reports he had read were true, that out of all these different people one would be one of theirs, for the county was infested with them, it was rotten with them, and the bastard would spot him and would then carry the information back that a new Guard had arrived and that his name was Anthony Daly and that he was a sergeant.

Once that happened it would not take the bastards long before they had his provenance and the full story of his work: how he had hammered Republicans in Listowel, Drumconrath, Ardee, Enfield, Kiltegan, Swanlinbar, Bawnboy and his last station, Ballingarry, and then the fuckers would do what they were best at: they would melt away like mist before the morning sun and vanish before he could root them out.

He decided that the New Inn Guards must be rank amateurs to send this fellow with a sheet of paper with his name on it but there might still be a way out of this.

He did not look at the Guard although he was aware that the fellow scanned his face as he had everyone else's face as they had filed out past the ticket collector. Instead he angled himself at the door to the outside and moved towards it. He kept his head down but as he passed the Guard he lifted his head a fraction and tipped a surreptitious wink his way and then he sped on and disappeared through the door.

On the other side he found himself in a covered area with a tarred forecourt in front and he saw a row of cars parked against a far wall that included a Wolseley that he guessed must be an unmarked Guards' car. He put his suitcases down: the smallish one and the big one with the pickaxe handle strapped to it. He heard the sound of footsteps behind.

"Excuse me," he heard. This was the Guard with the paper with his name on it; he had appeared on his right.

"I see you like to keep things quiet," he said. He tilted his head down and pulled his hat forward so that the brim obscured his face.

"I'm sorry, are you Sergeant Daly?"

Had this man heard what he had just said? Perhaps not, he thought. Anyhow even if he had it was obvious that an explanation about discretion would be wasted on this one.

"I am," he said. "I am Sergeant Daly. Now put away that bit of paper with my name. "

"I thought you were."

The Guard folded the piece of paper carefully in four, undid the button of his left tunic pocket and slipped it inside.

"You've the look of him," said the Guard. He re-buttoned his tunic pocket. He had grey eyes and thick eyebrows. Several of the eyebrow hairs were very long and stuck up into the air like the antennae of an insect.

"Really?"

"You do."

"And what is the look of him?'

"Fierce, they said."

"Fierce?"

"Yes."

"I look fierce?"

"You do."

"Oh no, I'll have to do something about that."

"Why's that – if you don't mind me asking?"

"I don't want to give myself away with my face, do I?"

"True," said the Guard, "but you'll find it very hard to stay anonymous. New Inn is small and they gossip quietly but with prodigious application."

"With prodigious application," he said and he laughed. "There's an idea – gossipers of prodigious application."

"I'm Gralton. Guard Gralton. Can I give you a hand with those cases? The car is over there."

He pointed a thumb at the black Wolseley that Sergeant Daly had already picked out as an unmarked car. Guard Gralton picked up his two cases. For a man in his fifties he was still strong. Gralton carried the cases to the car and put them in the boot. Sergeant Daly followed him over. As Sergeant Daly came up to the car Gralton turned.

"Front or back?" he said.

"Front."

46

Gralton opened the door for him and Sergeant Daly got in. Gralton went around and got in the driver's door. He started the car and nosed out through the gate and began to drive south out of Tipperary town in the direction of New Inn. Sergeant Daly was aware of people on the pavements with houses and shops behind them. It felt prosperous.

"So how's New Inn?" he said. "You like it?"

"Oh yes," said Gralton. "Mind you, I must like it, I've been there ten years, since 1930."

"Where were you stationed before?"

"I was eight years before that here in Tipperary town and before 1922 I was all over the west, Clifden and Galway, Adare and Ennis – you name it, I was probably in it."

"Ah," said Sergeant Daly.

Whereas he, Anthony Daly, was a Free Stater who had joined the Guards in 1922 after the Treaty, Gralton, he realised, was a Royal Irish Constabulary man who stayed on in the police after partition. He should have guessed from his age and his chattiness.

"When did you sign on?" said Sergeant Daly.

"The year of our Lord 1905: I was twenty. Enlisted in Limerick, I did."

"I won't hold it against you."

"What?"

He detected a thread of anxiety in Gralton's voice. He guessed Gralton feared he might be one of those Free State Guards who thought ex-RIC men were contaminated by association with the Dublin Castle administration and should never have been allowed to join the new force. In fact Sergeant Daly did not care. If ex-RIC men joined that was fine by him. In his opinion policemen were the same regardless of their masters.

"I won't hold the town against you was what I meant, that you joined in Limerick," said Sergeant Daly.

"Oh," said Gralton. He looked relieved.

"Limerick, what a dump," said Sergeant Daly.

He had done a month there quite early in his career, back in 1924, when three Republicans had caught him and took it in turns to pee in his face while the other two held him down and forced his mouth open with the barrel of a Webley revolver and after they had done with him they tossed him into the icy Shannon.

Over the two months that followed he had tracked the trio down. Then one night he had scooped the three and brought them to the barracks and locked them in adjacent cells. Then with a British Army pickaxe handle he had found in a storeroom he had beaten each in turn. He had concentrated on the hands and feet where he knew there were lots of little bones that would never set right and he had pulverised them. Finnegan, who had been the oldest of the three, had died of his injuries. Sergeant Daly's superiors had ordered him to Cork without delay. He had taken the pickaxe handle with him. Before every one of the great many beatings that he had since administered he nearly always told his victims about the origins of his weapon before he worked them over. He liked to think that the British Army provenance made his beatings more significant and less liable to be forgotten.

"So you're not a fan of Limerick?" said Gralton.

"No."

"I've not met many who are," said Gralton.

"Oh, there are a few people with strange ideas about. There's always one or two, I find."

They had left the town and were out in the country. Sergeant Daly saw hedgerows and trees and every so often when there was a gap he glimpsed green fields. He lifted his eyes. There were clouds in the sky but it was not cold. He wondered if rain was on its way and he thought that if it were then that would have been typical for an Irish summer's day.

"There's no rush," he said.

"What?"

"No rush."

"Oh."

Gralton lifted his foot off the accelerator a bit.

"I'm not going to do any work today and it's nice to be driven and talk," said Sergeant Daly. "I don't often get the chance to talk."

"I'm your man," said Gralton. "I love to yarn. What do you want to talk about?"

Sergeant Daly paused.

"Those gossipers of New Inn. The ones with the prodigious application, what do they talk about?"

"Anything, absolutely anything, nothing's too small or too trivial."

"Nothing much else to fill their time with, I suppose?"

"Right," said Gralton. There was a moment of silence.

The Guard cleared his throat. "At the moment they gossip about us."

"Oh. So what have the Guards in New Inn done?"

"We have this woman in New Inn," said Gralton. "Her name is Moll McCarthy, but everyone knows her as Foxy Moll."

"Red hair, I suppose?"

"Yes."

"How'd I guess? Perhaps I'm a Guard."

Gralton laughed. "She'd a series of children, every one a different father, and Superintendent Mahony went to law to get her children took off her."

"That sounds like a waste of Guards' time."

It was what he believed: proper Guards' business was to get the bastards who caused all the trouble and give them a good hammering and then lock them up; it was not to go around and take children from unfit mothers. That was Church work, he believed.

"It certainly was. He got rejected by the District Justice, Troy, not once, but twice."

Sergeant Daly shook his head. Moral Guards were an impediment to the kind of work he did and this one was his boss. He did not like the sound of this.

"Then the wife dies."

"Whose?"

"Superintendent Mahony's," said Gralton.

"Right." Sergeant Daly wondered where this was headed.

"Which changed him, made him think he'd been too hard, so, to make up, didn't he bring Foxy Moll into the barracks as one of the domestics."

Now Sergeant Daly knew just where this was headed.

"I see," he said, "so what the lovely people of New Inn are saying now is this: Superintendent Mahony's a lonely widower and he's brought her in to keep him company. But it isn't true. He's just a Christian man who's done a Christian thing and given a poor woman with a clatter of children a job as a cleaner."

"You are a remarkable man, Sergeant," said Gralton, "and I predict you'll go far."

"I wouldn't be so sure. Coming on nineteen years and I'm still only a sergeant."

There was a moment of quiet.

"What does Superintendent Mahony say?" said Sergeant Daly.

"About the gossip?"

"Yes."

"Nothing. He doesn't pay any attention to what the New Inn gossips say. He couldn't care less."

Sergeant Daly felt his feelings about his superior shift again. Perhaps Superintendent Mahony was a superior he could work with after all.

"What about the other Guards?" said Sergeant Daly.

"What about them?"

"What do they say about her?"

"I don't think any of them living in quarters mind in the slightest. And you'll be living in quarters and I can't see you minding either."

"Ah," said Sergeant Daly, "I imagine those Guards are unmarried, but I, alas, have a wife."

"Course you have, you're a decent upright fellow. Sure, haven't they told us? 'That Sergeant Daly,' Superintendent Mahony said to us all just yesterday, 'that Sergeant Daly,' he said, 'no better man for the straight and narrow.'"

Sergeant Daly snorted. "Really, I think reports of my sainthood are somewhat overstated."

Gralton said nothing. Sergeant Daly looked out the sidelight and watched the green hedgerows flash by. They knew all about him and the methods he employed to deal with Republicans, he thought – of course they did. That was what that last remark about the straight and narrow meant. In all likelihood they were sceptical or perhaps even anxious that he might make a bad situation worse but as soon as he had banged a few heads and reeled a couple of the fuckers in they would change. They would be grateful; they would even show admiration. In his experience it had always gone like that.

"I'm only in quarters until our rented place comes along," said Sergeant Daly. He explained that they had taken a house and the tenants who were in it were not due to leave until the autumn.

"Once they're gone, Sheila will come from Ballingarry to join me."

All this was true except he had omitted one fact. The landlord had offered to have the house available in June but Sergeant Daly had told the landlord that there was no need.

Let the incumbent tenants stay until the end of October, he had said. This would oblige him to spend five months in quarters in the New Inn Guards' station.

Would that not be inconvenient, the landlord had asked.

Oh no, he had said. It would be a good thing to have to stay in quarters for a few months because that way he would be able to socialise with the unmarried Guards. He would get to know the village and its people. For a new Guard there was no better way to get to know his patch.

In fact, what he really thought was that such a long time without Sheila just might give him the chance to meet someone and sleep with them if the opportunity arose.

Of course his story to Sheila had been different to the one he had told the landlord. He had told Sheila that the present tenants could not be moved for contractual reasons and he would have to stay in quarters until she joined him in November and it was a chore and a bore but there it was.

She had accepted his excuse and now five lovely months of freedom stretched ahead of him. Would he meet someone in that time? Well, from what Gralton had told him it seemed that there was someone there in the barracks already that might suit.

4 7

Gralton eased the car through a narrow gateway and drove across the cobbled yard. The car juddered and the wheels made a curious slapping sound. After the smoothness of roads the sudden agitation and commotion unnerved Sergeant Daly a little.

"You'd think they'd have got round to replacing these cobbles, wouldn't you?" said Sergeant Daly.

"You get used to them, like anything else."

Gralton pulled on the handbrake and turned off the engine and pulled the key from the ignition.

"Right, here we are, home sweet home. Welcome to New Inn, Sergeant."

Sergeant Daly and Gralton got out.

"Right," said Gralton. He pointed to the long L-shaped two-storey building at the back of the yard. "Those are the living quarters. Go through the door you see there and up the stairs. Your room is the one at the end of the landing, on the left. It has a lovely view of the yard, and before you say a word, yes, it is the best room in the place. I'll take your bags up."

Gralton opened the boot and heaved Sergeant Daly's suitcases out and set them down on the cobbles.

"That's the station," he said. He pointed at another long two-storey building covered with white pebbledash.

Sergeant Daly noted that the windows were the old-fashioned casement variety and they were all barred. This was an old RIC barracks.

"Through the back door there," said Gralton, "you see the one I mean?"

Sergeant Daly nodded.

"On the other side there's a passage. Straight on till morning and you hit the dayroom, but if you take the stairs on your right, you come out at Superintendent Mahony's eyrie. He's up there waiting for you."

Gralton closed the boot.

"Good to meet you, Sergeant Daly."

"Yes," said Sergeant Daly, "and likewise, good to meet you."

Gralton picked up his suitcases with ease.

"You haven't got a gun in one of these, have you?"

"A gun ... no," said Sergeant Daly. "Why do you ask?"

"Foxy Moll should be above in the living quarters. I'll get her to unpack for you and we don't want her getting any nasty surprises, do we?"

"Oh, right." Sergeant Daly understood now. "No, nothing untoward in my cases."

Gralton moved across the yard while Sergeant Daly went through the barracks' back door and up the stairs. He found Superintendent Mahony's door at the top. It was painted white and had a black metal fingerplate. He knocked twice.

"Come in," Superintendent Mahony shouted.

48

Daly went in. The room was square with windows that overlooked the yard. There were maps on the walls: they were large
scale maps with lots of fine black lines and fine print on a creamy
ground; the maps were of New Inn and environs and the towns
of Cashel and Caher and Tipperary and the whole of the county
of Tipperary. There were filing cabinets and tables piled with
dusty papers. It reminded Sergeant Daly of a country solicitor's
office. It smelled of lanolin. Superintendent Mahony nodded
from behind the desk.

"Ah, Sergeant Daly," he said.

"Yes, sir."

"I'm Superintendent Mahony. No need to call me 'Sir'. Sit
down."

Sergeant Daly sat in the wooden chair indicated. It had a
straight back but was not uncomfortable.

"Good journey?"

"Thank you, yes, I had a fine journey."

"Gralton collected you all right?"

Sergeant Daly pondered whether he should mention the sign that Gralton had waved around in the railway station which had announced his arrival to all and sundry but then decided not to say anything in case it had been Superintendent Mahony's idea.

"Yes."

"Good man, Gralton, reliable."

"Yes."

He was bored by these pleasantries. He was always bored by pleasantries. Back at the start of his career in the early 1920s there had not been time for this sort of guff. When men had met back then there had been decisions to make. There had been a country to run and an enemy to defeat. When men had met they had gotten straight to the point. Now two decades on this was a distant memory. Now the Guards were slow and ponderous and bureaucratic and more and more rather than take action they adopted a policy of observation: a wait-and-see brief, a sit-on-your-hands-and-do-fucking-nothing programme in the hope that the problem, whatever it was, would go away which of course it never did. Sergeant Daly was not of this school: he was one of the exceptions in the service or at least that was what he thought. He was a man who did things, who got things done.

"And that's what we need more than ever, reliable men," said Superintendent Mahony. "Don't you agree?"

"Yes."

The superintendent gazed at him, no doubt in an attempt to get his measure. Sergeant Daly was not surprised. Every time he went somewhere new (which was often) this was what he got, was it not? He did not mind. It was the superior's job to stare and Sergeant Daly's job to be stared at, was it not? He assumed his blank face so that he would not be read as insolent or contrary. Then he looked straight back and his gaze was level but neutral. Let Superintendent Mahony see him and in turn let him get a good look at Superintendent Mahony.

His superior, he saw, was a large fleshy man with a big head and a very wide face and a truly colossal nose. Sergeant Daly noticed that the nose was not red or swollen. It was not a drinker's nose. The poor fucker had been born with it.

From this the next thought flowed without effort. Superintendent Mahony was doubtless a pioneer. He glanced at the left lapel of Superintendent Mahony's brown suit jacket but there was no sign of the pin with the shield at the top that pioneers wore. Himself he did not care for pioneers. In his experience policemen who were pioneers were sticklers who liked to do things by the book and that always got in the way. He would have to find out which way Superintendent Mahony leaned. He could ask Gralton. A casual question: "Himself, upstairs, has he ever been known to darken a pub?" Then he remembered what Gralton had said about Foxy Moll and Superintendent Mahony. Would a pioneer have done what was insinuated? Maybe. Anything was possible. This was what he hated about the start in a new place. There was so much to work out.

Then a new thought came. There was something about this superintendent's face that was familiar. It reminded him of somebody but whom? It was on the tip of his tongue but he could not locate the name. It was somebody famous. Who? Damn his brain.

He was aware that Superintendent Mahony had spoken and he had not heard what was said.

"Sorry, I didn't catch that."

"I'm not here in New Inn much, that's what I said. I'm usually in Caher, or Cashel, or Tipperary: I have offices in all the barracks. I have to move around quite a bit."

Ah, thought Sergeant Daly, an attempt to impress. Well, he must show that he was impressed.

"Yes, I imagine that you would." Sergeant Daly said this in a quiet tone with a nice undertow of deference.

"I could be here quite a bit, though, this next while," said Superintendent Mahony.

Sergeant Daly thought he saw where this was headed.

"If you're everything you're cracked up to be and do the job right, that is."

Yes, thought Sergeant Daly, this was headed where he thought. Superintendent Mahony had high hopes and he expected Sergeant Daly to meet these.

"Will you get the job done do you think?" asked Superintendent Mahony.

"Yes, I'm going to try," said Sergeant Daly.

"Ah, but will you succeed?"

"I've not failed anywhere else."

"That's as may be, but the lovely Mr J.J. Spink is in altogether a different league from those you've dealt with heretofore."

My God this fucker was long winded.

"Yes, I realise he's slippery."

"'Slippery?'" Superintendent Mahony laughed.

Sergeant Daly saw into his mouth as he did. His superior's teeth were brown and his pink wet tongue was penned between them like an animal in a stone enclosure.

"We have a saying here in New Inn," said Superintendent Mahony. "'If J.J. swallowed a nail, he'd shit a corkscrew.' He's beyond slippery. He's a nasty, devious so-and-so. He's in a league with just him in it."

Sergeant Daly nodded.

"J.J.'s father was in the army and his family, essentially, were biddable Castle Catholics, certainly Home Rulers. J.J. loathed his father – actually, I always thought old man Spink was fine, but in the home, by all accounts, he was an old-fashioned Victorian of the 'do it my way or it's the highway' school of thinking. So, J.J., naturally, hating the old man, decided he'd do whatever the man wouldn't want him doing.

"He was out in 1919: he hid guns, he carried messages, he took part in various operations against Crown Forces. The Treaty signed, J.J. came out against it. Well, that was inevitable. He always was an awkward so-and-so. He became an Irregular, after which he caused no end of trouble round here. The Free State army chased him up and down the length of the county, God alone knows how many times, and then went away empty handed, leaving him thinking, 'I'm the king of the castle, I can do whatever I want.' Since then, he's been up to all sorts of nonsense, robberies mostly, though they're not called robberies ..."

"No," Sergeant Daly said.

"They are political acts, necessary, justified and so on. I'm sure you've come across this argument before?"

"I have."

"You've read the papers, so you know the whole miserable saga from top to bottom?"

The word saga took him by surprise. Superintendent Mahony was, without doubt, quite unlike your common-or-garden-variety Guard.

"Yes, I have read the files. They're in my suitcase."

The sentence out, he had a thought: a worrisome one. He wondered if the woman Foxy Moll would have a peek at the contents of his suitcases as she unpacked them? She might but if she was the cleaner she maybe was not so strong at reading so he was in all likelihood safe there.

"There's more for you here." Superintendent Mahony tapped a pile of manila folders bound with thick red rubber bands.

"I'll look forward to that," said Sergeant Daly.

"You read these. Then be here tomorrow, eleven o'clock. We're going on a little jaunt."

"That sounds interesting. Are we going to the seaside?"

"Very droll, Sergeant. We're going to meet a man. Well, actually, we're going to go with four burly Guards who will turn his house over and, while they do, we will be in his barn and I shall introduce the two of you."

"Is this the one in the files called 'the informant'?"

"Yes."

"Right."

"He's actually called Bermingham and he's a small farmer, Republican-minded, but he's got pretty strong feelings regarding right and wrong, and if he thinks something is wrong, he's not shy about speaking out. Let me tell you a story.

"Our friend J.J. fell out with a farmer – Finnegan, Eustace Finnegan. Don't mind what about ... a difference of political opinion."

Superintendent Mahony laughed again and showed off his tongue and little teeth.

"Our friend decided he'd teach Finnegan a lesson, but in a special way. Every cow Finnegan had, he would cut her tendons."

Sergeant Daly had heard of this but he did not think anyone houghed any more. This J.J. was some character.

"Our friend got a set of butcher's knives and made his plan. The night of the next full moon, he and his associates would creep onto Finnegan's land and cut every cow's hamstring. They'd never stand or walk after that, so they'd have to be put down. Finnegan would be ruined and J.J. would be even more respected.

"Now Bermingham, whose house was used by J.J. for meetings, which was how he came to hear what was planned, he did not like the sound of this. He thought it would turn a lot of local people against the movement. He did not want that. So he wrote me a letter, typed, no address, no name – he's a fly boy, Mr Bermingham is – and his sister, Mrs Harney, she came into this barracks on some pretext or other, a dog licence, tillage returns, I don't remember what exactly, and did she not drop his letter on the floor? It was found and it came to me and, to cut a long story short, we met and Mr Bermingham told me what was afoot.

"Forewarned is forearmed. I went to Eustace Finnegan. We agreed a plan. Eustace took his entire herd to the mart on the next sale day and sold them all, every single animal.

"It isn't done like that, as you know, and of course the man at the mart from the *Tipperary Democrat* covering the prices wanted to know why. Eustace and I had already agreed a story and Eustace now told it to the newspaperman.

"He said he had a sister in Australia, which was true. He said unless she had an expensive operation she was going to die. He said family meant more to him than his herd and that's why he was selling. Finally, he said this had all happened very suddenly and that was why he was doing everything in such a hurry.

"A few weeks later, I myself wrote a lovely little piece about the sister, her operation, her miraculous recovery, her wonderful brother, the whole kit and caboodle – there is no end to my talents, Sergeant Daly – and Eustace took my words to the paper and they ran it, along with a picture of Eustace, the good Irish brother who sold his herd for his lovely sister's sake. J.J. read it and believed it. And that's the real point of this story – J.J. believed it and that impressed Bermingham. He decided he trusted us – since when we've stayed friends. I think he'll be invaluable to you."

Sergeant Daly nodded. He had already decided he would be able to work with this man but now after what he had just heard he decided that he might even like him. To have someone like Bermingham lined up before he had done a tap of work was marvellous.

"Is he paid?" said Sergeant Daly.

"If only he was. No, he isn't. He's an informer with a conscience."

"The worst kind. The kind you can't be sure of."

"On the contrary, you can be sure of Mr Bermingham all right," said Superintendent Mahony. "When he tells you something you know it's true. The trouble is he won't always tell you everything."

The question returned. Whose face was Superintendent Mahony's like? It was there within his grasp yet he could not quite grasp it. Damn his memory.

Superintendent Mahony stood. Interview over, thought Sergeant Daly. Or so it would seem.

"Tomorrow?" said Superintendent Mahony.

"Here, eleven."

"Don't forget these." Superintendent Mahony pointed at the files.

"Oh, yes." Sergeant Daly gathered them up.

"Go to the dayroom and talk to the duty sergeant. There's meals organised for you and someone will be in to make the breakfast tomorrow. Nothing fancy."

Superintendent Mahony sat. He had not extended his hand when Sergeant Daly came in and he did not extend it now when Daly was about to leave. Peculiar, thought Sergeant Daly. Perhaps he had a thing about dirt or germs. A lot of Guards had. Criminals disgusted them and then the disgust spread out to include everybody, good and bad, after which a Guard would shrink from physical contact with anyone and everyone, even other Guards.

"Goodbye, Superintendent."

"Yes, Sergeant Daly, goodbye."

49

He saw someone about his meals and then walked across the yard and went through the door and climbed the stairs. They were bare wood. The walls were painted brown. The ceiling was white. The electric lights had coolie shades. Jesus, it would depress anyone. He got to the top. What was it Gralton had said? Go left to the room that overlooked the yard. Yes, that's what Gralton had said. It was always tricky to get one's bearings in a new place.

He turned left and glanced ahead. The corridor was brown. The bare floorboards were painted black. One of the electric lights was on and the light cast by the bulb was faint and watery in comparison to the afternoon light that came through the window at the end of the corridor.

He saw an open door. He approached. There was someone inside: a female. She hummed in a quiet way. He stopped at the threshold and looked in.

The woman was at the bed. She was tiny. She wore a blue day dress with an apron on top. The apron was white and was tied at the back in an extravagant bow. The bed was brass. Its brass smell filled the room. The woman wiped the rails and rods one at a time with a cloth.

He glanced about the room. There was a wardrobe on his right and he saw that his suitcases had been set on top of it. He was amazed that the small woman had managed to get them up there. He noticed a chair beside the wardrobe. It was obvious that she had stood on the chair but it must still have been an effort to get them up there. Perhaps she had pitched them up.

There was a heavy chest of drawers on his left that matched the wardrobe. The papers that Superintendent Mahony had sent him were on top of the chest of drawers. He had bundled them up and tied them with string before he had left Ballingarry. The string was still tied and looked the same as when he had tied it. She had not interfered with them. Of course she had not. He was safe in that respect. Of course he was.

He put the new set of papers he had just gotten from Superintendent Mahony on the top of the old ones and called, "Hello."

When she heard him the woman straightened up and turned.

From the front she looked even smaller than from behind. My God she was tiny, he thought. She had red hair and white skin and freckles. She was not unattractive.

"You're Sergeant Daly."

She hung her dusting cloth over the head of the bed. The cloth had been white once but was now almost grey with the dust she had lifted.

"Yes, that's who I am. And I know who you are too."

"And who might that be?"

She looked straight at him when she spoke. He had come across this before. Country people of a certain kind and age and vintage did that when they talked to you. They looked you right in the eye. There was no insolence about it. Nor was it meant to imply anything or suggest anything. To look was to be polite whereas not to look was to be discourteous.

"You're Foxy Moll. They call you Foxy Moll, don't they?"
he said.

"Who told you that? Was it Aidan?"

"Aidan?"

"Aidan Gralton."

"Yes."

"He's a lively one," she said. "I like him. How did you find
him?"

She still looked him in the eye.

"Chatty," he said.

"He's certainly that. I unpacked for you."

"I see that."

"You'll find everything where you expect to find it. Suits and
shirts here."

She went to the wardrobe. One door was mirrored and as
she reached for the handle she looked at him in the mirror. This
was a different look from the one he had received from her just
before. This was a look of appraisal. He saw this and she saw that
he saw this and she knew that he knew.

She turned the wardrobe handle and pulled both the doors
back. He saw that his uniforms and suits and shirts and ties hung
from the rail. She closed the doors. Again she looked at him in
the mirror. She turned.

"Everything else is in the chest of drawers."

She crossed in front of him to the chest of drawers. It was
made of some very dark wood and had decorations carved into
the edges. She opened one drawer after another showing him
where she had put everything. He murmured thanks.

"Now there's one thing of yours I didn't know where to put,"
she said. She reached into the corner beyond the chest of drawers
and produced his pickaxe handle. It was long and thick and it
was covered with stains and dents. "What is this?"

"That," he said.

"It's a big stick, isn't it?"

"No."

He took it from her and lifted it to his eye and looked down its curved length exactly as a hunter would look down the barrel of his shotgun.

"It's not a stick. It's my persuader and, me and him, we've been together all the years I've been a Guard and, I can tell you, we've seen some things me and the persuader, oh, yes, me and him … we have seen some sights."

"What made the stains?" she said.

"That would be telling."

He threw the handle from one hand to the other. After years of practise he was good at this.

"I'm going to turn down your bed," she said.

"Why don't you do that?"

She turned and tugged the candlewick bedspread from under the pillow and began to fold it back. When she reached across the bed to straighten the fold on the far side and her skirts rose up a little at the back he reached forward with his pickaxe handle and touched the insides of her knees with the point. She ignored him and went on with the job at hand and only once she had finished did she turn and face him.

"There's no need for that."

"For what? Can't I touch your knee?"

"I prefer men plain-spoken and direct."

"What's 'plain-spoken and direct' when she's at home?"

"You know."

He laid his pickaxe handle on top of the chest of drawers and walked back to Foxy Moll and took her left hand and stroked the back of it.

"Just speak your mind," she said.

"There's something about Superintendent Mahony. He reminds me of someone, only I can't work out who it is. He's got the same looks, the same manner and the same tone. Who does he remind me of? I have it on the tip of my tongue but I can't get it out."

A slow blush started: it began on her neck and moved over her chin and up her face to her brow and carried on right to her hairline.

"Why are you blushing?" he said.

"I blush sometimes, though nothing like I used to when I was young."

"Is that a good or a bad thing?"

"Mahony looks like W.C. Fields. That's what I hear the Guards saying. Is that the one you mean?" she said.

"You've saved me a night of torment. That would have worried me all night that would. That's exactly right. He looks just like him, doesn't he?"

"I don't know. I've never seen a film, never mind one with your man."

"Oh. Would you like to?"

"Maybe."

He lifted her hand and kissed the finger ends.

"Will you pull my curtains?" he said.

"I will."

"I'm going down the hall for a moment. When I come back, will you be here?"

"I will."

He went and peed and washed his hands and splashed his face and combed his hair with the comb that he carried in his left breast pocket. He went back to his room and opened the door and stepped in. She had pulled the curtains as he had asked and the room was quite dark. He stepped in and pushed the door shut behind. After a couple of seconds his eyes adjusted to the light. He saw that Foxy Moll had taken off her shoes and put them on the floor side by side and she had hung her stockings and her clothes over the end of the bed. She was under the covers with just her head showing and her hair was spread around like a puddle on the pillow.

"I'll lock the door," he said.

"Why not?" she said. "Though the two other fellows on this landing won't be up for a few hours yet."

She doubtless knows the movements of every man in the barracks, he thought as he turned the key.

The mechanism slid into place with a satisfactory click.

He undressed and slid in and went at her. His way was hot and urgent. As he worked himself up it struck her that this man was the same sort of animal as J.J. and she could tell, even though she had only known him for a little over ten minutes that he was a man who always had to win.

A few minutes later after it was done and they lay side by side in the curtained room she touched his wedding band and asked about his wife.

"She's called Sheila. She's in Ballingarry now, joining me in November. We're taking a house on the Cashel Road."

"Which one?"

He described the house as far as he could remember from the visit he had taken to see it some months earlier when he had been told he would be stationed at New Inn. It was white and had a slate roof and the front door was in the middle. It was like a house a child might draw.

Foxy Moll said she knew the house and pronounced it sound and then added, "Well, we've the guts of five months anyway."

5 0

The next day Superintendent Mahony and Sergeant Daly and four Guards drove to Boolakennedy and pulled up outside Bermingham's cottage. Everyone got out.

"Right," said Superintendent Mahony, "we all know what to do, don't we?"

The four Guards nodded.

Superintendent Mahony walked to the door and knocked.

"Bermingham," he shouted, "open up."

The door opened and Mr Bermingham came out with his pipe in his mouth. The silver lid was in the down position.

"There's no need to be shouting," said Mr Bermingham. "I heard you."

"We have a warrant –" Superintendent Mahony began.

Mr Bermingham waved his hand. "I don't need to see the warrant." He then addressed the four in uniform. "In you go, lads. You won't find a thing in my house, but away you go and no hard feelings."

"Go on," said Superintendent Mahony.

The four Guards clumped through the front door and within seconds from inside came the sound of bangs and thumps as they started the search.

"Right," said Superintendent Mahony, "in the shed."

Mr Bermingham went first. Superintendent Mahony and Sergeant Daly followed. Inside the shed was dark and smelled of turf. A nesting bird disturbed by their appearance flew out past them.

"This is Sergeant Daly," said Superintendent Mahony.

Mr Bermingham nodded. The shed had a slate roof and there were little holes here and there in the slates and the light came through these.

"If you write any more letters, send them straight to him."

"I won't be writing any more letters," said Mr Bermingham.

"Well if you do and they come to me, I'll pass them on to him anyhow," said Superintendent Mahony.

Mr Bermingham pulled on his pipe and exhaled. In the public road a passer-by in a long black coat stopped to gawp.

"You all right?" the passer-by called in to Mr Bermingham through the open shed door.

"As I'll ever be with four peelers tearing my home to bits."

"I'm going to hit you now," Superintendent Mahony spoke in an undertone and his lips did not move.

"Go on," said Mr Bermingham.

Superintendent Mahony hit Mr Bermingham on the chest. It was a soft blow but Mr Bermingham let out a terrible roar as if it had been a hard one and fell to his knees.

"You bastarding Free Stater," the passer-by shouted.

"Fuck off, you little cunt," Superintendent Mahony shouted without much enthusiasm, "otherwise we'll have to bring you into the barracks and kick the shit out of you."

The passer-by made an obscene gesture and ran off.

"Has he gone?" Mr Bermingham murmured from the floor.

"Yes," said Superintendent Mahony.

Mr Bermingham stood.

"Who was that fellow?" said Superintendent Mahony.

"Him? That's Andy Mulligan."

"What's he like?"

"Well, he's probably in the pub already, putting it out that the Guards are giving poor old Mr Bermingham another going over."

"I think our work is done," said Superintendent Mahony.

He sauntered over to the house and went inside.

"He told you, did he," said Mr Bermingham, "about Eustace?"

"Who?" said Sergeant Daly.

"Finnegan?"

"Oh yes," said Sergeant Daly. He knew who Eustace was now.

"He's a mouthy fucker that Mahony."

"Really."

Inside the house the bangs and thumps stopped. Superintendent Mahony and the four Guards came out. All the Guards had taken off their jackets and were hot from their exertions.

"I'm not, though," said Sergeant Daly.

"What?"

"A mouthy fucker. I'm a silent fucker. Anything I hear, it stays in here, in my head. Anything. Everything."

He tapped his temple twice and nodded to Mr Bermingham and sauntered out of the shed.

5 1

It was five months later, a dry still bright day in October. Mr O'Shaughnessy found Daniel McCarthy as he cleaned gutters in the yard.

"Are you going up home later?" said Mr O'Shaughnessy.

It was usually Daniel's practice to visit his mother for an hour every evening after work and then walk back to O'Shaughnessys' to sleep in the little box room they had given him behind the kitchen.

Daniel nodded. "Yes," he said.

"Well, I don't need you till a bit later tomorrow," said Mr O'Shaughnessy. He mentioned the name of another man who would help him milk the cows. "Stay at home tonight, and come in tomorrow at ten."

Daniel smiled. "Thank you."

"And when you've finished the gutters, go home early. I've help to milk tonight as well."

"Really?"

"Yes, you're a good lad, you work hard, why shouldn't you have a few hours off."

Daniel finished with the gutters, put the spade away and set off. It was still light.

Daniel was only gone half an hour when Mr O'Shaughnessy received word that a lorry would come at six the next morning for his pigs. To milk the cows and load the pigs onto the lorry he would need three pairs of hands. There was nothing else for it, thought Mr O'Shaughnessy, but to cycle over to Marlhill Cottage and tell Daniel to revert to his normal routine and to come back later that evening and sleep in the box room and be up bright and early the next day.

Mr O'Shaughnessy got out his bicycle and set off. It was a mild afternoon, and as he pedalled along he looked to his left and right at the high hedges and the trees. The leaves were turning from green to brown but they weren't fully turned yet.

When he was twenty yards short of the entrance to Marlhill Cottage Mr O'Shaughnessy was surprised by the appearance of a motorcar as it nosed slowly out the gateway. He recognised the make: a Wolseley. He knew that was a type the Guards used.

Without a thought Mr O'Shaughnessy braked and swerved sideways through a gate that led into a field opposite Marlhill Cottage. The gate was open so he sailed on into the field beyond and in a single fluid movement he dismounted and crouched out of sight behind the hedge with his bicycle. He did all this so quick and so sudden that Mr O'Shaughnessy felt sure that the driver of the car had not seen him.

A moment later the car glided past. It was as he had suspected: it was an unmarked Guards' car. The driver was the new Guard who had appeared in the summer, the one called Sergeant Daly, and the passenger was Foxy Moll.

After the Wolseley had passed Mr O'Shaughnessy cycled on to the cottage and knocked on the door. Judy answered.

"Can I have a word with himself?" he said.

"Daniel?" she said. Her voice was flat.

"Yes."

She went away. Daniel came out.

"Oh, hello, Mr O'Shaughnessy," said Daniel.

"You've only just got home?"

"I have," said Daniel.

"I'm afraid I have to go back on my word."

He explained about the lorry that would arrive the next morning to collect the pigs.

"It can't be helped," said Daniel. "Anyway, my mother had to go out, so it's not as if I'm about to miss out on seeing her. I'll just have some tea and then I'll walk back."

"You're a good lad," said Mr O'Shaughnessy.

52

A few days later J.J. and Mr O'Shaughnessy sheltered under an oak tree on the edge of one of Mr O'Shaughnessy's fields as cold rain fell from sky. Mr O'Shaughnessy told J.J. that he had seen Daly, the new sergeant, and Foxy Moll in an unmarked police car driving away from the cottage.

"Are you sure?" said J.J.

"I am," said Mr O'Shaughnessy. "I'm absolutely sure."

"Were they carrying on?"

"They just drove past," said Mr O'Shaughnessy, "but I don't suppose she'd go in his car just for a drive, do you?"

"No, you suppose right," said J.J. "And did they see you?"

"No," said Mr O'Shaughnessy.

"Are you sure?"

"Guaranteed."

J.J. thanked Mr O'Shaughnessy and stalked away. The rain fell hard on him but he paid no attention. His mind was turning. Of course his dealings with Foxy Moll were not entirely secret.

After all, she had the child. The midwife was there. The midwife might have known J.J. had seen Foxy Moll and guessed he was the father. Maybe. It was not impossible. And then the midwife might have mentioned this to someone, who would have passed the information to someone else, and gradually, by that means, everyone, and that would have to include the Guards, would have come to know his business. That was the thing about Ireland: in the end everything leaked out.

And of course, as J.J. knew from long experience, it was highly likely someone from his side of the house either already had or soon would tell the Guards about his relationship with Foxy Moll. So the only assumption to make was that it was known.

But until this moment this was not a worry to him because what was known was gossip and what could be done with that? He could not be arrested with gossip. The only things that could hurt him were facts and the only one with any dangerous facts was Foxy Moll. She knew the names of his associates and the whereabouts of his safe houses. But he had not worried before that she was going to tell anyone. She had told him she did not blab, of course, when they had finished, not that this could absolutely be relied on. However he had also observed over the years and when they were together that she never spoke about her lovers or the fathers of her children. Even if this information got out by other means, it was not because of anything she did or said.

But having Sergeant Daly involved changed things. He had a reputation. He was a violent fucker; he was also devious and a clever cunt. That made him dangerous. Did he know that Foxy Moll knew much that might be useful to the Guards? The only safe assumption to make was yes. He did. So there was the problem. Daly knew she had something and he would obviously want to dig it out of her. Now with any other man Foxy Moll could hold out and refuse to talk. But as she was a cleaner in the barracks, and as Sergeant Daly was in quarters in the barracks until he got his house, and given they were sleeping together,

Daly had her in his power in there. He could interrogate her if he wanted. He could lock her up and no one would know. He could bring such pressure to bear that in the end though she was not a blabber she would have to buckle and give the sergeant what he wanted: the names of J.J.'s associates, the locations of the safe houses, as well as everything else she knew about him.

Sergeant Daly's arrival in New Inn at the start of the summer had not troubled J.J. unduly. He had not been exactly delighted but he had felt he could manage the situation so long as he exercised guile and caution. However, now he knew Sergeant Daly was mixed up with Foxy Moll none of this would suffice. If Daly forced her to give up what she knew, J.J. and his unit would be destroyed. Foxy, he decided, would need to be watched and, if necessary, she would have to be made to keep quiet.

53

J.J. put out the word that if anyone saw Foxy Moll and Sergeant Daly together they were to be followed and their business noted. Two days later they were spotted together in Cashel. The man who followed them told J.J. that first they had gone to a chemist's where they had bought Beecham's powders and then to a shop that sold women's clothes where Sergeant Daly had bought a leather clutch bag that he had presented to Foxy Moll. Then they had gone to a hotel and had tea and toast and potted shrimps. The spotter reported to J.J. that there had been neither overt friendliness nor amorousness between Sergeant Daly and Foxy Moll.

The Friday after that they were seen again in Cashel only this time it was evening and the spotter was Screw. He followed them to the Lady Nelson, a quiet public house on the edge of the town. They went in. Screw followed a few minutes later.

Those who wanted to have a private drink favoured the Lady Nelson because the interior was partitioned into snugs. Screw found Sergeant Daly and Foxy Moll had occupied the corner snug at the back of the saloon. It was a good choice. They were well hidden. He considered sitting in an adjacent snug in order to eavesdrop but decided that was too risky. He went back out and stood at the side of the building from where he could watch the front but not be seen.

Some time later Sergeant Daly and Foxy Moll came out. Screw followed them to where Sergeant Daly's car was parked. He watched them get in and the car move off and then he went back into the the saloon of the Lady Nelson.

There was a barman at the fireplace who he presumed had served his quarry. The barman was throwing fresh sods of turf on the fire. Screw came up behind.

"Nice fire you have," said Screw, his manner genial.

The barman straightened up and rubbed the turf dust off his hands as he did.

"We keep a good fire in," he said. "We have to. Especially of a chilly evening like tonight."

The barman was middle aged, Screw guessed, and he had thinning grey hair and the sorry face and thin body typical of a drinker who never bothers to eat.

"Have you a nice malt?" said Screw.

"We do."

Screw took his battered wallet out of his jacket pocket and opened it and pulled out a green Irish one-pound note.

"It's all I've got, I'm sorry," said Screw.

"Well, there'll be plenty of change out of that," said the barman.

"I don't want any change. I just want a large malt with a little water and a pint of stout."

The barman took the note and went behind the bar to prepare Screw's drinks.

Screw got up on a stool. There were a few in the snugs but no one sat at the bar or waited there to be served. The malt whiskey and a jug of cold water with Dewar's Whisky written on the side were placed on the counter in front of him.

"I've started the pint, but it'll be a few minutes yet," said the barman.

"I have all the time in the world," said Screw.

"As I thought when I was a young fellow," said the barman, "but now I find I was wrong." He sighed and shook his head.

A few minutes later the pint came along with the change: a ten-shilling note and some silver and coppers. The barman set the money down: note first, change on top.

"You know the couple who were sitting in the snug in the corner there?" said Screw. "You'd have seen them from where you're standing behind the bar, wouldn't you?"

"I might," said the barman.

"I think you did."

"Fair enough," said the barman. He dipped his gaze and lifted it. Screw slid the whole of his change towards him.

"Put that in your pocket," said Screw.

The barman nodded and did as he was told. "Thank you," he said. "I'll have one on you after I finish."

"More than one, I'd say," said Screw.

The barman nodded.

"So what were they doing, the ones in the corner?"

"You mean what weren't they doing?"

"Was there kissing?"

"Was there kissing? Yes, there was kissing, and hand holding and arm stroking and knee squeezing and shoulder rubbing."

"Thought so," said Screw. "She's a cute whore, that sister of mine."

"That's your sister?" The barman looked appalled. He swallowed twice. His Adam's apple bobbed. "I'm sorry," he said, "I shouldn't have said what I did just now. It was wrong of me."

"Don't worry about it. She's a cross, but I bear her lightly."

"There was crying too, if that changes things."

"Crying?"

"Crying, yes. She was crying."

"Go on," said Screw.

"Your sister and the man, well, he has a wife, whoever he is, and the wife was away and now she's coming on Monday, and that's why your sister was crying, because when the wife comes, well, I don't need to say any more, do I?"

"No, you don't. What you've told me is all I need to know."

"She's also lost her job."

"Who?" said Screw.

"Your sister. She had a cleaning job ... in some barracks ... or maybe I've got that wrong, but anyway that's gone too, wherever it was."

"The job?"

"Yes, that's what I think I heard."

"Thanks," said Screw. "You've been very helpful."

The barman nodded and sidled away and Screw lifted his pint of stout and drank deep.

5 4

The next day Screw and J.J. met.

"She was in the Lady Nelson in Cashel and Sergeant Daly was with her."

"And?" said J.J.

"Carrying on."

"Carrying on how?"

"You know, carrying on like a man and a woman in love carry on."

"They're in love, are they?" said J.J. "Did they tell you that? You know that as a fact, do you?"

"All right, I don't know that as a fact," said Screw, "but I know they were carrying on. But don't take my word for it. Go yourself to the Lady Nelson and ask the barman. He'll tell you the same as he told me."

"Which was that they carried on?"

"And a bit more."

"And he had her knickers off, did he?" J.J. sounded incredulous.

"No. She was crying."

"Crying?"

"Crying. See, they're finished. Daly's wife is coming here, isn't she? She's coming this Monday," said Screw. "That's what the barman said. So, there – that's one less thing for you to worry about. They're finished."

J.J. stared away. His thoughts turned. Screw was wrong but then Screw was not a thinker, was he? J.J. had thought the danger point was earlier, when she was with Sergeant Daly and working in the barracks. But now he saw the real danger point was where they were now. Now was when she might choose to mention a certain house in Boolakennedy or a certain Mr Bermingham or any of the many other things she knew about J.J.'s world to Sergeant Daly. What better way to get his attention? What better way to get him to go on seeing her, just as she lost her job and his wife arrived, than with intelligence on Republican subversives?

"We're going to have to do something about her," said J.J. "There's no knowing what she might say to that cunt, Daly. We have to stop her talking."

"Right," said Screw. He shrugged.

He liked what he heard. He always felt more alive when they were engaged in some business and he knew that Nutley felt the same way.

"But whatever we do," said J.J., "we're not going to do anything stupid or precipitous."

"What does precipitous mean?"

"Look it up in the dictionary."

"I don't have a dictionary."

"It means anything reckless, anything that would attract unhealthy attention, especially from that fucker, Daly. We're not going to do anything that does that."

"No," Screw said. "We don't want attention, and we certainly don't want it from him."

"We need to get rid of her but in such a way that the Guards go after someone else."

"How will we do that?" said Screw.

"You mean how will I do that?" said J.J. "First I'll work out who that person should be and then I'll tell them who that person is, after which they'll be eternally grateful and make me a chief superintendent."

"You're not making sense."

"It will make sense, don't worry, you'll see."

55

Three weeks had passed. Autumn was sliding into winter and it was much colder. It was the morning of Tuesday 19 November 1940. Badger approached the dog pen. Lively Lady stood and waited. He always walked her at this time. He had done so for months. She knew to expect him.

He opened the pen. She came out and stopped. The lead had to be attached. It always was. This was another part of the invariable exercise routine.

Badger clipped the lead on. Man and dog struck out for the back gate. Lively Lady knew the way because the way that they went never changed. It was the same every morning. They walked down to the Dugout and came back by a different path that skirted the edge of the Stubble Field and that returned them to where they had started.

They reached the back gate. Badger opened it. They went through and he closed it. Lively Lady whimpered.

"Ready for Sunday?" said Badger.

He planned to take her hare coursing. It would be her first professional outing. The dog pulled and whimpered again.

"You just want to get going, don't you? You don't want to gas. Right you are …"

Badger and Lively Lady crossed three fields to the bottom boundary of the farm and turned right and passed the Dugout and then they turned right again. Here the path skirted the old fence that separated the Dugout Field and the adjacent Stubble Field and as they walked Badger looked over. He saw the earth around the stubble was dark and wet while the stubble stuck up brown and sharp like spears thrust from below up through the earth.

Halfway up the Dugout Field there was a small portion of fence missing. As a rule he kept this plugged with bushes and debris but this morning he saw that the material he kept piled there had been pushed back which left the gap open. Perhaps an animal had barged through but, whatever the explanation, the sheep would probably soon be let into the Dugout Field and if he knew sheep they would be through the gap and into the Stubble Field. Must fix that, he thought.

He slipped the lead and Lively Lady began to run here and there. She was excited and sniffed at the ground as she went. Badger walked over to the gap. The debris that he had blocked it with before had been scattered about. He gathered the stuff and put it back. Then he found a few good pieces of old hedge in the Stubble Field that had been left over from the hedge-cutting earlier that year and dragged these to the gap and piled them on top of what was already there until he judged that it would be impossible for any sheep to get through.

He climbed back into the Dugout Field and whistled twice and called, "Come on, come on, girl."

Lively Lady raced back. He reattached the lead. They followed the path back to the yard.

56

In his place behind the Dugout, Nutley saw Badger and his greyhound head up the path at the side of the Stubble Field towards Marlhill Farm. Once Badger had gone a good distance Nutley turned and crossed into Mr Byrne's fields that lay south of Caesars' and headed east; Nutley took care to keep low in case Badger were to turn and look back. Nutley did not want Badger to know he had seen him but Badger did not look back and he never knew Nutley had seen him repair the gap in the hedge of the Stubble Field and then walk home.

Nutley crossed a couple of small fields followed by a large field with an old ring fort at the top of a small rise in the corner and then he came to the ditch that separated Byrne's land from the bottom of Lynchs' which bounded Caesars' on its east side.

Nutley crossed the ditch and got onto Lynchs' land. He crossed a couple of tiny fields so small that they were in fact paddocks and he presumed they had once been for horses and then he saw ahead of him an overgrown garden with an abandoned house in the middle. It had a slate roof that looked to be in good condition. Behind the windows all the shutters were closed and the front door was shut. Once the home of an eccentric poet, the dwelling had stood empty for years. Lynch had long wanted to pull it down but his wife would not let him. She had said that it was a house with a literary history and she would live in it one day and so she had insisted that her husband kept it dry and paid the rates.

Nutley slipped through the rusty front gate and brushed past the high bushes that grew on either side of the path. He came to the front door and gave a soft rap.

"Nutley?" said a voice through the wood.

"Who do you think?"

The door was opened and Nutley saw Screw.

"Well?" said Screw.

"He filled in the hole we made."

Screw smiled. "That'll please himself."

Nutley stepped in. Screw closed the door. The two men walked down a passage and into a kitchen with a flagged floor. They had fitted the house up a week before. A storm lantern burned on top of a table. The light from the lantern was yellow. There was a bed with blankets and several chairs and another table piled with tinned food and a Tilley lamp for heat and a paraffin stove to cook on. There was also a drum with water. The water came from the well under the house and was drawn with the hand pump in the back scullery. One of the reasons that J.J. had picked this house was because it had water. The hard leather case with J.J.'s shotgun inside stood in the corner and under the shotgun case was a folded green tarpaulin.

"I'll make tea," said Screw.

He lit the stove and put a kettle of water on.

"Does J.J. still have his appointment later?" said Nutley.

"Yes, I think so."

"I hope they make their minds up. I'm too old to be traipsing around the fields and spending days in this kip," said Nutley.

He sat down and took out a cigarette and lit it.

57

When he got back to the yard after his walk Badger felt warm and happy. Lively Lady panted. He had no idea how often he had made this circuit down to the Dugout and back, perhaps many hundreds of times, but he loved it. It always left him happy. Many people hated routine but Badger was not one of them.

He put Lively Lady back in her pen with a dog-pan of fresh water and as Tommy was milking this morning he was free to attend to his other chores: he set off down the farm lane. There were sheep in the field at the mouth of the lane he needed to check. As he came down the lane Badger saw Foxy Moll and some of her children at the spring well. He often spotted her and different children drawing water there at this time of day.

He drew close to the gate of the field where the spring well was. He saw that this morning Foxy Moll was with the daughter Judy and the young lad Brendan and he also spotted a small brown dog he had not seen before. He noticed the buckets under the spigots that caught the water as it gushed out and more buckets at the side waiting to be filled. With so many in the cottage, he thought, and not for the first time, their need for water must be fierce – and they had to fetch it all. Up at the farmhouse they were lucky for their water was pumped in.

Foxy Moll turned and raised a hand in greeting. The brown dog turned and saw him and started to yap.

"Shush, you," Foxy Moll said.

The dog ran towards Badger who saw that the dog's strange short legs carried his long trunk with remarkable ease and aplomb. He was small and brown with white socks and a white belly and a white snout.

"Morning," called Badger.

The dog got to the gate first. Foxy Moll followed. This morning Foxy Moll wore an old coat and a black cloche hat. At the well, Brendan looked up from a pail, saw where his mother was and started after her.

"Who's this?" Badger nodded at the dog. The animal no longer yapped but eyed him in a wary fashion. "I've not seen him before."

"Little Sam," said Foxy Moll. "I just got him. He's only a pup, really. Well, nine months."

"He won't grow much more."

"No, but isn't he lovely?"

Badger looked at Little Sam: his breed was not obvious.

"What kind of dog is he?"

"Dachshund, Jack Russell, Corgi and some others I can't remember. Mr O'Shaughnessy gave him to me, for the children."

Brendan came up behind his mother. He wore a man's double-breasted jacket the hem of which hung lower than his shorts and an old pair of outsize Wellington boots.

"Now I don't like to ask," Foxy Moll began.

"But you're going to anyway," said Badger.

Little Sam had climbed through the gate and come up to

Badger to sniff around his ankles.

"Hello, boy," said Badger.

He bent forward and offered his hand. Little Sam went rigid and lifted back his lips with a growl to show his sharp white teeth.

"He's not friendly yet," said Foxy Moll. "I wouldn't stroke him. He might give you a nip."

Badger straightened. "I don't want to be bitten."

Little Sam jumped back through the bars of the gate and went behind Foxy Moll. Badger noticed that she wore a brown boot on her right foot and a black one on her left.

"We're right out of spuds," she said. "Isn't that right, Brendan? You'd no spuds to eat last night, had you?"

Brendan gave a slow solemn nod. He had a small white face with a pointed chin and a few freckles around the nose and curly black hair.

"The college are sending a food box on Saturday but, until then, could you spare a few spuds?"

Badger promised he would toss a sack over the gate when he passed later. Foxy Moll could pick them up when she was next out for water.

"Fair enough," she said.

Badger took a handkerchief out of his pocket and began to tie one corner into a knot.

"So I shan't forget," he said.

"You never forget," said Foxy Moll.

Badger noticed that the boy Brendan stared at him and he could not decide if the child's stare was amiable or curious or hostile. Brendan always stared at him like this when he was with his mother.

"Not at school this morning?" said Badger.

"Oh, he's going to school," said Foxy Moll. "You love school, don't you, Brendan?"

Brendan said nothing.

"I say to all my children, 'You have to go to school, you have to master your alphabet and your numbers, or else you won't amount to anything in life and you'll have to scratch a living, like me.' Isn't that what I say, Brendan?"

Brendan shrugged.

"He's very clever, very good at his sums and his letters, gets great reports from Master Murdoch, not that you'd ever know from the cut of him or how he carries on. A bit like yourself, Badger. You hide your lights under a bushel, don't you?"

"I don't know about that."

"Once Brendan's helped with the water, Mr Condon's going to give him and the others a lift down to Knockgraffon."

Badger nodded. "I've got to get on now. There'll be a few spuds later."

"Me too. I've got to draw the water."

Foxy Moll laughed and started back for the spring well and Little Sam and Brendan followed while Badger moved on down the lane and he put his handkerchief back in his pocket as he went.

58

In the potato store a bit later that morning Badger put some spuds in a grain sack. The sack had "McNeilly's of Cork" written on it. He had a pile of these sacks: he used them to carry and hold all sorts of things.

He tied the sack and lifted it onto his shoulder and carried it out of the store and into the yard.

He saw Tommy wheel a barrowful of hay towards the stables where the horses were. The horses had their heads over the doors and stamped and whinnied in anticipation of the food.

"I'm going down to the sheep again," said Badger. "The old ram was looking a bit poorly earlier."

"Fair enough," said Tommy.

Badger carried the spuds down the lane and dropped them over the gate near the spring well. As he walked on towards the field with the ram he took his handkerchief out of his pocket and unknotted it.

5 9

J.J. and half-a-dozen other men met in Mr Bermingham's house later on Tuesday afternoon. The visitors sat in the parlour and talked while Mr Bermingham stayed in the kitchen. He could hear their voices through the thin walls but he could not make out the sense of what they said and then he heard a name spoken loud and clear: Moll McCarthy. Ah, Foxy Moll, he thought, and he remembered the times when J.J. had brought her and he had to leave his own home and go for a walk. He had not liked that. A safe house was a place of safety and not a place to court women.

The men talked on for an hour. Mr Bermingham judged the conversation was heated: he also heard Foxy Moll's name several more times. Then the discussion stopped and J.J. came into the kitchen.

"Would you bring us through some tea?" said J.J.

"I will, surely," said Bermingham.

As a rule he did not like to make tea for meetings because

he saw it as women's work not men's but this afternoon he was pleased to be asked. If he got into the parlour and their conversation was still as loud and intense as it had been before then he might discover if they had something in mind for Foxy Moll and what that might be: he very much wanted to find these things out.

Mr Bermingham made a big pot of tea and set it on a tray along with cups and saucers, teaspoons and sugar. He was careful when he lifted the tray because he had filled the milk jug just a little too high and he did not want to spill any and then he proceeded across his kitchen and through the door and across the hall and through the door on the far side and into the parlour. No one looked in the direction of the doorway as he came in which was fortunate: at that precise moment all their eyes were on J.J. as he drew a finger across his neck. When J.J. heard Mr Bermingham he dropped the hand and straightened but he did not look around to check where Mr Bermingham was. On the contrary he gave the impression that he thought he had not been seen and he had mimed what he had mimed just before Mr Bermingham came through the door and therefore Mr Bermingham did not know what he had done.

However Mr Bermingham did know and when he returned to the kitchen he felt queasy. He sat down in his chair by the fire. He had made himself a mug of tea before he had carried the tray through and he looked down at where it sat on his hearth: the mug was striped blue and white and the tea was a dark brown like old wood and there were little bubbles around the side and steam rose from the surface. He had wanted it earlier when he had set it out but he did not feel in the least inclined to drink it now.

He closed his eyes and leaned his head against the back of the chair he sat in. They still talked in the parlour and he heard Foxy Moll this and Foxy Moll that said a few more times but he did not try to follow the talk any more. He did not need to. He knew what was planned and he knew that, despite his assertion that his letter-writing days were behind him and his having said so when Superintendent Mahony had brought the new man Sergeant Daly over, he knew now that he would have to renege on what he had said and he would have to write one more time.

60

It was later in the afternoon, still Tuesday.

"Will you come and help your mother get some spuds?"

Judy nodded.

"Can I come?" said Helena.

"We'll all go," said Foxy Moll, "and Little Sam will come too."

Foxy Moll and her children walked along the path that connected Marlhill Cottage to the spring well where they got their water. Little Sam scampered ahead and darted off the path every few moments because something caught his attention and then scampered back again.

They found the sack where Badger had left it earlier, tucked behind the hedge near the gate to the farm lane.

"Spuds tonight," Foxy Moll said. "That'll please Brendan. He was complaining he got none last night."

Foxy Moll and Judy carried the sack back to the cottage together. Little Sam and Helena followed and the child chanted, "Spuds tonight, spuds tonight."

61

J.J. and the others left Mr Bermingham's house. It was light but it would soon be dark.

Mr Bermingham locked his doors and closed the shutters on his windows. Then he opened his press and took the panel off the back and retrieved the typewriter he kept hidden there which nobody other than his sister knew that he owned.

He put the typewriter on the table and rolled in a piece of paper and typed in a slow laborious manner with just the forefinger of his right hand:

TUESDAY 19 NOVEMBER 1940 I WILL SEE YOU TOMORROW, WEDNESDAY 20 NOVEMBER AT NOON, SALOON BAR, HUNTER'S PUBLIC HOUSE. COME ALONE.

He took the paper out and rolled an envelope in and typed "Sgt Daly, Private & Confidential" on the front. He took the envelope out. He folded the paper on which his message was written and put it in the envelope and licked the glue line and sealed the flap. He put this envelope into a larger manila envelope and sealed this and addressed it to his sister Mrs Harney in New Inn and put a stamp on the top right-hand corner. Then he put the typewriter away and banked up his fire and put the fireguard in place and walked the mile to the post box. It was set into the side of an old demesne wall and was painted green but the initials on the box read "VR" because the box dated from the days of Queen Victoria's reign. He put his letter in and heard it drop. Then he retired to a copse that lay straight across the road from the box and stood behind a tree from where he could watch unobserved.

A few minutes later the post van drove up. He watched the postman get out and open the box with a special T-shaped brass key. The postman took his letter and a few others that were underneath it in the bottom of the post box and put them in a mail sack. He got back into the van and drove off. That was the last post of the day. Mr Bermingham knew that his letter would go now to the sorting office and be delivered in New Inn the next day. Other than a trip to New Inn to find Sergeant Daly in person, which was far too risky because he might be seen by one of J.J.'s many informants, this was the quickest and safest and simplest way to get a message across.

He came out of the copse and began to retrace his steps along the road. He felt gratified. He had done the right thing. By the following afternoon she would be safe and surely to God they were not about to do anything before then, were they? He thought about this for a moment and decided, no, that would not happen. The decision had only just been made. It would be a while before they moved. J.J. was careful. He was methodical. He did not like speed because speed caused mistakes and J.J. did not like mistakes. No, Mr Bermingham decided, the matter was in hand: she would be made safe.

As he walked on it began to get dark and night had come on by the time he got back to his house.

6 2

The manila envelope dropped onto the mat behind Mrs Harney's front door at ten o'clock in the morning on Wednesday 20 November 1940. Within an hour she was in the day room in the barracks.

"I want to report a dog," Mrs Harney said.

"A dog," said Gralton.

"It was fouling the footpath outside my house this morning."

Gralton bent down to get the day-room book in which details of all day-room business was written up. While Gralton had his head down Mrs Harney took her brother's letter from her coat pocket and dropped it. She stopped the letter's fall with her foot and then slid it onto the floor. It landed front upwards.

"Yes?" said Gralton.

He had the book open and a dip pen with ink on the end in his hand.

Mrs Harney gave him the details. They were all made up. She left the barracks. A few minutes later a Guard walked through the day room and spotted the envelope on the floor and saw that it was addressed to Sergeant Daly and put it in Sergeant Daly's pigeonhole.

Sergeant Daly came in half an hour later and saw the envelope and opened it and read the message.

63

Sergeant Daly drove home to his house on the Cashel Road. Sheila was in the kitchen unpacking crockery from a tea chest. There were wood shavings in her hair. The dishes were white and clean and there was a smell in the room of pine and tea leaves.

"I have to change," he said.

He went up to their bedroom, took off his uniform and put on a grey suit. Then he left without saying goodbye to his wife, hurried back to the New Inn police station and withdrew a revolver and a shoulder holster and twelve rounds from the armoury. Then he loaded the gun and put the six spare bullets in his pocket, strapped on the holster and put on his hat and his coat and got into an unmarked car and drove to Hunter's. It was a country pub off the road to Tipperary town.

He arrived not long before twelve. He parked and checked his revolver and got out and locked his car and went into the public bar. The barman told him that the saloon was down the passage at the side. He went through. The saloon was empty but he could smell pipe smoke. A few moments later Mr Bermingham came through a door from the back. He had the pipe with the silver cap clamped between his teeth. Mr Bermingham did not acknowledge Sergeant Daly. He went to a table in the corner and sat down.

"What can I get you?"

A barman had appeared at the saloon-bar counter.

"Red lemonade," said Sergeant Daly.

The barman poured the drink into a half-pint glass and Sergeant Daly paid and took the glass and went and sat at the next table to Mr Bermingham. Sergeant Daly took a sip of his lemonade. It was sharp and tasted of metal. Mr Bermingham took a sip from his glass. His drink was clear with bubbles in it. Soda water, Sergeant Daly thought. He did not think that Mr Bermingham was a man who would take alcohol; not on an errand like this one.

The clock behind the bar ticked. It was now a quarter past twelve. The barman had gone through to the public bar at the front. They were alone. Sergeant Daly watched Mr Bermingham reach into the inside breast pocket nearest his heart. Sergeant Daly slipped the fingers of his right hand under the lapels of his coat and the jacket he wore underneath and he found the butt of the revolver he had in the holster there. He did not think Mr Bermingham was about to try to shoot him but in this business one could not be too careful.

Mr Bermingham's hand came back the way it had gone. He pulled something out of his pocket. It was white and slim. Ah, Sergeant Daly thought as he saw what it was: Mr Bermingham had pulled a piece of paper out of his pocket. It was folded in two and there was typed text on the inside. Sergeant Daly could see typed capital letters through the back of the paper. There was also something drawn.

"Read it," said Mr Bermingham.

He unfolded then held the piece of paper up where Sergeant Daly could see it.

Sergeant Daly bent forward and read: "FOXY MOLL. RIP. IMMINENT." Above the words there was a picture of a stick woman in a dress hanging by a rope from a gallows.

"Got that?" said Mr Bermingham.

Sergeant Daly nodded.

Mr Bermingham walked over to the fire where he crumpled the paper up and threw it onto the turf embers. The paper caught. As the flame spread the paper turned first brown and then grey and then the grey crumpled into weightless white ash and the ash disappeared into the crevices between the embers and with that the paper was gone and there was nothing left of Mr Bermingham's deed.

Mr Bermingham returned to his table but did not sit down. He lifted his glass and emptied it. Sergeant Daly emptied his glass and stood.

"Why are you telling me this?" said Sergeant Daly.

Mr Bermingham pointed at a door. It was a side door and not the door that led to the front of Hunter's or the other door that went to the toilet at the rear and that he had appeared through earlier. Both men stepped outside. Mr Bermingham closed the door and looked around. They were in a corner piled with boxes of empty bottles and barrels.

"There are two things you don't hurt, if you can help it, in a war," said Mr Bermingham. "The first is animals, you don't deliberately hurt livestock, and the other is women."

"Fair enough," said Sergeant Daly.

64

Sergeant Daly drove straight from Hunter's public house to Marlhill. Foxy Moll's youngest, Helena, who had turned four in the summer stood near the gate with her back to the road. He did not stop at the cottage but drove past and parked in the entrance to the next field up and walked back. As he drew close he dropped to his haunches so that the hedge hid him from the cottage.

"Helena," he called.

The child was digging in the ground with a pointed stick. Beside her was a small brown dog that he had never seen before with a long trunk and ridiculous short legs.

"Helena," he called again.

When she heard her name the second time the child turned. The dog barked twice. Daly beckoned them over. They both came.

"Who's this?" said Sergeant Daly.

"Little Sam."

"What sort of name is that?"

"Mammy chose it."

Sergeant Daly nodded.

"Hey, Little Sam," Sergeant Daly said. "Come here."

The dog went closer to the sergeant but not so close that the sergeant could touch him.

"He's wary of strangers, I see."

Helena stared at him and said nothing.

"Is your mammy in?"

Helena nodded.

"Would you get her?"

Helena did not move.

"Please?"

Helena turned and skipped off. Her skirt was too long and full and the hem floated backwards and forwards as she tripped away. She wore old plimsolls a couple of sizes bigger than her feet. She would never see the other side of the winter in those plimsolls, he thought. Sergeant Daly made a note to give Foxy Moll a few shillings to buy the child shoes.

Helena disappeared inside the cottage. Little Sam remained out of reach a few feet away and watched him with his dark honey-coloured eyes. Foxy Moll came out and walked over to him. Sergeant Daly stood up. He saw Judy the older daughter at the door of the cottage. She watched him for a moment and then when she saw he had seen her she stepped back and closed the door.

"Hello," he said.

"Hello, Anthony," said Foxy Moll.

No one called him Anthony other than his wife although there was a world of difference between the way that Sheila said his name and the way Foxy Moll did. When his wife said Anthony fury and rebuke lurked behind the word but when Foxy Moll said it, even now, even when she tried to be neutral, there was warmth there and the suggestion of intimacy.

"How are you?" he said.

Foxy Moll shrugged. "It would be nice if I could see you. I know, you can't. Don't worry, I never plead, I never rebuke."

"You've got a new addition to the family, I see." He pointed at the dog.

"Yes," said Foxy Moll. "He cheers me up. Isn't he gorgeous?"

Speaking of the new dog brought out her warmth. It occurred to Sergeant Daly that it would be lovely to reach forward and stroke her face, her soft pink cheek, and then to put his arms behind her back and kiss her on the lips.

"Come here, boy," Sergeant Daly said.

The dog hung back still.

"Oh, Little Sam, you fool," said Foxy Moll.

She swept the dog up and carried him to Sergeant Daly.

"Say hello to Sergeant Daly," said Foxy Moll.

The dog regarded him with his honey-coloured eyes.

"Will he bite?" said Sergeant Daly.

"Not with me holding him."

Sergeant Daly extended his hand. Little Sam sniffed a knuckle and then gave it two cursory licks.

"Good dog," said Foxy Moll.

"Good boy." Sergeant Daly stroked the dog's head a couple of times.

"I don't suppose you've come to ask after my health?"

"Are you being a good girl?"

"What does that mean? I'm always good, aren't I?"

"You seeing anyone?"

"Is that why you're here, to check up on me? Did Mahony send you?"

"No."

"I wouldn't tell you if I was seeing anyone," said Foxy Moll.

"Well, don't see anyone."

"Why not?"

"Just don't."

"Anyone in particular?"

"Don't see anyone at all."

"What? Ever?" said Foxy Moll.

"For the next week."

"How's Sheila?"

"She misses Ballingarry," said Sergeant Daly.

"Friends, had she, in Ballingarry?"

"Yes. There's some family there."

"I could call in to see her, maybe, if she's lonely, your wife," said Foxy Moll. "Judy and I often pass your place."

"Really?"

"Yes, when we go to O'Gormans'."

O'Gormans' was a field with a sacred tree where supplicants left rosary beads or written prayers or little items of personal importance. Since Foxy Moll and the children did not go to mass, the sacred tree on O'Gormans' land was their only religious outlet and sometimes on Sunday afternoons Foxy Moll and Judy would go up there to leave offerings and to say prayers.

"Do you?" said Sergeant Daly.

"Yes, we do. Do you think your Sheila would welcome a visit?"

Sergeant Daly remembered the notion he had to give Foxy Moll some money for shoes for Helena. Now he revised the decision. He would not give her a penny.

"I don't think it would be a good idea to call at my house and I'd thank you to keep away from my door."

"You wouldn't want anyone seeing. There might be talk. I can see that."

"Keep yourself to yourself until I come and tell you otherwise," said Sergeant Daly.

He turned and began to walk back to his car. With Little Sam in her arms Foxy Moll started back towards the cottage and she stroked the little dog on the head as she went.

Sergeant Daly got back to the field entrance where he had

left the car. He shook. It was the dreadful idea of Foxy Moll and Judy on his doorstep as Sheila opened the door to them. With one hand on the side of the car he bent over and threw up. His sick was a mix of boiled egg and toast that Sheila had given him for breakfast and the red lemonade he had drunk in Hunter's.

He spat and wiped his mouth with the back of his hand and then he wiped his hand with his handkerchief. He got back into his car. His face was hot and he had a bitter taste in his mouth. Foxy Moll was trouble. He wished that he had never met her and the thought crossed his mind that it would be so much better if Foxy Moll did not exist.

He turned the key and set off for the barracks. The first thing he would do when he got there was to check the revolver and the holster and the ammunition back in. Yes, he thought again. Life would be so much better if Foxy Moll were gone. It was a shame that he could not have plugged her while he had the gun.

65

Screw stood behind the hedge across the road from Marlhill Cottage and watched Sergeant Daly drive away. This surprise visit of the sergeant's was not good, he thought. J.J. would not like it. No, not one little bit. If the sergeant was sniffing around, God alone knew what would happen next. Screw began to move away and he kept low so that no one could see him from the cottage. There was nothing else for it. He would just have to go and tell J.J.

66

"Right," said Foxy Moll.

She had just come in from her conversation with Sergeant Daly. She felt pleased. She felt that she had bested him with her quip about a visit to Sheila. As for what he said about seeing no one, she had not the slightest intention of doing what he said. How did he think she was going to survive if she did not see anyone; not that she had any regular callers at that moment in time although one would turn up. One always did.

"Who'll help Mammy peel some spuds for tonight?"

"Me," said Helena, "me."

6 7

It was nearly the end of Wednesday and Tommy was in the dairy. Tommy hung the milking stool over his shoulder by its leather strap and lifted two empty pails. He went out. He heard Badger in the turf shed chopping wood. Tommy crossed the yard and carried on up Caesars' farm lane until he came to the Crib Field on his left. Foxy Moll's cottage was ahead of him. He opened the gate and went in.

The Crib Field was small and six cows with full udders grazed there. When they saw Tommy come in the cows began to amble towards him. He milked them one after the other and as he milked he noticed that the light had started to go.

He finished. He swung the stool over his shoulder and hoisted the buckets. The shortest day was not far away, he thought, and as he did not want to have to mess around with a storm lantern when he did the afternoon milking he would have to remember to come out a bit earlier in future.

He started towards the gate. He could hear the cows move around behind and grass being wrenched from the ground. The buckets were heavy and there was the stool as well so he went slow. The milk in the buckets was still warm. He could feel faint warmth from the milk with his knuckles. He could also smell the fresh milk smell that rose up out of the pails, a lovely mix of cow and grass and dairy.

He got to the gate and set the buckets and the stool down and opened the gate and carried everything out and closed the gate. He felt the wind on his back as it blew from the south. He pondered. Would it bring rain? He hoped not. He did not care to milk in the rain on wet ground. The muscle at the top of his left arm felt tender. He circled the shoulder a few times and then began to massage the muscle with his right hand.

As he did this Tommy gazed at the point where the end of the farm lane met the public road. Tommy's mind was empty and he did not expect to see anything and he did not look for anything, so he was surprised when he saw that someone stood at the end of the lane watching him. Tommy saw the figure wore a trench coat and a hat. Even in the half-light he could make these out. He also thought by the way the figure stood that he knew who it was, although why he of all men should stand at the bottom of Caesars' lane and watch him come out of the Crib Field with two buckets of milk and a milking stool on a Wednesday evening was a mystery.

Then as if he had just realised he had been spotted, the figure began to move towards some thinned hedge at the side of the lane. As he did the figure's coat rose and Tommy saw that he did indeed wear the riding breeches that Tommy was pretty sure were called jodhpurs and which Tommy knew were the only type of trouser the figure wore. Yes, thought Tommy, he was right, it was the man he had thought it was, and then a second after Tommy thought this the figure slipped into the hedge and was gone.

Tommy picked up the buckets and the stool and began to move along the lane towards the yard and as he went he wondered what on earth J.J. had been up to at the end of the lane and why he had wanted to watch him at the twilit end of that Wednesday.

68

As he made his way from his hiding place behind the thinned hedge and back out to Caesars' lane J.J. wondered if Tommy had seen him. It had not been absolutely dark so perhaps he had. Well what odds, he thought. Even if Tommy had and could identify him, so what? The Guards would not be able to tie one sighting as night fell to what was to come, no way. He sniffed the air and as he did J.J. noticed that the wind was on its way from the south.

69

A few minutes later Tommy came into the yard. It was dusk now but still not night. The storm lantern was lit and hung on a hook over the outside tap. Badger, he saw, stood at the pen and talked through the bars to Lively Lady who was wolfing her dinner from a dog-pan. Tommy went into the dark dairy. He had no need of a light. He knew where everything went. He put the stool on the nail it hung from and the pails of milk in the cold store. Mrs Caesar would churn them into butter in the morning. She always churned on a Thursday morning.

Tommy came out of the dairy. He needed to wash his hands before he went in for supper.

He crossed the dark yard to the outside tap. Badger was there already, the top of his head and his white streak of hair lit by the lantern hanging on the nail in the wall. The tap was on and water streamed from the faucet. Badger washed Lively Lady's dog-pan. He was always very conscientious about everything to do with his dogs was the old Badger, thought Tommy. The older man had no girl and as far as Tommy knew he had not ever had a girl but then what did he need a girl for when the dogs were his life?

Badger twisted the tap off and turned and shook the dog-pan.

"Is the milk in the dairy?" he said.

"It is. Two good pails – plenty of butter in them."

"I think she has mince and onions for supper." It was what the Boss, as they sometimes called her, usually made on Wednesday evening and it was a dinner they were both partial too.

"Lovely," said Tommy. "I'll just wash my hands here."

He stepped forward and turned on the tap.

"Will you bring the lantern in?" said Badger.

"I will of course," said Tommy.

As Tommy rubbed his hands under the cold spear of water, Badger leaned the wet dog-pan against the wall to dry and went to the pen and said good night to Lively Lady. Then he headed across the yard towards the back door.

70

From where he lay on the hearth in front of the fire, Foxy Moll's dog Little Sam lifted his head and cocked his ears. Little Sam yapped. Someone was outside the cottage.

"Shush," Foxy Moll said.

Foxy Moll put down the stocking she darned. She stood and crossed the floor towards the door and Little Sam followed. She opened the door. Little Sam bolted out and ran down towards the turf house and began to bark at it.

"Who's there?" said Foxy Moll.

"Close the door, don't let the children out."

She knew the voice. She would have known it anywhere. She closed the door.

"It's closed, the children won't see," she said.

He came out of the turf house. Like his voice, she would have recognised his outline anywhere as well. It was J.J. Little Sam got behind him and barked twice.

"Little Sam be quiet," Foxy Moll said.

"Come here," J.J. said.

They went down and around the gable end. J.J. wore his hat pulled down on his forehead so that his eyes were shaded but she could just see the lower part of his face. He smiled.

"Hello," he said.

Foxy Moll felt herself tremble. It was a little relief mixed with a lot of surprise. She had never imagined that something like this might happen. Just as she had done with every man before him, once J.J. had left that was it, she had accepted he was gone and she would not see him again. Yes, she had pined and she had yearned but she had not and did not run dream scenes in her head nor did she ever allow herself to think that he would be back. No, when J.J. had left she had believed that she would never see him again, except perhaps at a distance in the street, and she accepted that it was over. It was not difficult. This was how she was with every man before J.J. and she did not doubt it was how she would be with every man who followed him.

"Little Sam you call your dog?" said J.J.

"Yes."

J.J. turned and clicked his fingers at the animal. Little Sam made a noise somewhere between a whine and a yap.

"He likes you," said Foxy Moll, "which is unusual. He doesn't like everybody."

"I'm honoured."

He bent forward and held his hand out. Little Sam ran past his hand and began to sniff at the boots into which his jodhpurs were tucked. J.J. rubbed Little Sam's back.

"Good boy, Little Sam," he said.

He straightened up, pushed his hat back and looked straight into Foxy Moll's eyes.

"I've come to take you out. Are you busy?"

Foxy Moll thought of her half-darned stocking which she had left by the fire with the needle threaded through the top. That could wait. She thought of the children. Judy would mind them.

"Will we be long?"

He shook his head.

"Are we going to the Dugout?"

He shook his head again.

"Where are we going?"

"That's for me to know and you to find out."

"Oh, a surprise," she said. "How long will we be? An hour? Two?"

"Two," he said.

"I'll get my hat and coat."

She slipped back inside and closed the door. She lifted a lit candle and went to the bedroom. She found an old lipstick with a stub of red at the bottom. She went to her mirror. It was set in the door of a rickety wardrobe that Miss Cooney had given her. The mirror was freckled and around the edges the silver had flaked away. She leaned towards the middle where the reflection was best. There was not enough light to see very much but she knew right well what she would see if there were. Lines had started to show around her eyes and her mouth and across her forehead.

She coated her lips and rolled them. The red was quite lovely, she thought – at least she remembered it as such. She lifted her eyes from her lips and tried to see the image that floated in front of her. All she was able to see was the shape of her head and her hair pinned up behind. It had begun to lose its lustre. It was not as red as it had been when she had been younger; the colour seemed to have faded out of it over the previous couple of years. There were grey threads as well around her temples and behind her ears. She was getting old and she had started to look like her mother when she had gotten old. Well what did she expect, she thought. She was thirty-nine.

She dabbed on some eau de toilette that had been another gift from Miss Cooney and then she found her hat and her coat and put them on. She carried the candle back to the other room. She gave instructions to Judy about when the children were to go to bed: they were all there other than Daniel, although he was expected in a short while. He always came over after work.

"Tell Daniel to hang on," she said. "I'll be back in a couple of hours, about nine."

"Why are you going out?" said Brendan.

"I have to, but I'll be back and I'll give you a big kiss."

With Little Sam at her heels she went out and closed the door. She found J.J. where he waited beyond the gable.

"Well, I'm as ready as I'll ever be," she said.

"Is he coming too?"

J.J. pointed at Little Sam.

"He won't be parted from me," she said.

"Fair enough."

She glanced at J.J. She wondered had he noticed the lipstick. Would he comment? No, he would not – it was too dark to see.

"I'm sure you look as good as you smell," he said.

She felt gratified and a lovely surge of warmth rose up from somewhere deep inside.

"Let's go," J.J. said.

He linked her arm and started to walk her towards the gate at the back of the cottage and Little Sam ran on ahead. This was the way they always took when they went to the Dugout. She was puzzled.

"I thought we weren't going to the Dugout?"

"We're not. But we'll walk past it."

"So, where are we going?"

"I said, it's a surprise."

The dark fields were damp and dank and to protect their shoes they stuck to the edges where the grass was longer and the ground drier. As they went they talked about the weather and the prices of goods and the shortages occasioned by the war. It was inconsequential but pleasant. She felt cheerful and hopeful. Although she found the idea incredible, perhaps they were about to start again. That would teach Sergeant Daly a lesson, she thought. That would put him in his place.

71

After a good walk they arrived at the abandoned house that belonged to Mr Lynch whose farm was on the east side of Caesars' place: a gloomy structure under a dark night sky. There were no stars and no moon.

"I've never been here before," said Foxy Moll although she had always known of its existence. "Didn't that man – what was he called?"

"Cormac Mercer," said J.J.

"Yes, him, didn't he live here?"

"He did."

"He wrote stories and poems."

"He did, and they're not very good either."

"Oh," said Foxy Moll.

"It's all guff about the little people and Irish colleens and wily peasants tricked up for an English audience."

Although she had never read any of the writer's work she had always understood that he was rather good and she felt perplexed by J.J.'s opinion but then she reminded herself that he liked his opinions and the more they ran contrary to established opinion the more he liked them so it was no wonder that J.J. did not like Cormac Mercer.

She followed J.J. through the old gate and along the path through the unruly garden. She thought she heard a noise from inside the house. This surprised her. Who could be in there? Screw? Nutley? She dismissed the thought but still she was sure she had heard something.

"Is there someone in there?"

J.J. rapped on the door twice. Now she did hear a definite and identifiable noise inside: the sound of feet as they advanced in the hallway behind the door.

"Yes," J.J. said in a low tone.

At Foxy Moll's feet Little Sam let out a strange quiet bark.

The door opened. It was Screw and Nutley. Both men greeted her by name. Their manner was jocular. Foxy Moll's reaction was cool and considered. Why were they here? Why had J.J. not mentioned them? Her thoughts turned grim: well one thing was for sure, if they were about J.J. could forget any ideas about her and him starting again.

"Who's this?" Screw nodded at Little Sam.

"My new little dog," said Foxy Moll.

"In you go, Foxy Moll," said J.J.

They all filed in and Little Sam followed as they went through to the shuttered kitchen that was lit by lanterns and some candles. Little Sam began to run around the kitchen and sniff at the furniture and the corners where the floorboards and the wainscoting met. Foxy Moll noticed the tins of food on the second table and the bed with the blanket and the water drum. J.J. and his associates had been here for a while, she realised.

"I've a surprise for you, Foxy Moll," said Nutley.

He held up a bottle of Powers whiskey, one of the extra big bottles that she knew they had in pubs behind the bar to dispense shorts out of. She wondered if it were stolen.

"You'll have a drink, won't you?"

Her vague sense of disgruntlement began to recede. A drink, she thought, yes, she would like a drink.

"I will," she said. "Why not?"

There were glasses on the table lit by the yellow gentle light of the lantern.

"You have glasses," said Foxy Moll.

"Nothing but the best for the lady," said Nutley.

He uncorked the bottle and poured out four measures. The cork went back into the bottle's neck. Screw took a glass. J.J. took two glasses and handed one to Foxy Moll. Nutley took the fourth glass.

"Foxy Moll, your health," said J.J.

The four clinked their glasses together and drank. The first mouthful made the inside of her mouth hurt and she shivered. The second went down easier. The third she scarce noticed. Within seconds of the third gulp that emptied the glass, Foxy Moll felt the liquor warm and soften and loosen her deep inside.

"Another?" said Nutley.

Foxy Moll held out her glass. As Nutley poured she noticed J.J.'s shotgun case stood against the wall and the folded green tarpaulin on which the bottom of the case rested.

"What's the gun for?" she said.

"To shoot a fox," said J.J.

He held his glass out for a refill and so did Screw. The measures were generous. They must want to be drunk, she thought, and they must want her drunk too.

"What fox?" she said.

"The one who's been worrying your birds," he said.

"Where did you hear that?"

"Mr O'Shaughnessy heard it from Daniel."

"He must have taken something up wrong, so he must. I haven't had a fox around this last while."

"Oh," said J.J. "Well, I'm still going to get the gun out later and have a blast, whatever the case. Haven't fired her in ages."

"In the dark?" she said. "You can't shoot anything when it's dark. You can't see."

"You'd be amazed what I can do in the dark," said J.J.

She heard Screw and Nutley giggle.

"Well, lady and gentlemen," said J.J., "I'd like to propose a toast: to quieter, calmer, slower times."

All clinked and drank. Little Sam, she noticed, had gotten onto the bed and lain down.

Nutley refilled the glasses with generous measures again. So they had brought her here to get drunk with her and to get her drunk. Why did they want to do that? Were they about to ask her to do something for them? She decided that was in all likelihood what this was. This was the prelude to a request. Well, whatever it was, whatever they wanted, she was not about to do it. No, she was not, although she would take their drink. She was happy to take their drink. She would take their drink but she would not give them anything in return.

They pulled out the chairs and sat around the table. They drank on and she began to notice the smell of the room. It smelled of male sweat and old plaster with a vague hint of semen. Drink did that to her: it gave her an uncommon sensitivity to smells.

While she pondered these smells, and revelled in them too, she listened as J.J. and Screw and Nutley began to talk about the past and their exploits as renegades who would not have the Treaty. She was not surprised that Screw and Nutley became heated and excited and boastful but she was surprised that J.J. did. Was he drunk? Yes, he was, she thought, but why? He was always so careful and so sober and so controlled and she had always thought that he was not the sort of man liable to ever let himself be affected by drink.

Then she had another thought, a revolutionary thought that startled her. Maybe he was a little gone, maybe he had let himself slip because he was sorry he had thrown her away. He had gotten drunk because he was sad or even miserable and he wished he had not thrown her over and he really wanted her back.

Foxy Moll enjoyed this thought for a second or two and then decided that it was tomfoolery. If J.J. had wanted her back, if he really wanted her back, he would not have arranged to meet Screw and Nutley here. Oh no, if he had wanted her again he would have ensured that they were alone but here they were: J.J. and Screw and Nutley. J.J. did not want her back, she thought. So why had he gotten drunk if not because he missed her? The answer came to her in a flash. It was not that complicated, she decided. He was drunk because they all were. Everyone else had taken a drink so he had just followed suit. It was as simple as that.

72

It was eleven o'clock and the McCarthy children were fretful. Where was their mother? Why was she not back?

Daniel had not returned to O'Shaughnessys'. Now he took the storm lantern and went through the dark windy fields all the way to the Dugout. He went inside the Dugout. There was a rat in the corner but there was no sign of his mother. He went up the Stubble Field. He passed the place in the hedge that Badger had filled earlier. There was no sign of his mother anywhere. He went back through the darkness to the cottage. Everyone was still up.

7 3

Foxy Moll was very drunk now and her thoughts were rapid and they churned. Each time, over the course of the evening, the four of them had clinked glasses she had always looked J.J. in the face but not once had he met her gaze, she thought, not once. Why was that? Perhaps the reason was the sergeant. He must know about Sergeant Anthony Daly and he must disapprove. Well, of course he must. She decided that, even though she and Anthony were no longer together and since his wife's arrival at the start of the month she had not even seen him till he had visited that afternoon, J.J. was furious and jealous and actually that was why he had not once given her a proper look and, what was more, it now occurred to her, that was why he had brought her here: that was what he actually wanted to talk about. No sooner had she formed this thought than she began to feel annoyed. What business of his was it what she did and who she saw and whom she consorted with? None of it was any of his business. No, of course it was not. He was the one who had finished with her so he only had himself to blame. If J.J. had stuck with her she would still be with him. Oh yes he only had himself to blame. He had thrown her over and now he had to live with the consequences. He knew her history. He knew the sort of woman she was. Everyone in New Inn did. She was loyal for as long as something lasted but once it was over she never brooded. If she was abandoned she moved on and she had moved on. He had finished with her and she had moved on to Anthony who had then finished with her and now she was free and ready to start with someone new. It was as simple as that and J.J. could just lump it.

"I can't get stocious," she heard J.J. say. "I need a clear head. I have to shoot a fox."

J.J. stood and stretched his arms over his head. His shadow appeared on the ceiling above.

"Sure, you've not enough taken to make you drunk," said Nutley. "It's sharpened you, that's all."

"Will it rain?" said J.J.

She considered this question. It had felt like rain, she thought, when they had walked here but it was also very cold. She noticed J.J.'s stiff leather gun case again. Earlier in the evening it had been in the corner stood on top of a folded tarpaulin but now it was by the door. How had she not noticed him move it? She must be drunk, she thought, drunker than she realised. Or maybe she was so caught up with the surge of her thoughts that she had just not noticed.

Foxy Moll shifted her gaze from the gun case to the bed, where Little Sam lay and watched her with one ear cocked, and then back to J.J. Her attention was drawn to the bulge in the right-hand pocket of J.J.'s trench coat. That was a box of cartridges, she guessed. They were Eley Grand Prix cartridges No.5. That was written on the side of each cartridge. How did she know this? She must have been told. She must have asked J.J. and he must have told her, although she could not remember that conversation. Maybe he had shown her one. Yes, that seemed more likely because that would explain how she not only knew their full name but she also knew the look of the Eley Grand Prix No.5 cartridges with their dark red waxy covers and the brass discs at the bottom with the indentation in the middle where the hammer struck to fire the charge and unleash the contents.

"I'm going to have a sniff about," said J.J. "I'll be back presently."

J.J. stepped towards the door.

"Don't touch the gun," he called back and then she heard him go down the passage and out the door.

Why did he say that? He knew, did he not, that she would never touch it? She had never fired a gun. She had never even held a gun. She did not like guns. She did not like the noise of guns or the oily smell of them. She did not like what a gun did either and now that she came to think about it she did not want this fox he planned to shoot to die and the thought that it would die made her feel wretched. Then she told herself to stop being sentimental. It was a fox. It had to go. Of course it did. It had to die so her hens could live. She needed her hens. She needed their eggs. She had mouths to feed and children to raise. That was what J.J. cared about and that was why he had come to do this. Yet how had he heard about this fox? He had said Mr O'Shaughnessy but surely that was wrong. Daniel would not have said there was a fox when there was not. Perhaps Badger had seen this fox. He took his hound out for a walk every morning, did he not? Yes, she decided, that was it. Badger had been out with his dog and he had seen it – it was entirely possible that his hound had raised the fox – and this information had then gotten back to J.J. as everything that ever happened in New Inn had a habit of doing. Then she remembered again it was now night and she wondered again how J.J. could see enough in the dark to shoot. Well, it was not possible, was it? So what was all this talk about shooting the fox? It was nonsense. It was just flannel. It didn't mean anything. In which case, why had J.J. brought her there? Earlier she had thought it was because of the sergeant but since nothing had been said about him she assumed that was not the case. So why had he brought her? Was it really just to ply her with drink? Was that it? Incredible, she thought, but maybe that was it. They were men. They were lonely. They missed the company of a woman. That was why J.J. had brought her: it was so they could drink and talk with her. Well, why not? Sometimes people did not have motives or secrets but instead they had needs and desires and in this instance what these ones needed and desired was a woman to talk to and she was the only one available.

Now Foxy Moll's thoughts drifted to later in the evening. As she no longer felt angry at J.J., indeed, on account of the drink, as she now felt warm and friendly towards every living thing including these three, she decided she would take J.J. and Screw and Nutley back to her cottage. They would all sit by her fire. They would all have tea. They would all have spuds and butter. They would wake her children. They would all sing songs and tell stories and they would all be happy and perhaps they would even talk of the fox and how clever J.J. would shoot it later with his long gun.

The thoughts swirled in her head. Then she remembered something that her mother had always said when she had come home from the orphanage to live with her: "Ah, Foxy Moll, you're always thinking, will you never stop?" Her mother had been right. She had thoughts all the time. They never stopped. These had turned to questions and she had put these to her mother and her mother had given her answers which had given rise to more thoughts and more questions and then more answers and on and on it went and it never stopped: "Ah, Foxy Moll, will you never stop?"

Screw materialised in front of her. Where had he come from? "Here," he said.

He handed her a glass. She drank.

74

It was his habit to shave last thing at night instead of first thing in the morning and so, late that Wednesday night, Sergeant Daly was soaping his face in his kitchen by lamplight when he heard a car pull up outside his house. He turned his head. Was it a Guards' car? He did not think so. He looked at the clock on the mantelpiece over the stove. It was after midnight. But if it was not someone from the New Inn station then who had come to see him at this time?

He dried the soap from his face and carried the lamp into the hall. He put the lamp on the hall table and turned up the wick. The front door at the end had two glass panels. The glass was frosted and he saw the blurred outline of someone as they approached. From the sound of his footfalls and the swagger in his step he could tell that, whoever it was, the visitor was a man but that was all he knew. He realised that if he did not get to the door and open it quick then the visitor would rap on the door and that might wake Sheila above and he did not want that. Any time that she was asleep and got woken she could never get back to sleep again and would be an awful weasel the day after.

"I'm coming," Sergeant Daly called in a quiet tone.

He sped down the hall to the door and pulled the top and bottom bolts and opened the door back. He was very surprised to find Johnny Spink, the infamous J.J., stood on his doorstep in a trench coat and jodhpurs. Since Sergeant Daly had arrived in New Inn they had glimpsed one another in the street a few times but they had never spoken.

"What do you want?" said Sergeant Daly.

It was then that he noticed the smell. His visitor did not appear intoxicated but the whiskey reek was unmistakable.

"You've been drinking."

"Really?" said J.J. "I'd wait until I've finished before saying any more. "

Although he did not summon it, the memory of Mr Bermingham and his bit of paper came straightaway to Sergeant Daly and with his inner-eye he saw the typed words: "FOXY MOLL. RIP. IMMINENT" with the awful picture of a stick woman hanging by a rope from a gallows. He knew this visit had to have something to do with that. He knew it for sure. The muscles of his thighs trembled. His knees felt rubbery.

"Foxy Moll ..." said J.J. as if he had just read the sergeant's mind.

Sergeant Daly felt hot and he felt the vessels in his temples throb. There was the taste of sick at the back of his mouth.

J.J. drew a finger across his throat.

"She's dead," he said. His tone was blunt and his voice was quiet.

Was this a subterfuge? Was this a ruse? It took Sergeant Daly a second to decide no, it was neither. This was true. She was. He heard a roar in his head, and then the roar stopped and he knew he was in terrible trouble: the worst.

"The person who 'finds' the body," said J.J., "will be the one you'll want to arrest and charge. As it won't take you long to discover, he did it, or that's what everyone will think, which comes to the same thing."

Sergeant Daly's bladder ached. He wanted to pee. "I've a mind to find the right person, not any person," said Sergeant Daly.

"And I've told you who that is."

"The one who finds her?"

"Yes," said J.J., "that's what I told you."

"Why?" said Sergeant Daly.

"Generosity. Big heartedness."

Sergeant Daly let out a snort.

"Sergeant, it would not be good for your health for anyone to know how friendly you and her were. You need to keep your name well clear of what's coming. Even you can see that."

Sergeant Daly kept his expression neutral but he knew what had just been said was true. For a start there was the carry-on before Sheila's arrival, on top of which Mr Bermingham had told him what would happen, he had not stopped it and now it had happened. If his meeting earlier with Mr Bermingham was ever discovered by anyone in the Guards, well, he'd be out the door so quick his feet would not touch the ground.

"You do what I say," said J.J., "you'll be in the clear. You'll keep your uniform, your rank – you might even get promoted."

"What if I don't do what you say?" said Sergeant Daly.

"You're finished."

"What's to stop me coming after you?"

"You do that and I'll do a Samson. I'll pull down the temple. I'll take you with me. I'll say you stole her from me. Imagine the talk then? I'll say this one last time: the person who 'finds' the body, he's the one."

J.J. turned to go and then turned back.

"Oh yes, Tommy Reid, you'll have to shut him up or he'll blab and ruin everything. But you're good at that sort of thing, aren't you, shutting people up? Good morning."

He walked off. Sergeant Daly closed the door and bolted it. He felt dizzy and light-headed and nauseous and fearful.

He took the lamp and went back to the kitchen and sank onto a chair. He heard J.J.'s words in his head: "I'll do a Samson … I'll say you stole her from me … Imagine the talk then …" It might be news to him about J.J. and Foxy Moll but he saw immediately how dangerous this was to him.

It was twenty minutes before Sergeant Daly felt strong enough to stand up and resume shaving.

When he finished he went upstairs and slipped carefully into bed. Sheila stirred but stayed asleep and he thought that was a blessing.

He lay in darkness with his eyes open and stared up: it was so dark that he could not see the ceiling boards. He felt his heart pumping. His thoughts churned. If J.J. really did put it about he had stolen Foxy Moll from him … and if Mr Bermingham weighed in and revealed how he had warned him … well that would destroy everything: his marriage, his career, even his pension. He would be finished in the Guards; he would be finished in the Free State. He would have to go to England and work in a factory or on a building site and he would die old and forgotten and ashamed in a bed-sitting room in some awful town like Coventry where the Irish were hated and no one would come to his funeral.

He told himself to stop thinking the way he was thinking but his mind would not obey. All he could think about was his exposure and destruction. There was nothing else for it, he decided after several minutes: he would count. If he counted long enough and hard enough he would lose himself in the numbers and then his mind would go quiet and blessed sleep would come. He counted first to one hundred then five hundred then one thousand, two thousand, three thousand, four thousand, five thousand …

75

At Marlhill Cottage the McCarthy children stayed up, sat around the fire and watched the door until two o'clock on Thursday morning. Then Judy put Brendan and Helena to bed in their mother's room and made the settle beds in the kitchen for the rest of them. Outside the wind started to move around from the south to the north and it began to rain. As he lay and waited for sleep Daniel calculated that he would have five hours of sleep and wake at seven and get dressed and creep out without waking the others and walk to O'Shaughnessys' farm. When he got there the first thing he would have to do would be to apologise that he had not come back the night before or sent word that he would not be back either. He would tell Mr O'Shaughnessy that the reason why he had stayed at home was because his mother had gone out and had not come back. Daniel hoped that would placate his employer. Mr O'Shaughnessy was not a bad fellow and Daniel did not imagine there would be a problem.

76

Foxy Moll had her head on her arms that in turn rested on the table when she was woken by something. She heard something. What was it? She heard rain. It was hard rain that threw itself against the walls and the roof above. There was also wind. She opened her eyes and was most surprised to see rested on the edge of the table a few inches away from her face the barrels of J.J.'s shotgun. She also noticed that the lantern and the glasses and the whiskey bottle had been taken off the table.

Was this a dream? She let her eye wander along the barrel until it came to the triggers. There was a finger around the first. Beyond the hand there was the cuff of a trench coat. It was J.J.'s. What was he at? Why would he want to point the gun at her face with his finger on the trigger? Not long after this thought she sensed furtive movement behind her and the sound of something heavy being unfolded.

She looked again at the end of the gun that was pointed at her face. She saw the ends of the two barrels. What was it they were? Yes, they were an eight, the number eight, she remembered, but this eight was not stood up. This eight lay on its side. It was a sleeping eight, a drunken eight, she thought. No it was not those. It was something else. What was that phrase? Yes, yes she had it now. They were the dead eight, that's what they were, the dead eight.

Now she knew what she had seen on Screw and Nutley's faces all evening. What she had seen was shame and excitement. They had known that this was what was to come. They had known it when they had come and opened the door. They had known it when they had clinked her glass with their glasses and drank to her health. They had known it all along and that was why they had gotten drunk. That was why J.J. had gotten drunk. They were ashamed by their knowledge of what was to come.

Her children flashed before her inner eye: her six living children and her single dead child at different ages and different stages and she wondered would Daniel and Judy manage with her gone and she wondered if Miss Cooney might help?

Only one thing could happen now, she thought.

"Go," she heard J.J. say.

There were rustles and something fell on her, something heavy like a blanket, not a blanket, no, the tarpaulin, it was the tarpaulin she had seen folded in the corner, it had been thrown over her – that would be Screw or Nutley or the two of them – and she felt its weight now and she smelled its smell now, a smell of engine oil and a smell of grass, and there was no light or much less than there had been although it was not darkness she was in, no, not complete darkness for the light of the lantern came through the tarpaulin but it only came through very faint, almost not at all, and she heard a bark that would be Little Sam on the bed and far away he sounded, ever so far away and sad and desolate as if he knew – what did he know, what did he know: what she knew, that was what he knew, and then Little Sam barked again and it seemed even further away this time and even sadder, it sounded like he said "No" and she wondered was it possible that a dog could say a word, could say to someone, to J.J. who rested his gun on the table with the end in under the tarpaulin a few inches from her face, and she thought to herself she was drunk, oh yes, very drunk, and her mind was woozy and her mind was full of these strange thoughts that surged and churned, and her children were at home sat by the fire and they watched the door and waited to hear her come up to the door with Little Sam behind and call ahead to them, "It's your mammy, children, I'm home," and then the door open and her come in but that was not about to happen, it would never happen because in a fraction of a second the hammer would fall and then a great wall of metal would stream out of the gun and strike her, finish her, end her, give her … the dead eight.

77

Badger woke. It was very dark outside and his bedroom was very dark. He heard two sounds: the faint tick of the alarm on the table by his bed and the loud sound of the rain that banged on the glass of his window. The rain came from the north and it fell hard and heavy and he guessed that the wind that moved it blew hard and heavy from the north. He wondered about the cows out in the Crib Field. He would have to see how wet the ground was and how wet they were. It might be time to bring them inside.

He looked in the direction of his clock. Did he want to light the candle and see the time? He considered. No. It was night: deepest darkest night. It did not matter what the time was. Whether he knew the time or not would not change a thing. It would still be deepest darkest night for a while. Then light would start to show around the edges of his curtains and the walls and the ceiling and everything in his room would become dimly visible. The alarm would go. He would wake and fumble and push the switch that controlled the bell from "On" to "Off" and lie there and think about the day to come.

He began to drift as he came to the end of this thought and fell asleep. Later he woke again. It was still very dark. Perhaps it was now three in the morning, he thought. It still rained but the noise made when the rain struck his window was no longer hard and insistent; it was softer and gentler. The rain had slowed and thinned. With luck, he thought, it would have stopped by the morning.

78

It was very early Thursday morning and it was not night and it was not dawn. It was the time right in between and the light was pewter. Screw was first. He had one end of the rolled-up tarpaulin. Nutley followed. He had the other end. J.J. followed with the gun. Little Sam followed J.J. and whined and whimpered for his mistress who was wrapped up in the tarpaulin.

It was very quiet out in the fields at this time. There was no birdsong. No cows lowed and no sheep bleated and no dogs barked and no donkeys brayed. The only sounds were the gasps and rasps of their breath which got heavier the further they walked and the sound of their feet as they scuffed on the ground and now and again the noise as a gate squeaked or clanged when it was opened and then a few moments after as it was closed again and just twice, when they had to negotiate ditches, there were very hard pants and grunts because the body was awkward to carry and once there was a clatter at a stone wall when a couple of stones tumbled from the top and thumped onto the ground and then soft scrapes as J.J. put these back and then finally the sound of Little Sam as he jumped the wall.

They got to the hole in the hedge of the Dugout Field that Badger had repaired the day before. J.J. pulled away the bits of brush and bush. Screw and Nutley went through and put down their bundle and opened it. There was Foxy Moll on her back in her mismatched boots with a large hole in her neck and the lower left side of her face.

"Put her there."

J.J. pointed at a spot a bit further back from the gap and further into the Stubble Field. Screw got the corpse under the armpits and Nutley got the legs and together they manhandled the body to the spot that J.J. had indicated. Nutley dropped the legs and then bent down and lifted the left leg and crooked it over the right.

"She's wearing different boots," he said.

Little Sam jumped up onto the corpse.

"Get the dog off," said J.J.

Screw lifted Little Sam away.

"Pull the tarpaulin back."

Nutley obliged.

J.J. pointed the gun down at Foxy Moll's blasted face and pulled the trigger. The pellets tore away the left side of her head and buried themselves in the ground below and bits of bone and tooth and skin and sinew and tissue and vein were scattered around Foxy Moll's head on the damp ground.

"What do you think?"

Screw dropped Little Sam and the dog jumped onto the body. Screw examined the ground around Foxy Moll's head.

"Yes," he said, "I think you'd think this was where she was shot."

The three folded the bloody tarpaulin and headed off. They reached the Dugout.

"You two go on," said J.J., "and get packed up. I'll stay. I want to be sure our boy finds her. I'll see you back at the house."

"I'm gasping for a smoke," said Screw.

"Me too," said Nutley.

J.J. took a packet of Sweet Afton out of his pocket and gave two cigarettes to Screw. "Have you matches?"

Screw took a packet out of his pocket and shook them.

"See you later."

Screw and Nutley headed away and J.J. went behind the Dug-out. As it grew light he thought about the evening before and the moment when Tommy saw him on Caesars' lane and he realised that he would have to change how he dressed in case Tommy put two and two together. Just to be on the safe side.

79

Sergeant Daly got to the Guards' station in New Inn some minutes before eight o'clock. He went straight to the day room. Gralton was behind the counter. He had just taken over from the night man.

"You're early," said Gralton. "Good morning, Sergeant."

"No, it isn't," said Sergeant Daly.

"Oh dear, that bad?"

"Worse than bad."

"Oh dear, oh dear."

"If anyone comes from Marlhill, Mr or Mrs Caesar, or Badger, or that other employee ..." said Sergeant Daly.

"Tommy Reid."

"Him, or anybody from the cottage, any of those McCarthys, or the man O'Shaughnessy, or anybody from Marlhill, you put them in a side office and you lock the door and you do not let them talk to anyone in this station and you come and get me from my office immediately, do you understand?"

"I do," said Gralton.

"And when you go off, you tell the next man the same."

"I will."

Sergeant Daly hurried out.

80

The alarm went off. Badger sat up in bed and turned it off. It was eight o'clock on Thursday 21 November. He could see some light around the edges of his curtains. He got out of bed and pulled the curtains but the room was still dark. He lit the candle. It did not make much difference but it cheered him up to see the flame burn. He liked the smell of melted wax and always had done ever since he had been a boy.

He washed his face and ears and hands in cold water at the ewer and basin. He took off his pyjamas and pulled on his underwear and his work suit. He wet his hair and combed it down. He ran a hand around his chin. He needed to shave. Perhaps he would do it that night; he would have hot water then.

He put out the candle and lifted his boots and went downstairs in his socks. The Caesars slept downstairs in the winter and he did not want to wake them.

In the kitchen at the hearth he bent over the fire and cleared off the ash that lay on top of the fire to reveal a clump of embers that glowed orange. He threw on paper and kindling and added a few sods of turf on top of these and got the fire going and then he swung the crane with the kettle into place, the water in the kettle slopping about as he moved it.

Then he lit the cooking stove after which, still in his socks, he climbed upstairs and knocked twice on Tommy's door.

"Tommy, Tommy," he said.

"What?" came Tommy's voice through the wood.

Badger opened the door. The room was dark. It smelled of candle wax. Tommy often fell asleep and left the candle to burn out. The figure under the scrunched up bedclothes stirred and lifted its head.

"Is it that time?"

"It is, Tommy."

Tommy yawned. "Is it cold?"

"It is. I've the kettle on."

"I'll be down, so."

Badger went back to the kitchen and opened the window shutters back then lit two lamps and trimmed the wicks. The kettle boiled and the steam fluttered the lid. He made tea and poured it and cut slices off the loaf of wheaten and fetched butter and apple jelly from the larder. Tommy arrived. Although the fire blazed the kitchen was still chilly so rather than sit at the table they both stood with their backs to the fire and drank the tea and ate the bread and apple jelly.

"It was pouring last night," said Badger.

"It was," Tommy said, "but now it's stopped, thank God."

When they had finished breakfast Badger and Tommy went out to the yard. Although the rain had stopped some time earlier every surface was damp and a sharp wind blew down from the north as well and within seconds Badger felt his nose start to run. The two men fetched milk-pails from the dairy and two milking stools and went to the Crib Field. The ground squelched as they crossed to the cows. The animals were in the corner under an old beech where the ground was driest. They had huddled here overnight and kept themselves quite dry but despite the shelter of the tree the turf was soft and sodden and when Tommy and Badger sat on their stools the wooden legs sunk down several inches.

They milked the cows and carried the milk back and left it with the previous night's milk in the dairy. Then Tommy said that he would chop wood and went to the woodshed. Badger got Lively Lady from her pen and put her on a lead and set off. He followed the path as he did every morning. In the first and the second fields there were sheep and he counted these as he walked to check if any had strayed: none had. The numbers tallied.

He and his dog came to the third field along: the Dugout Field. It was an empty field so after they were through the gate and the gate was closed behind he slipped the lead off and let Lively Lady free. She bolted away in the direction of the Dugout and he watched as she moved here and there to follow scents. She moved well, he thought, and she might win at the weekend trial.

He started to move forward. He stared ahead and watched his dog and then he looked around and checked the field to see if anything was awry. Away to his right he noticed that the gap, which he had only just plugged the previous day, between the Dugout Field and the Stubble Field gaped open again. Perhaps the winds overnight had blown aside the debris that he had piled into the space. He would have to fill it in. Then he became aware that not only was the gap open but someone lay on the other side of the gap just inside the Stubble Field. It was a woman, he thought, and worse he had a good idea who it was and then he decided that no, it was only his imagination and once he got over and checked it would turn out not to be what he suspected but just a bush.

He left the path and started to stride across the damp ground towards the other path that ran alongside the fence that he followed each morning on his way back to the farm with Lively Lady. He had his hands in his coat pockets and his collar turned up. Lively Lady ran ahead of him towards the gap then turned and ran back and came up beside him and huddled close to his leg and made a noise he had never heard her make before.

He felt his stomach flutter. His hands, which had been cold only a few moments earlier, were now hot and damp. His head was hot too. He stopped and took off his cloth cap and let the wind blow through his hair and cool his scalp. He wiped the now cold sweat droplets off his brow with his cuff. He put his hat back on. Rather than go all the way down to the gap he decided that the simplest and quickest thing to do was to cut over straight ahead to the fence and to climb up on it and use the height of it to see if he could make out what had happened lower down.

He hurried to the fence and climbed up and looked down to his left. The first thing he saw was a dog. He knew the dog. The dog was brown. The dog was Little Sam. The second thing he saw was what Little Sam sat on. It was a body. It was a woman's body. She lay on her back. She wore a blue dress (he saw the hem) and over the dress she wore a coat and from where he was the clothes she had on looked dry. He also noticed that one leg was crooked over the other and on one foot there was a black boot and on the other a brown one. Until now the head had been hidden by Little Sam but now he moved off the woman's chest and down to her pelvis and Badger saw her face was gone and in its place there was a deal of red pulp and behind the head he saw that her bright red hair was matted with gore and spread like a shroud and of course he knew full well who it was: it was Foxy Moll.

He was about to jump right over the fence and go down for a closer look but as he climbed up a rung Little Sam turned and saw him and growled. It was a terrible noise: very fierce and very angry. He decided not to go over and provoke the dog but to go back and report what he had seen to Mr and Mrs Caesar. They would know how to proceed.

He jumped down and put the lead on Lively Lady and began to run.

81

J.J. watched Badger sprint away towards the farmhouse while his greyhound loped at his side. For a man of his age he was pretty nifty, thought J.J., but then he had seen a sight that would make anyone run.

J.J. threw down the butt of the cigarette he smoked and stamped it into the ground and then he turned and began to walk away in the direction of the house on Lynchs' land.

8 2

Badger ran into the yard and put Lively Lady in her pen and did not stop to give her a drink of fresh water as was his usual routine but instead ran inside the farmhouse through the back door. Now he was in the scullery. On an ordinary day he would have removed his boots here but under the circumstances he did not take them off: he just ran across the kitchen and down the hall and up to the door of the Caesars' downstairs winter bedroom. He knocked twice very hard.

"Hello," he shouted.

"What is it?" Mr Caesar called from inside in a groggy voice.

"Can I open the door?"

"Course you can."

He opened the door. The curtains were closed. It was dark. There was a smell of perfume and also, he thought, a salty smell of pee.

"What is it? What's the matter?" said Mrs Caesar.

She had sat up in the bed. She had curlers in her hair and wore a white nightdress with roses embroidered on the shoulders.

"There's a woman," Badger said, "and she's in that gap in the fence between the Dugout and the Stubble Field, lying on the ground."

"Well, do you know who it is?"

When he had knocked on the Caesars' bedroom door he had planned to say who it was because he knew right well that it was Foxy Moll. Of course it was. He knew exactly who it was. He had seen her nearly every day for years and so he knew the cut of her and, even if he had not, the dog would have told him.

However, in between the moment when he had knocked on the door and the moment Mrs Caesar had asked her question, something had occurred to him: given Foxy Moll's pedigree it might be best that he did not recognise her. That way no one would think that he had anything to do with whatever had happened to her.

"No," he said. "I don't know who it is."

"And she's on the ground?

"Yes."

"A woman lying on the grass, really? Why would she be on the ground? The ground's soaking after last night's rain, isn't it?"

"Yes."

"Well, is she sleeping or what?

"I don't know."

"Did you go up to her?"

"No," said Badger.

"Why not?"

"I couldn't go near her because there was a dog on her chest and he was growling and that and I thought he'd bite."

"I don't follow," said Mr Caesar. "What exactly did Badger see?"

"A woman stretched on the ground and a cross dog sitting on her."

"And because of the dog I couldn't see her face," said Badger.

"How strange," said Mrs Caesar.

"It is," said Mr Caesar. "And you really couldn't recognise this woman?"

Badger shook his head. "No," he said.

"You'd better go to the Guards," said Mrs Caesar. "Don't bother with the pony and trap. Take the Mass Path, it'll be quicker. You'll be there in fifteen minutes or so if you're fast."

83

Gralton looked up and saw Badger hurtle in through the day-room door. Ever since Sergeant Daly had spoken to him earlier he had half expected something like this.

"You look hot," said Gralton. "What's the hurry?"

"The Guards must come to Marlhill Farm now," said Badger. He sounded very frightened and very troubled.

"Why do the Guards have to come to Marlhill Farm?" said Gralton.

"There's a woman."

"A woman?"

"Yes, and she's either sleeping on the ground near the Dugout or … I don't know …"

"Is she dead?" asked Gralton.

"Well, she's lying there anyway."

"How do you know it's a woman?"

"She's wearing women's clothes."

"Do you know who she is?"

"I don't."

"You've never seen her before?"

"I couldn't see her face."

"Oh," said the Guard.

"There was a dog ..."

"Yes."

"Stretched out on top of her."

"Right."

"And the dog stopped me seeing. I don't know who it is. I just know it's someone, stretched out, on the ground."

"Right. I'll get Sergeant Daly and we'll drive over and take a look." Gralton opened a door into a side room. "You wait in here. Get your breath. I'll be back in a tick."

Badger went in. Gralton closed and locked the door. A few minutes later he returned with Sergeant Daly. The sergeant asked Badger to tell him what happened.

"Every morning I take my dog for a walk, for exercise," he said. "She's a greyhound. We go down the fields by one path to the Dugout and back by a different path that comes up by the Stubble Field."

"So, this morning you were doing the same you do every morning?" said Sergeant Daly.

"Yes," said Badger, "and as I was going down towards the Dugout, I looked over to my right and saw there was a gap in the fence between the Dugout and the Stubble Field and there was someone lying on the ground in the gap, I thought, and then I went over and saw there was. It was a woman."

"How do you know it was a woman?"

"By her petticoat and her shoes," he said.

"Do you know the identity of this woman you saw?" said Sergeant Daly.

"No," said Badger. "I don't."

"But you're certain she's a woman?"

"Yes."

A replacement for Gralton in the day room was organised

and then the three men went out and got into a Wolseley car and began to drive towards Marlhill Farm.

"This woman, is she from the locality?" said Sergeant Daly.

"I don't know," said Badger. "I didn't go near her. I didn't know her or the dog and she might only have been sleeping."

They parked in the yard and got out. Badger led the two Guards through the back gate and then down the path that he usually travelled in the reverse direction because it was the way he went when he returned to the yard from his morning walks with Lively Lady. When they came into the Dugout Field he led them along the side of the fence.

"There's a gap in the fence further down and that's where I saw her," Badger said.

"Did you go through the gap earlier this morning?" said Sergeant Daly.

"No."

"So, how did you see her?"

"I climbed up on the fence and looked down the back."

"Show us where you climbed up," said Sergeant Daly, "and we'll look from there."

Badger brought them to the place and the three men climbed up on the fence and looked down to the left.

There was the body and the dog sat on the chest and the boots were mismatched: one was black and one was brown. Sergeant Daly remembered that he had noticed these boots the day before and as he did he knew just who it was.

"It's Moll McCarthy," said Sergeant Daly.

"God, it must be; look at that foxy head," said Badger.

"What's happened to her face?" said Gralton.

"I'll go," said Sergeant Daly.

He climbed down into the Stubble Field and jogged towards the body. Little Sam watched him but did not growl. Sergeant Daly bent over and lifted Little Sam up. The dog whined and wriggled a bit but otherwise did not object. Sergeant Daly saw that from her chin to her eyebrow the left side of Foxy Moll's face was gone. He noticed that there were white teeth and bone shards on the ground around her.

He stood and walked back to Badger and Gralton.

"Put the dog in the car and bring a sheet back."

84

Badger hurried off and returned. They put the sheet over the body. The sheet was a coarse flannel one with a huge yellow stain in the middle. The three then returned to the yard of Marlhill Farm. Little Sam yapped inside the car. Sergeant Daly told Gralton to start the car. He went into the farmhouse with Badger. He found Mr and Mrs Caesar and Tommy sat in the kitchen.

"What terrible news," said Mrs Caesar. "Who'd shoot a creature like Foxy?"

While Badger had gone back to get the sheet, Sergeant Daly calculated, he had told what he had seen and what he thought had happened. He should have told Badger not to say a word but it was too late for that now.

"We don't know that yet, Mrs Caesar," he said.

"But Badger said about her face. It must have been a gun, mustn't it?"

"You're all to stay here," said Sergeant Daly. "No one leaves, understand? No one, until the Guards come back."

"My wife has to churn in the dairy and we've a few cows need to be milked," said Mr Caesar.

"Is the dairy in the yard?" asked Sergeant Daly.

"Yes."

"That's fine, churn away. Now where are these cows you need to milk?"

Mr Caesar described the field. It was up the lane and well away from the Dugout.

Sergeant Daly agreed they could milk but do nothing else outside; then he swept out and got into the car.

85

A few minutes later the car with Sergeant Daly and Gralton pulled into the yard at the rear of the Guards' station.

Sergeant Daly went in and issued instructions in the day room: Superintendent Mahony was to be telephoned and given the news and four Guards were to go to Marlhill Farm: two to ensure that no one left the farmhouse and two to watch the body.

Sergeant Daly went back outside. Little Sam was in the front passenger seat. Gralton stroked him. Sergeant Daly threw Little Sam into the back and got in.

"Foxy Moll's," he said.

Without a word Gralton drove to Marlhill Cottage and nosed through the gate and stopped. The cottage door opened and Judy appeared with all the children except for Daniel. Sergeant Daly guessed that he must have gone to work.

"I wouldn't like to be in your shoes, having to tell them," said Gralton.

"I've done far worse," said Sergeant Daly.

He got out and closed the door. He opened the back passenger door and Little Sam jumped out. Little Sam bounded to the cottage door. Sergeant Daly took his hat from the back window ledge and put it on. He closed the back passenger door and assumed a solemn expression and then strode across the flags after Little Sam.

"Hello, Judy."

She nodded. She looked terrible. Her eyes were bloodshot. Her face was pale.

"Is it about Mammy you've come?"

Her speech was flat and sullen and, just as he always had on the rare occasions when he had spoken to her in the past, he found it tedious to hear. The local opinion was that she was a bit retarded and this was an opinion he regarded as charitable. She was not just a bit slow: she was very slow.

He sensed the smaller children behind and below her: they all looked up at him. He felt the pressure of their gaze. He would not look or engage or make eye contact. He would only deal with Judy.

"Yes." His voice was neutral and rather quiet.

Her response was a little instinctive shudder. He knew that she knew, even if she did not have the details. He had been in this situation before with other relatives and he knew from past experience that when a relative already had an inkling then breaking the bad news was not too bad. It was when they had no inkling and would not believe or got angry and refused to believe that it was difficult but that was not about to happen here.

"Yes, I've come about your mother," he said.

As he expected she started to cry. She made very little noise as she cried, while the tears themselves were heavy and thick. He wondered if that was a skill one developed in a cramped small cottage: the ability to cry in a heavy and meaningful way without any noise or fuss. It would be a good skill to have, he thought, perhaps even essential.

He knew what he had to do in the next couple of minutes and he was not worried about that. First he had to wait a bit and then take her around the corner and then tell her and then bring her back and then maybe tell the other children. It was his other bigger problem that had his attention and even as he stood at the door of the cottage his brain turned this problem over. He had his suspect but before he moved against him he needed to work out how to make the charge stick. What would make everyone believe he was the one? That was his problem.

As he had these thoughts Sergeant Daly felt someone tug the tail of his coat. He looked down. It was Foxy Moll's fourth child, the nine-year-old boy, Brendan. What struck the sergeant was Brendan's expression. He looked miserable, of course, but there was also awe and relief mixed in with the pain. To Sergeant Daly's mind it seemed that the child believed he was some kind of a saviour. He was not, of course, but that look prompted a sudden flutter in the recesses of his psyche.

He felt a tiny throb as if a fish had just nudged the hook at the end of a line. It was not his first experience of this feeling. He had felt it a couple of times before when he was searching for an answer to a problem so he recognised it. It was prescience mixed with certainty. He did not have all the details. He would have to make a lot up. He would have to improvise. He would need to be creative and nimble but the feeling was undeniable. He could get away with this. Yes, he was going to get away with it and already he knew one thing for sure: Brendan was part of the solution. He did not know how – that would come – but he knew for sure that this boy was his key.

"Right, I want all you children to go and sit inside at the fire, except for you, Judy. I want a word with you." Sergeant Daly pointed at the corrugated turf shed tacked to the gable furthest from the road. "Come with me."

The children made no move. They did not want to go to the fire. They wanted to hear. Judy turned to them.

"You heard what he said. Go and sit down. I'll be back in a minute."

Judy stepped out while behind her the children moved back to the fire. Sergeant Daly closed the door and led Judy along the front of the cottage and around the end and on to the far side of the turf shed. He stopped.

"How old are you?"

"Sixteen," Judy said.

He looked into her face. As well as being stupid and dim Judy had neither her mother's clean pure complexion nor her lovely red hair. She must take after the father, he thought. Had he been told the father's name? As he pondered this, Sergeant Daly lifted his eyes from Judy's pale and miserable face and he stared up at the sky. The clouds above were thick and black and very low in the sky. The crime had only come to him that morning and attached to it was the name of the culprit but a name alone was not enough. He needed a reason, a motive: he needed a narrative. What was that? No sooner had he framed the question in his mind but the answer came.

Foxy Moll had a pedigree and Badger was a lonesome man. They were intimate or had been and Badger was the father of one of the children, the last one, the dead one ... what was her name? Edwina. Yes, that was her.

The story's next section, and it followed in a logical fashion from what came before, was that Foxy Moll and Badger had argued about this and she had threatened to expose him.

Now if this happened, then Marlhill Farm, the seventy-five acres that Badger had laboured on all his life and that were meant to go to Badger when Mr and Mrs Caesar died (all New Inn knew about this), could not then go to Badger.

Yes, if the truth came out the Caesars would change the will, of course they would, because it would not be right for a fellow who had given Foxy Moll the baby who died, it would not be right for such a fellow to inherit a seventy-five-acre farm. The

Caesars would take the farm from Badger and give it to another member of the family. They were a large family and there were lots of other deserving candidates.

Obviously Badger would not want this to happen and the only way to stop it was to ensure Foxy Moll never spoke about it to anyone and the way to do that was to kill her, and so that was exactly what he had done. He had gone and killed her.

As Sergeant Daly saw that he had the culprit and he had the culprit's motive, even if he did not have all the details yet about how the culprit had done the deed, he had a second moment of clairvoyance.

The great virtue of this culprit, as he knew from his deep experience of rural life, was that once he was arrested not a single person, not one single person in New Inn, or County Tipperary, would stand up and say Badger was innocent. Not one.

Of course they would not, and they would not because if they did they would have to admit all sorts of terrible things, which would include details of all the different men that Foxy Moll had gone with, both those who had not fathered children with her and those who had. Over the years, Foxy Moll had had relations with a lot of men who in turn had wives and sisters and mothers and families, and this enormous community of interested parties would not want any of what Foxy Moll had done for New Inn's men-folk to be revealed. Of course they would not. The shame and the humiliation of it would be ruinous. So nobody would say a word and everybody would be happy and relieved for the Guards to take one person and construct their case against him.

Sergeant Daly saw all this and then he saw who would give him the information that Badger was Edwina's father, that Foxy Moll had been about to expose him and there had been many arguments about this between the two of them in recent months.

It was Brendan who would give him the story first and then he knew that he would get Judy and the older children to endorse what Brendan said and he knew they would endorse it because they were malleable and desperate. Now he had this worked out he saw how the story had to go.

Foxy Moll and Badger had been in dispute for a while and then some time on the afternoon or the night of the previous day Foxy Moll had left the cottage and gone to the Dugout by prior arrangement to meet Badger. There Badger had shot her with a gun. He had shot her with the Caesars' gun. Sergeant Daly wondered if Mr Caesar had a weapon, then concluded that every farmer did so it was inconceivable that Caesar did not, so Badger had shot Foxy Moll with Mr Caesar's gun. Then on the morning after the murder Badger had pretended to stumble upon the body when he had been out with his dog and then he had hurried to the Guards' station and reported his find. Sergeant Daly realised that his visitor the previous night had been right: Badger was the perfect culprit and it was a beautiful and simple and elegant solution to the problem.

He lowered his gaze from the sky and looked at Judy. She pressed the heels of both hands into her eyes to staunch the flow of tears. What was the point of crying now, Sergeant Daly wondered. He had not even told her yet.

86

"Right, Judy," he said. "Yesterday, when I was here, you saw me from the front door, didn't you? I had to give your mammy a message about something. Do you remember?"

She nodded.

"So, when did you last see your mammy after that? Was it yesterday, about teatime or a bit later?"

"No," said Judy slowly, "after ... we'd all had our tea, but Daniel hadn't come yet."

He nodded. "Go on. Tell me what happened."

"She put on her hat and coat and went out."

"Just like that, no explanation, nothing, she just went out?" said Sergeant Daly.

"Yes."

"Did she go to the Dugout? Did she say anything about meeting someone at the Dugout?"

Judy looked at him. "I don't remember."

"I know she went down to the Dugout and that was where

something bad happened to your mammy. Now prepare yourself for a shock, Judy."

She looked at him. Her lip quivered and her brow furrowed. She began to wring her hands and pull in her breaths in short hard gulps.

"I've just seen her in a field below, the field next to the Dugout Field, but she wasn't alive, Judy. She was dead."

Judy nodded and let out a long shrill cry. Then she closed her eyes and gulped in a frantic manner. As she gulped tears forced their way out from between her closed eyelids and ran down her cheeks.

"She went down to the Dugout. She'd an appointment. I think I know with whom. Now say to me, Judy, say 'I understand'. I want to hear you say 'I understand'."

She opened her eyes. She stopped the gulps. She wiped her eyes to clear the tears clogged there. She nodded.

"I understand."

"All you know is this. She left yesterday, Wednesday, after tea, went to the Dugout and you didn't see her since. Have you got that?"

"Yes."

"Say it, then."

"She went away after teatime to the Dugout, and I didn't see her since."

"Good girl," said Sergeant Daly. "We'll go in and tell the other children now. Has Daniel gone to work?"

"Yes, he went this morning, and he said I was to send a message if Mammy came home."

"Will you send someone for him or go yourself?"

"Brendan can go," she said.

"I don't know about that. I need to talk to him."

They retraced their steps to the door of the cottage and went in.

87

As he sat behind the wheel and cleaned the dirt from under his fingernails with the blade of a little fruit knife he always carried, Gralton fancied that he heard wails and sobs coming from inside the cottage. Then he heard the cottage door open. He looked up and saw Brendan come out with Sergeant Daly behind. Sergeant Daly closed the cottage door. Sergeant Daly had a sack. It was a light brown grain sack with "McNeilly's of Cork" written on the side.

He watched Sergeant Daly move over the flags and push Brendan ahead. He went behind the car and shouted, "Open the boot, Gralton."

Gralton pulled the boot release. Sergeant Daly threw in the sack and closed the boot. Then he opened the back door behind Gralton and Brendan got in and Sergeant Daly closed the door. He went to the rear door on the far side and got in beside Brendan.

"Gralton, get out your notebook and write down what Brendan has to say."

Gralton took out his notebook and opened it to a fresh page. He licked the end of his pencil.

"Now, Brendan," said Sergeant Daly. "Tell me your full name."

"Brendan."

"Brendan what?"

"Brendan McCarthy."

"Age?"

"Nine."

"Residing Marlhill, New Inn."

"Yes."

"Good lad. Now that wasn't hard, was it?"

"No."

"We need to go over what you told me inside. How long have you known Badger?"

"Since as far back as I remember."

"And where did you usually see him? Go on. Tell me what you told me inside."

"Mammy and Badger bumped into each other around the fields and sometimes they'd just stand and talk and sometimes, if I was there, Mammy would turn to me and say, 'Go home, Brendan, go on, go home, I'll be with you in a while.'"

"Got that, Gralton?"

"Yes," said Gralton.

"And this happened often, didn't it, your mammy and Badger stopping and conversing?"

"Yes."

"Would you say they were friends?"

"Yes."

"Did you ever see them kissing?"

"No."

"Or holding hands?"

"No."

"But they stood close to each other when they met, didn't they?"

"Yes."

"Tell me about the spuds."

"Sometimes when they met Mammy would ask for spuds and Badger would say she could have some. He would leave them behind the hedge near the well for us or sometimes he'd meet her other places and give her the spuds."

"Was one of those other places the Dugout?"

"Yes."

"Say it."

"And sometimes he'd meet her in the Dugout and give her spuds."

"Good boy. Was Badger a friend of your mother's?"

"Yes."

"Say 'Badger was my mammy's friend.'"

"Badger was mammy's friend."

"But sometimes they didn't get on, did they?"

"Yes."

"These past few weeks they'd argued, hadn't they?"

"Yes."

"What did they argue about?"

"Edwina."

"Who's Edwina?"

"She's my little sister who died."

"And why did they argue about Edwina? Didn't you tell me Badger was the father of your little sister who died and your mammy wanted to tell people he was and he was against that?"

"Yes."

"Say it."

"Sometimes Mammy was cross with him. Badger was baby Edwina's father and Mammy wanted to tell people he was and he was against that and that's why they argued. He didn't want Mammy to tell anyone he was Edwina's father."

"That's excellent, Brendan, excellent. Have you got that, Gralton?"

"Yes, Sergeant."

"Can you remember the last time this happened, Brendan? You told me inside."

"Last week, they were arguing and Mammy said to Badger that Edwina might be dead but he still had to pay for her so Mammy was going to the judge."

"To the judge, good boy, Brendan, I like that. Now tell me the last time you saw Badger."

"We were at the well, getting water."

"Was that yesterday or the day before? It was the day before, Tuesday, I think."

"Yes …"

"Say that, then. Say 'The last time I saw Badger was the day before yesterday, Tuesday.'"

"The last time I saw Badger was the day before yesterday, Tuesday."

"Add in a bracket, Gralton, 'Tuesday 19 November 1940'. Right, Brendan, on Tuesday just gone you were at the well, and it was morning … go on … tell me again what you said inside."

"I was at the well with Mammy and Judy before I went to school and Badger came down the lane and we went over to the gate and Mammy asked for spuds and Badger said he'd leave a sack in the usual place near the well."

"Did they talk about Edwina?"

"No."

"They seemed friendly enough?"

"They did."

"Now, Brendan, this is the most important bit. You have to be absolutely clear about this. It's vital you tell the truth. You said that yesterday, Wednesday 20 November, you didn't go to school. You were at home all day and during the day she told you she was going to meet Badger at the Dugout in the evening. Isn't that what you told me inside?"

"Yes."

"Say it: 'I didn't go to school on Wednesday 20 November and in the day Mammy said she was going to meet Badger at the Dugout later.'"

"I didn't go to school on Wednesday 20 November and in the day Mammy said she was going to meet Badger at the Dugout later."

"And what were they going to talk about? Didn't you say inside that your mammy said they were going to talk about Edwina?"

"Yes."

"Say it."

"Mammy said they were going to talk about Edwina."

"And then?"

"And then after tea she left and went out to meet Badger in the Dugout and I never saw her again."

"Did you get all that, Gralton?"

"Yes."

"Let's get you back inside, Brendan," said Sergeant Daly.

Sergeant Daly pulled a small leather wallet out of a pocket and opened the change pouch and took out an English shilling.

"Here," said Sergeant Daly. He put the silver coin in the child's outstretched palm.

Brendan closed his fingers around the shilling.

"Buy yourself something nice with that," said Sergeant Daly.

Sergeant Daly led the child back inside the cottage and re-turned. He got into the front passenger seat.

"Badger did it?" said Gralton.

"Of course he did," said Sergeant Daly. "It's as plain as the hand in front of your face. Can I see those notes?"

Gralton took his notebook out and gave it to Sergeant Daly.

"They're a bit rough and ready," said Gralton.

Sergeant Daly found the first page and began to read.

"They'll do," said Sergeant Daly. "I'll get a statement made up out of these and the lad can sign."

"That's not quite regular," said Gralton.

"If we did everything regular we'd have to close all our jails because we wouldn't have a soul to lock away." Sergeant Daly shut the notebook and gave it back. "Right, back to the station."

As he drove Gralton wondered about Sergeant Daly and Foxy Moll and how after the time they had spent together the sergeant could now be so calm. Perhaps Foxy Moll had not meant much to him. After all he had a wife.

88

The cows were milked, the butter churned and now Badger and Tommy sat side by side on the sofa in the farmhouse parlour. Mrs Caesar stood in front of the fireplace. There was paper and kindling in the grate but the fire had not been lit.

"I am going to ask each of you a question," Mrs Caesar said, "and I want each of you to answer with the truth, the absolute truth. Do you understand?"

The two men nodded.

"Did either of you have anything to do with this?"

Neither man spoke.

"Badger?"

He shook his head. "No. I swear to God. The last time I saw her alive was Tuesday morning, the day before yesterday. I was going down the lane to the field with the sheep to count them and she was at the spring well with Judy and Brendan. Then the next time I saw her was below and she was dead."

"Tommy," Mrs Caesar said, "had you anything to do with this?

"No," he said. He sounded appalled. He was appalled. What sort of question was this?

Mrs Caesar nodded. "Listen to me," she said. "Listen very carefully. Neither of you have anything to do with this. That's clear. Now, in a situation like this it is vital you say nothing and you do nothing. Do you follow? You are not to talk about this to anybody, either of you, not a soul, and you are not, under any circumstances to go near the Guards. And I'll tell you why. Whatever you say the Guards will take it and twist it and use it. Do you follow? You do not volunteer one thing to them, not one word. Now, it's true, they may ask you things, in which case you will have to reply, though you mustn't say anything without carefully thinking first – but otherwise no contact, nothing, understand?

The two men nodded.

"Light the fire," Mrs Caesar said. "I'll bring some tea through. We'll wait here till the Guards come back and tell us we can get on with our business."

89

In the middle of the morning of Thursday 21 November Father O'Malley's curate Father Blackburn administered last rites to the corpse. Sergeant Daly and Gralton searched the potato store at Marlhill Farm and removed a pile of sacks marked "McNeilly's of Cork". Doctor O'Connor of Cashel examined the body.

Superintendent Mahony arrived in the early afternoon with a large waterproof lorry-cover to put over the body. He asked Doctor O'Connor what kind of weapon had been used.

"Shotgun," said the doctor, "and there are certainly pellets that can be recovered. And, once they are, there's a good chance that we can identify the type of cartridge that was used."

Superintendent Mahony drove back to the barracks and found Sergeant Daly. They went into an office. Sergeant Daly outlined what he knew.

Badger was the father of Moll's last baby, the one who died, Edwina, and Foxy Moll intended to expose Badger unless he paid her money. Brendan, the nine-year-old, had heard

Badger and Foxy Moll arguing about this and Daly already had a statement from Brendan to this effect.

Badger knew he would lose the farm if the truth came out so he had arranged to meet Foxy Moll the previous night in the Dugout to discuss the matter. That was the pretext. At that meeting he had killed her with Caesar's gun. Sergeant Daly assumed Caesar had a gun. Every farmer had. Or he'd borrowed a gun from somewhere. Anyway, a gun was easy got. This detail didn't matter. The point was, he shot her dead and then the next morning, which was that morning, when he was out walking his dog, Badger had "found" the body and gone to the New Inn police to report his find.

When Sergeant Daly got to the end Superintendent Mahony smiled and clapped his hands together. Caesar had a gun, he said: he had signed the licence. And they had their man. When he broke the news to his superiors they would be delighted. There was nothing better with a vile crime than a speedy arrest.

"You're going to make us all look very good," he said. "Now let's get the murder weapon."

In the dayroom, Superintendent Mahony gave instructions for all guns to be brought in. Then they drove over to the farm in the Wolseley Sergeant Daly used and got out and knocked on the front door of the farmhouse. Mrs Caesar opened it.

"I want to talk to your husband," said Superintendent Mahony.

Mrs Caesar brought the two Guards into the front parlour. The fire had been lit since earlier and the room had warmed up. Tommy and Badger were by the fire. Superintendent Mahony glanced at them and then nodded at Mrs Caesar.

"Badger, Tommy, go out to the kitchen for a tick, will you?"

They left.

"I'll fetch my husband," said Mrs Caesar. She left.

The Guards stood in front of the hearth and warmed the backs of their legs. Mr Caesar appeared without his wife. He wore a blue pinstripe suit and a dark shirt and a tie. Both Guards wondered if Mr Caesar had expected them and had gotten togged up in advance.

"I need your gun, Mr Caesar," said Superintendent Mahony.

"Why?" said Mr Caesar.

"We're calling in all guns."

"But why mine? My gun hasn't been used for weeks. It's been in my room on top of the wardrobe. If it had been used, I'd have known but it hasn't so why call it in?"

"We're calling in all guns, I said. We have to. That's the way you run an investigation. You leave no stone unturned."

"We'll only need to keep your gun a few days," said Sergeant Daly. "It'll be checked, eliminated from the list and you'll have it back in a week, ten days at most. We'll also need the cleaning rod and any wads that might have been used to clean out the barrels and all your cartridges."

Mr Caesar went to his ground-floor bedroom and got everything from the top of his wardrobe. The gun was a double-barrelled English nineteenth-century piece: the maker's name was Prentice. The cleaning rod was dark brown oak. There were two boxes of Eley Grand Prix cartridges No.5.

He carried everything back to the parlour.

"Here we are," he said. He put the gun and the other paraphernalia on the sideboard.

"I'll just check the cartridge numbers," said Sergeant Daly. "Got to keep the records right."

He opened the first box: there were twenty-five cartridges in it, which was the number that would have been in it when the box was purchased.

"Box one, full," he murmured loud enough for Mr Caesar to hear. He opened the second box: only twenty-three cartridges. Perfect, he thought, and he scribbled again but he said nothing and then he pointed his pencil at the gun lying stretched on the sideboard.

"Does your farm manager, Harry Gleeson, use this gun?"

"Badger, you mean. Of course," said Mr Caesar. "He shoots pigeon and rabbit, but he hasn't had it out for a while."

"What gun shop do you use?" said Sergeant Daly, his notebook in one hand and his pencil in the other.

"Feehan's hardware shop in Cashel."

"Feehan's. Nowhere else?"

"No."

"So, every transaction relating to this weapon will be in their Firearms Register?"

"It's not up to me to keep the record," said Mr Caesar.

"No, of course," said Sergeant Daly. "When did you last make a purchase in Feehan's?"

Mr Caesar shrugged.

"Never mind," said Superintendent Mahony, "it'll be in Feehan's register."

Sergeant Daly folded his notebook and put it and his pencil in his pocket.

"This is a working farm," said Mr Caesar. "You said we could only do milking this morning. We did. We stayed in since then. But can I send the lads out to work now, please?"

Superintendent Mahony looked at Sergeant Daly who gave a slight nod.

"Of course," said Superintendent Mahony in his most reasonable tone, "but they're not allowed down the bottom of your farm and they're not to go near the Dugout or the Stubble Fields. Do you understand?"

"Of course."

The two policemen carried the gun and the rest out of the Caesars' farmhouse and put it all in the boot of their car and then got into the car. Sergeant Daly got into the driver's seat and Superintendent Mahony got into the front passenger seat.

"That was good work," said Superintendent Mahony. "We've

hardly started and we have the murder weapon."

Sergeant Daly nodded and turned the key. The engine started.

"Caesar's cartridges are Eley Grand Prix No.5," said Superintendent Mahony. "You won't forget that, Sergeant Daly?"

"No," said Sergeant Daly.

"So Mr Caesar doesn't remember when he last visited Feehan's to buy shells. I've a mind it was on 3 October. I think that's a weekday. Check the calendar and come back to me."

"I will," said Sergeant Daly. He put the car in gear and drove on.

90

On Friday morning the state pathologist Doctor McGrath arrived. In the Dugout Field he made a preliminary examination of the body and then ordered its removal to the Guards' station. Along with Doctor O'Connor he spent several hours examining the corpse there. He determined that some time between Wednesday afternoon and the Thursday morning when Badger had found her Foxy Moll had been shot twice. The first shot had killed her: she had died of shock and haemorrhage. The second had shaved off a lot of her face – her chin right up to her eyebrow – and when that had happened a lot of information had been lost. He presumed that had been the reason for the second shot. He had however managed to retrieve a few cartridge-wads and some pellets. In his opinion, given his past experience, the cartridges in the shotgun used to shoot Foxy Moll were Eley Grand Prix cartridges No.4 or No.5 – he could not tell which.

Doctor McGrath passed this information on to Superintendent Mahony. He in turn told Sergeant Daly.

"Did you check the calendar?" asked Superintendent Mahony.

"October third is a Thursday," said Sergeant Daly.

"Don't do anything yet but that may have to be in Feehan's register. I'll give you the nod as and when."

91

On Friday evening in the New Inn Guards' station Doctor Stokes, the local coroner, opened an inquest with a jury. Superintendent Mahony announced that he would call evidence of identification only and then he would seek an adjournment. This was the usual procedure when a criminal investigation was underway. Only two witnesses gave evidence, Sergeant Daly and Guard Gralton, and both men described the events of the previous morning and the discovery of the body and both confirmed the identity of the victim. In addition Sergeant Daly said he had last seen the deceased some time during the middle of Wednesday afternoon when he had called to her cottage in connection with her application for a dog licence.

After the proceedings ended Miss Cooney appeared with the same small man with the papery voice who had made Edwina's coffin. She had heard about what had happened from Father O'Malley, she explained to Superintendent Mahony and Sergeant Daly, and it was his idea she take charge of the body.

Father O'Malley did not want to conduct a funeral, Miss Cooney said, not given the pedigree of the deceased or the circumstances she had died in. Superintendent Mahony and Sergeant Daly were quick to agree with the wisdom of Father O'Malley's decision. A public funeral would only provoke. Better to do things quietly and without any fuss.

The coffin maker ran up a box for the corpse. Miss Cooney paid him and he left. Sergeant Daly and a couple of other guards put the body in the box. The lid was screwed shut. Sergeant Daly and the others put the coffin in a Wolseley along with a couple of storm lanterns and followed Miss Cooney in her car along the dark roads and through the gate of Garranlea House and along the lane below the beech trees to the crypt.

Sergeant Daly lit the lamps and then, guided by Miss Cooney, he and the other men carried the coffin into the crypt: they stowed it on the same shelf as Edwina's coffin, with the smaller coffin resting on top of the bigger one.

After the crypt was shut and the lanterns extinguished, Miss Cooney brought Sergeant Daly and his two fellow Guards up to the kitchen in Garranlea. She gave them hot port and cheese sandwiches.

92

The following Monday morning as he drove the cart away from the creamery Tommy saw that Guard Gralton waited on the road in front of the barracks. The guard lifted his arm and flapped his hand.

"Tommy," said Gralton, "they're wanting you inside here to give a statement. You can tie up in the yard."

Gralton rode round with Tommy on the cart to the yard. He got off the cart and hitched the donkey to a ring set in the wall.

"There's Chief Superintendent Reynolds for you," said Gralton. He pointed at a man in a suit who stood at the back door of the front building where the offices were. Tommy had never seen this man before. "He's a very important man is Reynolds, so be sure and be nice to him," said Gralton.

Tommy walked across. "Hello," he said. "You want me for something?"

"Come in," said Chief Superintendent Reynolds, "and follow me."

Tommy went inside and Chief Superintendent Reynolds led him up the back stairs and into a small room that was bare of furnishings apart from two metal filing cabinets and a blind on the window that was drawn down. Sergeant Daly and two guards stood in the middle of the room with their jackets off. Their shirts were white and their sleeves were rolled up to their elbows.

Chief Superintendent Reynolds shut the door.

"Hello, Tommy," Sergeant Daly said. He held a pickaxe handle.

One of the guards came forward. Tommy saw that he had thick forearms and large red hands. The guard curled his big right hand into a fist and punched Tommy hard in the face just under his left eye.

"What?" Tommy fell to his knees and put his hand to his face. "What was that for?"

"You want to know what that's for?" said Sergeant Daly.

A heavy boot delivered a sharp blow to the small of Tommy's back and he was propelled forward to sprawl on the wooden floor. Tommy cried out in shock and pain.

"I'll tell you what that's for," said Sergeant Daly. "That's for silence. Do you know what silence is?"

Tommy felt a heel grind into the back of his neck and his face was pushed hard against the floor. He smelled wood and dust. His eyes leaked and so did his nose.

"I asked you a question," said Sergeant Daly. He jabbed the end of the pickaxe handle into Tommy's back. "Do you know what silence is?"

"Yes," shouted Tommy.

"What is it, then?" Sergeant Daly jabbed again.

"It's not saying anything."

"You're quick, Tommy, but you're not quick enough."

Both guards began to kick Tommy up and down his body. He curled his arms around his head and drew his legs up to his chest. A kick caught his right elbow and a jolt of pain shot through his arm. Numbed by the blow his arm fell away from his head and a boot connected with his jaw. He felt dizzy and sick.

"Give him a minute," said Chief Superintendent Reynolds. The kicks and blows stopped.

Tommy registered that the sergeant had moved over and stood right over his head and he wondered if it had been Sergeant Daly who had kicked him in the face. He wondered what the sergeant would do with the pickaxe handle.

"Let's see if you're getting quicker. What do you need to be silent about, Tommy?"

Sergeant Daly slapped the side of Tommy's head with the pickaxe handle.

"I don't know."

"Off you go," said Chief Superintendent Reynolds.

Sergeant Daly and the other two kicked and stamped at his body. Tommy realised that he was wet. At some point, although he did not know when, he had pissed himself. His clothes around his middle were warm and wet but the warmth soon cooled. Tommy began to cry. Snot filled his nose and leaked out into his mouth and down his chin. There was a salty smell from his piss and a salty taste in his mouth from the snot and the tears. The kicks stopped.

"Badger Gleeson," said Sergeant Daly, "is he your friend?"

"Yes."

"Wrong."

The tip of pickaxe handle dealt two savage blows to Tommy's right hipbone. The nerves there jangled and he cried out.

"No," he shouted. "No."

"Right," said Sergeant Daly. "Badger Gleeson is not your friend. Good. Now, say after me, 'Badger Gleeson is not my friend.'"

"Badger Gleeson is not my friend."

"If he is not your friend, it therefore follows that you know nothing about him, and if you know nothing about him, it therefore follows that you have nothing to say. Nothing. Do you understand? You have nothing, nothing to say about what he might have done or not done last week, especially last Wednesday and Thursday and Friday. Do you understand?"

One of the Guards got on the back of Tommy's knees and began to jump up and down. The other kicked his head and neck and shoulders.

"Yes," shouted Tommy. "Yes."

"He's getting there," said Chief Superintendent Reynolds, "but he hasn't learned all his lessons yet. I think we need to teach him a little more. Keep the hurting going, lads, keep it going. I have to go and do something. I'll be back in ten minutes."

Tommy heard the door open.

"Help," he shouted.

"Shut up, Tommy," said Sergeant Daly. "No one can hear you scream in here."

Tommy heard the door close followed by a hard kick to his shoulder.

"Oh God," he shouted.

93

While Tommy lay on the floor in the barracks, Superintendent Mahony and Inspector Reilly knocked on the door of Marlhill Farm. Mrs Caesar answered.

"I'm afraid you're for the Guards' station, you and your husband," said Superintendent Mahony. "We want the place clear so we can talk to Badger."

"Is he in trouble?"

"No, Mrs Caesar, he is not. We just want him to go over everything and we want the place clear, like I said, when we do that. Your other man, Tommy Reid, is already at the barracks. He stopped in on his way back from the creamery run and we've a car here to run you and your husband over. We've a room ready and there'll be tea and sandwiches, you'll be well looked after, and if you wouldn't mind waiting there, then we'll get on with what we have to do here as quick as we can and we'll have you back as soon as is humanly possible. Does that sound reasonable, Mrs Caesar?"

The room prepared for the Caesars at the police station was at the other end of the building from where Tommy was. Mr and Mrs Caesar did not therefore hear his screams.

94

Statement of Harry Gleeson, taken at the dwelling house of John Caesar, at Marlhill, New Inn, Co. Tipp. at 12.10 pm on Monday 25 November 1940, after the said Harry Gleeson had been cautioned by Superintendent Mahony that he was not obliged to say anything unless he wished to do so and that anything he might say would be taken down in writing and might be used in evidence:

My name is Harry Gleeson, but I am known as Badger on account of the white streak I have in my hair. I am about forty years old. I have been living with my uncle Mr John Caesar and his wife Mrs Caesar for many years. My uncle does not pay me a wage, but any time I want a pound or three pounds or more I can get it from my uncle or his wife. I have no promise from my uncle that I will get his farm at any time. The way things are, if my uncle and his wife were gone I believe I would have the best right to the farm and that if I did not get it then I would get a fair thing out of it. I have always been on excellent terms with my uncle's wife, just as if she were my mother. I never had a row with my uncle or his wife but if I was out late, my uncle might say something to me but I know it would be for my own good. I drink stout but I was never drunk except maybe once.

*

Questioned by Superintendent Mahony:

QUESTION: How long have you known Moll McCarthy?
ANSWER: I have known her since I came to this side of the country from my own home.
QUESTION: Did she ever work here?
ANSWER: No.
QUESTION: Will you give us an idea of what dealings you had with her since you came to live here?
ANSWER: I will. We often cut trees on the other side of the road near where she lived and I used to tell her she could have the light branches. The same thing happened when we cut furze off bushes at the ditches. She often took branches or bushes without permission. She often got water from the spring well in the field at the back of her garden that is our field. That was happening generally since we came here by agreement. She always had goats and they used to trespass on my uncle's land. She used to be after them. I met her frequently when she was taking away bushes, drawing water or running after her goats. I was always friendly with her and spoke to her always when I met her. I often cautioned her about the goats trespassing.
QUESTION: Did you ever give potatoes to Moll McCarthy unknown to your uncle?
ANSWER: I did but he wouldn't have minded because there were other times when I gave her potatoes and he knew.

QUESTION: But you did sometimes give potatoes to her unknown to him?

ANSWER: Yes.

QUESTION: When was the last time you gave Moll McCarthy potatoes?

ANSWER: Last week.

QUESTION: When? What day last week?

ANSWER: I think it was Tuesday.

QUESTION: Tuesday 19 November?

ANSWER: If that's the right date, yes.

QUESTION: What happened?

ANSWER: I met her in the morning. She was at the spring well with her daughter, I think you call her Judy, and the lad Brendan and she said they needed spuds, could I give her some? I said I could and we arranged I'd leave a sack under the hedge near the spring well for her to collect later. It was lunchtime when I filled the sack with spuds. Then I carried it back and left it where we'd arranged, lying under the hedge near the spring well.

QUESTION: And did you make an appointment with Moll McCarthy that same day (Tuesday last) to meet her on Wednesday evening at the Dugout?

ANSWER: No, sir.

QUESTION: Did Moll McCarthy ever suggest to you that you were the father of her last child?

ANSWER: No, sir.

QUESTION: Have you ever heard that she said you were?

ANSWER: No, sir. So far as I know, she never named anybody for it.

QUESTION: Did you ever meet or see Moll McCarthy late at night?

ANSWER: No, but I heard she used to be out late herself.

QUESTION: Your uncle has a shotgun. Did you ever use it?

ANSWER: I did. I'd shoot for crows with it after cutting

the wheat the odd time but mostly I'd go after rabbits for Mrs Caesar for a stew.

QUESTION: Did Tommy Reid ever use your uncle's gun?

ANSWER: Never to my knowledge.

QUESTION: Who cleans your uncle's gun?

ANSWER: The boss. I never cleaned it.

QUESTION: Where was the gun kept?

ANSWER: In the boss's bedroom.

QUESTION: Where was the gun on Wednesday and Thursday last?

ANSWER: The gun is always kept in the boss's bedroom.

QUESTION: Do you know when the gun was last cleaned?

ANSWER: No, but I know a yoke was there to clean it. I could not tell you what that yoke was.

QUESTION: Will you tell me what happened last Thursday morning?

ANSWER: After breakfast, Tommy and I went out to the yard. It had rained in the night but the rain had stopped. Everywhere was wet and there was a cold wind. We fetched milk pails and milking stools from the dairy and went up to the Crib Field. We milked the cows in a corner under a tree where the ground was driest. Then we carried the milk back and left it with the previous night's milk in the dairy. Then Tommy said he would chop wood. I got my dog Lively Lady from her pen, put on her lead and set off on the walk we make every morning, the same walk exactly. When we got to the Dugout Field and the gate was closed, I slipped the lead and let Lively Lady free. She was after the scents, mad for rabbit. I began going down the field with her ahead of me. Away to the right of me, I noticed the gap between the Dugout Field and the Stubble Field was open again. I wondered if the wind in the night had blown away the bushes I'd piled up there. I started walking towards the gap to plug it again. As I got closer, I realised there was someone lying on the other side of the gap just inside the Stubble Field. The quickest thing to do was to cut straight over and get up on the fence and look over, which is what I did.

QUESTION: What did you see?

ANSWER: The first thing was a dog. The dog was brown. The second thing I saw was the dog was sitting on something. It was a person, a woman.

QUESTION: How did you know it was a woman?

ANSWER: From the clothes she was wearing, from her petticoats, her shoes.

QUESTION: Did you recognise the woman?

ANSWER: No.

QUESTION: Did you know the dog?

ANSWER: No, sir.

QUESTION: You didn't know either the woman or the dog?

ANSWER: No, I did not.

QUESTION: You knew Moll McCarthy when you saw her at the spring well on Tuesday and she asked for potatoes. How is it that you did not know her when you saw her on Thursday?

ANSWER: The dog was in the way.

QUESTION: When you stood up on the fence and saw the woman lying on the ground what impression did you get of her?

ANSWER: My impression was that she was lying there and she was either sleeping or dead.

QUESTION: Did you notice anything wrong with the woman's head that morning?

ANSWER: No.

QUESTION: Where was the dog when you first saw him?

ANSWER: He was lying on her breast with his tail to her knees.

QUESTION: What position was the dog in when you arrived with the Guards?

ANSWER: He was in the same position as when I first saw him.

QUESTION: When did you first recognise the woman?

ANSWER: When I went back with the Guards.

I have heard this statement read over to me and it is correct,
Harry Gleeson.
Witness: Thomas Reilly, Inspector, 25.11.40
Patrick Mahony, Superintendent, 25.11.40

95

"Tommy? Wake up."

Tommy opened a swollen eyelid and looked up. It was Sergeant Daly.

"You're free to go, Tommy."

Sergeant Daly helped him get up from the floor and assisted him down the stairs and out into the yard. It was dark outside. The cart and donkey were where he had left them hitched that morning.

Sergeant Daly untied the reins. Tommy pulled himself up onto the cart with difficulty. His body ached and his upper right gum throbbed. The Guards had kicked two of his teeth out.

"Don't forget now, Tommy. No talking." Sergeant Daly put a finger to his lips. "Never forget, whatever you do, say nothing."

Tommy took the reins and shook them. The wheels turned. He drove out the gate and began to move up the street. He guessed that it was at least midnight.

A while later Tommy rolled into the yard at Marlhill Farm. He saw that the lamps were lit downstairs; lamplight shone through the windows. Someone had decided to wait up for him. The back door opened and Mrs Caesar flew out with a lamp in her hand.

"Is it you, Tommy?"

"It is."

She came up to the cart and raised the lamp to look at his face.

"Oh, my God," Mrs Caesar said. "What have they done to you?"

Tommy began to cry. The tears were hot and big.

"They beat me," he said. "They beat me and beat me and they never said why."

"Who?"

"The new one – Daly I think you call him – and two others and some big boss was there too – you call him Reynolds, I think – a chief superintendent, I think they said."

"Oh, Jesus Christ," Mrs Caesar said. "Oh, Jesus Christ."

96

On Saturday 30 November Badger was arrested at Marlhill Farm and taken to New Inn Guards' station. Superintendent Mahony charged him with the murder of Mary "Moll" McCarthy in an interview room that smelled of wet tweed and wellington boots and was painted two different shades of grey: battleship grey and dove grey. The charges had to be read twice because of his poor hearing.

"I had no hand, act or part in it," Badger said. "And when do you say I'm supposed to have done this?"

"On Wednesday, the week before last."

"What day was that?"

"Wednesday 20 November."

"Right, I can account for my movements; you have your duty."

Later that day Badger was brought before the peace commissioner, Mr Philips, at a special court in Cashel Guards' station.

"Do you have anything to say?" said Mr Philips.

"No, sir, whatever statement I gave, I gave," said Badger.

Mr Philips remanded Badger into the custody of the Fethard District Court until the next Friday, which was 6 December 1940, and after this he was taken to Limerick Jail in a police car and put into a single cell on the committal wing. It was the first time in his life that Badger had been out of County Tipperary.

The same day, Saturday, at Mr Caesar's request, John J. Timoney, a solicitor with a practice in Tipperary town, called to Marlhill Farm early in the evening to meet with him and his wife.

The next day, Sunday, nothing happened, but the day after, Monday 2 December, Mr Timoney went to Limerick Jail where he met Badger for the first time and agreed to take his instructions.

At the end of that week, on Friday 6 December, Mr Timoney appeared on behalf of Badger for the first time at Fethard District Court; Badger was remanded to Caher District Court for 19 December.

The Monday after his first appearance on his new client's behalf was 9 December and on that day Mr John Timoney went by train to Dublin and met Seán MacBride, who accepted the brief as junior counsel for Badger.

On 19 December at Caher, Seán MacBride opposed a request for a further adjournment. District Justice Seán Troy fixed 2 January 1941 as the day the depositions stage would commence at a full District Court hearing in Clonmel, adding that there would be no more adjournments.

97

It was Monday 23 December, about 3 o'clock in the afternoon, when Sergeant Daly opened the door and entered Feehan's hardware shop. There was a smell of twine and gun oil and sacking. There were dark wooden counters on three sides. There was no one around other than a man in a brown coat at the back of the shop who weighted out nails and bagged them up.

"I'm looking for the manager, Mr O'Driscoll," said Sergeant Daly. "Is he about?"

"I'll get him for you now." said the man.

He limped away and returned with an elderly fellow who had grey hair that his white scalp showed through. The man's eyes were dark and brown and magnified by the spectacles he wore.

When he saw Sergeant Daly in his uniform he looked startled.

"Mr O'Driscoll?" said Sergeant Daly.

Although the shop was known as Feehan's it had been owned and managed by the O'Driscoll family for forty years.

"Yes."

"I'm Sergeant Daly. Is there an office where we could have a private word?"

Mr O'Driscoll brought him to his own office. It was a small room with a tiny window that overlooked a yard full of paving stones and sand and gravel and timber. There was a desk and there were chairs but Mr O'Driscoll did not invite the sergeant to sit.

"I'm from New Inn," said Sergeant Daly, "where we've had this unfortunate business with this woman, Moll McCarthy. You've probably heard."

Mr O'Driscoll nodded. Some colour left his face. "I did ..." he said. His voice was faint.

"I understand Mr John Caesar of Marlhill, New Inn, buys his cartridges here?" said Sergeant Daly.

"Yes."

"Can I see the Firearms Register?"

Mr O'Driscoll fetched a large old ledger book. He put it on the desk.

"I want to see the last two months of entries," Sergeant Daly said.

Mr O'Driscoll opened the book at the pages with the information the sergeant had requested.

"Here we are," he said.

His hands trembled as he spoke. He reached up and pulled his spectacle frames down hard onto his nose as if he feared otherwise they might fall off. This was going well, thought Sergeant Daly, and in a few minutes he would have this one reeled in and landed on the bank.

Sergeant Daly sat down at the desk and looked at the page at which the register was open. He ran his finger down the column of names. He huffed and sighed as he did. His finger came to the bottom of the list. He huffed and sighed again and then went, "Tut, tut." He looked up. Mr O'Driscoll stood on the other side of the desk. His mouth was open.

"Is something the matter?" Mr O'Driscoll said. "I hope we haven't done something wrong. Did we do something wrong?"

"Yes," Sergeant Daly said.

"But we keep very precise records."

"We'll come to your so-called records in a minute," said Sergeant Daly. "But first let's talk about your record as –"

Sergeant Daly stopped and stared. Mr O'Driscoll's expression was grim.

"Your record as an uncle," Sergeant Daly continued.

Mr O'Driscoll removed his glasses and wiped them and put them back on. "I don't understand," he said. "What are you talking about?"

"Helena McCarthy, Moll McCarthy's daughter, that's who I'm talking about, and she's your niece, you are her uncle."

"I'm afraid I ..." Mr O'Driscoll could not go on.

"Of course," said Sergeant Daly, "confusingly, McCarthy's the name on the birth cert but you and I both know what name should be there, don't we?"

Mr O'Driscoll began to blink. He did this at speed.

"No I don't ..."

"You do. It should be O'Driscoll, shouldn't it? You know that! Your brother certainly knows that. As the father, of course he does. I don't know if your brother's wife knows that. What's she called? I can't remember."

It occurred to Sergeant Daly that it must seem very strange to O'Driscoll that he found himself in the place where his employees doubtless stood and he, Sergeant Daly, sat in his place behind the desk.

"I said, what's her name?" said Sergeant Daly.

Mr O'Driscoll swallowed. "Veronica."

"Veronica, yes, that's a lovely name. Is she French?"

"No."

"No?"

"No," said Mr O'Driscoll.

"I thought Veronica was a French name, so that's why I asked if she was French, you see. But she's not French you say?"

"No."

"She understands English so she would understand me if told her that her husband was the father of the late Moll McCarthy's child Helena? And I know Helena would understand if she were told who her father was, and I think I can say pretty categorically that, given her tragic circumstances, if she knew Mr O'Driscoll were her father and you were her uncle that one day she would come here to this shop, just like I have today, and she would ask for help."

Mr O'Driscoll dropped his head, examined his shoes and looked up again.

"But the only way that is going to happen is if we fall out today, and we don't have to fall out, because you can now do something very simple, which at a stroke will guarantee we won't. Would you like to know what that is?"

Mr O'Driscoll nodded.

"Mr Caesar from New Inn came here and bought two boxes of Eley Grand Prix cartridges No.5 on 3 October, a Thursday if my memory serves, and it isn't here on your so-called register.

"Now I see before me, on this desk, an inkstand and a pen. I am going to leave this office, and I am going to go out into the shop, and then I'm going to go on out into the street, and I'm going to make my way to Milligan's the stationer. I'm going to buy myself some Christmas cards, and then I'm going to come back, and when I do, I expect, Mr O'Driscoll, uncle of Helena McCarthy, I expect to find that on Thursday 3 October just past, according to this book, Mr Caesar, of Marlhill Farm, New Inn, bought two boxes of Eley Grand Prix cartridges No.5 here at Feehan's in Cashel town. Have I made myself perfectly clear? Good. I shall be ten minutes."

Sergeant Daly left Feehan's and went to the stationer's and made his purchase and returned. The lame man waited for him just inside the door. He had the Firearms Register under his arm.

"Mr O'Driscoll left this. He had to go home, but he said it's all in order."

Sergeant Daly opened the book at the last page. He saw that an addendum had been inserted between two lines: "Thurs. 3 October 1940, Mr John Caesar Esq., Marlhill, New Inn, registered gun owner N50686, Eley Grand Prix cartridges No.5, 2 x 25 boxes."

Sergeant Daly nodded and left. He found his car and drove to Knockgraffon National School. It was a white building with two classrooms. Lessons had finished and the children had gone home but the tremulous yellow light of an oil lamp lit up the tall windows and told him that there was someone inside as he had hoped. He parked and went in. There was a smell of oil and floor polish and underneath that the smell peculiar to children who did not wash.

He found Master Murdoch where he sat at a table at the top of a classroom marking scripts. Sergeant Daly stated his name and business.

"Can I see the roll-book?" he said.

The master took the book from the drawer of the table he worked at and gave it to Sergeant Daly. Sergeant Daly opened the roll-book at the last page. He saw that Brendan was marked as having attended school on the last Wednesday his mother was alive; this was unfortunate because in his statement Brendan had claimed to be at home.

"I'll have to take this," said Sergeant Daly. "I'll write you out a receipt."

Sergeant Daly went back to New Inn. In the Guards' station he put the Firearms Register and the roll-book for Knockgraffon National School in the small safe that he had in his office.

98

The District Court hearings started on 2 January 1941. They lasted six days, spread over three weeks. At the end of the final day District Justice Seán Troy spoke.

"I have only heard one side of the case," he said, "but I am satisfied the State has made a case against Mr Gleeson. I therefore order him to be sent for trial by the Central Criminal Court."

He looked down at Badger.

"Do you have anything to say?" he asked.

"I had neither hand, act or part in it," said Badger.

As the police led him away Badger passed Tommy Reid in the courthouse hallway.

"Tommy," Badger said, "they'd hang you with lies here."

"Don't I know that," Tommy said. "Don't I know it well."

Badger spent that night in Limerick Jail and the next day was driven to Dublin in a Guards' van and put into Mountjoy Prison. He had never been in the capital in his life.

99

From the Tipperary Democrat, *Tuesday 18 February 1941:*

FIRST DAY OF TRIAL OF HARRY GLEESON

(From our court correspondent)
The trial of Harry "Badger" Gleeson, a well-liked figure
from Marlhill Farm, New Inn, Co. Tipperary, began yesterday in Green Street Courthouse in Dublin. Gleeson is
the manager of a farm owned by his uncle, Mr Caesar, and
his wife, Mrs Caesar.

Harry Gleeson is charged with the murder of Mary
McCarthy at Marlhill on 20 November 1940. Acting
for the defence on the instructions of Mr John Timoney,
the well-known Co. Tipperary solicitor, is James Nolan-
Whelan SC and his junior counsel Seán MacBride, while
leading the prosecution is Joseph A. McCarthy SC, aided
by his junior counsel George Murnaghan. The judge is Mr
Justice Martin Maguire.

Following the swearing in of the jurymen, the election of the foreman and some remarks from Mr Justice Maguire, the charge was read; this had to be done twice as the accused has difficulty hearing. His answer, however, delivered in a loud, clear voice, was unequivocal: "Not guilty," he said, adding, "I had neither hand, act or part in it." In January, earlier this year, when the Clonmel District Court ordered that he should be sent for trial at the Central Criminal Court, the accused used the same form of words, exactly. "I had neither hand, act or part in it," he said.

The preliminaries completed, the proceedings began in earnest with a request by Mr McCarthy that the charge be amended to read "on or about 20 or 21 November", that is, it was either on the Wednesday when the victim was last seen alive, or the Thursday when Mary McCarthy's body was found, that the murder was committed. Mr Nolan-Whelan, noting his client, the defendant, Harry Gleeson, was most anxious to have all the facts fully investigated, consented.

It was then the turn of Mr Nolan-Whelan to make a request. He asked the judge to direct the court stenographer to record the opening address to the jury by the State. He hoped, presumably, that knowing his comments were being recorded Mr McCarthy would make a less emotional appeal. Mr Justice Maguire turned down the request.

For the State, Mr McCarthy now made his opening speech, outlining the State's case against Gleeson and providing the jury with a summary of the evidence the prosecution would offer in order to prove the charge.

He opened by describing the morning the body was found, and described in graphic detail the brutal injuries the deceased had sustained to her head and face. He then described Gleeson's arrival at the police station, "the first intimation the ... authorities got of a murder that was as crafty, as cold-blooded and as black-hearted as the mind of man could conceive", he said.

He next dwelt on Gleeson's strange assertion on reporting the news in the New Inn Police Station that he did not recognise the dead woman or the small brown dog sitting on her chest, "one of the many steps taken by the accused to conceal his association with the act he had committed ..."

The prosecution, he continued, would demonstrate, beyond reasonable doubt, that "the murder was committed by ... some person who knew the victim ... whose presence on Caesars' land would not be a surprise to her ... someone who had knowledge of where Mary McCarthy would ... go and had easy access and means of escape". That person, McCarthy continued, who had "cunningly contrived an ambush, trapped and shot her and ... endeavoured to mutilate her beyond recognition ... was in the dock".

Mr John Caesar, he continued, Harry Gleeson's employer, owned a licensed shotgun and bought two boxes each containing twenty-five cartridges on 3 October, a Thursday, and those were the same type of cartridge that was used to kill Mary McCarthy. The defendant, he said, regularly used the gun to shoot game and occasionally vermin. He had no difficulty obtaining it whenever he needed it and no questions were asked. He simply took it and returned it at will.

The victim, Mary McCarthy, was a neighbour who lived "in a humble little cottage on a little plot of ground", inset into Caesars' farm and lying just at the mouth of the Caesars' farm lane. She was "the unfortunate mother of seven illegitimate children", who obtained her potatoes by stealth from various sources in the neighbourhood, one of these being Harry Gleeson, and a sack in which Gleeson had provided her with potatoes the Tuesday before her death would be produced which matched a pile of sacks at Caesars' farm at Marlhill.

Once they heard the evidence, Mr McCarthy continued, they would be in no doubt that the relationship between the dead woman and the accused was an immoral one. They would further understand why this was so problematic. The defendant was the father of the victim's seventh child, now sadly dead, Edwina. In the weeks and months subsequent to the child's death the victim had warned the defendant she intended to obtain financial compensation from him for this child and to do this was fully prepared to go to court and to name him as the child's father. As the prosecution would make clear, Mr McCarthy continued, here was the defendant's motive: he knew that should this happen then his uncle and aunt, a pious and conservative couple, would not leave Marlhill Farm to him, which heretofore was his and their understanding, and it was therefore in order to make certain this did not happen and that he did inherit the seventy-five-acre property that he killed the victim.

Mr McCarthy next outlined the State's version of events. On Tuesday 19 November McCarthy and Gleeson met at the spring well on Caesars' land where McCarthy drew water and, witnessed by McCarthy's son Brendan, Gleeson agreed to provide potatoes as he regularly did, this being his means of paying her. On the afternoon of Wednesday 20 November, Mary McCarthy was at home and Harry Gleeson was on his uncle's farm. At some point in the late afternoon, Mr McCarthy said, Mary McCarthy told Brendan, who was absent from school that day, that she had to meet Gleeson because of their dispute about Edwina's paternity. She then left the cottage where she lived followed by her little brown dog, Sam, and went to meet, by arrangement, Harry Gleeson at their regular trysting spot, an old Civil War dugout at the bottom of Caesars' farm. And at some point that night, he shot and killed Mary McCarthy.

Mr McCarthy then summarised the events of the night and the following morning, with particular reference to Brendan and the interview he offered the police concerning his mother's last words to him, words which threw so much light on the unhealthy and unhappy relationship of McCarthy and Gleeson. Then he previewed the evidence that the State Pathologist would provide as to the probable time of McCarthy's death.

Finally, bringing his peroration full circle, he returned to what the prosecution regarded as the key event: Harry Gleeson's insistence to the police when he went to report the discovery of the body that he recognised neither the victim nor the dog. This subterfuge, Mr McCarthy ended, was intended "to divert attention from his own responsibility, [and] to endeavour to convey to the Guards his willingness to assist, and to put himself forward as a person whose conduct was consistent with innocence."

The accused sat impassive throughout the prosecution speech, probably because, with his imperfect hearing combined with the bulk of the speech having been directed at the jury, he would not have heard much of it. We understand, however, that his junior counsel, Mr MacBride, who took notes throughout, will give him sight of these later.

The State's opening speech having lasted five hours, the court adjourned and the accused was returned to Mountjoy Prison.

100

From the Tipperary Democrat, *Tuesday 25 February 1941:*

SEVENTH DAY OF TRIAL OF HARRY GLEESON
– DEFENDANT FINALLY TAKES STAND.

(From our court correspondent)
The trial of Harry "Badger" Gleeson who is charged with
murdering Mary "Moll" McCarthy at Marlhill, New Inn,
County Tipperary, continued yesterday. The day was
mostly given over to routine but, after much anticipation,
at 4.15 in the afternoon the defendant entered the witness
box for the first time.

In his direct examination Mr Nolan-Whelan, counsel
for the defence, asked the defendant roughly forty questions.

First he dealt with Gleeson's statement to the Guards,
pointing out it was made without legal assistance. Gleeson

said he had not seen a lawyer until he was brought to Limerick Jail after the Clonmel hearings.

In response to further questions from Mr Nolan-Whelan, Gleeson agreed Brendan McCarthy had made the allegations against him that Superintendent Mahony and Sergeant Daly had testified to: he added he had denied them when they were first brought to his attention and he denied them again now.

He then swore the deceased Moll McCarthy had never threatened to bring him to court over her last child. He said he had last used his employer's gun, with which he is accused of shooting Miss McCarthy, at the start of November, well before the murder, and he had not used it since.

Asked if he had ever been in court before, he said the only time was when he went into a public house in Cahir to buy cigarettes after closing-time, and the technical charge had been dismissed.

Finally, he told the jury he was not the father of Moll McCarthy's last child, he had never had an immoral association with the dead woman and he had "no hand, act or part" in the murder.

The trial continues.

101

From the Tipperary Democrat, *Thursday 27 February 1941:*

TRIAL OF HARRY GLEESON – DRAMATIC INTERRUPTIONS

(From our court correspondent)
Yesterday, Wednesday, the ninth day of the trial, started with closing speeches from Joseph A. McCarthy SC for the prosecution and James Nolan-Whelan SC for the defence and was then followed with Mr Justice Maguire's charge, spiced here and there with some of his own observations and thoughts. His principle criticism was the failure of anyone from the Caesar household to give evidence. He thought this strange, he said, especially as the accused was from that household. He said this not once but twice, and the second time was too much for Mrs Caesar, who had sat in the court with her husband every day of the trial. In a loud clear voice she shouted back at Mr Justice

Maguire, "We were not called." The judge directed the Guards to eject Mrs Caesar. She was carried out shouting and, order restored, Mr Justice Maguire continued until one of the jurymen collapsed with a suspected heart attack. Mr Justice Maguire determined he would finish his charge the following day and adjourned until ten o'clock on Thursday 27 February.

After the day's interruptions, the mood of the court was sombre. Nobody spoke as they filed out, with the exception of the accused who was heard distinctly saying to a friend from New Inn who had come to watch and to show support, "Say a prayer for me, Billy, say a prayer."

102

From the Tipperary Democrat, *Friday 28 February 1941:*

CONVICTION OF HARRY GLEESON

(From our court correspondent)
After ten days, the trial of Harry Gleeson, a farm manager from Marlhill, New Inn, concluded yesterday, Thursday 27 February. The juryman whose collapse on Wednesday caused an adjournment had been pronounced healthy overnight by the court doctor and was back in his place with his peers.

His jury restored, Mr Justice Maguire continued his charge. He finished in the afternoon and the jury retired to consider their verdict. After deliberating for two hours and twenty minutes, they were back at 6.30 pm. They found the defendant guilty but with a strong recommendation to mercy.

Mr Justice Maguire asked the defendant Harry Gleeson if he had anything to say as to why the sentence of death should not be imposed, though he added it was not mandatory that the defendant reply to this question. Harry Gleeson, in the dock, appeared confused and it seemed as if he had not appreciated the verdict owing to his impaired hearing. The Guard sitting in the box with Gleeson whispered to him and Gleeson nodded, suggesting he did now understand, and then called out in a strong clear voice, as he had several times already, "I had neither hand, act or part in it."

Mr Justice Maguire then gave the formal order "that on the 24th day of March, 1941, you, Harry Gleeson, be taken to the common place of execution in the prison in which you will be confined, and that you be then and there hanged by the neck until you are dead, and that your body be buried within the walls of the prison".

He assured Gleeson the jury's recommendation to mercy would be communicated to the relevant authorities and the condemned man was taken back to Mountjoy Prison. His defence is expected to appeal, though as yet no formal application has been lodged.

Mr and Mrs Caesar were later seen in the hallway of the Green Street Courthouse weeping.

103

From the Tipperary Democrat, *Saturday 1 March 1941:*

APPEAL AGAINST CONVICTION OF HARRY GLEESON LODGED

(From our court correspondent)
Yesterday a notice was lodged in the Court of Appeal by Mr John Timoney, solicitor, Tipperary town, of his intention to appeal the conviction of Harry Gleeson of Marlhill, New Inn, Co. Tipperary for murder. Until the appeal is heard, the notice for Gleeson's hanging is suspended.

104

Mr Bermingham sat in his usual table in the saloon at the back of Hunter's public house. The room was empty. It was ten in the morning. A small fire burned in the grate. Sergeant Daly came in and sat down at the table beside Mr Bermingham.

"I got your letter," said Sergeant Daly. "I hope this isn't about Gleeson because if it is I don't want to bloody well hear it."

Mr Bermingham lifted the lid of his pipe, struck a match and put it to the bowl. The tobacco caught. Mr Bermingham sucked. His spit in the pipe stem gurgled. A plume of blue smoke left Mr Bermingham's mouth and rose towards the ceiling. Mr Bermingham waved his hand and the flame at the end of the match went out. He stood, walked to the fire, threw the dead match onto the turf embers and went towards the door.

"And don't write again," Sergeant Daly called after him, "unless you've something important to tell me."

Mr Bermingham went through the door and was gone. Sergeant Daly sighed and shook his head and closed his eyes.

105

Father O'Malley felt the confession box shift as a person came in and sat down on the other side of the partition. He heard them close the door they had come in through. Now they were sealed in and invisible like he was, whoever they were. He moved the slider and opened the hatch between the two spaces, his half and the confessor's half.

"I was a Republican," he heard, "but now I'm a police informer."

Father O'Malley did not recognise the voice. He could see the outline of a head through the hatch but it was too dark to make out the face. There was a strong smell of pipe tobacco.

"Go on," said Father O'Malley.

"Gleeson's innocent. It's J.J."

"Why do you say that?" said the priest.

"Because he had a meeting with Republicans in my house about Moll McCarthy two days before she died. She was carrying on with this new guard, Daly; they didn't like that. So a decision was made: she had to go. I heard this. I got in touch with Sergeant Daly immediately, here in New Inn. I met him. I told him they would kill her. Then they did and now, on the strength of this cock-and-bull story that he and this woman had a child and she was going to expose him and he was set to lose the farm and so he killed her, Harry Gleeson is going to swing. Well, even the dogs about here will tell you Gleeson wasn't the father. The child was J.J.'s."

"Why are you telling me this?" said Father O'Malley.

"Why? I thought that would be obvious. The State won't listen to the likes of me. I'm only an old farmer. But you tell them and they'll sit up and take notice. You're a priest. You have to tell them."

"Oh, do I? I tell them the father of the last child wasn't Gleeson but J.J. and then what?" said Father O'Malley. "Let me tell you. People will say, what about the sixth child and the fifth and the fourth and so on and who were their fathers, maybe it was one of them murdered her? And before you know it, all Ireland will know of Moll McCarthy and who she carried on with.

"Now, it may not matter to you but all these men, not just the fathers but the all ones she was with, they are my parishioners and so are their families and they're not going to be happy if everyone in the country knows what went on even if it were wrong what those men got up to.

"Yet you would have me speak up and ruin every member of my parish, a horror which, mercifully, thanks to the prompt and correct action of the authorities, so far we have avoided. You're mad. I'm not talking to anybody. Now get out of my church."

1 O 6

Mr Bermingham left the confessional and went out. He got his bicycle. He cycled to Garranlea House. He knocked on the kitchen door. A small maid with a freckled face let him in.

Miss Cooney saw him in a chilly room with a small fire. He told her everything. Then she told him all the McCarthy children other than Daniel were in St Bridget's (where their mother had been) and as she was not a family member she was not allowed to see them. However, she would try, she said, as maybe they had information that would help.

107

Superintendent Mahony heard a knock on his door.

"Come in," he said.

The door opened. Superintendent Mahony heard someone enter. He looked up. It was O'Rourke. He had a white envelope in his hand.

"Superintendent, I want to give you something," said O'Rourke.

"Is it in that envelope?"

"Yes."

"Give it to me."

O'Rourke handed the superintendent the envelope. The superintendent opened it, took out the paper that was inside and read it.

"Fine," said Superintendent Mahony. "If you want to go, O'Rourke, who am I stop you? I'll sign the necessary papers. I'll have that done by the end of today. You work your final days and you'll be free to go."

"Thank you, Superintendent."

"Why do you want to leave us, as a matter of interest? I thought you liked the work."

"Personal reasons."

"Meaning the Gleeson business?"

"Yes, and what was done to Tommy Reid."

"You should know by now, O'Rourke, if you want to make an omelette you have to break eggs. Don't you know that?"

"No, Superintendent."

"You don't know that?"

O'Rourke shook his head.

"All right, O'Rourke, get out."

108

Badger and two officers played whist in Badger's cell. All the tricks had been played except the last. Badger to lead. He threw a jack of clubs into the middle of the table.

"No," said John-Joe.

He was a bulky fellow from Mayo with a wide heavily creased face. He looked like a large contented man who enjoyed his food but his disposition was nervous and his nails were bitten to the quick.

"And now look what I have to sacrifice." John-Joe threw down a ten of clubs.

"Billy?" said Badger.

The other prison officer was a small wiry Londoner who had come to Ireland with the British Army and married a woman from Ringsend. After partition he had stayed on and had gotten a job as a prison officer in Mountjoy.

"You might be sad to lose your ten, but that's nothing compared to what I'm feeling." Billy put down the queen of hearts. "I've got nothing else I can throw away."

The cell door opened. It was Gordon Dunlop, a Scot who was known to his colleagues of course as Jock. He was another British soldier who had married and stayed on after partition and gotten a job in the jail. Many of the prison staff were ex-British Army.

"Badger," said Jock. "I've been sent by the governor. I wish I hadn't been."

"It's about my appeal?"

"I'm afraid I've bad news for you."

Badger nodded. "Don't tell me, the governor just heard. It was rejected."

Jock nodded.

"Well, just as I expected," said Badger.

He gathered up the cards from the game they had just finished.

"Another?" he said.

"No, you can't," said Jock. "I've got to bring you to the governor."

"Why?"

"You know. He's to tell you the day. At least I haven't had to do that."

Ten minutes later Badger was in the governor's office. He stood in front of a desk and the governor sat behind it. He wore a pinstripe suit and dark blue woollen tie and there were ink stains on his fingers. His head was bowed as he studied a piece of paper on the desk in front of him. He looked up. His face was a surprise. He looked like a film star. He had a strong jaw and neat even features and very clear bright blue eyes. He was not much liked in the jail and he had a reputation for being bad tempered and morose.

"April twenty-third," he said.

He came from the Dublin suburbs and had a flat Dublin accent.

"What's today?" said Badger. "I lose track in here."

"April eighth, Tuesday," said the governor.

"I've the guts of three weeks anyhow," said Badger.

The governor nodded to Jock, who stood at the door. Jock took Badger's arm, turned him and took him out.

109

Anastasia Cooney to the Minister for Justice, Gerry Boland:

Friday 18 April 1941

Dear Minister,

I am writing from the Dublin house of my brother-in-law with whom I am staying, District Justice John H. Rice, and I am writing in connection with Harry Gleeson. I know his appeal has failed: however, I have information that goes to the very heart of this case, information that I believe has not previously been in the public domain and that I feel bound to communicate. This information concerns the paternity of Mary McCarthy's children.

I live in New Inn and I was on exceptionally friendly terms with Mary McCarthy for many years. Although she told me (with one exception) who the fathers of all her children were, she at no time mentioned Gleeson in this or any other connection. She did not and would not tell me who was the father of her last child (Edwina, who died in infancy) and evaded my questions on the matter. Before this case I never heard Gleeson's name mentioned by anyone as being in any way connected with Mary McCarthy or her last child. I did, however, hear the name of another man mentioned as being the likely father of her last child and from my own investigations I believe what I was told was true and I am prepared to identify this man to the Gardaí. I also believe that Mary McCarthy kept this man's identity a secret because, given his political affiliations, she believed the truth would damage him. But now we have passed that stage and I think it is a matter of extreme importance that, before Harry Gleeson is hanged and something is done that cannot be undone, the matter of the paternity of Edwina, Mary McCarthy's seventh child, is re-examined and that once this has been done the State will see it has no other course but to grant Harry Gleeson a reprieve. Naturally I am prepared to provide the Guards with all the information I have.

Yours sincerely,
Anastasia Cooney (Miss)

1 1 0

Miss Cooney's letter was received on Saturday April 19, opened and read by an official.

After he finished, the official wrote in pencil on the bottom: "It has been decided that a reprieve cannot be granted and that accordingly the law must take its course."

Unseen by the minister, the letter was filed away.

111

Governor's log – Tuesday 22 April 1941:

Albert Pierrepoint met at Dun Laoghaire by the Deputy Governor and brought to Mountjoy Prison by car. He is shown his quarters and then spends day in execution room checking equipment.

The governor checks Gleeson's grave and confirms it has been dug to the depth he had specified and then drafts the death notice to be posted outside Mountjoy after the execution. The governor confirms that the prison doctor and the local sheriff will be present (with the governor) at the execution. They confirm they will be.

In the afternoon the governor interviews Harry Gleeson. The condemned is asked if he has a last request. He asks to see Seán MacBride. Arrangements are made for MacBride to visit Gleeson in his cell in the evening.

MacBride arrives at the prison at 18.00 and is brought to Glee-son's cell: Officer Dunlop also present and remains in the cell for duration of meeting. Conversation of condemned man and MacBride (as reported by Dunlop) as follows:

Gleeson begins by asking MacBride to let his uncle and aunt and his friends know that he does not at all mind dying, and moreover he is well prepared and he will pray for them as soon as he reaches heaven.

He assures MacBride he is calm and happy.

MacBride promises to pass on Gleeson's message.

Gleeson then tells MacBride that he would not care to change places with anyone else.

MacBride asks why.

Gleeson explains that on account of his "ordeal" he has un-dergone his purgatory in this world and he knows of no one else so well prepared to meet his death as he is.

MacBride asks is that why he is so cheerful.

Gleeson says yes. The condemned man then says he spec-ially wishes to thank MacBride for all the work he (MacBride) has done on his behalf. Gleeson adds he will pray for Mac-Bride.

Inconsequential extended conversation about the execution follows.

At the end of forty minutes Dunlop indicates time is up. MacBride and Gleeson stand. Gleeson tells MacBride he has one final thing he wants to say. He says he will pray that whoever killed Moll McCarthy will be discovered and then the whole sto-ry will be like an open book. He says he is relying on MacBride to clear his name and he has no confession to make, only that he did not do it. Gleeson ends by saying he will pray for MacBride and he will be there at MacBride's side whenever he (MacBride), Mr Nolan-Whelan and Mr Timoney are fighting and battling for justice.

Officer Feeney subsequently reports as he comes on duty seeing MacBride in his car, which is parked outside the front gate of the prison. MacBride is writing, Feeney reports.

At 21.00 Gleeson is seen by Fr Bertram. The light is turned off in Gleeson's cell at 22.00. Orders are issued to check on him every 15 minutes through the night.

*

Governor's log – Wednesday 23 April 1941:

Harry Gleeson is woken at 6.00. Two chaplains from Clonliffe College attend him at 7.00.

At 7.55 Harry Gleeson mounts scaffold, is hooded and bound. The prison doctor, the local sheriff and the governor, present.

1 1 2

The hood was made of a material he did not recognise. It was thick and black and no light came through to him at all. There was wood below his feet. It felt firm. It felt solid. It would not always be firm. It would not always be solid. He knew that. Oh, he knew that. The air came in and out of his mouth. It was hot under the hood. He had only been in it a few moments but already, because the air that he exhaled could not escape, he could feel his face start to flush with the heat. He was aware of movement around him as the ones doing this did whatever they had to do. What did they do? What did they wait for? He felt calm if hot. He had an itch. It was at the side of his nose. He could not lift his hand to scratch his nose. His arms were bound. He wrinkled his nose but that did no good. He turned his head and tried to catch the itchy spot on the inside of the hood but that did not work either. The itch was right in the crease where his nose met his face and he could not get the itchy spot to rub against the material. It was about to happen. He knew it was. It had to be.

An image flashed up before his inner eye. He saw Marlhill Farm, the house where he had lived for so long. He saw the farm lane. It ran ahead in a straight line past the Crib Field and on to the road with Foxy Moll's cottage just there on the left behind the high hedge. Then, to his surprise, he saw he was on the lane. It was strange to see himself like another person might see him. He had Caesar's old gun. It was broken and it hung on his right arm. His right hand was stuck in his pocket. He went forward. He looked around as he went. He came to the gate of the field with the spring well. Foxy Moll was there. She left her pail under the spout to catch the water that came out and came over to the gate. He stopped. They talked. "It's not loaded, is it?" she said.

"No, of course it isn't."

She touched the barrel ends. "It looks like the number eight but it's lying down … the dead eight."

That was new to him. He had never heard it. Nor her, she said.

"I only heard it myself yesterday and it means killing something, giving it the chop. That's what I was told."

Yes, the dead eight, that was the first time he had heard tell of it. He smelled tobacco smoke now. Someone close to him was smoking. What was it? A cigarette? No, it was heavier than a cigarette. It was a cigar, yes, that was what it was. There was someone with a cigar nearby. They puffed away nearby. More smoke. Why not? If you had to do this job you would smoke. He had never tried cigars himself. Maybe he should have. Why did he not? It had not appealed. So he had not. One of so many things he had not done. So many. So many. Yes, so little done. So little known. The dead eight the dead eight yes Foxy Moll gave that to him yes she did … the unmistakable noise of a metal mechanism grinding … the smell of cigar smoke … the dead eight …

113

Governor's log – Wednesday 23 April 1941 [cont.]:

At 8.00 Albert Pierrepoint pulls the lever.

The body is taken down. There is a brief formal inquest. Harry Gleeson is pronounced dead.

At 8.05 the notice goes up outside Mountjoy recording Harry Gleeson's execution. A small crowd is waiting to read this. They disperse by 8.30.

114

On Thursday 24 April, using the notes he had made, Seán MacBride wrote a letter to John Timoney. The letter was mostly an account of what was said at his and Gleeson's last meeting, but at the end he made a personal observation. Gleeson, he wrote, not normally noted for his eloquence or fluency, was never so eloquent or fluent, nor so charged with feeling and emotion, as he was at their final meeting.

MacBride concluded by saying it was his understanding that their client had remained calm and quiet right up to the moment the trap opened and he fell to his death.

115

Miss Cooney to Mr John Timoney:

1 May 1941

Dear Mr Timoney,

I am now in contact again with the McCarthy children. Harry Gleeson was not the father of Mary McCarthy's last child and Brendan has admitted to me he only offered the contrary testimony (that Harry Gleeson was the child's father) because, one, he thought that was what Sergeant Daly wanted him to say and, two, he believed if he said it Sergeant Daly would give him money as a reward, as indeed Sergeant Daly did: the sergeant gave him an English sixpence, Brendan has told me.

I am sure, with your legal experience, you will appreciate the significance of this admission.

Yours sincerely,
Anastasia Cooney (Miss)

Written in pencil at the bottom of the letter:
Replied, promising to bear her information in mind and
promising that Seán MacBride and I would not rest till we
proved Harry Gleeson's innocence.
    John J. Timoney, 10 May '41.

116

It was a mild June day and the meadows were yellow with buttercups. The Guards' car from New Inn Guards' station nosed up and stopped in front of Marlhill Farm. Superintendent Mahony and Sergeant Daly got out. The driver opened the boot and Sergeant Daly lifted out a large box. It was brown cardboard and written in pencil on the lid was "Gleeson, Harry – AW808".

As the Guards began to walk towards the front door of the farmhouse they realised that someone had come out of a shed behind them.

"Hang on, Sergeant," Superintendent Mahony said.

Sergeant Daly turned. To his surprise the man who moved towards them had the same build and the same long flat face and the same eyes and neat features as Harry Gleeson. He even wore his flat cap turned to the left as Badger had. It was not the dead man but it was very like him. Sergeant Daly felt disoriented.

"Who are you?" said Superintendent Mahony.

"I'm Pat."

"Pat?" Superintendent Mahony was also puzzled and troubled as he considered the name.

"Pat Gleeson," said the man. "Badger's brother. I'm managing the farm for Mr and Mrs Caesar now."

Superintendent Mahony nodded. Now he remembered being told that the brother had taken over. He wished he had also been told of Pat's resemblance to his brother.

"Is Mrs Caesar about?" said Superintendent Mahony.

"I'll get her," said Pat.

He did not go in through the front door but disappeared down the side of the farmhouse. It was obvious to Superintendent Mahony that he would go in through the back door.

Time passed. A crow cawed. The front door flew open. Mrs Caesar shot out. She wore a black dress and over the dress she wore a dark pinafore. Her mouth was open. Pat followed behind. He had taken off his work boots and he was in socks. His socks were grey and thick with black speckles and looked to be new.

"What do you want?" said Mrs Caesar.

"We've Badger's clothes from Mountjoy for you," said Superintendent Mahony.

Only the week before, Mrs Caesar had buried Badger's fiddle and his dogs' leads and his dogs' collars and his dog-pan and his razor and his strop and his shaving brush and soap and his collar studs and the Fyson's Salts tin he had kept his collar studs in and his best brogues and the shoe trees which had kept his best brogues in shape and his best suit and various other personal effects in the corner of the Dugout Field and once she had finished that task she had imagined that she would never have to look at anything connected to the dead man again. However it seemed from what the superintendent said that she was wrong.

"Murderers," she shouted. "Murderers. You are murderers."

Her vehemence shocked the superintendent and the sergeant. They both felt nervous. Sergeant Daly pushed the box at Pat and as soon as Pat had taken it they turned and hurried back towards the car. Mrs Caesar shouted after them.

"You're murderers, the pair of you, and you'll rot in hell. That's what happens to murderers. You'll rot in hell."

The two Guards got into the car and the car drove away.

117

From the Tipperary Democrat, *Saturday 10 May 1941:*

McCarthy Children in State Care

(From our court correspondent)
A sad epilogue to the murder of Mary McCarthy occurred
yesterday, Friday 9 May, in the District Court in Caher
when District Justice Seán Troy directed the permanent
committal to State care of the surviving children of the
murder victim Mary McCarthy: Judy (17), Maria (13),
Brendan (10), Dermot (7) and Helena (5). The oldest,
Daniel (21), is in employment and another, Edwina, born
1939, died a short time later.

On the advice of the New Inn police, District Justice
Seán Troy also directed that the McCarthy cottage at Marlhill be secured, its windows boarded, its doors locked and
its gates chained, to prevent its occupation by itinerants.

118

Superintendent Mahony to Mr John Timoney:

Monday 9 June 1941

Dear Mr Timoney,

Thank you for your letter with respect to the revocation of Mr John Caesar's firearms licence. We are revoking your client's firearms licence on the foot of the Firearms Act (1925). In our view Mr Caesar is (and I quote) "a person who cannot be permitted to have a firearm in his possession without danger to public safety and the peace".

Instead of confiscating the weapon, I am prepared to allow your client to sell it privately, providing this is done within two months and I am presented with a bill of sale signed by the purchaser.

   Yours sincerely,

   Superintendent Mahony.

119

Mr Nolan-Whelan, Harry Gleeson's senior counsel, died in 1950. Father O'Malley died in 1953. Mr Caesar died in 1954. Mrs Caesar died a few years later. Pat Gleeson inherited the property and stayed on to work it. We would meet him sometimes, my father and I, when we were in New Inn. My father would say hello when we met. He would respond. They would exchange pleasantries. That was the height of it.

Pat Gleeson was wary, almost timid. That was to be expected, my father said. A terrible thing was done to his brother Harry. He was convicted of a murder that many people about New Inn knew he did not do and yet they did not speak out but kept quiet and let the system grind on and hang him, an innocent man. Little wonder Pat Gleeson was withdrawn and a little suspicious, my father said. He was living amongst those who had killed Mary McCarthy as well as those who had let Harry hang.

John J. Timoney died in 1961. Mr Justice Maguire died in 1962. Mr McCarthy, the senior prosecutor, also died in 1962. Nutley and J.J. died in 1965 within a week of one another, Nutley dying first.

120

My bedroom was in the roof space of the little gate lodge we had off Miss Cooney. The roof sloped. There were wooden beams. The room smelt of pine.

One evening in March 1966, I was in my room. I was home from school at least an hour. My school blazer and shirt and tie and trousers were hanging up and I was in my home clothes. I was at the table. I was at my homework, I would think. I don't remember. The table was in front of the little window. I looked out. Perhaps I had heard him. Perhaps that was why I looked out. Or I had sensed him there. I don't know. It was a man and he stood at the gate in the demesne wall. He faced our house. He had his cap in his right hand and his left hand was over his face. It was difficult to make out what he was doing but after I had stared a while I realised he was crying. It looked to me as if he wanted to come forward. He wanted to come through and walk to our door. But something held him. Something stopped him.

I heard our front door open. The door was right below. I saw my father. He went towards the man. He put his hand out. He put his hand on the stranger's shoulder. He took hold of the stranger's arm. Something was said but I could not hear. They began to walk back towards our front door, the stranger and my father. After the two had gone a few steps my father looked up. He nodded at me. I opened the window.

"Come down, Hector," he said.

I went down. I found my father and the stranger in the kitchen at the table. My father sat on one side and the stranger sat on the other. He wept. My mother stood at the sink. I went over and stood by her.

"What is it," said my father, "why have you come, Screw?"

I knew that name. I knew exactly who this was. Oh, yes.

He took his hand away from his face and mopped his tears with the inside of his cap. "I'm not very well," he said. "I'm not very well at all."

Screw looked old and tired.

"I heard you were in hospital."

"I haven't long. It's the old ticker. It's falling apart, the doctors say."

"Are you here to make your peace?"

Screw nodded. "J.J. and Nutley have gone," he said. "I'm the last one left. I am here to make my peace."

"Will you tell me what happened?"

Screw put his cap over his face and pressed his eyes.

"I will try," he said. The cap muffled his words.

My father looked over at me. I looked back. He moved his gaze to Screw. It was a different look to any I had ever had before from my father. I was to listen. I was to pay close attention. That was what his look said.

"There isn't much in it." The cap was there still held up to his face. It made his words sound strange and far away. It would not come down either. I knew that now. He had to keep it there. He could not look at us. Not given what he had to say.

"Tell me what you can," said my father. "Tell me everything you know."

"We had a meeting over in Boolakennedy in a safe house," said Screw, his voice distant yet audible. None of us in the kitchen made a noise. We did not move. We were still.

"It was the house of a fellow called Bermingham. We often met in his house. He was one of ours. Anyhow, at this meeting it was agreed … you know what we agreed, we agreed … That was the Tuesday. Then the Wednesday J.J. brought her and that little dog she had over to the poet's house on Lynchs' farm. We had it all ready. We'd decided to get her drunk. We gave her a feed of whiskey. But we forgot not to drink ourselves. Soon we were all drunk. Well, not J.J. maybe. J.J. went off and he told the sergeant, the man Daly, that she'd be found dead the next morning. Then J.J. came back. Your mother was passed out with the drink by this stage. We put the tarpaulin we had over her head to catch anything and J.J. pulled the trigger. Then we carried her in the tarpaulin with her little dog following and we brought her to the Dugout Field and put her in a gap in the hedge where we knew Gleeson would find her. He walked past the gap every morning with his dog. We shot her again. Her little dog was there. She had odd boots on. I've never forgotten that. We left. It was a dirty thing we did, a filthy dirty deed, and I am heartily sorry."

"Thank you, Screw," my father said, "thank you."

Screw took the cap away from his face, closed his eyes and let out a long cry.

1 2 1

Screw died a few weeks later in hospital. We heard he refused the priest at the end. But that might just have been a story. Sergeant Daly died in 1971. Justice Troy died in 1972. Mr Bermingham died in 1973. Pat Gleeson died a bachelor in 1974. Marlhill Farm was sold. The new owner demolished the farmhouse and the outbuildings, rooted out all the hedges and pulled down all the fences. All that was left from the 1940s was the spring well where Foxy Moll drew her water and the cottage, although by this time it was in disrepair and the corrugated iron roof had collapsed.

Superintendent Mahony died in 1980. Seán MacBride died in 1988. Mr Murnaghan, the junior prosecutor, died in 1990. Miss Cooney died the same year. She was a hundred. I no longer lived in the lodge by this stage. I was long married and lived in New Inn. Garranlea was sold.

122

All of the official figures from The People v. Harry Gleeson were gone and Miss Cooney was gone but there was one participant in the story still alive.

Tommy Reid had a breakdown after Harry Gleeson's execution; he spent a year in hospital in Dublin and recovered and worked for the rest of his life as a foundry man. He never married. He retired to Adare in Co. Limerick and early in 2008 I heard he was living quietly there. He was very old, I was told, but he was alert. I wrote to him and he wrote back to me. His handwriting for one so very old was surprisingly clear. The letters went to and fro. Finally he agreed I could visit him on the last Monday in September 2008, Monday 29. He asked me to come at four. He promised he would provide me with a good cup of strong tea.

1 2 3

I found the bungalow and knocked. I could hear the sound of the television in the front room. Tommy opened the door. He was a small compact man with a small compact face. He was much smaller than I had expected. His hair was the colour of old linen: it was white with yellow in it. It was also very fine. His small hand when I shook it was cold.

"I've poor circulation," he said. "The hands and the feet never get warm nowadays."

He brought me into the bungalow's small front room. The stove was lit. I heard the coal roar on the far side of the glass door. The heat from the stove was fierce.

Tommy went off to make the tea. I looked at the television's screen. The programme was about the life of Seán MacBride. I watched some shaky black-and-white footage of Republicans with guns on manoeuvres while the voiceover explained that for two years in the thirties MacBride was IRA Chief of Staff and that later (this voiceover was carried by period footage of Dublin in the forties and fifties) he was a successful barrister, Minister for External Affairs and a founder of Amnesty International. Tommy came back in with a huge brown teapot.

"Look," I said. A photograph of MacBride in a lounge suit was on the screen.

Tommy made a snort and put the teapot down on the hearth near the stove to draw. He was a spry fellow, I thought.

"He may have done great in the world," said Tommy, "and what was it he won?"

"The Nobel?"

"That, yes, but what did he ever do for poor Harry Gleeson?"

Tommy took the remote and pointed it at the set and pressed a button. The picture collapsed and the screen went black. He closed the doors to the hallway and the kitchen and came back. He sat down. He asked about my journey and then my father. He remembered him, he said. He had seen him around Marl-hill and on the road to O'Shaughnessys'. He fetched the brown teapot and poured tea into cups. He invited me to add my own milk and to take a biscuit from the plate. I did. The milk was already slightly sour because the room was so warm and the skim of chocolate on my biscuit was moist and nearly runny. I decided not to drink my tea.

"It was terrible what they did to your grandmother," Tommy said. He was ready to speak, I thought. So I waited. I said nothing. He had to say what he needed without guidance from me. This was the only chance I would have to get his knowledge without its being contaminated.

"The day before Badger found her was a Wednesday," he said. "I know it was. It was me to milk. I got the stool and the pails and I went up the lane to the Crib Field. The Crib was small and there were six cows in it. I milked them, one after the other, just as the light was going.

"Then I swung the stool over my shoulder and hoisted the buckets and started for the gate. The buckets were heavy so I went slowly. I felt the heat off the milk in them and I nearly tasted the smell of it too.

"I carried the buckets out the gate and closed it. I was sore and I didn't pick the buckets straight up. I stood there, working my shoulder, and I looked down the lane towards the public road.

"I wasn't expecting to see anyone so I was surprised when I saw, standing at the end and watching me, a man in a trench coat and a hat. I know who that is, I thought, though why he should be watching me lug buckets of milk and a stool on a Wednesday evening was a mystery.

"Then he realised I had seen him and he began to move towards the hedge. As he did, his coat rose up behind him and I saw he had on the riding breeches – jodhpurs, aren't they called? – that he always wore. Then I knew for sure it was J.J., Johnny Spink. Then he slipped into the hedge and was gone, and I knew he wasn't pleased I'd seen him from the way he bolted.

"I've thought a good deal about the next part. I heard things too while I was still in New Inn and I put them together, what I thought and what I heard.

"After I seen him, J.J. went and got her, he went and got Foxy Moll. Her cottage was just there. He was the father of her last one, the one who died … what was she called? Don't tell me … Edwina. Yes, J.J. was her father. I'm sure the Guards didn't know that, or if they did they soon forgot it. If they had known who the father was, the real father, and that it wasn't Badger, everything would have been different. Well, for a start, there'd have been no case would there? But there we are. Either they didn't want to know or they didn't know, which amounts to the same thing.

"Where was I? Yes, J.J. went to her cottage after I seen him, and he took her away that Wednesday night. I'm sure of it. And wherever he took her, that's probably where he would have shot her, and then he carried the body back and left it for Badger to find when he was out walking his dog – which was not hard, as Badger always followed the same route, day in, day out. Badger found her, ran to the police station and, well, you know the rest, I'm sure."

Tommy took a biscuit and began to nibble it. I think his teeth were false. I heard clicking inside his mouth. He took a mouthful of tea and swallowed it.

"When I was in Dublin in the hospital," said Tommy, "after my nervous breakdown, Mrs Caesar came to see me and do you know what she told me?"

I looked at him. "I don't."

"By now she knew I'd seen J.J. watching from the end of the lane, and she told me that was the last time he ever wore jodh-purs because the next time she saw him, she said, and every time after that, he was in ordinary trousers."

We sat in silence. It started to rain outside and the room was suddenly dark. Tommy got up and turned on the electric light.

Epilogue

I wrote the story of my grandmother and Harry Gleeson and I put everything I knew into it. Then I put a copy of the manuscript in an envelope and went out to Garranlea House. The new owners were away but I met the bony Lithuanian caretaker by arrangement at the crypt under the beech trees.

It was a winter morning. Snow was imminent. The caretaker took the key from the niche at the top of the right-hand side pillar and unlocked the crypt's metal door. I turned on my torch and I went in.

The crypt was cold and there was a smell of dusty wood and limestone and what I took to be old bone, wrinkled skin, shrivelled organs and dry blood.

I shone the torch around. There were stone ledges on three sides with coffins on them. On one shelf a child's coffin rested on top of a small adult one. Unlike the others in the crypt these were plain and simple. I felt sure the man with the papery voice had made these. I fed my envelope into the slot between Edwina's coffin and the bottom of the ledge above. Then I went back out. The boughs of the beeches creaked overhead. I heard the metal door grate as the caretaker closed it, and then as he turned the key I heard the click of the lock.

"The ugly fact is books are made out of books," said Cormac McCarthy in an interview in the *New York Times* on 19 April 1992. "The novel depends for its life on novels that have been written," he continued, though he might have added that novels also come out of all sorts of other types of book. This is certainly the case with *The Dead Eight*, which owes its existence to *Murder at Marlhill: Was Harry Gleeson Innocent?*, a forensic examination of the Gleeson case by the late Marcus Bourke. I freely acknowledge that without both Mr Bourke's research and his encouragement (in his last letter he wrote, "I would accordingly urge you to make a formal decision to try a work of fiction based on my book") I wouldn't have written this novel.

Readers, however, need to remember that *The Dead Eight* is *not* a documentary recapitulation but a hybrid that combines some factual content with a great body of invented speculative material. From Bourke I've taken many key dates and many key events (though I've simplified and even altered the chronology when it suited), many real names (though I've conflated characters in places), the topography (simplified where necessary), several lines from Harry Gleeson's police interrogation and trial, some of Anastasia Cooney's letter to the Minister of Justice, the details of what was said during Sean MacBride's final interview with Gleeson and a last scene with Tommy Reid, – and the rest I have *invented*: that includes every scene up to the moment when Foxy Moll's body is discovered, all the minor characters (and their names), all the men that Moll has relationships with, including her murderer and his accomplices (and the names of all these many men), and all the sexual acts that are described. The notion of the family of one of Moll's lovers owning Feehan's (a real shop) is also invented. Finally, but most importantly, all Foxy Moll's children are inventions and so is her grandson, the narrator, Hector, and for story-telling purposes, I've ignored usual legal protocols about the identification of children by newspapers in custody cases.

Carlo Gébler